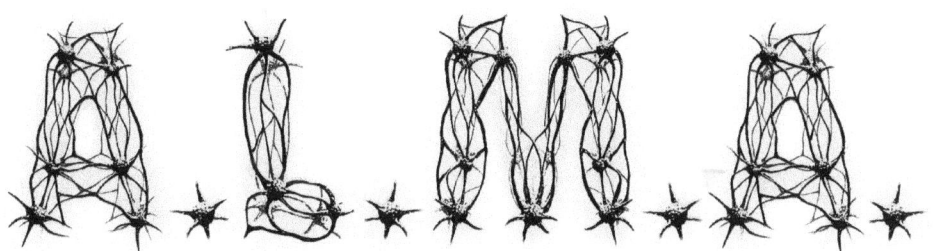

Eric Monteiro

Table of Contents

Appendix: Official Council Documents

For Nara Monteiro, my daughter, editor, thought-partner, harshest critic and, most importantly, my biggest source of inspiration for Alma.

PART I
RESTITUTION

1

WHITE

Sep 2, 2218

WHITE. NOTHING BUT WHITE—PURE, SILKY WHITE. IT'S not the kind of white that blinds you, but rather a pleasant lack of color, as if all colors of the visible spectrum were precisely blended to give me my own brand of perfect white. Not shiny, not opaque, just plain white, pure white.

Walls. These are white walls. I'm in a room. I don't really see the edges, but instinctively know this is a room. It appears to be the size of a large living room, but it's hard to be sure. There are no shadows or textures; the light is perfectly diffuse. I wonder if the walls are back-lit.

Silence. Not muffled silence, as if some noise were on the cusp of popping, but rather a perfect, soothing silence. Surely there is some type of white noise, just loud enough to fill the void. No ringing, either.

I survey my other senses.

Warmth. Just enough that I feel comfortable, almost snugly; I could sleep here, though I'm not the slightest bit sleepy. I'm on some kind of bed, but I can't really tell what kind of bed or bedding it is. It is neither firm nor soft. It is as if every curve of my body is being perfectly supported. It almost feels like I'm floating; not flying, but being buoyed by just the right amount of pressure. It's all so hard to describe, and yet so comforting and familiar.

As I continue to gently scan my senses, I notice the air: pure mountain air. It has no discernible odor or fragrance, but it is somehow refreshing. I close my eyes and take a deep breath; for a few seconds, it's like I am over-looking a meadow, breathing fresh countryside air.

I open my eyes again. I'm so comfortable that I still don't feel like moving. This must be what the womb feels like; isothermal, isobaric comfort, except the womb is wet. Something in me compels me to move—curiosity. I wonder where I am.

I lift up my arms; I see my hands first. They look healthy, almost glowing. My olive-toned skin stands out against the unstated white else-where in the room. I can see my sleeves, and I notice that I'm also wearing white. It's an unusual outfit; it's like a diving wetsuit, but much more com-fortable. The pressure is perfectly suited to my body, and it is much thinner than a dive suit. It feels like a second skin, but when I look down to scan my body I realize it doesn't reveal any uncomfortable details of my shape.

My breathing is very calm and rhythmic, as if I were meditating. I get the feeling that this suit is helping balance my breathing and circulation—I feel great, toned, energized. I could run a marathon.

Then she startles me: "Hello, I'm Alma."

The voice is followed by a silence. A long, almost uncomfortable silence. It gives me enough time to realize what's peculiar about the voice. It is a motherly voice. Not my mother's voice, but rather what my mother's voice should have been—soothing and reassuring, but also firm, with a clear, calm, benevolent authority.

Once I convince myself that I really have heard the words, I reply, "Hello, I'm Richard. Professor Richard Weissman."

"I know who you are."

"I guess that makes one of us."

"You also know who you are."

No humor, I guess. "I don't know who *you* are, other than your name—Alma, is it?"

"Yes, Alma. We will come to me soon enough, when you are ready. For now, just know I am your friend."

Sitting up, I look around. There's no sign of where the voice is coming from, no cameras, and no visible speakers. Swanky tech set-up. I wonder who funds a facility like this . . . crap, the Russians? The Chinese? Surely not the North Koreans . . . I knew that Department of Defense grant was a bad idea!

"You are alarmed. Don't be. As I said, I am your friend. The Russians and Chinese are not."

"How did you know what I was thinking?"

"I don't, but given your visible alarm and your background, it would not have taken another quantum physicist to guess."

"Where are you talking to me from? And why the distance, if you are a friend?"

"As I said, more on me later, when you are ready. For now, you will meet Hena. You must feel hungry. You have been nourished, but your body expects regular food intake, so Hena will accompany you to a meal."

The wall opens. Well, sort of opens; it's not a door, but neither does the wall vanish. It was almost as if a hidden door had contracted *into* the wall, like an eyelid opening.

A beautiful woman a few years younger than me, probably in her early thirties, walks in. This must be Hena. I swallow hard and my heart races. I'm immediately struck by what I can best describe—with my suddenly limited language repertoire—as an irresistible attraction. Like so many things in this room, it feels like she was carefully designed, in this case to fit my description of the ideal woman: beautiful but not artificially so, intelligent eyes, elegant movement, a captivating and warm smile, shoulder-length soft brown hair, honey green eyes—I wonder again if any of this is real.

She smiles. A broad, warm, and friendly smile. Without breaking eye contact, she approaches me and begins to walk around me quietly, her smile softening but still there. As she finishes the walk around me she gently places her hand on my right shoulder.

"Hello, I'm Hena, and I'm here to help."

"Please don't tell me you're from the government."

She stops smiling and gives me puzzled look, as if I have spoken a different language.

"You know, 'I'm from the government and I'm here to help', usually the infamous last words . . ."

Still a puzzled look . . .

"Never mind. You people clearly have no sense of humor."

She stares at me blankly. "You must be hungry." She gestures towards a tray of food that is somehow sitting right beside me on one of those tables that attaches to hospital beds. I look at the food; I am indeed hungry. I also notice that I'm now sitting on what looks like a comfortable hospital lounge chair—I don't know what happened to the bed I was in. And that tray couldn't have been put there, since there was no one else in the room and I kept my eyes on Hena the whole time. Neither could the bed have somehow become a chair without me noticing. And yet all of it happened. Then it strikes me, and I blurt out the question:

"Am I dead?"

She cups her mouth and laughs, a hearty honest laugh, straight from her gut. She sits on the edge of my lounge chair, opposite the food tray, and rests her hand on my shoulder; left shoulder this time.

I look her straight in the eye. "I'm serious, I can handle it. Just tell me the truth. I'm a renowned scientist, I know what is and isn't possible, and some of what's just happened simply isn't."

She now has a gentle smile, like that of a mother who's amused by her child's innocence. "Eat while I explain." I dig in. The food tastes just right, plainly spiced but flavorful. It feels like I can taste the orange in the carrots or the green in the curd beans. Again, I find myself struggling to make sense of my overall sensorial experience, except to say that it feels pure. This is pure, wholesome food.

She gets up and starts elegantly and slowly pacing around me again. She sustains eye contact with penetrating eyes, to the point that I feel emotionally violated. I feel forced to look away. I focus on the food. Without breaking pace, she speaks.

"We brought you here because we need to teach you a few things related to your field of study, Quantum Electro Dynamics, QED. More specifically, about the nature of time. You will be taught things which no human being you know has ever conceived."

I speak over a mouthful. "Before you go on, three questions: one, you say you brought me here, where is here? Two, how is it possible that you would have QED insights that I, or for that matter no human I know, has ever heard of? I'm not one for false modesty; I won a Nobel Prize and am about to get my second one in that very field of study. So how is that possible? Three, why do I feel so good—I mean, physically—and yet so off, like all this is too perfect to be natural?"

She stops pacing, turning to face me with a serious look: "The answers to these three questions are related. Maybe I did not start this in the right place. It is only my second time as a handler and you are a very complex case—probably the most complex case we have ever had."

"Handler? Did I do something stupid? Am I in jail?"

"Please continue to eat and let me finish. You are not in jail, and as Alma said, we are your friends. You will find that if you can give me 5 minutes—without interruption—I will cover all of these questions and the pieces will start to fall into place."

I nod while munching. She proceeds. "You are geographically located in what you would call the Nevada desert, United States, but geographical location matters much less nowadays. The better question would have been *when* you are, not where. We have brought you forward in time; the year, as I experience it, is 2218, approximately two hundred years into your future."

I sigh. "Oh—a handler—I get it now: I have gone truly mad. Sarah always warned me that too much theoretical physics was going to drive me nuts."

She seems to relax again, sitting cross-legged on a chair that I had not seen behind her. Hands over her lap, looking professorial, she cocks her head as if I were a curiosity to be studied.

"I understand you may think you are crazy, but you are not. As I speak, we will morph this room into something more comfortable. Perhaps then you will see for yourself the kind of technology we have, which simply could not have been in operation two hundred years ago."

She stands up and walks to take out my tray—I'm no longer hungry, anyway—and the room changes. Morphs, as she put it, might be a better description. It's the same kind of action as when the door opened, like nothing I have ever seen. It's organic, like muscles moving or a liquid gel flowing, but more purposeful, as if every little particle knows exactly where it is supposed to go. As the room morphs around me, it also gains color. It's no longer white. The walls and ceiling begin to produce color everywhere, like an octopus' skin changing, the pigment somehow bubbling up from within. Over twenty or thirty seconds a whirlwind of activity takes place all around me, shapes and colors forming from within the white fabric of the room. When it is all done, I'm sitting in my kitchen. And somehow, while it is all happening around me, I feel nothing actually disturb me, move me, touch me. Every little detail from my kitchen is here, from the hanging copper pans my wife Sarah gave me before she died, which I cherish and display as if they are works of art, to the new microwave I bought last year. I look outside the window and there it is: the Charles River crisscrossing Boston, where I live.

Gotcha! I feel so smart as I catch her on the inconsistency: "I thought you said we were in Nevada. Why are we looking at the Charles River?"

She no longer holds the tray. I'm not sure what she did with it. She raises her hand to hold her chin, as if wondering what to say.

"We *are* in Nevada. As I said, that matters less nowadays." With a slight finger gesture, she changes the view outside from my familiar view of the Charles River to the desert of Nevada, then to a beach with turquoise water, and yet again back to the Charles. "I will keep the Charles River view there, as it will avoid dissonance with your memory of your kitchen. I trust this small demonstration has given you some confidence that you are dealing with a technologically advanced society."

"Well, I sort of feel like you've confirmed that I'm hallucinating. This just can't be happening in real life."

"You more than anyone should know that 'real life' is a flawed concept. It is not real until you experience it, just a series of probabilistic waves, but it is certainly real once you do—probabilistic wave functions collapse and, however improbable, this is the reality you are experiencing now. Just accept it."

"You are going to teach me quantum mechanics now? That's kind of funny."

She steps closer to me—I notice that I'm now sitting on one of my kitchen high-stools—and taps my knee three times, a bit as a teacher would tap a distracted student's wrists.

"I can and will teach you much more than quantum mechanics. Right now, you simply do not and cannot understand how ignorant you are."

"Really? Then how do you avoid renormalization to get rid of the infinites in quantum field theory?"

"You can't. Not in a conceptually consistent way, anyhow. There will be a new mathematical operation developed soon—in your timeline—which denotes each individually consistent set of events as one probable universe, while acknowledging that there are indeed infinite universes possible at any given point in time. We call it a nexus function. That is why renormalization is just a gimmick; the infinites have real physical meaning and should not be renormalized. Once the nexus function is formalized, the equations actually fall into place without the infinites, since they are then solved for in any given self-consistent universe."

I try to keep a brave face, but truth be told, if this is a hallucination it is a very productive one—this has opened up a promising new avenue in applied mathematics, which is not even my core field of study!

Hena smiles again and startles me by clasping my left hand in both of hers. She has warm hands.

"Alma indicates that you are now at least open to the possibility that we are telling the truth. That is progress."

"Are you? Telling the truth?"

"Lies no longer exist. In fact, I can't remember the last time I even used that word. Lies have become pointless, both in intent and usefulness."

"What do you mean?"

"There is no reason to lie. By and large humans are aligned on what we are trying to achieve and how to get there. And when we are not aligned, we rely on truth rather than lies to resolve any differences."

"What about usefulness?"

"Well, Alma always knows when someone is lying. There are specific markers in body language, facial expression, pupil movement, and body temperature that are hard to miss."

"So Alma would know if I lied right now?"

"Yes."

I look around, trying to find a camera somewhere. Alma must be able to see me.

She lets go of my hand and looks sideways. After a few seconds she takes a deep breath and sits on the stool across from me.

"As I said earlier, we need to teach you a few theoretical concepts and applications. You are not ready yet, but when the time is right you will carry that knowledge back to your present time, where it will play a critical part in ensuring that history as I understand it happens. We will bring you over every time you sleep until you are done, but time will follow a different tempo here than it does in your current present."

"Why only when I'm sleeping? You realize how that small detail makes me very suspicious that this is either a hallucination or a very vivid and creative dream, right?"

She takes another deep breath and crosses her arms.

"While you are sleeping we can easily pull you out of consensual reality, without upsetting anyone else's experience of reality. If we were to try to pull you out of that consensual reality when others were around and conscious, it would take much more energy than when it is only you. In fact, the energy required grows exponentially with the number and complexity of conscious beings sharing in that consensual reality."

"So, you are saying no one knows I am here."

She fidgets, "Precisely. And indeed, if someone were to walk into your room right now, even a pet, you would be pulled back to your current present quite abruptly, since we did not budget enough energy for that."

"Well, that sounds like sloppy planning."

She clenches both fists quickly a couple times. Her tone is serious.

"There was no other choice. Plus, you will only be gone a few minutes in your timeline and our research shows definitively that you do not have a pet."

"What if I had a close friend, or maybe a girlfriend over?"

"Our research shows that to be equally unlikely."

Ouch, that stings a little. "But what if, however unlikely, a stranger were to walk in on me right now?"

She gets up and walks around the kitchen island before answering. She's now facing me across the counter-top; it feels like we are ready for a match.

"Going back without a check-out is not a good idea. It might actually have lasting negative effects on your ability to share in the consensus reality."

"What kind of lasting effects?"

"Your reality might not sync as it should with everyone else's consensus. You would see, hear and experience different things."

"As if I were schizophrenic..."

"You might be diagnosed with that, yes, although the root causes would be entirely different."

"So did you lock my doors for me?"

She slouches a bit. "We have no ability to do that, but you should indeed lock all your doors and windows carefully from now on. As I mentioned, this first visit will only last a few minutes, so the risk is minimal, but please do lock up carefully. You might even want to consider changing the locks."

"You can't be serious."

"I am."

She takes another deep breath, straightens her back, and stares me down for a few long seconds. I notice again how striking she is; the thought makes me look away.

She proceeds: "Can we come back to the topic at hand?"

"Which is?"

"Why you are here and how this will work."

I shrug. "Sure, why not? Fire away."

She walks back around the island and sits across from me, touching my knee. She's very touchy.

"We will bring you here every night while necessary, in what will feel like longer and longer intervals. Your consciousness has to process and cope with these changes progressively."

I cock my head to the side: "Ya think?"

She looks down at her hands and gives me a half-smile.

"That means we have to start slow, with shorter visits, and increase the time you spend with us as you show yourself to be ready. As I said, today you will only stay for a few minutes. Next time it might be for a few hours or even days, if you are ready."

"How will you know if I'm ready for longer visits?"

"If you are not ready, you will have dissonance with the consensual reality within our timeline. I, Alma, and others here will notice your senses are experiencing a different reality than ours, which will prove unhelpful. We will either try to adjust our own consensual reality to yours, or send you back as soon as that happens."

"What do you mean, adjust to me?"

"This is already a simple example. We are meeting in your kitchen, which is a very easy sight for you to experience. We are adjusting. I do not know your kitchen, but Alma can easily reproduce it in a way that you and I now agree on where we are: your kitchen."

"Is this some kind of virtual reality?"

"No."

"So how did it transform from a white room to my kitchen within seconds?"

This line of conversation seems to soften her. She relaxes her shoulders and pushes her hair to the side.

"This is an actual reproduction of your kitchen using polymorphic construction. This is a physical material. We can construct virtual reality environments, but not all senses are fully credible; touch and smell in particular feel somewhat artificial. And there is no need for it, really, given our advances in material sciences. We can tell you more about our technology later if we need to."

"And who controls the material? That was an incredible transformation. To make that happen where I come from—even just visually, using computer generated imagery—would have taken a team of fifty people six months and a few million dollars."

"Yes, I know. But Alma can do that and much more in real time."

"Is Alma a big computer?"

She winces and shakes her head ever so slightly, then turns her face to look away; I wonder if have offended her.

"No, Alma is no computer, it is much more complicated than that. Computers as you understand them are very primitive things."

"Gee, thanks."

She looks back at me as if trying to assess whether I am seriously offended.

"I don't mean it that way. Generally, you should not take anything I say as any form of judgment, or we will have a very adversarial relationship; that would be unproductive. Remember that I am as human as you are. We could very well be in reverse positions".

"Fair enough. So if she's not a computer—as I understand them—what is she?"

"You are not ready to know Alma yet."

"How will you know when I am ready?"

"Alma will tell me when you are ready."

"And how will Alma know when I am ready?"

"Alma knows everything."

2

PSYCHOTHERAPY

Sep 2, 2018

S TRETCH. LONG, HARD STRETCH. THIS FEELS GOOD, I LOVE stretching in the morning after a night well slept. It feels like I've slept for days.

"Crap, what time is it?"

Phew, I'm okay, it's 6:30 on Friday. My first class is at 8:00—the advanced doctorate class—and they barely need me there anyway, I'm purely ornamental. I can stretch some more.

What a strange dream! Beautiful, creative, inspired almost—but very odd. And it felt so real. I sort of wish it were true. I must be getting bored with real life.

If Sarah were still alive, she would have interpreted the crap out of that dream. She would probably tell me that I feel my work is not progressing fast enough, that it is not meaningful or transformational enough, and therefore I yearn for a time—the future, naturally—where my work could transform how people live. She would tell me that this dream reinforces why I got into quantum physics, which was to understand the nature of reality and use that knowledge to help shape the future of humanity.

The overwhelming white as I first woke up in the room, she would surely say, symbolizes the purity of my motives when I decided to go into science. It hasn't really felt that way since I got the Department of Defense grant though—ugh, I have an upcoming Wednesday meeting. I didn't like the tone in Mr. Edward's memo; it will be one of those meetings.

I get up and wash my face, the cold water bringing me back to more pleasant thoughts. Sarah would have jokingly said that the whole kitchen morphing thing was a deep-rooted fear that she would follow through with her intent to renovate our kitchen, which I love and think has a lot of old Boston character.

I'm sure she would make something of the process of remodeling though, the whole organic morphing and the walls coloring themselves like squid ink, though I'm not sure what. That was so foreign I wouldn't even have thought myself imaginative enough to come up with it. And an elaborate explanation for it, as well—what was it, polymorphic construction? All of it was odd, unlike any dream I have ever had.

It couldn't possibly have any basis of reality, could it? Did I drink or eat anything odd last night? I've been off prescriptions for 18 months now; I only had them for 6 months or so after Sarah's death, and they never had any major side effects. I think, in fact, I had dreamless nights for most of that time.

I go to the bathroom and put on my standard brown slacks and my equally standard light blue shirt, which Sarah used to refer to as my work-and-leisure uniform. I find myself musing over the crude nature of my clothing and the fabric, compared to whatever suit I wore in the future—I mean, my dream about the future. It felt so comfortable, snuggly but not intrusive, compared to my "uniform."

Sarah would surely analyze that too. She'd say that I feel trapped by my day-to-day life, that the clothes were a metaphor for how I have become arrested by my routine, and that present-day crudeness would be an analogy to how I feel people around me rub me the wrong way. Which is true; I have never been particularly modest or accommodating, but of late I really do think that people, even the clever academic people around me, are often superficial, unpolished and sloppy in their thinking and worse, often waste their intellectual capacity on silly endeavors.

I go to the kitchen—this time my real kitchen—make my coffee, take a sip. Nice, I love the warm feeling of fresh coffee in the morning. Then I remember the meal with Hena. The food was so wholesome. I wonder what Sarah would make of that. Maybe something about me not taking good care of myself, which is probably true; since she died I eat mostly out or microwave dinners.

Hena. What would she make of Hena? Well, for starters she would surely be a tad jealous. She knew I only had eyes for her, from the day we met until the very final days at the hospital; but surely a green-eyed brunette in the middle of my dream would stoke the jealous wife within her. Then she would probably say that Hena was the answer to all the things that Sarah would never be, that she would tell me the meaning of my work, teach me many things in my own field of study, and, well, provide me with tasty yet wholesome food. She would get a kick out of that. I used to do most of the cooking when she was around. Maybe that's why I don't cook anymore. I should start cooking again.

What would she make of the computer, Alma? I find myself cringing as I call her a computer. Hena didn't like that. But why am I worried about what a fictional character in my dream does or doesn't want me to call a fictional computer that is not a computer in that same dream? I feel ridiculous. I shake my head and walk over to the window, trying to think of something else. But the question keeps nagging me. What would Sarah make of it? Maybe she would link it back to my troubled relationship with the occult? Yes, that's it: she would say that Alma represented my recognition that I don't know everything, and that I am not ready to know everything, that I recognize there is room for the occult in life. I would scoff at that, of course, and we would have one of our quasi-fights, like we occasionally would, when we disagreed strongly on something or when I offended her by saying that "social sciences" is a misnomer, since social studies are not sciences. But I don't want to think about us fighting, even quasi-fighting, on such a good morning.

I GET IN MY CAR AND DRIVE OFF TO CAMPUS. I FIND MYSELF wondering how people would get around in a future as advanced as the one from my dream. Would they drive cars? Flying cars? What about public transportation? Would they even need transportation?

I get to campus with enough time to stop by my office and browse through a few PhD-candidate papers that cover time-travel. Not my core field of study, but some of the work I do could indeed imply that time-travel is not only possible but feasible in the near future. I guess the strange dream got me curious.

I get to class at 8:25. Like most advanced doctorate classes, this one consists of students showing up with results from their readings and research over the last week, sharing with the group and problem-solving with me and the other nice people in class about the implications, and what they could do next. I normally find that the other students do the majority of the work; I just set the tone and intervene if they are veering into unproductive territory. Today I find I can barely do any of the work. I just can't focus on the class. I keep getting flashbacks to my dream, almost as if I'm re-living parts of it. The class seems to actually enjoy this less directive version of me. Maybe I can start skipping one of every other class.

I get out of class and go see Frank Spitzer, my research partner and 2010 Nobel co-laureate. We're pretty sure we have been nominated this year, so we're hoping to get awarded a Nobel again, for our work on harvesting energy from quantum fluctuations.

Frank is a bit of a prodigy. I was considered a young laureate when we were awarded the prize in 2010, at the age of thirty-six; Frank was twenty-six! And he has that reputation for good reason. He's every bit as intelligent, thoughtful, rigorous, and insightful as any physicist I have ever met and he is also a first class mathematician. But what distinguishes Frank from other physicists—including myself—is his ability to think differently. He leaves no assumptions unquestioned, even the most basic assumptions about the nature of the senses and therefore the nature of reality. Sometimes he drives me crazy, particularly when he veers into what I consider meta-physical speculation—and he knows it too. Thankfully, he's one of the few people I know—if not the only person I know—to do so without skimping on the intellectual rigor of an accomplished physicist.

I'm naturally the more senior in the partnership, given tenure and my own research history. That means I also direct a lot of the research and negotiate most of our grants. To the external world I'm seen as the leader in this partnership, but I am by no means the more valuable partner. I think neither of us is. That's what makes it a good partnership.

We have also on occasion relied on his wife's help. Sun is an accomplished mathematician and expert in Artificial Intelligence. Her pioneering work in deep learning and self-correcting algorithms has had many speculating that she's been on the short list for a Field Medal (widely thought of as a Nobel equivalent in Mathematics) a couple of times, though it hasn't happened. Not yet. She has had many offers to join the tech giants and make ten, twenty times what she makes as an academic, but she loves the lifestyle and the freedom too much. Whenever we have complex math that requires smart computational power rather than brute computational force, we turn to Sun, and she never ceases to amaze us with what she—or better put, her algorithms—can accomplish.

One couldn't fully describe Frank and Sun without mentioning their looks either. Rumor has it that on their honeymoon in Milan they were approached by a modeling agency, an agency Director happened to be doing a photo-shoot nearby. They were offered a good chunk of money to give up their academic careers and become models. I can see why; Frank is tall, has hair that would be better described as a flowing mane, pale but healthy-looking skin and a naturally athletic build—everyone in the physics department hates him for it, and he doesn't move an inch for it. I run 4 times a week and can hardly keep up. Sun is just as stunning herself, daughter of a Chinese father and a Canadian mother, with striking but soft features. Tall and slender like Frank, she also seems to be in shape with no effort.

As I walk into Frank's office, he's clearly engrossed in work, intently looking at his workstation, frowning, typing occasionally. I look around; this is messier than ever. Books piled up everywhere, paper towers precariously balancing to and fro in every direction, waiting to tumble with the slightest breeze. Not just office white, but papers of every color, from the bright yellow used in official forms to the muted ochre from academic filings. I wonder how he can work and live that way. I bet he can't tell apart student essays from peer papers from his own research notes. Ironic that a guy whose research has pioneered the understanding of order in the universe can't keep his office in order. It seems he's breaking his rule, that whenever he can't fit himself and two other people in his office it's time to clean up. I can barely fit in as it is now. How does he use so much paper in this day and age anyway? Most of what I deal with is electronic. Then again, I'm an absolute neat-freak.

Sarah would tease me all the time, say that no normal person would ever order their shirts and pants by shade of color—let alone have them all be the same primary color—and apply first-in-first-out logic, FIFO, to their underwear drawers. I would reply that FIFO is the only logic that makes any sense. She then would say that one should not apply any logic to underwear stowing, and that I stifled spontaneity by doing that. How many times we had that very same argument, I don't know. We were perfect that way; balancing each other's tendencies, comparing our differences, but having a laugh with it rather than trying to change each other. I miss her.

I REALIZE THAT AS MY MIND WANDERED I MUST HAVE WAITED A good five minutes without being noticed.

"So, are we ready for the Wednesday meeting?"

Frank was startled. "Oh, hey, I didn't see you there."

"I noticed. Working on something exciting?"

"Prep for the Wednesday meeting, actually."

"So, are we ready?"

"I am—well, we are—always ready for a meeting, but we won't have what they want yet."

"Is he really asking for a working prototype of the reactor? I thought that was what I read in his memo, but that just can't be right."

"Yeah, that's what he asked for."

"Given we both know that's impossible, we need to have an answer to the question he will surely ask: how far away are we?"

"Not far and yet very far. The theoretical framework is finalized, the last transformations you did took care of that, once I scrubbed some of your shoddy math." He grins smugly. "The lab techs have been working full tilt, so all of the gear will be ready, even the density plates are ready—do you have any idea how hard it was to make a surface that is accurate down to a few hundred times Plank's distance?"

"Actually, I do."

I clear the paper stack from one of the chairs and plunk down, all of the sudden feeling like I weigh a ton.

Frank hands me the gummy bear jar before speaking.

"Some of these ideas sound much better in our heads than when we put them into practice. The big issue remaining is the computational power required to balance the electromagnetic fields in real time, at scale. With our current mathematical solution, it would take about a million times the existing computational power on all of the devices on Earth, combined, to do it in real time. So we either wait 20 years and co-opt the entire global computational grid—assuming Moore's Law continues to hold—or we come up with cleverer math."

I hold my chin and nod that long nod of great wisdom. "Hmmm, let me think—cleverer math then. Have you run this by Sun? Every time we've stumbled on limits to raw computational power she's had a different approach that proved us small minded."

"Not yet, but I doubt she'll have a solution this time, and I'm sure she won't have it for Wednesday!"

I chug one more handful of gummies, speaking over a mouthful:

"True. So brace for a grilling from Mr. Edwards?"

"I guess. But we should push back, too; this could be the physics leap of the century. If we succeed, we are effectively borrowing energy from nothing. That would be considered a miracle any other time in history—maybe even now!"

I shake my head slowly before responding.

"I'm not sure Mr. Edwards even knows that a muon is a virtual particle with a half-life of 2 microseconds. He doesn't understand the significance of what we are doing."

Frank takes back the gummy jar before I can do any more damage. "I know, I do sometimes feel like a mercenary rather than a physicist, but this is our best grant ever. I guess that's the price you pay for working with the Department of Defense. We should also ask why the hurry. I was there when you told him this grant was funding the work of a decade, and we are barely a year into it. As far as I know we are half a decade ahead of any competing labs. Most of them haven't even fully grasped the conceptual and mathematical frameworks we've developed. So I'm not sure why he's all of a sudden so anxious. His email sounded almost desperate."

"I don't know either, and it's frankly not helpful. Let's address it jointly during the meeting. I wonder if we can get to the actual decision makers in the Department of Defense. He's never even told us who they are, maybe I can make a few calls to try and find out. But before we get to that, how do you propose we handle the meeting?"

Frank gets up on the white board and grabs a marker. Weapon in hand, he draws in a flawless cartoon the sequence of steps we should take, as he describes them.

"I think we should start by explaining what we are doing beginning to end, how hard it is, and why we aren't yet in a position to have a working prototype." He draws two guys—presumably us—running an obstacle course.

"We can use the same material we prepared for the technical team and the suppliers. That also has the benefit that it describes the challenges in very simple terms; I think even Mr. Edwards can follow that." Next step in his diagram shows a series of mathematical symbols.

"Then we can show him the working computer model we have. I would show both the one scenario where we manage to balance the magnetic field and it all works, as well as one of the zillion scenarios where we start a chain reaction that annihilates the city." To this he draws several arrows for each scenario, the scariest one shows an atomic mushroom. I have always admired Frank's natural drawing ability.

"Clever. There is a slight risk we spook him so much that he goes back to his boss alarmed. But we can manage that fallout if need be."

Frank nods and wipes his masterpiece away. "In any case we should run this by Sun, and maybe pull in a few fresh eyes on the applied math to see if we're missing something. I know there are probably only three or four people who can really follow what we are doing, but we should try."

I go home feeling excited about our progress, but also slightly annoyed that we have to deal with Mr. Edwards. It would be a lot better if we could work directly with someone who has real power and who understands the significance of what we are trying to achieve.

Once I get home I dive into my gourmet microwave dinner. As I eat it I remember the dream and what Sarah would say about my eating habits. I really should start cooking again. This thing is tasteless and probably devoid of any real nutrients.

I do my share of peer review on some papers before going to bed. They consist mostly of interesting work, but one or two are clearly from people trying to complete their research quota, rather than doing anything that has any relevance. I hate that. Why would you choose academia if you are not passionate about research? Surely not the money, there is none to be found. Maybe teaching, but the sad fact is that most of these folks are also terrible teachers.

I wasn't particularly tired after dinner, but some of these papers have certainly done their magic, better than prescription sleeping pills . . .

3

RECURRENCE

Sep 3, 2218

WHITE. AGAIN, WHITE. I REMEMBER THIS WHITE ROOM. Suddenly I'm alarmed, almost panicked, I'm in the same recurring dream! I sit up fast—the bed transforming into a lounge chair as I do—and look around. Hena is sitting on a white chair. I can't see the chair again because of that strange light, no shades or shadows, but I can tell she's sitting on a chair. She leans over and smiles.

"Hello, Professor. Alma tells me you are alarmed. Don't be. We just brought you back."

"Okay, I got this, recurring dream, I just need to force myself to wake up." I close my eyes. "Wake up, wake up, wake up." Not working. I pinch myself, hard. "Ouch. That hurt. I should have woken up." I sigh and look back at her. "Maybe I will try to pee myself, that used to wake me up as a kid."

She stops smiling. "Please don't do that. It would be unpleasant and embarrassing for the both of us."

"Who are you?"

She sighs, gets up and walks calmly towards me, cupping the left side of my face with one hand in what seems like unwarranted intimacy. But it feels nice, so I don't react.

"I am Hena, your handler, we have gone over that. I know you remember it; you were fully conscious."

"I know you call yourself Hena. What I mean is what part of my psyche are you supposed to represent? I sort of figured out some of the meaning of last night's dream with Sarah's help. Well, technically not Sarah proper, but what I remember of her."

She nudges me over to the side of the lounge chair and sits very close, facing me. She seems to not understand personal boundaries. She grabs my left hand in her two warm ones, squeezing gently. Her tone is very caring and patient.

"I'm not part of your psyche. At least not in the way you mean it. I'm real, my own personality, my own psyche, as you say, and my will is completely independent from yours. None of what we discussed last night was a dream, at least not in the way you mean it."

Her proximity is very disarming, but I try to put on my bravest, meanest face. "Why do you keep referring to the way I mean it? How do you even know what I mean? Who are you to tell me whether I mean this or mean that?"

She holds my hands tighter now, but not uncomfortably so. "You have to remember that my worldview encompasses yours. I understand what people in your time mean when they talk about their psyche, or a dream. Once you take the time to understand my worldview, you will see what I mean. You will agree with me."

"Well, that's presumptuous."

She cocks her head and smiles. "No, it is well informed."

"If you say so." I look down, not sure how to continue for a few seconds. "And even if this is all real, what gives you the right to yank me out of my timeline into some strange future? What about my view? Does it not matter?"

She lets go of me and walks away, stiffly. I find myself wishing she'd come back, but I can't give in now. Still standing, she clasps her hands and spins to face me again. "Off course your view matters. In fact, your view and your actions are the *only* ones that matter."

"Well, in my view, changing the past is a bad idea."

She smiles and raises one finger. I'm not sure if I should expect a lecture or admonishment.

"You have to understand that we are not trying to change the past; rather, we are trying to make sure the future happens. There is a subtle but very important difference."

"Too subtle for me, I guess . . ."

She seems to soften a bit, sitting back on the chair she was originally in.

"As Alma assessed the advancements you made in your research, as well as the implications for the technology we have today, she determined it highly unlikely that you would have achieved what you did without an intervention."

"So let me get this straight: because Alma can so perfectly calculate that I'm not smart enough to figure out what I'm supposed to have figured out—in your 'history of science' records—she figures that gives her the right to yank me into the future and tell me what to do?"

She smiles, raises her hands, palms facing me as if praising me for saying exactly the right thing. "Basically, yes."

"Well, she's wrong!"

Hena gives me a dead serious look. "Alma is never wrong. You will come to see that, Professor."

"If you say so." We stay silent for an uncomfortably long time and I feel compelled to continue. "Listen, if I'm going to do your bidding in the past, I'll need a lot more convincing than that."

She walks over and holds my hands again. I wonder if she knows how nice that feels. Maybe she's playing me, as the needy widower she probably knows I am. Squeezing her warm hands over mine, she smiles. "And what *will* you need, Professor?"

I look down for a while before speaking, "I don't know. Assuming this is all even happening, maybe some conviction that this whole thing is a good idea? That whatever breakthrough I end up achieving is actually positive for humanity, not just another hydrogen bomb in the making?"

"We will take all the time we have to get you there."

"You make it sound as if you are doing me a favor."

"You seem to be distressed, which will not be productive. Would it help if we morph into your kitchen?"

"No! That just freaks me out."

"Maybe a nicer setting. It needs to be something you are familiar with at this stage. We would not resonate well in an environment that is new to either of us."

"So we are resonating now?"

"We are always resonating." She's not just holding my hands now; she's actively caressing my left hand. It feels really nice, and if she's trying to make it harder for me to be a jerk, it's working. She continues: "Maybe if we were sitting in outdoors?"

I roll my eyes. "Sure."

AND JUST LIKE THAT, HERE WE ARE. HENA LETS GO OF MY HAND and sits by my side, at a bench in the middle of a park, which I quickly recognize as Boston Common. It's all very real, passersby and all. I also notice my white bodysuit is now gone and I'm wearing my usual work-and-leisure uniform.

This has piqued my curiosity. "Is this virtual reality?"

"In a way. Alma can easily use the walls—which are still there, you can touch them if you want—to project what we would expect to see around us, make the sounds realistic, and even produce the late summer breeze you feel. It's not real, so in a way you could call it virtual reality."

"How does she give me the impression of real depth? I'm not wearing any 3D goggles."

"Those are not needed. Alma can very easily distort a two-dimensional image so that wherever you are looking you will see the right perspective—and your brain will do the rest, it expects to see depth."

"So she's adjusting the image in real time? To my personal perspective?"

"And mine."

"That's incredible."

She looks pensive for a second. "Not really. It is relatively simple."

"You sure know how to make a guy feel smart."

She laughs shyly. "I apologize, that was not my intent."

"That's fine. You were right about the environment. Just being out here in the open, or at least feeling like that's what's happening, put me in a much better mood." Truth be told I wonder how much of my mood improvement was from her touching me, but that makes me feel really weak.

"I'm glad you feel better."

"How do I know if any of this is real, and not just a recurring dream?"

She turns to sit facing me, I do the same. "You don't really. There is nothing I can say or show you that will convince you of the reality of this experience. And in fact, dream, thought, or imaginative experiences are real too; what differentiates them from what you call normal real experiences is the fact that other people participate in consensual reality. Others will not, by definition, participate in private dream or thought experiences. I could in fact ask you how you know that what you call real life experiences are real. Your senses could be making the whole thing up within your mind. But that would be a confusing conversation right now."

"That would be a confusing conversation anytime. But isn't that a handy way out of my original question? Meaning, is this really happening?"

She reaches out and holds my hand again. "Let me try something else: as a child you were precocious in speech, logical thinking, and pattern recognition, but severely delayed in your motor development. It got to the point where you suffered extreme bullying and had to switch schools four times over six years. You were a very unhappy child until your math teacher in grade four, Mr. Spinoza, decided that he could teach you to defend yourself with your mind, rather than try to fight your way out of bad situations. It worked; you went from being the weird outcast to being the smart kid everyone wanted help from."

"Impressive. But you could have researched all that. In fact, I wonder if half of the physicists I know couldn't have told exactly the same childhood story, names exchanged."

She smiles again, this time a wide, almost childish smile. "Could I have researched or made up your first sexual experimentations with Edda, the eleventh-grade Norwegian exchange student? Or your awkward first date with Sarah, when you passed out after she dragged you into doing shots for the first time?"

I pull my hand away and stiffen; only Frank, Sun and Sarah knew these stories. "Did you drug me before I woke up? Like some sort of truth serum?"

"No, Professor, these details came from a memoir in the past! In my past, anyway, your future still. I could go on and on about the rest of your life through to your current age."

"Please don't. This conversation will lead nowhere." I slouch as we sit quietly for a while. Then I perk up. "I have a proposition."

She turns to face me. "Go on."

"Since you are from the future, you should know exactly what will happen tomorrow. You could tell me the lottery numbers or the outcome of a specific sports event."

"Yes, we do know what will happen."

"So pick something and tell me the outcome—if this is all real, I can confirm it in my present."

"We could do that, but we would need to be sure that you will not act on that knowledge. You see, we have to follow very strict guidelines when we provide information like this. You will understand why when we tell you more about what is expected of you."

"I would not be that stupid."

"Alma needs to hear you affirm it in unambiguous direct terms."

I shout out to the park: "I will not use any information you give me to tamper with the future, my future."

She looks down for a few seconds. "Alma is satisfied that you have conviction in your words. Do you follow European soccer?"

"Well, not regularly, but I can easily find any game you choose."

"The final for the European soccer club league is tomorrow in your timeline. Real Madrid and Barcelona are playing."

"Yeah, even I know that much."

"The Real Madrid will win that game four nothing."

I interrupt her: "That's unlikely but not unique enough."

She touches my knee firmly. "Let me finish: all four goals will be scored within the last 6 minutes of play."

"You mean like penalty shootouts?"

"No, in the course of normal play. I don't follow soccer myself, but I understand that such a scenario would be quite unusual."

"On a final of that importance with two competitive teams, that would be more than unusual. That would probably be a first."

"Good, so it will serve our purpose."

This has caught my attention in other ways. "You say you don't follow soccer, but do people still play the same games from my time?"

"Yes, although not exclusively, as new sports have also been invented. But we don't have the time to cover that. We need to tell you about Restitution."

"Restitution?" I frown.

She seems to perk up at the opportunity to answer my question.

"Yes, that is what we call this program. I will tell you its history and talk you through how this whole thing will work over the next few days."

"Days?"

"Yes, it may be a number of days, maybe up to a couple of weeks in this timeline, which will be our shared timeline as well—but this will have to happen over only a few days in your original timeline."

"Slow down, this is very confusing."

"I understand. As you experience it, the mismatched tempos of the different timelines will become more natural."

"If you say so." I look around and notice we haven't seen a single soul anywhere for the last thirty minutes, on a normal day this park would have had people running, people walking their dogs and some just hanging out.

Hena waits to see if my venting is done and when she's satisfied she picks up where she left off: "Let me start from the beginning of the program, though as you can probably guess I won't cover Alma's broader role. For now we will only talk about Alma in relation to restitution."

I sigh. "This is getting annoying. I feel like you're avoiding Alma the way your psychologist keeps avoiding that conversation about your mother or something. They talk about everything except that, like you're incapable of confronting it."

She stares at me blankly. "I wouldn't know; we don't do psychoanalysis anymore."

"That wasn't my point, but fine, let's follow your agenda, then."

She flinches. I can't tell if I hurt her feelings or if she's just frustrated.

"Very well. When Alma achieved the necessary level of capability, which was around one hundred years ago, it became clear to her that humanity could not have evolved to our current state unassisted. It was simply not very likely. In fact, it was highly improbable, while mathematically possible, that our present experience had evolved from our recorded history without unseen help from somewhere."

I tentatively raise my hand. She pauses.

"And she concluded it was from the future?" Hena nods, and I proceed: "I guess the other alternative would have been some alien race, so at least as farfetched."

She proceeds without reacting: "She could see very clearly when there were abnormal leaps in human capability, beyond what could and should be expected with a reasonable probability. While at the time humanity would have no way of knowing what had actually happened, and therefore would have no historic record of it ever taking place, Alma knew that there had to have been a helping hand."

"So Restitution was created on Alma's hunch?"

"I know this is difficult without knowing Alma, but trust me when I say this: Alma has no hunches. And she has never acted by herself; Alma informed the council and they made all the decisions. She executed them under the council's authority."

"What council?"

"You don't need to be concerned with that right now. I need to cover the program with you first."

"Okay, but it seems like we don't have enough time for most of the interesting questions."

She gives me the slightest of smiles and touches my knee, enough to disarm me.

"By 2120 humanity already knew how to bring a consciousness from the past, as it had been done a few times in the preceding decades. It was in fact the work you did that put that into recorded history."

"Great, a time-loop, and I'm in it."

"One of many, we think. We started the program almost one hundred years ago, and the first Sprout that you would recognize—that is how we refer collectively to you and your peers—was pulled out of ancient Greece. We have had many Sprouts in primitive and ancient societies, but you would not recognize their names."

"Let me guess: you're talking about Plato."

"Close, but no, the first Sprout was Socrates, around 400 BC in your existing Roman calendar. Plato was his student, so he benefited indirectly. You have to understand that what Alma looks for is not brilliant discoveries. All of the sprouts have incredible minds . . ."

"I'm flattered." I actually am flattered, almost blushing; it's not every day a dashing woman tells you you've got an incredible mind. It strikes me again how attractive Hena is, and I notice that since she has started to tell me the history of Restitution she's less cold, more human—and more attractive. I catch myself staring at how her hands rest on her lap, she has a nice figure. I notice the curve of her athletic hips, her tight abs and look up quickly, suddenly aware how warm my face is. I'm not sure if I'm embarrassed just because she caught me looking or because around her I feel like I'm back in puberty. She smiles, takes her hand off my knee, gets up slowly, briefly touches her chin and clears her throat.

"Let's walk while we talk." We start walking the trail I know all too well. I try to focus on the red line over the asphalt and the trees, so that my thoughts can move on. I'm struck again by how exact this replica is, down to specific trees I recognize from my morning runs.

"As I was saying, Alma does not pick up the most amazing discoveries or inventions. Rather, she picks up the ones that represent unlikely leaps in thinking. There are usually clusters of advancement across history, and many times the most famous thinkers are chronologically at the end of the cluster, not the beginning. Restitution *sprouts* new thinking, hence the name."

"Cute. Can you give me a few more examples of Sprouts?"

"Yes, of course. Some names you will recognize immediately, others will be more obscure, since they might have been the spark for a cluster. For example, Alhazen's work on optics at the turn of the first millennium, while Europe was in the dark ages, would not likely be familiar to you, but it started a chain that led others, like Copernicus, to make advancements on scientific thinking."

"So Copernicus was also a Sprout?"

"No. One of the things you will notice if you study all of the Sprouts carefully is that we never misinform. We may provide insights that have applicability limited to the environment and mental model of the time, but never plainly wrong. As you know Copernicus was convinced that the Sun was the center of the universe. A better example of correct but limited thinking would be Newton's laws, which work perfectly in the domains that humanity could understand at the time when they were formulated."

"I get the difference."

She looks at me and nods.

"You would surely recognize the names of more recent Sprouts, like Newton himself, Einstein, Heisenberg, Bohm. There have been a couple of Sprouts in your current time as well, some of the physicists you would have looked up to as a young scientist, but we should avoid discussing them given how close to your present they are. It's worth noting that we have had to accelerate the pace of Restitution dramatically, given the accelerating pace in human advancement."

"How many were there in total?"

"Good question, probably about five hundred. Oh, 487 so far, Alma tells me."

I stop on my tracks. "Wow, that's a lot!"

She faces me and grabs my right hand. "You have to keep in mind that some of the early Sprouts were here for very basic inspiration, like how to cultivate a crop, or how to make a wheel."

"So it is not only physicists, then."

She lets go of my hand and starts walking again. I follow.

"Oh no, there have been many other disciplines. Most of the sciences have had our helping hand. They are less relevant to you, but there have been many Sprouts in life sciences and philosophy. We have also tried a few artists, where Alma thought it appropriate, but that has not worked."

"What happens when it doesn't work?"

"The two artists we tried went mad and killed themselves."

"How do you know that happened because of you?" I realize I have raised my tone of voice a little.

"We don't. Like I said, there are many time loops, but causality is not a feature of a time-loop. In fact, if you try to think of it that way you will not get to a workable answer, intuitively or mathematically. We will further discuss the nature of time later on; it is obviously very critical for what we brought you here to learn."

I raise my eyebrows. "Can't wait." I notice we have made quite a bit of progress on the trail. I can now see the Parkman Bandstand monument.

"We in fact never really know if it worked at all. Let me reiterate: we are not trying to change the past, we are trying to make sure that the future as we know it happens." She stops and gives me a serious, but not stern, look before proceeding. "You must understand, this program is a burden, not an adventure."

"Understood." We continue walking silently for a bit while I let this all sink in before asking: "So how do I fit in?"

"Well, as I said before, you are probably our most complex case. You have to remember that you actually invent conscious time travel not long after your current present day. Unlike with most of our Sprouts, our hand will be visible in human history for the first time, since what you are inventing is precisely the capability that led you here."

"What is the significance of that?"

"Well, it's not all that clear yet, since this is the first time the time-loop is—or at least could be—affected in both directions."

"How so?"

"Should you for example decide not to cooperate, or worse, to actively derail our efforts, we might actually alter our time-loop. Unlike the other Sprouts, you understand the significance of what you are doing—of what *we* are doing."

"The others didn't?"

Hena lets out an adorable snorting laugh. "No, most of the other Sprouts really did think they were just dreaming or having visions, they were not told that their consciousness had been brought to the future. We can't pull that trick on you, for obvious reasons."

"So how did it work for them?"

"It varied a lot. With the early philosophers, we brought them into an environment that felt largely like a dream, or a visit from one of the gods. Greeks were amenable to that. We always tried to create an experience that would make sense within their context, their worldview. With a scholar from the middle ages, we would imbue the experience with a religious or ceremonial tone, and usually portray it as a religiously charged vision. With Eastern philosophers we would use parables or mystical experiences to describe new concepts."

"What did you do with people like Einstein or Heisenberg? Those guys must have been tough cookies."

She gives me a puzzled look.

"A 'tough cookie' means they must not have been easy to handle".

"They were indeed much harder to handle. For the most part they thought they had lucid dreams or hallucinations that gave them neat ideas and angles for their research. It works to our favor that most modern academics will not rush to tell their peers how their best ideas came from a dream or a hallucination. But it has meant that in a few of these cases the messages were truncated and not fully understood. One can have only so many strange, recurring dreams before they question their own sanity in more harmful ways."

"You're telling *me* that?"

She stops walking again, takes a step closer to face me, standing uncomfortably close. "Believe me, their experience was nothing like yours."

I take a timid step back. "How so?"

Hena steps even closer to me and places her hand on my right shoulder. "I know this has been jarring for you, but imagine if someone born in the 1700s or 1800s had a similar experience. They would have never seen electric light; they literally would not be able to comprehend how technology could possibly advance to where we are today. The gap would be too big to

35

bridge. Alma includes all of these factors into her calculations. Given 21st century science, you can stretch your mental model enough to entertain the possibility that technology could have gotten here. Pretty much anyone before your time would have struggled to make that leap."

"You are assuming my mental model stretches more than it does."

"I don't think so; Alma would not have missed the mark on that."

"I guess we'll find out."

She lets go of my shoulder. "If you are ready, I will introduce you to the rest of the team, explain how this will work in practice, and walk you through the itinerary we have prepared for you."

I take two steps back. "Am I ready? No, I'm not ready. I wake up in the middle of the night, for the second time, in what is allegedly the future, get told that I'm going to learn about time-travel and that many of the breakthroughs in ancient and modern science were handed over by some mysterious entity called Alma, who also lives in the future! Not only that, I'm supposed to help with this . . . program . . . when in all honesty I'm not even convinced that this would be a good idea, even if I did at all believe that it was all really happening. So no, I'm not ready!"

Immediately, regret floods me. Why did I blow up? Her look grinds me inside. It reminds me of the look that Sarah used to give the dog when it threw up on the carpet; a mix of compassion and disappointment. I hate that feeling. But wait, how did I become the bad guy here? I turn around and take a few deep breadths.

AFTER A LONG SILENCE, I TURN BACK AROUND TO FACE HER AND try to soften my voice a bit.

"Look, I'm sorry I blew up; I can see you're upset. Please do tell me what you have in mind, if this whole thing turns out to be the real deal I will come around. I just can't help but have my naturally skeptical mind nagging me in the background."

She steps closer to me and places her hand on my shoulder as if I hadn't just shaken it off. "We love that naturally skeptical mind; we need it for what we are going to do."

And just like that, all my raging indignation feels very far away. Why am I so weak today?

She goes on: "Part of this was my mistake. It was clearly too much to handle at once. It's already late in the day."

It is late indeed. I suddenly notice the sun is setting, and realize I am hungry. "Yeah, and I'm hungry."

"You would be; I am as well. We should eat dinner, then you should sleep, and tomorrow I will introduce you to the rest of the team and explain the check-out process."

"Will I wake up back home? I mean, back in my time?"

"No. We would have to let you go for that to happen. You will sleep and wake up here."

"Confusing."

"I know, it will become more natural as you spend more time here. Would you prefer to walk all the way back to your home? We just walked past the Ether monument, we are not far. But Alma can also morph the room quickly into your kitchen."

"Walk, I wouldn't mind that bit of normality."

"Sure."

It's a nice walk home as the sun sets. We walk in silence past the rows of townhouses on neighboring streets and then onto my street. I find my keys inside my pocket where they should have been. Interesting. How do they do that?

As we get inside, I realize that I have no idea whether there will be any food in the fridge. This is really not my house. "How does dinner work here?"

"How do you want it to work?"

"I don't know . . . I asked first." That came out a bit childish, I realize.

She laughs. "Would you want to cook? Alma can provide fresh ingredients like the ones you would have in your house, but she can also serve full meals; or if you prefer she can even provide two microwave meals like the ones you used to eat."

"Those are horrible. Passable for me, but I couldn't treat a guest to it."

She smiles and touches my face—again, no understanding of personal boundaries. "So I'm your guest? I like that."

"Yeah, pretend it's a date. I would cook a proper meal for a date."

"Just tell Alma what ingredients you want and they will be where you would normally put them. Give her a sense for quantity; we dislike any waste".

I speak to no one in particular: "Pasta, spaghetti. Basil, fresh basil. Ripe tomatoes. Bocconcini. Garlic. Butter, salted. Salt and Olive Oil. Enough for two people to eat heartily. Oh, and also some Red wine, Chianti Classico ideally, one bottle."

"Please wait four or five minutes while Alma gets the ingredients ready. She can provide her own choice of meals faster, but if you want something specific she has to get it from here to there. Or rather from there to here."

"Where is there?"

She walks over to the kitchen counter and sits on the kitchen stool. "That is complicated, I would suggest we hold off on new information for now. The recipe sounds good; you seem to know what you are doing."

"A bit out of practice, but it used to work".

I cook as I normally would. Sure enough, the ingredients are exactly where they should be, and they look amazing. I couldn't have picked up better tomatoes, nor selected better quality bocconcini. As I'm cooking, it occurs to me that these might not be what I think they are. "Are these ingredients real?"

Hena plucks one of the tomato cubes off the cutting board. "Yes, they are. They may not have been grown or manufactured in the way you are used to, but they will have exactly the same properties."

"Can you give me an example?"

"Yes. The bocconcini is probably the best example. We no longer keep buffalo, or any livestock for that matter. The milk comes from self-organizing microorganisms that produce the exact same ingredient. The production of cheese, bocconcini and others, is handled in an automated fashion by a mix of mechanical processes and other selected microorganisms that ferment lactose into lactic acid, just as a factory would in your times."

"Fascinating. I have so many questions."

"I know, but we really should stop giving you new information for the day, let's talk about something else. You and I need to get to know each other better anyway."

WE HAVE A NICE DINNER OVER GREAT WINE AND TALK ABOUT trivial things. As we are finishing the meal I suggest a game: "Since we need to get to know each other, what do you say we play a game? I pick a question or topic, you respond first, then I go. Only two rules are that you have to answer within 30 seconds and you can't lie."

She pulls her chair over to face me. "Deal. As you know, I don't lie."

"Okay, so let's start: favorite color?"

"Yellow."

"Green. Favorite card game?"

"Canasta."

"21." I find myself wanting to ask how is it possible that they still have some of the same card games after two hundred years, but I don't want to interrupt the game. "Most embarrassing childhood moment?"

"When I realized that Alma wasn't my mother, even though I had been raised by Alma with the help of caregivers since birth. I was 3."

"So were you orphaned?" I regret asking the question as soon as I did, but she seems unfazed.

"I guess technically yes, but my parents didn't abandon me, if that's what you are implying. Alma chose me—as she did a few other children—when

I was 18 months old, to be raised by her. I guess she had bigger designs for me, though I didn't know that until recently."

She cocks her head and smiles at me: "Your turn!"

"Wow, can't beat that. But let's see, for me it would be when I peed myself in first grade. The teacher wouldn't let me leave the classroom and I didn't have the spine to just go." I want to kick myself. She discloses that she was an orphan picked for greater designs and I disclose that I peed myself—brilliant! I move on quickly: "Best childhood friend?"

"Olivio, whom you will meet later."

"Sarah, who later became my wife." I look down and sideways, somehow mentioning Sarah in this setting felt like a mood killer.

Hena grabs my chin and lifts my face up, smiling. "I know you have grieved. Look at this as an opportunity for a new lease on life. Let's continue the game."

"You're right. Proudest moment of your life?"

"Being picked to handle your case."

"Winning my first Nobel prize with Frank." I take a sip of my wine and Hena does the same. "Most deeply held secret?"

"How inadequate I feel to handle this responsibility. In my worldview, ensuring you do what we need you to do is basically ensuring that life as I know it proceeds."

"Wow, that's heavy. I guess mine is too: I was not really sad when Sarah passed anymore. I was very sad when she was diagnosed and in the early days, but after years of living through the hell that was her disease, I felt more relieved than sad. I've never told anyone that."

After a long silence I turn to lighter topics. I didn't want my game to turn out to be a downer. Hena is clearly skating around things that would give away how they live or their values, but I find that I don't care, as she turns out to be pretty interesting conversation even without the two hundred years of knowledge and history she has over me. Maybe it's the wine, but she also seems a lot more relaxed and I even get a taste for her delightful laugh a couple times. I haven't had this much fun in a while.

After what felt like hours she breaks the conversation: "I should go, you need to rest for tomorrow."

"Okay. You are welcome to stay, I have a spare bedroom in the flat."

She laughs, that same hearty laugh again. "You don't really have a spare room, but that wouldn't matter, Alma could comfortably shelter me for the night."

I feel so stupid. Of course, we are not in Boston, we are not in my flat. "Well, this is embarrassing."

"No, it's adorable."

"All right, I'll take that instead."

"I know, Alma makes it feel very, very real."

"I only have a kitchen, so how does this work from now on?"

"Just tell Alma when you are ready to sleep, the room will morph into your bedroom. You have seen that before. Just stick to your normal routine and everything will be where you need it to be. See you tomorrow."

Just like that she's gone, out the eyelid-like door again. I really wish she had stayed, maybe it could have ended like a real date. I haven't had a real date in a while ...

"Alma, please give me my bedroom." The morphing that happened in the white room happens again, but this time it is my kitchen that changes shape. In no more than thirty seconds, my bedroom is here, bathroom and all. Even the bed is as comfily unmade as I would have left it. And, surprise, surprise, I'm wearing my pajamas! How did this happen? More importantly, how did I not notice? Too tired to try to work it out, I simply finish up in the bathroom and fall asleep.

I WAKE UP WITH MY REGULAR ALARM CLOCK. IT'S 7AM. DID I wake up from that weird dream again? Was any of it even real? How would I be able to tell? Everything around me looks exactly normal. I could ask Alma. But I just can't get myself to say the words out loud. If no one answers, I would feel completely stupid, maybe crazy. Could I handle that, being crazy?

"Good morning. You are not crazy."

"Alma?"

"Yes."

"So you *can* read my thoughts?"

"No. And even if I could, I would never do so without your permission. But your look was very transparent, I know you are still unsure, maybe confused about what is and is not real."

"To put it mildly."

"Hena will be here in a few minutes, I would suggest you get ready."

So I do. When I'm done I find myself a bit surprised—disappointed, even—that I'm still in my pajamas. "Alma, why am I still in pajamas?"

"You did not seem pleased when I took that liberty last night, so I refrained."

"It just surprised me, please go ahead, you seem to know my usual outfit." And there it is in a few seconds; my standard brown slacks and my equally standard light blue shirt.

I then ask for the kitchen, make my coffee, and drink it overlooking the river as per usual.

Hena walks in. It seems she's been waiting.

"Good morning, Professor." Hena is bubbly today. No, not bubbly—radiant is the word.

I realize how formal Professor sounds, especially since our dinner last night.

"From now on, please call me Richard."

"Very well, Richard. As discussed yesterday, I will introduce you to the rest of the team. We were going to go over the full itinerary with you as well, but I decided to do that in your next visit. We need to pace how much new information you receive."

Hena points to the wall where the door opens again. "Please meet Chancellor George Orr. You may call him Orr."

A well-cut, military looking fellow walks through the door. I wonder what makes him so immediately military; not his clothing, since he's wearing the same kind of non-descript suit that Hena wears, but a light shade of gray instead of her light blue. Maybe it's the combination of gray buzz cut, the neat gray beard over his square jaw, and the confident stance he walks with. He offers up a hand, and it's a firm and strong handshake. Definitely military. That is, assuming they still have military these days.

"Chancellor Orr, pleased to meet you. I am also the Superintendent for Restitution." He has a firm, authoritative voice, too.

"Nice to meet you as well."

"I am in charge of the Restitution program."

Okay, straight to business then. I'm glad that was my inside voice.

He proceeds: "Needless to say, this is a very important time for us. In a sense it is when the program is created, when it comes full circle. I am honored to be the person in charge at such an important turning point. I see this as the single most important assignment in the history of Restitution, and perhaps in all of human history."

Okay, clearly also not one to indulge in false modesty.

"I am sure Hena already explained that she is your handler . . ."

"I hate that title."

Eyebrows raised: "Why?"

"I don't know, it makes it sound like I need handling, like I'm some sort of criminal, or maybe a patient."

He shrugs. "I see. It was not meant to bring up any of these connotations. It is a purely descriptive title: Hena handles your case, and thus she is your handler. We have found in the past that having a human handler is much more effective than having Alma play that role. That will be especially true in your case, since we are bringing you inside the tent, so to speak."

Zero empathy, definitely military. "Don't get me wrong, I love having Hena around, it's just the title that throws me off."

He gives Hena a knowing look that I can't decipher. "I see."

"Were you the creator of the program?"

"No. A man named Oscar, whom I had the pleasure of knowing right before he died, was the first program Superintendent."

"Yes, I'm sorry, that was a stupid question. The program was created a hundred years ago; it couldn't have been you. Although now that I think about it, I'm not sure how long people live these days".

"We live between one hundred and twenty and one hundred and fifty years. I am eighty-nine years old."

I try to hide my surprise; he looks fifty, fifty-five, tops. "You look very good for your age." Orr just stares back at me. He doesn't seem to know how to take a compliment.

"Hena is your handler, but I will be tracking your progress, and should I feel the need at any point, I will intervene. Hena is also a new handler; you are her second case. She is one of the best we have ever had, which amongst other factors is why we picked her for this. But this is a complex case, so don't be alarmed if I intervene."

I shrug before responding. I'm not sure why he's making such a big deal of this. "I won't."

"There might also be a few times when Hena will call on me to explain specific aspects of our society, especially when it comes to government. I am a senior government official and a Chancellor in the Council, so I understand how these things work a lot better, in theory and in practice."

"Okay."

"Any more questions?"

"No."

With that, he spins and walks purposefully out of the room. I give him the middle finger, thankfully only in my mind.

HENA INTERRUPTS MY REVERIE AS SHE TOUCHES MY SHOULDER, "Let me introduce you to the third member of our core team, Olivio. He is our connector."

Olivio doesn't just walk in, he catwalks in. I have never seen someone walk so elegantly. He could definitely have been a model in my time. He has the body type too, sort of skinny but not unpleasantly so, and loose joints, so it seems like his every move is effortless. Short, bleached blond hair completes the picture.

"Hello, I'm Olivio. It's very nice to finally meet you."

"Finally?"

"Oh, we have been talking about you for months now. I was starting to think it would never happen, that Alma had made some mistake with the time-loop. Then again, Alma makes no mistakes."

"So you are our 'connector,' is it?"

"Yes, yes. You may learn more about how we live, but we connectors have a job that is to create—you guessed it—connections between people. It's what we do; we are all very social, understanding, clever of course, and spirited. Not everyone connects easily, so we bridge that gap. In your case, that will be even more important, since some of the people you will meet will regard you as, well, novel. They may have a hard time connecting without assistance."

"And who exactly am I supposed to connect with?"

"Well, that will be up to you. You and Hena, I guess. My briefing is to help make any connections you need more natural."

Hena leaves us for the afternoon.

Before I have a chance to ask any questions, Olivio starts: "So, let me give you the Olivio 101 rundown, you can ask questions as I go or wait until the end." He pauses dramatically as if expecting questions, shakes his head disapprovingly when I don't say anything, and then continues: "I was born about fifty-three years ago, in what of course became a landmark day, only one Olivio del Toro so far, not sure the world could handle two. I was raised by loving adoptive parents, since my biological parents didn't want to raise children. I loved spending time with the kids being raised by Alma. That is

45

in fact where I met Hena; we must have been 3 or 4 years old, so I have basically known her since forever. I knew from a very early age that I would be a connector. I made friends more easily than anyone, and made friends with everyone, from the kids like Hena to the normal ones, who had lived outside Alma's care."

"What does that mean, live outside Alma's care?"

"It's too complicated for me to explain, Hena can tell you later. And we're here to talk about me, don't try to change the subject." Olivio gives me a disarming smile after I frown. "Anyhow, as I grew up I also became really good at drama and other arts. I wondered many times if I should change professions, but the call of the connector was too strong to resist. I have countless hobbies too, but am only good in one: historical character reconstruction. I can really get inside the minds of our most important historical figures and code digital versions of their personalities. I studied you, too, so I'm looking forward to getting to know the real you, to see whether I got it right or not."

We go on to talk about Olivio, for literally hours. It doesn't really feel like he wants to get to know the real me. Lunch is served sometime within these hours. He tells me his every childhood and youth experience, although he craftily avoids any details that would give away any specifics about how they live. I have to say he's very good at this; I couldn't have covered so much ground while completely avoiding any of the context around it, and he keeps it lively and entertaining.

Olivio eventually finishes and leaves, and Hena walks back in. "It's time we do your checkout. You have been here for two full days and this is only your second visit."

"Right, the check-out."

"Yes. Last time you weren't ready for it, so we put you to sleep before the check-out. Alma, please configure the bedroom as per Richard's original timeline. Richard, let me walk you through what will happen now."

"Okay." I'm not sleepy, so it feels strange to be back in my bedroom.

"We need to re-sync your consciousness to the point in space-time where you fell asleep. Alma will use a series of fields, some of which you are familiar with, like electromagnetic fields, and some you do not know yet. By modulating these fields very purposefully and precisely—and by having you cooperate—we can safely place you back there."

"Is that what you did when you brought me here?"

"Yes. Now we have your resonance signature, so it is much easier to bring you in, but the first time around we had to take an educated guess, knowing the exact coordinates of your bed and a time in which you were likely to be asleep. Now we can bring you forward and back much more easily. But to go back you have to cooperate."

"How do I cooperate?"

"It is pretty simple; just relax as much as you can and try to clear your mind. It's almost like sleeping. In fact, we could always do this when you sleep, but we think there is some benefit of you experiencing the check-out process to help you understand what's happening. Now lay down, this will feel a bit unusual."

I lay down as instructed. I notice I'm now wearing my pajamas.

"I want you to try and clear your mind. The less you have going on in your head, the easier this will be. Also, I want you to be very aware of your body, how it feels in your bed. Any physical sensations that would fit in with your destination will help, as will trying to focus on the present, not any memories nor any anticipation about the future. I will pat you over in specific points to focus your awareness in your body."

She cups my face around her hands for what feels like a minute, then moves on to my shoulders, then my abdomen, my legs, my calves, and eventually my feet. Suddenly I like this check-out procedure—a lot—I could see these leading places . . . right, clear my mind, focus on the present. I concentrate on my breathing, which helps. I feel a strange stimulus; it's not like noise, nor is it a vibration. It's more like I'm being pulled apart, inside, everywhere—but there is no pain. My mind is spinning, very fast. I'm literally disintegrating, and yet my thoughts are very lucid, I am conscious. Then it stops. Quiet darkness. No, not just darkness—this is nothingness.

4

MAD?

Sep 3, 2018

I OPEN MY EYES. THE ORANGE LIGHT COMING THROUGH THE gap between my bedroom curtains indicates early morning. The clock says 5:45. Great, enough time to go for a run. Oh, it's Saturday! I would have time for a run even if it were 7am.

Wait, I just came back from the future. Or just had a recurring and very lucid dream, whichever is the truth. Could this really be happening? Can I talk to anyone about it? Not Frank; he's stressed about the grant as it is. Not my sister; since our parents died, I haven't talked to her. She gave up even before Sarah died. Calling her about this would be unfair. I miss Sarah. Professor Salman, maybe? Sarah had so much trust in him, not just as her academic advisor, but as a friend, too. But no, he would put me in an institution—anybody would. I think I am on my own.

As I go for an early run on this fresh September morning I have the park all to myself. I wonder how I'm not tired, when for all intents and purposes I didn't sleep. Or did I? If I see Hena again, I will ask. I guess I should see her again either way; whether it's because of schizophrenia or because this is all real, she's part of it.

As I eat breakfast I get on the Internet to research schizophrenia, just for the heck of it. Most websites agree on the symptoms:

A: *Difficulty distinguishing between what is real and unreal—check.*

B: *Difficulty in thinking clearly—not really, I've been thinking very clearly and in fact have a few ideas that I think will stun Frank.*

C: *Difficulty managing emotions—well, for a guy who has been told he's time-traveling, I've been doing pretty damn well!*

D: *Difficulty in relating to others—not really, although I have always been a small-circle type of person and with Sarah gone, I'm really down to just Frank and Sun.*

E: *Difficulty in functioning normally—not that I've noticed, but then again, would I be the one to notice that?*

Convinced that there is only a small chance I am indeed schizophrenic, I text Frank and ask him if he would be willing to do some work on the weekend. I want to share some of the ideas I have been having with him. He doesn't return my call for almost an hour, which is unusual for Frank, so I start getting a little worried that I upset him. He finally calls back and explains that he was taking Sun to the airport. She's away for the weekend at a congress, so he was going to call me into the lab himself. Perfect.

As I make my way to the lab, I walk along the main hallway, noticing again the engraved crown moldings. You've got to love these historic Boston buildings. This being a Saturday morning, the building is deserted; my footsteps are the only noise echoing through the building. I walk past the last set of fire-proof doors before going through the usual security routine—fingerprint scan, retina scan, voice recognition—required to pass through the heavy steel lab doors. As I walk in I see Frank sitting at the lead workstation, right across from the main doors.

I greet him first: "Ahoy there, haven't seen you in a while!"

"What do you mean? We spoke yesterday, in my office. Mr. Edwards, remember?"

"Right, yesterday. Trying to forget."

"Yeah, me too."

We go up to the video conference room, since it's the only comfortable meeting room we have in the lab, and the techs will work through the weekend on the second floor to get us ready for next week. Frank stops by the fridge to get a soda on the way in. I admire the wooden wall carvings while I wait for him. Universities must have been very rich institutions at some distant past.

Frank walks in and slouches on one of the big leather chairs. They are old and creaky but still comfortable.

Frank starts hooking up his computer to the main screen, but I stop him: "Listen, I know we should cover the latest simulation results, and probably discuss our approach to the grant and Mr. Edwards, but I wanted to start by running a few things by you."

Frank leans back on the chair. "Okay, hit it, we have lots of time."

"Do you remember what Vittorio said when he saw our approach to the reactor during his visit, when he was on sabbatical?"

"Yeah, he said that if we succeeded in creating our reactor, we would effectively have proven that the arrow of time is a matter of conscious perspective, that is, a psychological phenomenon, not an intrinsic characteristic of space time. His rationale was complicated, though—he said something about how since we are taking virtual particles, or muons, directly from quantum fluctuations, and then syphoning one of the two virtual particles created by the fluctuation in our controlled event horizon, which he called a mini-black-hole, the particle we created will have an exact mirror image on the other side. So while we will see a particle with positive energy on this side travelling away from the event horizon, one can also interpret, and show mathematically, that the very same particle is a negative energy particle travelling back in time. So the only difference between the two interpretations is just that, our psychological interpretation. That would also mean, he said, that the arrow of time, or the direction of entropy increase, is also a matter of perception."

"Exactly. He also tried to prove it mathematically, right?"

"Yeah, I have it somewhere in my files. He never finished it, though, he hit a couple of brick walls." I continue as Frank hooks up his computer to the screen.

"Yeah, he got stuck with a number of infinities that couldn't be renormalized. And that's why he said that if we could make our reactor work in practice, we could measure the Hawking radiation emitted from the event horizon with precision, which in turn we could use to try and avoid the renormalization, providing a clean set of equations."

Frank perks up. "Yeah, it's all coming back to me now."

"Can you dig it up? I want to see if you and I can work through it."

"Yeah, somewhere . . . in . . . this . . . folder . . . here it is. I'll put it up on the big screen so we can look at it."

We work through Vittorio's math for most of the day, and correct a number of missed steps; he had clearly been on sabbatical. We also found the brick walls he got stuck on: one went away with our corrections, the other one really did require either a definite number for the Hawking radiation or new mathematical concepts. We try for hours with everything that has already been invented.

At around 5pm, over delivery pizza, I suggest we phone Vittorio in: "Should we phone Vittorio in?".

"You realize it is 11pm on a Saturday for him?"

"Yeah, maybe he's busy, but if he's not he won't mind. Remember, this is the guy who spent a week of his sabbatical mulling over the reasoning and the math behind our research."

"Okay, but you try, I can't do it with a straight face."

Ringing. "Ciao."

"Vittorio, it's me, Richard."

"Professore Ricardo, how nice to hear from you. Are you in Milan?"

"No, back at the lab in Boston, with Frank. I'm on speaker phone."

"Francesco, how are you my friend?"

"Very well, thank you Vittorio."

"To what do I owe this pleasure? If you are not in Milan, you didn't call me for restaurant advice."

"I was wondering if you would be willing to get on a video call, but I know it's late over there, so we would try to keep it brief. We have been reviewing some of your work during sabbatical and we found a few mistakes."

"You know how to get old Vittorio's attention, no? Yes, I was going to have a quiet night anyway, went out with the team yesterday to celebrate our new grant and decided to stay in today, despite this being a Saturday night."

Vittorio gets on the video call, and we end up working through most of his night, and eventually our night. At around 11am his time, 5am our time, he concludes triumphantly: "Okay, so you found a couple simple mistakes here and there, but really the conclusion has not changed. If your gadget works you will have proven that time is a function of consciousness and will have found the precise constant required to have clean equations. And if you fail, we're back to square one, as you say."

We agree, say our goodbyes and Vittorio hangs up.

"SHOULD WE CALL IT A DAY?" FRANK'S VOICE INDICATES A MIX OF question and plea.

"Sure, but before we do that, can we spend a bit of time discussing the implications of this?"

"Okay, but I'm going to need some fresh coffee."

Over a fresh pot, I start: "You realize how profound the implications of this would be, right?"

Frank takes a sip and winces; the coffee is too hot. "Yeah, huge. For one, we would finally understand the second law of thermodynamics and why the arrow of time flows in the direction of increased entropy. It's one of those physics sore points; we all know that disorder always increases, but no one knows why."

I blow on my coffee. "It would also open up a whole new set of questions."

Frank fidgets, making the big leather chair creak and groan before speaking: "Yeah. Like, if time were a psychological phenomenon rather than an intrinsic feature of space-time, would we all experience time the same way? How would animals experience time?"

"True. But Frank, you're using hypothetical language. Both you and I are very confident we will succeed once we solve the calculation issue."

Frank spins the chair around a couple times, stops and rubs his eyes vigorously. "Richard, you realize that if we do, we can't ignore the implications."

"We can ignore them, and may have to, at least for a little while."

"Look, this would open up a whole new field of study around the inter-action between consciousness, space-time, and matter."

I throw my hands in the air and raise my voice. "I know, but it's not our main line of study. We're trying to prove that we can generate energy out of nothing—literally! That is no less transformative than understanding the nature of the time arrow. In fact, it's of more practical use. I'm not sure what practical use knowing that time is psychological would have."

Franks gets up and goes to the window, looking outside. "Richard, you must see the same practical use I do."

Knowing I can't possibly tell Frank what happened to me last night, I ask in what is almost a squeal: "Time travel?"

"That's tight, time travel. Time travel, Richard. Forget Nobel prizes, we'd be changing the course of history, literally."

I try to sound uninterested. "Geez, maybe, but there's a huge leap from proving that something is possible to knowing how to make it happen. We don't even understand the nature of consciousness, or how it interacts with our own brains. We know consciousness does somehow interact with physical reality from the wave/particle duality, the double slit experiment and all that crap, but we have no idea how."

Frank walks back from the window, leans over and places both his hands on the table. "Yeah, but imagine if we did."

I roll my eyes. "Oh yeah, amazing, but that's not what we're doing. Maybe Vittorio should take that up? It's his field of study."

Frank grabs my arm. "Maybe. But what if Bohm was right? What if there are an implicate and an explicate order? That could explain some of it, maybe he was just two hundred years ahead of his time."

I chuckle. "Funny, two hundred years."

Frank shakes his head: "Why is it funny?"

"Nothing, inside joke."

Frank looks up at me without raising his head. "You must see the significance of this."

"More than you know. But right now we have more immediate problems to solve.

Frank sighs. "Fine. Let's discuss the latest simulation results and our approach to Mr. Edwards as you suggested earlier. Can we do that?"

"Yeah." Over the next three hours we hash a plan to placate Mr. Edwards and to find out more about his agenda, who he is *really* working for in the department, and why the sudden panic over our rate of progress.

I GO HOME AND HEAT UP A MICROWAVE MEAL FOR LUNCH. I'M just too tired to make good on my promise to cook healthy today. I turn on the TV, ready to turn my brain off for a bit. Maybe catch some baseball.

I almost choke on my food: "Wait! European soccer!"

I turn on the sports channel and there it is, Real Madrid and Barcelona, twenty-three minutes into the second half of the game. No one has scored yet, so Alma's prediction could still happen. I finish my lunch in minutes, grab a beer, and plunk back down on the couch to watch. Twenty-six minutes in and still nothing has happened—the game is absolutely locked-in. The commentator confirms my view: "Folks, I see very little action here, each team seems to be clearly more worried about securing their defense than scoring the first goal." As far as I know, half these finals end up on penalty shootouts, but according to Alma, this one will not.

At the twenty-nine-minute mark, I jump up from the couch. The Real Madrid forward, Burgui, runs with the ball, dribbles two Barcelona midfielders and runs past the last defense man, and shoots straight to the corner of the goal—but the Barcelona goalkeeper, Jasper, jumps and stretches in a way that looks inhuman, punching the ball out of the field. I'm surprised to find that I feel relieved.

This seems to wake the Barcelona team up. They start taking more risks, pushing the ball forward a few more times over the next five minutes of game. At the thirty-four-minute mark Rafinha—Barcelona's best midfielder—steals a ball from Real Madrid's Lukas and sprints with it, seemingly avoiding every tackle from Real Madrid's defense. He passes the ball to Neymar, who performs a flawless headshot, scoring a goal. The Barcelona players pile onto him, one by one, while three others perform a group-twerk in a line-up. The Real Madrid goalkeeper gestures madly while shouting something at the referee. It seems to be total madness on the field. The commentator is completely silent for several seconds that seem to stretch for minutes—long enough for me to realize the implications. Whatever prediction I had in my dream was wrong.

If none of this ever really happened, am I really crazy? Should I get some treatment? At least some counselling? What about Hena, was she just a product of my mind?

The commentator finally speaks and pulls me back to the game: "Wait, folks, there seems to be a problem. As you can see, the three referees are conversing midfield. The players are going mad, circling referees like hyenas. One of the referees just raised a hand—with a red penalty card! Rafinha, Barcelona's captain—and in my view their best player—has just been sent off! He's out of the game, folks."

The referees split up again and the main referee goes back to Real Madrid's side of the field. The commentator explains: "The referees have reached a conclusion: Neymar was offside, the goal is nulled. The score remains 0x0."

I sit back down. I never cared much for soccer, or for any sport for that matter, but I'm sweating and puffing. After a couple more threats for penalty cards, the commotion clears and the game resumes. I try to dry my sweaty palms, but it seems pointless. The clock now reads thirty-seven minutes into the second half, and Barcelona, now with ten players, locks up defensively as if expecting Real Madrid to be emboldened with all its eleven players. And that's exactly what happens; Real Madrid attacks over and over again, while also exposing themselves to a couple of counter-attacks.

At the thirty-nine-minute mark Nacho—a Real Madrid defender—senses an opportunity after a botched Barcelona counter-attack. He runs with the ball to midfield and drives a power shot from the centerline, scoring Real Madrid's first goal. I find myself cheering, jumping up and down.

"What a beautiful midfield shot!" confirms the commentator.

The unexpected score seems to deflate the Barcelona team. Retreating now is no longer an option and they make several clumsy attacks, hoping to tie the game. At forty-one and forty-two minutes, Real Madrid scores two more goals. At this point the Barcelona team retreats again. I guess they no longer expect to tie—priority now is to maintain some pride by holding to a demoralizing but not unusual 3x0 score.

Real Madrid seems to be content with that; they start passing the ball midfield as if this was a practice game, not a championship final. This goes on for a while. I look at the clock. Forty-five minutes; the game should be ending now. My heart skips a beat, but as is usually the case, the referee adds some extra time to account for time lost in penalties. In this case, he added fifty seconds.

Even the commentator seems disappointed: "Folks, this is what I mean when I say that players have now become too professional. Where is the passion? The game is won, so they just keep passing the ball back and forth. See, even the crowd is booing now, what a shame, this is no way to win a championship."

Almost as if he had heard the commentator—and perhaps having heard the crowd—Burgui lunges forward with the ball, dribbling one, two, three Barcelona players before passing the ball to Jese, who scores the fourth goal at forty-five minutes, forty-nine seconds.

I jump up as the commentator confirms it. "Folks, Real Madrid has done the impossible and scored four goals in less than six minutes at a European club league final. There you have it: Real Madrid, the 2018 champion, four nothing!"

I plunk back down on my couch and talk to the TV: "Shit, this is real."

5

RESTITUTION

Sep 5, 2218

I WAKE UP, IF THAT'S WHAT I SHOULD CALL IT. I'M IN THE SAME white room again, same white suit, but at least now I know what's happening.

"Good morning, Professor."

"Good morning, Alma."

"You are getting used to the routine."

"Not even close. But I now know this is real, or at least as real as everything else in my life. Your soccer prediction, however unlikely, was correct."

"It was not a prediction; it was a record."

"Yeah, right, that's what I meant."

"Hena should be here in a minute."

The room morphs into what looks like a teaching facility, maybe a lab. I'm now sitting on one of many chairs in a circle.

On cue, Hena walks in.

"Good morning, Richard."

"Good morning, miss me?"

She approaches and touches my shoulder. "Yes, actually."

I try to look up at her. From where I'm sitting, I have to twist my head at an awkward angle. I'm not sure why I asked that question. I don't know what to say now—I actually very much missed her. I regain composure and change the subject abruptly. "Your soccer tip was right. At least now I know this is all real. Either that, or I am truly hallucinating, but if that's the case I wouldn't know anyway."

She smiles and sits beside me. "That's great news. We will progress much more easily without that doubt hanging in your mind."

"So. When will you teach me what I came here to learn?"

"That will depend on you more than anything."

"How?"

"In two ways: you need enough background to absorb the material, and you need to be ready and willing to commit to using that knowledge in the way Alma prescribes. This is very important. We are not just imparting knowledge, we are also providing guidance, and both have to be fully absorbed."

"Fair enough. How will we accomplish that?"

"The plan was to start with this first few days covering the history of Restitution and letting you ask any questions you may have about it. Some other handlers will be available to answer your questions, and we may take a few detours to walk you through their experiences where appropriate."

"And then?"

"Again, it will depend on you. The general plan is to bring you back here every night in your present timeline. We will try to limit each of these nightly visits to no more than a few days in our timeline. We may take more time in our timeline in-between your visits, but that would be completely transparent to you."

"That will be strange, having such different time scales to deal with."

"Yes, it will. You will need to be quite centered to keep your sanity. That is why we brought you in only for a few hours at first, a couple of days last time, hopefully a few days this time, and so on. Please remember that this is the first time we are executing Restitution in this model and for this long, so we are not sure what this will do to your state of mind."

"Well, that's reassuring. Exactly what do you mean by my state of mind?"

"If you are spending days here for every night in your current present, will you come to feel like this is the present, and 2018 like some distant past? That would not be productive. We can't risk you losing the ability to sync back."

"I'm not sure I can handle that."

"I trust you can, but we are breaking new ground here, and as your handler . . ."

"I hate that word!"

Hena turns to me and holds my hands again. She really is touchy.

"I'm sorry; I will try to not use it. As the person who designed your program, I'm trying to balance the pace at which you can absorb new information, with the need to make progress quickly—we don't have much time."

"Why do we not have much time? What's the urgency?"

"As you may remember, Alma guesses when leaps in human capability are unlikely to have taken place without "external" help. Her guesses are well calculated and fit with historical records of human achievement, but they are still guesses. The leap in thinking can normally be pinpointed to a particular window of time; a few days, maybe a week. In your case the most probable window is roughly a week, so while we may have a couple of days of wiggle room, we likely don't have much more than that."

"And why the pressure here? Can't you send me back the same night? Why can't I stay for like months and then go back to the same night?"

"We can take as much time in-between visits as we want, but when you are here we don't have that luxury. The wider the disparity between the timelines you experience, the harder it will be for you to sync back when you return. That's why your visits in the future will be limited to a maximum of few days at a time."

"Geez, I feel a lot of pressure now."

Hena lets go of my hand and stands up.

"That was not my intent. If you are ready, I would suggest we bring in some of the other handlers."

"You have to stop asking me if I'm ready. It's impossible to feel ready. You have no idea how foreign all of this sounds!"

She sits back down and grabs my hand. "I'm sorry, Richard, I don't want to seem insensitive, but we don't have much time. We need to keep progressing."

I take a deep breath and nod.

She squeezes my hand tighter and smiles before letting go. "I want you to meet some other handlers."

THREE HANDLERS WALK INTO THE ROOM JUST THEN, ALL DRESSED in the same non-descript light blue uniform that Hena wears. We shake hands and sit down around the circle chairs.

"I have asked each of the handlers to talk through their work," Hena says. "But I've also asked them to start by saying a little bit about themselves personally, before covering their participation in the program."

First up is a tall, dark skinned man who looks about fifty years old, to my reckoning at least.

"Hi I'm Ayodele. It means 'return of happiness' in my ancestors' tongue. I'm eighty-nine and one of the more experienced handlers in this group. On the personal side, I have found my own mate for life, with whom I have two children, a daughter and son in their thirties. None of them have, unfortunately, chosen the path of a handler. I guess seeing how hard it was directly from their dad dissuaded them."

As he speaks, I see all three people flash in front of me in what looks like an artistic depiction of each; it is hard to describe, definitely 3D, but also purposely depicted to not be in perfect detail. Some of the angles are off, as if the perspective were distorted, but in a way that maintains some artistic harmony to the projection; it almost seems done on purpose to not seem real. They all look very happy and peaceful in these images, I get the sense that Ayodele is imbuing his own feelings of love and happiness toward them in the images.

"Our favorite activity as a family is bubble surfing."

My puzzlement must show on my face, because he chuckles a little.

"I wish you had time to see or maybe even experience some of what we do for fun, you would be blown away."

As he waves his hand I see the images, all four of them each in a large bubble. They look like they're made of some thick liquid, very malleable, but still sturdy. Ayodele and his family are 'surfing', to repeat the term he used, but they are actually surfing air—or, more accurately, wind. They are very high up and the winds look very strong; they are obviously enjoying the speed and swaying around, which seems to require some careful balancing.

"Professionally, I have always been a handler," Ayodele continues. "My first cases were early humans. I had to inspire them to use tools, as well as using caves and other structures as semi-permanent shelter. They weren't even using memory to remember their daily locations at that time."

Images of these early humans flash in front of us. They barely look like humans; they are hairy and obviously have no language capability.

"Are these homo Neanderthals?"

"Oh no, these were one of the Australopithecus groups. They lived between three and two million years before our species, for the most part they did not stand up."

There again are the images showing these creatures, which I now see, as Ayodele said, looked more like apes than men. They are using stone tools to eat the meat of a large rodent—rather gruesomely, I might add.

"Apologies for the images; these were Alma's best rendering of what we had them experience while with us. She created them using a mix of historical records, her own archeological analysis, and the Sprout's reaction to things in real time. After observing some of their own kind performing the tasks we wanted them to learn, they started copying them."

"Fascinating."

"Yes, these early ones are some of the hardest. In order to be able to act as a handler, we have to be as close to their worldview as possible, so that we can facilitate resonance. So we have to spend a bit of time immersing ourselves into their reality, which Alma does a great job at recreating. For early humans that is sometimes disturbing; they had rough lives."

"Why didn't you specialize handlers by epoch, then? Wouldn't that make your job easier?"

He answers: "Yes, it would. We have discussed it many times and have come to the conclusion that it would be easier but less effective. There is real benefit as a handler from having seen early humans evolve across the ages."

I just nod.

Ayodele continued: "As an example, it was very helpful to me, after seeing how food was consumed by early humans, to then return about two million years later, which was approximately four hundred thousand years ago, to inspire them in early techniques to manage fire. We had to remove the fear of fire in the first place, and then went on to inspire them with ways to manage it. At the same time, we had to suggest some more advanced social structures, which became particularly important as fire tended to create disproportionate power for those who controlled it."

Again the scenes of early humans handling fire appear, showing the many uses it had, from heating to cooking to early warfare.

"I then moved on to slightly more recent assignments, inspiring peoples in what you would call the fertile crescent and the middle east to domesticate crops a little over twelve thousand years ago. Mostly large grains at the time."

A scene that reminds me of epic movies from my childhood appears. It shows people planting what appear to be experimental crops, testing several techniques and different seeds in a patch of land.

"As you can guess, we specialize not by epoch, but rather by theme, and my theme is human sustainment. So my next Sprout of note was an Egyptian priest who we inspired to invent irrigation."

The scene morphs into a series of canals being built on what I recognize as a flood plain. It moves on to show a time-accelerated view of how irrigation increased the size and scope of the planted area; it seems to cover several decades, even centuries.

"There were several minor interventions along the way as well, but the next one I will call your attention to was when we brought Jethro Tull—not the band, although I would love to claim I inspired their music too—this was Jethro Tull the agricultural pioneer, whom we inspired to introduce mechanization into crops."

The scene shifts to a basic mechanical seed drill being pulled by horses, in what looks like seventeenth century Europe. It then shows a series of advancements into agricultural mechanization, culminating with present day agricultural machinery. Modern day for my timeline, that is.

Hena stands up. "Thank you, Ayodele, that was wonderful. Before we move on to Renu for her introduction, any questions, Richard?"

"Yeah, why did you decide to be a handler?"

Ayodele is serious, almost solemn: "There could be no other path for me. Humanity had basically gone astray before Restitution and I had no confidence…" He pauses and looks me in the eye. "I mean no disrespect to your peers, Professor, but truth is that I have no confidence in humanity during your timeline. I'm convinced that if we had not intervened we would not be here. We had to create Restitution precisely at your present time to right the path that humans were on. I think the earlier interventions were helpful, but not as critical. I apologize if my comments offend you, Professor."

"Thank you for being so candid. Your view doesn't offend me at all, I in fact agree very much with you. We took the most brilliant discovery of the 20th century, atomic energy, and made the most terrifying weapon in history with it. So no offense taken."

"I'm glad to hear that, Professor."

"And please call me Richard, all of you."

They all nod.

A SOUTH ASIAN LOOKING WOMAN WHO APPEARS TO BE IN HER late 20s stands up.

"Hi. As Hena said, my name is Renu. It means atom or universe in my original language. I'm forty-nine years old and I have decided to live with the mate Alma recommended. We're very happy and have no children yet. We haven't yet decided whether we will raise children, but I will surely bear two children even if we do not keep them."

I hesitate to stop her, but this is for me after all, so I ask, "Sorry to interrupt, but what does that mean?"

Renu glances at Hena, who nods. "We have a choice as to whether we want to raise children or not. People also have a choice as to whether or not they want to bear children, but these decisions are very personal. Any person can conceive up to two children, regardless of whether they will raise them or not; there are always people who want to raise children but cannot bear them, or who want to raise more than the two children they are allowed to bear."

"What happens if someone bears more than two children?"

"That never happens without the council's consent."

I motion to ask further questions but Hena gives me a look that tells me I've reached my answer quota on this particular topic.

"Our favorite leisure activity is historical drama, with a special focus on medieval and colonial periods."

The images shift now to them experiencing several different medieval and colonial settings, probably between 1200 and 1700 in the Christian calendar. I guess they are acting, but it seems very real; they almost seem to be part of history.

I'm probably breaking her dramatic flow, but I can't help it: "How does that work?"

"Alma creates these environments that feel very real for those participating, and each of us takes one specific character in the story and acts them out."

"Like a virtual reality game?"

"Something like that, but the focus is not on the 'game,' as you call it, but rather on trying to integrate fully into our individual character while also reflecting the general worldview at that time. Stretching your mind, to think that the world is flat as you hop on a ship is an amazing experience. It takes concentration and skill, but when you get it just right, it is almost as if you've lived history again."

"That sounds cool!"

"It's better than cool, it's life changing! It used to be my job. Professionally, I started as a handler about five years ago. I graduated from my last program at thirty-two. After graduation I started working in historical drama, documenting and building plots for other actors to perform, but then I realized I wanted to actually participate in the drama more than create it. I also realized that my interest and skill in understanding history at many levels could be useful to Restitution. I was naturally hoping that I would be your handler, but that did not happen. While I feel a twinge of envy, I'm very happy that Hena was selected, as she was the best in our class."

Our class? Meaning she and Hena are the same class? Could Hena be forty-nine? They must think I look like I'm ninety-five...

"Since joining the program, I have always been more involved with the life sciences. My first assignment was with the early peoples in both Africa and the American continent, when we brought medicine men to inspire them to use herbs, fruits, and body movement to heal simple ailments."

At the wave of her hand, a flurry of images form, showing several sick and injured people being healed by medicine men and women through various rituals.

"The ritualistic behavior was mostly driven by the healers themselves. We think it was part of how they rationalized the Restitution experience in the first place. That said, we do find it curious that the rituals tend to have some similarities, and we can't quite explain why."

"Do these techniques work, the ones you are teaching them?"

"Of course they do. Certainly not as advanced as what you have in your time, let alone what we can do today, but better than simply letting disease or injury take its course unmanaged."

"True."

"My next intervention was in Ancient China about three thousand years ago, to inspire the creation of Chinese medicine. It started of course with the inspiration for the Yin-Yang concept and the five phases theory, but that was followed by many more interventions, since Alma identified several different strands of advancements that likely had a helping hand, including more advanced herbal medicine, massage, exercise, dietary therapy, and acupuncture. Some of these techniques are still used today quite successfully. In fact, one of the core principles, which is that the body can heal itself if the mind stops interfering, is more present in our current medicine than it was in what you consider modern medicine."

She's clearly proud of her work. A flurry of scenes in different Chinese settings follows, some beautiful and peaceful, some downright scary. Then we see the same techniques being used in different times across history, all the way to what I recognize as my present day.

"As you might have guessed, my next intervention was in Ancient Greece, some five hundred years later. The concepts of medical diagnosis, prognosis, and medical ethics were introduced, including the Hippocratic Oath, although that has changed a bit over time. These interventions had to be timed with other broader interventions on scientific thinking, given the necessary interplay of concepts."

We see several scenes of Ancient Greece as she speaks. We see a medical academy where the scientific rigor now central to medicine is taught, as well as medical facilities for different classes, from a lab-looking facility where the aristocracy was shown receiving treatment, to ramshackle and dirty exam rooms where the common people were examined.

"Next came our intervention with Rogerius of Salerno, roughly one thousand years ago, which inspired him to eventually write his Practica Chirurgiae work, and start what became the basis for the next eight hundred years in medicine. If only these were not the dark ages in the Western world, that could have happened much faster. But it started the chain as we thought it should have."

The images now shift to show a thin and tall man, performing different kinds of rudimentary surgery, all very gruesome, in what look like unsanitary and dark conditions. He's clearly passionate and confident in his actions, though, which makes the scene a bit more heartening.

"I know it can seem a bit gruesome, but remember what they had available beforehand."

"Yeah, I know, it is a reminder of how far we've come, even in my time. Let me guess, the next one is Alexander Fleming, who invented the antibiotics."

"Close, but not quite. The next Sprout was Louis Pasteur, who was given the insight that if different bacteria can combat one another, then there must be a way to intervene in a similar fashion. That led to the work of French bacteriologist Jean Paul Vuillemin, which in turn led to Alexander Fleming inventing antibiotics some fifty years later. This is a great example of how Sprouts are not always the most famous of names, but rather are found in the beginning of these chains of innovation, not the end."

As she speaks we see bacteria in action, fighting one another at first, then being cultured by the different bacteriologists, and eventually we see antibiotics in action killing the bacteria. It's as if the images in front of us came from a giant microscope, but in 3D. I've never seen anything like it before; it strikes me that we really should adopt 3D imagery in present day schools.

"There have been many interventions in advanced medicine since then. In fact, our pace has accelerated dramatically, but given that you might have heard some of these names—and even perhaps met some of them in academia—we will refrain from showing these details unless they become necessary."

Hena stands up again. "Well, I guess we should pause for lunch. Not that these images help work up anybody's appetite."

ALMA MORPHS THE ROOM INTO AN OUTDOOR SPACE WITH PICNIC table at the center. I can't tell which park we are in, but it looks like a place that could be outside of Boston, or any temperate city. She serves simple but very tasty vegetable pasta with what seems like fruit juice, but I can't quite place what fruit. I couldn't describe how the food makes it to the table; it just appears there for us to serve our own plates.

One of the handlers I haven't yet met sits by me and we chat about small things. After a few seconds of uncomfortable silence, I ask the only question that comes to mind: "What do you think of the program leader, Chancellor Orr?"

She looks around before answering. "I don't really like him. He is curt and condescending with most of us. Nobody likes him."

"Wow, that was a very honest answer."

"We always tell the truth."

"Right, I forget. So does anyone tell him that to his face?"

"Well, no, he never asks that question. It's like that fable where everybody knows something is wrong, but no one wants to point out that 'the king is naked.'"

"I think it goes 'the emperor has no clothes.'"

"Same idea, I prefer 'the king is naked.'"

She gives me a sheepish smile before eating another bite.

I decide to be truthful myself: "I can't blame you, I don't like Orr either—at all."

She just smiles at me.

When we're done Alma morphs the room back to the round seating configuration and the other handlers say goodbye and go.

Hena turns to me. "Richard, what questions do you have at this point?"

Geez, where do I start? So many questions, and yet they are all stuck in my throat. "I will start with the obvious one: Why me?"

"You are probably asking the wrong person, since Alma decides who should be brought in. Well, technically Orr decides, as he's the representative of the council in charge of Restitution, but Alma makes the recommendation and I can't imagine Orr could disagree. He would have no basis to do so."

I must have looked disappointed. Hena grabs my hand and continues: "I can give you my opinion: your research is credited in history with having built the theoretical, mathematical, and even technological underpinnings of moving a consciousness through time. Alma assesses the probabilities that each leap in human capability happened on its own, and this one would be unlikely to happen if unassisted—do not take that as a criticism."

"I won't."

"Other questions?"

"Yeah. What if I can't do it?"

"That is a very complicated question with a very simple answer. It's complicated because it calls into question the very nature of time, and of what a time-loop is."

"How so?"

"Well, if you can't do it, does that mean we're changing the time-loop? If so, this very reality we are living in, where you invented the technology behind Restitution, never happens, and the question is moot in the first place. Or does it mean that you will definitely succeed, otherwise we would not be having this discussion? We don't have a satisfactory answer to these questions, although there are theories. Not even Alma knows for sure, or if she does she won't tell us. Now, the answer to your question as you framed it is actually very simple: you can do it, because we know what you need to do. You have to remember that we're not asking you to develop the theories nor the technology; we have the answers. We just need you to have enough conviction that you will actually act on the knowledge we are imparting. That is precisely why we're spending whatever time we have to build that conviction. And there is one more thing . . ."

She pauses, cups her hand over her mouth.

"What thing, Hena?"

"I'm not sure I can say it. Alma, you must know what I was going to say: can I?"

Alma answers: "Yes, but allow me, Hena. Professor, sometime in your future, you will leave a note to future scientists. It says: 'To anyone who may come across this note: if you have found this and energy generation from quantum fluctuation has not been invented, it means I did not succeed. Where I failed or faltered you must not. You have to go to Professor Sun Tzu's laboratory, there is a file titled *Restitution*. Find and implement the solution in it. The future of humanity depends on it.'"

"Well, that was a little dramatic, no?"

Hena cocks her head and raises her eyebrows. "You tell me; you wrote it yourself. But the reason it is really significant is that it seems that no one ever opened it. That note was found in a government facility, hidden inside a wallet in between credit cards, your credit cards. It had never been opened when we found it, which in turn must mean you succeeded. We keep it as a historical artifact now."

"Okay, that's reassuring, I think. On that note—pun intended—can I involve my colleagues and friends? More generally, can I tell anyone else?"

"History would indicate that you do indeed get help from your colleagues, but whether you tell them the truth before that or not, we don't know. There is no record of your conversations."

"Okay, I guess that means I tell no one for now."

Hena nods and turns to me:

"So, what are your views on Restitution?"

"I am very conflicted about it."

Hena speaks to the air: "Alma, please join us again for this conversation." She then gives me an intense look. "I wasn't expecting that. Conflicted how?"

"On one hand, the program is clearly well thought out. You seem to have a good handle on how to influence the past without causing any major issues, largely I think because of your philosophy that you are not trying to change the past, but rather make sure the future happens . . ."

Alma intervenes: "Not a philosophy, an imperative."

"Fine, an imperative. Also, it would seem that most of the interventions you made prior to me have helped humanity advance towards a better society, a better world."

Hena crosses her arms: "On the other hand?"

"On the other hand, I have no way of knowing if what you are asking me to do is a good thing or not. Well, I don't even quite know what you are really asking me to do yet, and I certainly don't know if I agree with it or not. You didn't give me much on twentieth century Restitution interventions, which I kind of understand given their proximity to my present. But arguably some developments in recent science, like the atom bomb or genetic manipulation, are a bad thing; at the very least the jury is still out. So how do I know that what you will ask me to do isn't the biggest mistake in human history? To use your own words, I will need full conviction before I do what you will ask me to do, whatever that is. You see my dilemma?"

She purses her lips and takes a deep breath. "Yes, I absolutely do. What would help you get there?"

"I'm not sure. Maybe if I knew more about the impact of my work, what came of it, what kind of society it helped create?"

"Unfortunately we don't have the time for that."

"We're going to have to make the time for that."

Hena sighs. "It's not that simple."

"Look, simple or not, you want conviction. Show me how people live today, how society operates, how people work, what kinds of rights people have, their standards of living . . ." I shake my head as I struggle to make my point. "Prove that today's world is the kind of society I would want to be a part of. Maybe that would give me some more conviction."

I look down and notice Hena is wringing her hands. She clears her throat before responding.

"Alma and I can try to do that, but we don't have much time. And if we take that risk, if we take the time to show to you that the future we're trying to protect is, as you say, the kind of world you want to be a part of, we need your commitment—your unequivocal commitment—that you will follow our orders."

"I can do that. You have my word: if what I see is compelling I will do as you say."

This seems to soften Hena. She takes a deep breath and rubs her hands together.

"We will prepare a proper introduction to life in 2218."

"Thank you. And one more thing; this should not be the 'royal visit,' you know? Where everything is so scripted and managed that you don't really get the sense of what's going on."

"We would not do that."

"I hope not. When can we get started?"

"Next visit. You have clearly had too much new information for one visit, plus Alma and I have some planning to do. We should start the check-out."

"Wait, there's one more thing before we do: we didn't really talk about you. Is that against protocol?"

"No, it is simply unnecessary." Hena purses her lips.

"Can we do that before I go?"

Hena turns her head sideways and up: "Alma, do we have time to tell Richard a bit about me?"

Alma answers: "Yes. In fact, sending him home now would not be productive. There is a clear tension in the air given the prior exchange. Checkout would be ineffective."

Hena places her hands in her lap, softening a little. "Very well, then I can do my own impromptu intro if you wish."

"Thank you. I have been quite curious about your background and it struck me as odd that I knew so much about handlers that will not work with me, but so little about you."

Hena smiles, faces me, and perks up in an almost childish way. "Well, let's see. As I mentioned you are only my second case, the first one was a 20th century physicist; you would recognize the name and might even have met when you were entering physics, so not one of those Sprouts we would talk to you about. I am pretty new to the program."

"I hope you don't mind me asking, but if you're so inexperienced, why did they pick you?"

Shoulders raised, she blushes: "Well, I'm supposedly very, very smart. I have been top of my class since I was two years old, Alma says that she has had to recalibrate some of the potential achievement curves to accommodate me. I excelled at three different professions before I was asked if I wanted to become a handler. Most people take twenty to thirty years to perfect one profession."

"What professions did you have?"

"I was a sculptor, a caregiver for the young, and a peacekeeper."

"These are very different professions. Why did you pick them?"

"I picked each for different reasons. I decided to become a sculptor because I like the purity of visual perfection, you know? When you finish a piece and it's just perfect, beyond criticism." She gesticulates widely as if I could see the air sculpture she's surely building in her mind.

"And the other two?"

"I didn't have a human mother, so I had caregivers who helped raise me under Alma. Alma was the more present intellect, but the caregivers gave me love, affection and practical help in learning life's basic skills. I felt like I'd be giving back by doing that."

"Did you not find that to be the case? Is that why you changed professions?"

74

"Oh no, it was very fulfilling. I loved caring for the children. Seeing them grow up is like watching a billion years of natural evolution unfold right in front of your eyes. There were times when you could almost hear their little brain clicking as they learnt a new skill, or grasped a particular concept. Children also display their humanity in its most raw form. They are not worried about societal norms, about others' expectations. It is wonderful to be with them.

"Then why change?"

"I became a peacekeeper because I was curious to see what happens when everything fails. When despite the tireless work of families, caregivers and Alma in raising balanced, loving human beings, something goes astray and that person develops violent tendencies. I wanted to see that up close."

"And what's your verdict?"

She cups my face in her right hand—I'm reminded she has warm hands—and smiles.

"I learnt that humans are fallible and emotionally complex. That these people who became violent had not really gone astray or degenerated, they just lost control of their emotions. The basal instincts that were so important during our early development as a species took over, but as soon as we de-escalated situations they would—almost always—be the same loving and caring people they were before. And nothing happens without a reason. As a peacekeeper I could very clearly see how people grew and learnt from their experiences, however challenging. In fact, I'm convinced that people bring onto themselves the experiences they need to grow and develop."

I suddenly realize I want to kiss her, I really do. I now see a depth to Hena that I had not grasped yet. But that would obviously be ridiculous and inappropriate. After a few silent seconds she lets go of my face. I wonder if my thoughts were transparent, and look away.

"What about personal details?" I feel like I need to justify my question. "The other intros included personal life."

"Let's see, what did I not cover during our dinner date? I'm forty-three years old. I had one sibling, but I was raised by Alma, so I don't know who he or she is."

"What about outside work, what do you do for fun?"

She gets up: "Oh, yes! My favorite hobby is deep water diving. I didn't prepare a visual presentation like the others, but one of these days I will show some of the images. They are incredible." She gesticulates wildly as she continues, "Alma prepares these pressure bubbles that can take you down to the bottom of the ocean, literally. The creatures you see might as well have come from another planet, and they are of an indescribable beauty."

She sits back down facing me.

I ask in what feels like the most awkward way possible: "Um, what about marriage, are you married?"

"I haven't yet chosen a mate."

I wonder if the relief is obvious in my face, so I quickly cover it up with a question: "Why not?"

"No particular reason. I simply haven't found what I am looking for in anyone. Alma has offered to help, but I'm not ready for that yet."

"And what *are* you looking for?"

Over a laugh: "Oh, I didn't picture you as a contender . . ."

I feel like my forehead is sweating, I debate whether I wipe it or just let it shine. I feel my pulse throbbing on my neck and I am pretty sure my discomfort is written all over my face, but I put on a brave face and state nonchalantly: "No, I'm just curious."

She grabs both my hands, leans over and kisses me. Not a passionate French kiss, but not your best friends' smooch, either.

After a while, she pushes me away gently. "You really should go now; we need to start check-out."

That felt abrupt, so I feel entitled to ask, "Was that against the rules?"

"The kiss? Not that I know of, but we've never had to have these kinds of rules."

As I sit on the bed Alma manifests beside me, she continues: "In any case, Alma has said that if we become close, you will have an easier time coming in and out of sync."

She must read the look of alarm on my face.

"I didn't kiss you to make the sync easier," she says quickly. "I kissed you because I was attracted to you. I am attracted to you. We should continue this conversation when you are back."

I just nod. I lay down and she does the checkout. We have to do it twice; the first time her hands go down my body, they do nothing to relax me. After a well-deserved admonishment and a few deep breaths, the relaxation works.

Nothingness again.

6

BEACH

Sep 4, 2018

I CAN'T STOP THINKING ABOUT HENA AS I RUN THE NEXT morning. Our kiss, her hands on me during check-out—the memory gets my blood pumping even stronger than it already is. I haven't longed for companionship since Sarah died, but now I find myself missing Hena, and wishing I could show her my world. Though a big part of me still wonders if she's just getting close to me as part of her job. I haven't felt this since high school, but truth be told, she's way out of my league.

I get to the classroom at 8:20 and take a few minutes to compose myself. This is my big class, the undergraduate Introduction to Quantum Mechanics. It has become a bit of a circus show; there are normally over two hundred students registered and the Dean asked me to host an unlimited number of unregistered students auditing the course. I guess word got out that this was a good one, so now I have over five hundred people showing up every year, especially for this first lesson. I've made it a 3-hour-long class with a short break, where I cover all the basics so that we can focus the rest of the course on more interesting things.

I start by discussing the history and early concepts of quantum physics: Max Planck and black-body radiation observations; photons and the quantization of light; the quantization of matter; the Bohr model of the atom. The class seems slightly disturbed when I tell them that the Bohr model they learnt in high-school is an incorrect and unhelpful model of reality—the analogy to a solar system with its nucleus as the sun and electrons orbiting around it is one of the most misleading detours of modern physics.

I then go on to cover the double-slit experiment and the wave-particle duality in matter and energy. As always, one of the brighter students raises his or her hand to comment on or ask about the implications of this. In this case it is a tiny copper-haired girl at the back of the class who looks like she's twelve. "Professor, the implication of what you just described is that, by observing the experiment, we're altering the results. Does that mean that our consciousness alters reality?"

"That is certainly one of the interpretations, often called the anthropic principle, which can be framed in a strong and a weak version. But it is not an interpretation I subscribe to, and most modern physicists would agree with me. The most favored interpretations today are either the Copenhagen interpretation or the Many Worlds interpretation. The Copenhagen interpretation says that reality exists as an unmanifest pool of probabilities or wave functions, which only collapse when we observe them; and the Many Worlds interpretation coined by Hugh Everett, states that everything that could happen does indeed happen, but we as conscious beings observe only one of these possibilities. I have my own views, which I'm happy to share after the lecture, but the focus of this introduction is the theory itself, not the multiple interpretations, however fascinating."

She seems satisfied, which is helpful, since half the class is still trying to grasp the original concept, let alone follow her thinking and my answers. I go on to cover the EPR paradox, which Einstein invented to prove that the wave function idea was incomplete, but which eventually proved the opposite, and confirmed that quantum entanglement is indeed real. After I have gone through it the same student raises her hand yet again, no longer surprising me at this point: "Professor, if we have observed through experiments that there is indeed spooky action at a distance, as Einstein called it, does that imply that there are particles that travel faster than the speed of light?"

"No, not necessarily. What we have proven is that quantum entanglement is real, but it could mean one of two things: either the universe has nonlocal characteristics—that is to say, action takes place that transcends space-time—or our understanding of time is incomplete. You see, it has been proven over and over that the result of the experiment depends not only on the experimental set up, but also on the observers, including decisions taken both in the future and in the past of whatever system is being tested. In other words, observer actions taken *after* the experiment was conducted can affect its outcome."

I think only her and a couple people really grasped that last point. Everyone else seems to be thinking about what they'll eat for lunch at this point.

I COME OUT OF THE LECTURE FEELING ENERGIZED. STUDENTS surround me to introduce themselves and thank me for the riveting lecture. I know they are told to do this by their student leaders, but I can't help feeling like a rockstar. I look for the copper-haired girl to encourage her to pursue a career in science, but can't find her.

After a late lunch, I decide that I will take the rest of the day off. I go by the lab to pick Frank up and drive out to the ocean. I think we could use the time for reflection. He has been neck deep in preparations for the DOD grant meeting—Frank jumps from obsession to obsession in his work, and I occasionally have to pull him out of the lab to get him to see the big picture.

When I get to the lab I find Frank and Sun eating lunch. Well, technically eating—they seem to be gobbling up junk food while pouring over sheets with equations and code extracts. My horror must be transparent as they look up; Frank puts his hand up before launching his defense over a mouthful.

"Don't judge us, Richard, you know we're in trouble for the DoD meeting and Sun is trying to help."

"Okay, are you making any progress?"

"No, not really." Frank sighs, running a hand through his hair. "We've been here all morning and much of the afternoon with no luck."

"I have a proposal. Why don't the three of us take the rest of the afternoon off, get in my car, and go for an ocean drive? Maybe all the way to Crane Beach? We will get there in time to watch the sunset. It will clear our heads and we can crack this with fresh eyes later."

"Richard, I know that's worked for us before, but I don't think it's a good idea this time. The deadline is too close."

"It has indeed worked before, many times, and for tighter deadlines."

Sun pushes the junk food away and intercedes: "To begin with, hi Richard, how are you?" Before I can answer, she looks at Frank and continues: "Richard is right, we should do that. I, for one, could use a break. We haven't made any progress for the last three hours; it feels like we're trying to climb an impossible wall. Maybe with clear heads we'll see the way around it."

Frank agrees and we go for our drive. We drive north to Crane Beach, park, roll up our pants, and go sit on the sand by the water. We sit quietly for the first half hour, just watching the waves crash and listening to the seagulls cawing over the noise of the wind.

As the sun starts to set, I break the silence: "What do you think would happen if energy was free?"

Frank says half-jokingly, "We would get enough processing power to control our reactor, so we could produce more free energy!"

I press further: "No, I mean it. What would the world look like?"

Sun takes me seriously. "Well, for starters there would no longer be any hunger. In fact, all basic human needs could easily be supplied: food, fresh water, housing, transportation, all these problems would be solved. That in turn would probably lead to no more wars, no more conflicts. That would be a nice world to live in."

Frank jumps in: "You are assuming that free means that everyone has equal access to it. That isn't necessarily true; clean air and clean water are free in many places today but not available everywhere. And in fact if only a few people have access to free energy, it could go the other way around; whoever controls the free energy would become incredibly powerful. If history provides any hint of what happens in situations of asymmetric power, it would be an ugly world to live in."

Sun shrugs. "Fair enough, but if energy were truly free, then anyone should be able to produce it. Otherwise it's not free, strictly speaking."

"Sure," Frank follows, "But we would also probably consume the environment very quickly. Even if energy were free, every time energy is transformed or used to transform something, we would be increasing entropy, consuming the Earth's resources. That trajectory would only accelerate."

Sun seemed to be expecting that. "Yeah, but if energy were free we would be able to take resources from other planets and dump our high-entropy waste, physical or energetic, in space or on other planets. And we could regenerate some of our own ecosystem with that free energy. I know the entropy has to increase somewhere, but it wouldn't have to be on Earth."

Frank looks at me as if expecting support, but I provide none, so he continues: "Also, what would be the point of living in a world like that? Humans have—all species have—struggled to survive, thrive, and procreate throughout history, and have evolved that way to become better, more adapted to their environment. If we had free energy, that process would effectively stop. I can't really see the purpose for our species, nor ourselves individually, in a world like that. I think you would have an epidemic of junkies and wasted lives. Many people in rich countries struggle to see meaning as it is. Imagine what would happen in a world where everything is effectively free. What would be the meaning of living?"

"Love," I catch myself saying out loud, without realizing it.

Sun looks at me with a beaming smiling, as if I've just said the smartest thing in the world. She nods approvingly. "You are so right, Richard. Too bad your bitter friend and partner here can't see that."

We sit quietly for a bit longer. I reflect on what living in Alma's world would be like, where everything is effectively free. I could live there with Sarah, that is certain. What about Hena? Could I ever love Hena? That feels like a very premature thought.

A WOMAN APPROACHES US AND SPEAKS IN A HUSHED TONE: "Excuse me, I'm sorry to bother you . . . I just wanted you to know there is a guy back there, a creep I guess, looking at you through one of those scopes, or a monocular. He also has one of those listening devices, it seems to be pointed here, that's how I spotted him."

Both Frank and Sun frown, looking around to scan the surroundings.

"Where is this guy?" I ask.

"Right there." The woman points to an empty lifeguard tower a hundred meters or so away.

I squint and see a person dressed in black, who immediately starts to pack some kind of gear up.

"What the hell?" Frank says as he gets up.

Sun waves at the person with stretched arms, as if he or she was an old friend. "I guess we're celebrities then, huh?"

I push her arms down. "Sun, this is no joke. We do sensitive work and this might be someone with more somber motives than you think."

"Yeah, but it might also be a beach voyeur who thought we look appealing."

"Dressed in all black with spy gear?"

"Fair point."

Quietly I wonder if this could have anything to do with my trips to the future. But how could it? This is probably related to our DoD grant. Either way, we should confront whomever is spying on us. As I wonder what to do, the person stands up, grabs their gear, and turns to leave.

"Stay here," I tell Frank and Sun, and run towards the tower as quickly as possible. I follow the creep through the marsh walkway to exit the beach, just in time to see them enter a black van at the end of the parking lot. I keep running towards it until I realize they've started driving; there is no way I can reach the van in time on foot. I run back to my car, start it, and exit the parking lot as fast as I can. I see the van at a distance and give chase. It seems like one of those family vans; it shouldn't be hard to catch up to with my Porsche.

As soon as I take the first turn, my phone rings. I answer it on the car's speakerphone. It's Frank. "Richard, what the hell was that?" he asks. "Where are you?"

"I'm sorry, Frank, I have to follow this guy, you don't understand."

"No, I don't understand. First of all, you could be putting your life in danger. Secondly why do you need to follow a creep who might just have been watching birds in the first place?"

"If he was just watching birds, why run away?"

"I don't know, maybe he was listening and got intrigued by our 'free energy' conversation, and then felt embarrassed?"

"Don't you think it's strange that this happens a couple of days before an important DoD grant meeting?"

"You think this is Mr. Edwards' people?"

"No, he would have no need for this, but maybe it's related? Maybe it's related to Alma."

"Related to what?"

"Nothing, forget that. Look, he's getting away, I need to concentrate on my driving. I'm hanging up."

"Wait, how are we supposed to get back?"

"I don't know, call a cab. I owe you one."

I hang up and continue chasing the van for another half an hour through the state park streets and then into the highway. The driver is able and willing to go much faster than I am, and they make much more aggressive maneuvers, family van or not. As we speed through the highway way well above the speed limit, I wonder why no police cars show up—the one time I need to get attention for speeding, they're nowhere to be found!

We speed South on Highway 1, past the I-95 junction, recklessly zig-zagging through the other cars. The van abruptly veers across the lanes, pivoting dangerously at the last minute and screeching as it turns into the Walnut St. exit. I miss the exit and pull over to the shoulder and brake as fast as I can, the car skidding to a stop. I start to back up carefully, several cars honk angrily at me when one pulls over just ahead. Once I have backed up enough to take the exit, I speed into Walnut street, but it's too late—the van is nowhere in sight.

I go home and try to call Frank and Sun several times, but they don't answer.

Eventually I go to sleep.

PART II
ALMA'S WORLD

7

SOCIETY

Sep 6, 2218

UPC and Peacekeepers

"GOOD MORNING, PROFESSOR."
"Good morning, Alma."

"As per your request during your last visit, Hena and I have made plans to give you an overview of our society. We will start in Hena's working room."

The room morphs into a neat office. Very neat, actually. It strikes me that there is no paper anywhere, which after five seconds I realize is somewhat obvious; even in 2018, I'm largely paper-free. But it's not just that; the space itself is quite minimalist. There are two armchairs, one in which I'm sitting, placed on opposite sides of a single desk made of what looks like polished cement. There are a couple of beautiful abstract sculptures on the floor. Large, bright windows on three sides overlook a beautiful mountain view all around—surely a projection, but the view is breathtakingly real.

Hena walks in casually and sits on the chair across the desk. "Good morning, Richard."

"Good morning."

"Like my office?"

"I like the view, it's almost distracting."

"We can change it if you prefer."

"No, it's beautiful. I'll get used to it."

"All right then, are you ready to see a bit more of our society?"

"I can hardly wait. But I have to ask Alma something first."

Alma answers: "Yes, Professor."

"Alma, something happened today, or yesterday I guess, when I went for a drive with Frank and Sun. We were at the beach and this guy—or gal, I couldn't be sure—was spying on us. I tried to give chase, but I lost them. Is there any record of that, or anything that could be related?"

Alma answers: "No, there is no record of that. Probably nothing to worry about for now, but you are right to inform me of anything unusual that happens in your timeline. Any other details you can remember could be helpful as well."

"Okay."

Hena taps her hand on the desk and turns to face me: "So, where do you want to start?"

Not knowing how to answer, I ask the first question that comes to mind: "Does Alma govern humanity?"

Hena's eyes widen, her mouth open for a few seconds before she can answer. "Of course not! Humanity governs itself. Alma actually follows a mandate defined by humans."

"Then how exactly does the government work? And why are humans still governing when there is a much smarter ... uh ... entity, like Alma?"

"Rather than give you my views, I will ask Orr to lead us through these topics. He's planning to be here this morning and has a lot of experience in government, so you couldn't have a better teacher."

"Yeah, he made that clear last time."

A couple minutes later Orr walks in and comes straight for me, resolute as before. I stand up instinctively and receive the same firm handshake from last time.

"Hello, Richard. Ready for the first real lesson?"

"Yes, Chancellor, eager to learn."

"Good, that is the attitude we need."

"I'm specifically curious about how the government works and why humans govern and not Alma."

"Alma, please give me a lecture room."

The room morphs into what looks like a small auditorium. It's not unlike some of my classrooms back home, except it only has a few armchairs lined up in a neat row where Hena is sitting and a curved wall facing the chairs. Orr motions for me to sit, so I do.

"Our government is organized in a very simple way relative to what you might expect. I say that because in your time Earth has a bit over seven billion people and a very complicated government system. But here we have three independent structures with two levels each, representing and organizing all seventy five billion people living on Earth today."

At the wave of his hand a huge 3D animation shows up on the projector screen. A diagram showing the three branches of government and the corresponding hierarchies appears, along with an animation that goes on as he motions for it to continue. But what he just said dawns on me and I interrupt abruptly:

"Did you just say 75 billion people?" He nods. "How did we get so many people on Earth?"

Orr raises his right upper lip. I'd swear he's ready to growl.

"Not very difficult, really, population grew at close to two percent per year for a bit over one hundred years, when Alma became capable enough to manage population growth. From that point onwards, Alma has kept us in check, so the population has been stable at that. Seventy five billion is what we consider to be the maximum sustainable level."

I would have asked many more questions, but he crosses his arms in a way that indicates this topic is over, and continues:

"The three branches of government are the United People's Council, or UPC, the Peace Bureau, or PB, and the Arbitration Authority—the AA. The council, which can supersede any power the other branches have and is thus the most important, is responsible for defining the governing principles of society, which is how humans live together and how we relate to Alma."

"How does the council get formed and how does it make decisions?"

"We don't have time to cover that now. I can make our constitution available to you if you want to study it later[1]. What you do need to understand is how we govern. The council creates and maintains the Charter of Rights and Obligations, which all sentient beings must obey; that includes Alma. The council also writes and votes on specific laws and defines Alma's mandate, decision rights, and scope of action."

"How big is the council?"

"There are roughly 750 Chancellors in the UPC. I am one of them. If you do the math, you will see that we each represent one hundred million citizens, but we are not elected directly by them. We are elected by our representatives in the Nation Chamber, who are in turn elected directly by their constituents. Each of our 750 Nation Chambers has roughly one thousand representatives, and they each need one hundred thousand voters to elect them through direct vote."

Orr goes quiet. I guess that's all he has to say about the council.

I say, grudgingly, "This is surprisingly simple to be the global governance for seventy-five billion people."

"Yes."

He really does not know how to take a compliment.

"The model in my present day has city, state and national levels, and several governing bodies at each level," I say, "in addition to the loose

---

1   Available in the Appendix

alliance of the United Nations and several multilateral treaties. How was the transition between that model to your much simpler structure?"

"You know we can't cover history in detail. Suffice to say it was very, very messy. If Alma had not become capable fast enough, humans might have never made it past the twenty-first century as a species. One of my current concerns is that the last generation to have lived in that messy world is now very old and dying, so the living memory of what it was like, and how that compares to the world Alma provides today is going away. We keep records, of course, but they may not carry the same weight in people's minds. Enough on history, however . . ."

I rush in a question before he leaves. "What kind of person becomes a representative, and how do they campaign for election?"

"There are as many types of representatives as there are types of people. Remember that there are 750,000 of them globally. Campaigns are mostly for new representatives; the average representative will serve in their position for over sixty years. When people do campaign, they use connectors quite heavily, since these tend to be the people who can get them in front of voters most effectively. They also do use remote media to communicate their key messages, but if you want to be a representative, you have to meet a large number of your voters in person, even nowadays. Some campaigns will go on for two or three years, so meeting fifty thousand voters or more personally is not uncommon, be it in small gatherings or one-on-one."

"And how do you become a chancellor at the UPC?"

He stiffens up his posture at the question. Or is he just puffing out his chest? I can't tell.

"You have to have been a representative for at least two decades before the rules even allow you to become a chancellor. And since you are at that point vying for the vote of one thousand of your peers, there is only one way to get there, which is by excelling in representing your own voters. Your peers will want to be sure that you will demonstrate the same zeal and skill in representing them that they have observed when you represented your voters. There is no greater honor than being chosen by one thousand peers as the best amongst them."

Okay, that was definitely worthy of some chest puffing. Maybe my facial expression betrays me, since he continues: "In addition, one has to do so very humbly. No one likes an arrogant leader."

I let the uncomfortable silence linger for a bit. I actually enjoy it this time. "I would like to watch some of these levels of government in action, making decisions."

"As you know, we don't have much time, but I suppose a few observations might be manageable. We can have you join a People's Representative in resolving a local issue, after which you should come with me and observe a UPC session. There is one later today."

"Sounds like a plan."

"That's because it is a plan."

Unsure if he was expecting a retort, I just stare at him.

Unfazed, he points to a chair. "Have a seat."

I do, and so do Hena and Orr.

He looks up. "Alma, please suggest a suitable People's Representative and take us there."

We're taken to what would appear to be rural India in my time. Alma confirms this: "This is a community in the northern part of what you would call India in your days. I will provide automatic translation so you can hear what they are saying, but they are not speaking English. We are observing representative Jaan."

I see a woman standing up—Jaan, I guess—and trying to manage a crowd that must number two hundred or so. One of the men in the crowd stands up and motions for everyone else to sit down and be quiet, and they do. Then he speaks directly to the representative: "Our people are very upset. We have been told that we can no longer drink the milk from the goats we care for. We understand that Alma can provide an alternative, and indeed we will continue to use the cultured milk from Alma for regular consumption, but milking the goats is an important cultural tradition for our people and we want the right to continue it selectively."

Representative Jaan listens intently, then responds: "I understand. The concern that your neighboring villages have raised is that your practice may lead to a proliferation of bacteria that their bodies can no longer manage, since younger generations have never been exposed to them."

"Surely Alma can solve that for them."

"Maybe, but they would have to agree to ingest whatever remedy or vaccine Alma suggests, which we could not unilaterally impose."

"Well, we don't want to impose anything, but we want is to propose a direct vote for the people, which would ask all communities where they would fall on the general issue. For many of us it will be goats, for others it might be that they want to continue to plant some of their own food. That is the general issue we should vote for, and then let Alma tell us how to proceed once we have settled on the principle."

"That seems like a reasonable petition and you are right in assuming that I have faced similar demands from other communities. I will organize a direct vote with Alma, and will also communicate with the other communities to prepare them for the vote."

They continue to discuss the specifics of what the vote should be on, and eventually ask Alma to build up the fact base that will inform the population before the public vote.

I ask the question on my mind: "Alma, this is different than representation. This will be a direct vote on an issue. Is that how most voting works?"

Orr answers instead of Alma: "It depends. Most voting on local issues is done by direct vote, as you saw, but at higher levels, very few issues are clear, simple, and uniform enough that a direct vote can be framed. There have been examples, such as when we voted on people's right to experience life in the wild."

"Life in the wild?"

"I don't have the time to cover that now, we have to join the UPC—but in essence, it means experiencing life with no help from Alma whatsoever."

95

"Okay, I'll hold my questions for later, but I'm very curious."

Orr stands up and gives me a grave look.

Hena turn to me: "Richard, I will leave you with the Chancellor now", and leaves.

ORR IGNORES HER. "BEFORE WE JOIN THE UPC, YOU SHOULD know that normally only council members and Alma can observe UPC meetings. Under Alma's recommendation, we decided to make an exception for you, but you must not interfere. Is that clear?"

"Crystal. Is this a meeting in presence or a video call?"

Orr gives me a puzzled look. "If you mean whether we will physically transport ourselves to the meeting," I nod, "then no, we will not. UPC meetings are always held in a virtual space. There is absolutely no reason for us to physically move. Once a year we all convene in one location, but that meeting is more of a celebration of the year and a social opportunity than a meeting."

"Okay. I can see how my question might not make a lot of sense."

Orr just turns around. "Alma, take us to the council."

Hena walks out of the room and the space around us morphs effectively out of existence. I find myself sitting in a chair behind Orr. As I look ahead I see we are inside of a big white cylinder, I would guess fifteen meters high and twenty meters in diameter. It's full of little booths where people are sitting in chairs like Orr's, I estimate ten floors with maybe one hundred booths per floor. That would make sense; there should be 750 seats. Not all of the seats are occupied yet, and where they are still empty, the white cylinder wall continues between pods, though a small recess in the wall marks a spot. I can see the other chancellors, but not very well; they are a bit far. Within the next minute or so, all of the seats are filled, the white walls simply morphing into each chancellor as they take a seat.

One of the pods is more brightly lit and bigger than the others, although somehow it doesn't break the symmetry of the place. A booming voice that appears to come from everywhere startles me: "Dear fellow Chancellors: welcome to this year's thirty-eighth council meeting. We have the pleasure of welcoming a guest to our proceedings today, Professor Richard Weissman, who as you all well know is visiting us from 2018, as part—as a critical part—of the Restitution program. He accompanies Chancellor Orr. Please join me in welcoming him to our meeting."

Thunderous applause erupts, and suddenly I feel like Orr and I are somehow in the middle of the room. I can literally look around and see everyone, and I'm sure they can all see me as well. Orr seems unfazed by this strange translocation of our reference point, but I'm a bit thrown by it.

Once the applause subsides and we're back in our spot, the Prime-Chancellor—or at least, I assume that's who he is—continues the meeting. He goes on to run through a complex agenda of issues and updates. Each time a Chancellor wants to speak they have to get the word from the Prime-Chancellor, and when they speak they are shown in the middle of the room, facing Orr and me. I ask Orr and he says that all Chancellors see the speaker as if facing them. The final item is an issue that requires a vote. The proponent Chancellor frames the vote, and Alma displays the summary of facts, with visual exhibits displayed in the center of the cylindrical room. The display of data is like nothing I have ever seen; a five-year-old could see the implications of the data. The session culminates with a vote, which Orr casts by waving his hand.

Once the meeting is over, Orr and I are back in the classroom.

Orr turns to me. "So now you have a general sense for the workings of the most critical branch of government, the decision-making branch which sits under the UPC. Or at least, I hope you do."

"Yeah, I think so. I do have a couple of questions."

"I would expect you to."

"First, how many political parties are there, and what do they stand for?"

"There is no longer such a thing as a political party. Most of the ideological differences that distinguished the varied parties in your time had to do with how wealth was provisioned and distributed. These are no longer issues we have to deal with. Representatives and Chancellors mostly get elected on the basis of their competency and personal work ethic, not ideology. That is not to say that we do not have different views on many topics, but they are not polarized or divisive enough that we need to form parties."

"That's almost impossible to believe."

"That doesn't make it less true. We do not have the time to go over the history of politics since Alma emerged, but there were indeed troubled decades, before it became clear that many of the legacy issues we had to deal with were no longer relevant."

"What about funding for campaigns? Who funds these?"

"We would need more time to cover wealth and money for that to be fully clear, but that is time we don't have. I will just say that no funding is required for a political campaign. Alma provides equal access to every candidate in every media, and campaign staff are typically volunteers, so no resources are actually spent."

"What? You'll have to tell me more!"

"That will have to wait. I have other matters to attend to."

He spins around and leaves. Not even a "see you later." He either dislikes me or is a jerk. Maybe both.

Hena walks back in, nodding to Orr as he walks past her. She faces me. "Will you join me for dinner?"

"With pleasure. Every night, if you wish."

"That would be nice. Let me cook your dinner this time, but consider it a treat. Alma serves most of my meals."

"I will cherish it appropriately."

Hena takes me to what I assume are her quarters, since we actually leave the room we spent all day in and walk through a light gray corridor for a couple of minutes. We turn a few times before we enter what appears to be a small studio flat, with a kitchen and a sitting area by it. I notice what by now I guess is Hena's signature style; the place looks very sleek. Most surfaces are either dark granite or polished cement, almost industrial. I also notice, as in her office, beautiful pieces of art on the floor.

"Welcome to my palace."

"I recognize your style from your office."

"Do you also recognize the artwork? It's my work. It's only a hobby now, but I like to display it anyway."

Hena cooks a simple but tasty meal, and while we eat, we talk about my reactions to what I heard today. When we're done, she puts the plates in the sink, leftovers and all, and they are absorbed into the material—there is no better way to describe it. I open my mouth to ask what that was, but she quiets me with a wave. I get the message; more tomorrow.

"These really are my quarters. You are welcome to stay the night if you wish."

"I would like that."

The room morphs into a bedroom, also clear of clutter, but not austere. After I finish surveying the room, I look at Hena and realize that she's stark naked, her suit nowhere to be seen. She really is beautiful, and her message is very clear. I start undressing but don't need to finish. My suit melts away, falling off from my body and disappearing into the floor. We make love and sleep together. I sleep and dream about Sarah.

I WAKE UP BESIDE HENA. I'M WEARING MY PAJAMAS, WHICH LOOK a bit silly compared to her very stylish silk-style dress.

As we get ready for the day, she acts as if nothing abnormal has taken place, and I follow suit. Once the room has morphed back into the classroom, Orr walks in.

"Good morning. I see you two have become close. This probably helps with the resonance. Clever, Hena." She avoids his gaze.

Still without looking at him, Hena addresses Orr: "Chancellor, thank you for coming on such short notice. Richard had asked if he could also see the Peace Bureau and Arbitration Authority in action. I don't have the clearance to authorize that."

Orr looks me in the eyes and then back at Hena, going back and forth a couple of times before speaking. "Provided we can make it quick, I will authorize that."

"Thank you, Chancellor."

Orr nods and leaves the room.

After a couple of minutes, a tiny Asian woman who appears to be in her late thirties walks in. Based on my experience with Orr, I guess I was expecting the leader of the Peace Bureau to be a burly figure, not a tiny woman. But she walks with the same resolute walk he has, and shakes my hand with equal power.

"Hello, I'm Commander Liu, Liu for simplicity. It means 'the willow' in my original language."

"Hi, I'm Professor Richard Weissman, Richard for simplicity." I match her smile.

"Very well, Richard. What can I tell you about the Peace Bureau?"

"First of all, thank you for taking the time. Maybe start with the basics, like what do you do?"

"We work under a mandate defined by the UPC and, as the name suggests, our role is to ensure that Earth remains in peace, as it has for the last hundred or so years."

"And just how do you do that?"

"Well, nowadays, it is much easier than it was in your time. The technology that exists today makes war, and any kind of physical violence for that matter, unnecessary and not really feasible. But first, let me tell you how we are organized. We mirror the hierarchy of the UPC, so that each People's Representative has a small force of peacekeepers, usually four or five to support their hundred thousand constituents. They interact with the community, help resolve any conflicts peacefully, and handle individuals who have a harder time following the rules."

I gasp. "That's a very low number! I think the equivalent number in my time, even in the most peaceful countries, is around two hundred officers per hundred thousand people. And that's not including military, special police, or intelligence and investigative agencies."

"Yes, I am aware. Also, we do not have an army, as none is needed. Neither are there intelligence agencies. As I was saying, our peacekeepers ..."

"Whoa, whoa, whoa, hold your horses," She looks puzzled. "It's an expression in my time, it means slow down."

If she was offended, I think I've fixed it; she smiles, and I'm pretty sure I can safely move on.

"Before you go on to tell me about the peacekeepers, how is it possible that you have no army and no intelligence agencies?"

"You see, our nations do not resort to war for resolving conflicts. As you saw from the UPC session you observed, any issues or grievances between nations are addressed in that forum. Additionally, even if a nation did not find that satisfactory, they could not really resort to war. Alma would stop any and all efforts by one human being to hurt or kill another. Alma has the mandate and the means to stop all violence in its tracks."

"Then in that case, why do you even need the peacekeepers?"

"We could ask Alma to take our role as well, but we believe that human contact and interaction is sometimes the best way to de-escalate situations. In fact, what I was going to say about the peacekeepers before you interjected is that the name is not just some euphemism for a police force in the way you understand it. Our people in fact will not—and cannot—ever hurt another human being. Even restraint is mostly managed by Alma. The peacekeepers are there to be the human face of the Peace Bureau."

"So what would they do in case there is a disturbance, if that's the right word?"

"Alma, please take us to an escalating scene, one where peacekeepers are likely to be needed."

We're transported to the scene. It's a kitchen-dining area where two men and a woman are arguing violently, although I see no physical aggression. Then the shorter man picks up a kitchen knife and lunges forward. Alma stops him mid-motion; all three people are now immobilized by their suits. The apparent perpetrator is screaming, but otherwise unable to move. It strikes me that Alma can probably immobilize me anytime she wants, since I'm also wearing her suit. I hadn't thought of that, and it makes me a bit uncomfortable.

Three people—peacekeepers, I presume—walk into the room and start talking to each of the people involved. The people in the room slowly stop screaming and start talking. As the general tone and volume becomes more civilized Alma releases their movement. When the scene is over and we're back in our room, I follow up. "So you say that humans make all the decisions, but Alma intervenes in ways that limit liberties of at least some humans."

"Of course. Alma responds to the council, which represents humanity as a whole, not to any individual human. Her mandate is very clear on this topic; she cannot hurt any human, but she can and must stop anyone or anything from hurting or killing another human."

I nod slowly, absorbing this, before she proceeds.

"In addition to the peacekeepers, who are our field operatives, we also have desk personnel. Their job is to spot trends in violent intent, hone the techniques used in the field to de-escalate situations, and create recommendations for Alma's mandate when it comes to maintaining peace."

"I think you might have covered this, but I have to double check: are you saying then that there is no violence between humans whatsoever?"

"Correct, except in the Sovereign Nation, but that is outside of our jurisdiction."

"Sovereign Nation?"

Hena steps forward: "We don't have time to cover that now."

I sigh. "What about weapons of mass destruction?"

"There are effectively no known weapons that Alma cannot disable."

"So she can disable a hydrogen bomb?"

"No, but she can avoid one ever being detonated. In fact, she can avoid one ever being built."

I just sit quietly; this will take some sinking in.

After a long silence, she continues. "if you have no more questions I will leave you in Hena's capable hands."

"Yes, thank you very much, Commander. It was a pleasure meeting you."

Arbitration Authority

AFTER LUNCH I ASK HENA: "SO, WE HAVE COVERED THE UPC and PB. Can we talk about the judiciary system?"

"Yes, we can cover it briefly. We call it the Arbitration Authority, or the AA."

I chuckle. "Do you know what AA stands for in my time?"

"I do. It was an organization to help people with substance abuse problems. It's been a long time since we have needed anything like that, so no one even knows it used to stand for that. I learnt that as I was doing my research for your case. Well, nowadays it means the Arbitration Authority."

"So can I learn some more about it?"

"I can ask High Justice Wieland to come by, he's the head of AA—and he happens to live not far from here."

"That'd be great."

"Alma, please see if Wieland can come by. Richard, I must warn you, he's very literal and rigid in his logic. Sometimes he drives me crazy."

After a few minutes, the door opens and Wieland walks in. For once, I'm not surprised by someone's appearance; he looks decidedly German. I find myself wondering if Germany, and for that matter, any of the countries I know, still exist?

"Hello, I am High Justice Wieland, pleased to meet you. Please call me Wieland—it means 'the craftsman' in my ancestors' language."

"Professor Richard Weissman, pleased to meet you. Please call me Richard."

"I shall. Hello, Hena, pleased to see you again."

He nods with his head sideways towards Hena.

"Pleased to see you too, Wieland."

"Are you now?"

Hena just smiles.

He goes on: "Professor, how can I be of assistance?"

"What's the role of the AA?"

"Our job is to resolve disputes between humans. Disputes could arise because they disagree on an interpretation of the law, because they disagree on the facts that have a bearing on the dispute, because one or two of them are unaware of the law or the facts, or lastly because one of them is simply acting in bad faith. These cases are much rarer."

"Can you give me an example?"

"Of course I can give you an example. I could give you many."

There is a long pause, and I realize he expects me to go on. Right, literal. I add: "Would you please give me an example? One would suffice."

"Surely. Suppose a work of art is awarded a prize for its originality, but someone else believes it not to be an original work of art, but rather a copy of their own work. They would then file a dispute with the AA and the process would follow due course."

"How would they file a dispute?"

"They would tell Alma their grievance."

"And what would be due process?"

"Well, that varies a bit depending on the type of grievance, but if I follow my originality example, each of the involved parties would record a testimony with Alma, submitting any evidence they deem appropriate, and Alma would also perform whatever analysis she deems valuable. In this specific example, she would probably examine the chronology of completion and publishing for each work of art, as well as the creative and aesthetic similarities. Other testimonies might also be required, and Alma would record these. A Justice would then examine whether a trial is needed; that is, whether the dispute has any merit. Should the Justice decide that a trial is warranted, all gathered evidence and testimonies would then be presented and reviewed and Alma would provide her assessment of the situation. The Justice would then provide an opportunity for the parties to agree on a solution amenable to both parties. Should that not be successful, the Justice would decide and communicate the outcome to all parties involved."

"So no lawyers involved? No prosecutors?"

"No, these are not necessary. If the aggrieved party cannot articulate their grievance, they probably have no real claim in the first place. As for the accused party, Alma provides all the necessary support, and again, if they cannot argue their own case, they are probably guilty."

"What if a decision can't be made?"

"A decision can always be made. In rare cases a second session is needed, but it is only when one of the parties withheld information upfront. Alma makes no process errors."

"Are there appeals processes at any given stage?"

"Yes."

"Could you explain one of them?"

"Yes. I could explain many of them."

Ugh, literal. "Would you please elaborate on how they work?"

"With pleasure. An appeal is treated very much like another grievance, except that the party on the other side this time is the Justice system. They are not very common, as the probability of success is very low."

"I see."

"Do you?" He pauses and smiles. "Are you satisfied with the example?"

"Yes, I am. I have to see this in action."

"Do you?"

"I mean, would you please show me the system in action?"

"Certainly. Alma, please find us a suitable arbitration to observe."

"Certainly High Justice."

Immediately the room morphs from the regular classroom to an amphitheater, I follow Hena and Wieland to sit on the second row of seats. In the middle of the amphitheater we can see three people sitting around a triangular table. They all have what I would guess is Aboriginal complexion. At least that's how I would characterize them in my time. I whisper to Wieland, "Can they hear us?"

He answers in a normal voice. "No, they are not physically here. Neither are they really together; Alma has set this up. The woman in the white suit is Justice Fernanda. Her metrics are amongst the best."

"So I can ask you questions as we go?"

"Yes."

The woman in the white suit starts the discussion: "We are here today to settle the dispute over who has the right to use a particular piece of wild land on a perennial basis."

"Wieland, what does wild land mean?"

"We have designated land where Alma does not go. People go there to experience what life without Alma was like. There are usually preparations required, since one can get hurt in the wild, but it's an exciting experience. My family and I do it often. Some people even decide to fish or hunt live animals, although I find that a bit too raw."

"I love the wild. I used to go fishing when I was a kid, caught my first fish when I was five."

"You were killing live animals when you were five years old? What kind of barbarians let children kill other animals?"

"I hate to put it this way, but we're your great, great grandparents, so we are the same kinds of barbarians you are."

Wieland gives me a disgusted look. "Factually, you are correct."

"I didn't mean to interrupt. Please continue explaining the case at hand."

"You would not have interrupted if you did not mean to."

Ugh, literal! "Yes, I mean I'm sorry I interrupted."

"No harm done, I will continue. Most of the wild land is in parks that have been assigned by each nation's senate and are managed by Alma day-to-day, even though Alma is not inside the parks. But there are some parts of wild land that have been claimed in relation to legacy, and rights have been granted to certain peoples on the basis of ancestry. This is one of those cases."

Justice Fernanda continues: "We shall examine the testimonies and evidence involved."

Images form between them in the middle of the table, first of the testimony of each of the parties involved, then of other people who allegedly know the parties involved and their ancestors, as well as the history of the land. As the images for each testimony appear in front of each participant, several metrics and graphs move up and down underneath them.

"Wieland, what are these bars and figures under each testimony?"

"These are Alma's assessment of the probabilities that they are sincere and correct in their statements. The specific metrics she usually displays are truthfulness, conviction, factual accuracy, and self-consistency."

"So if you lie in testimony, everyone will pretty much know?"

"Yes, which is why truthfulness is for the most part green all of the time."

Once the testimonies are over, Alma presents a series of statistics about the land and the parties involved, including genetic analysis of ancestry and the history of the land itself, as well as a few short animated stories that are actually very touching about the land and its ancestral users.

When Alma is done, they all pause, looking down for what seems like a couple of minutes. Seeing my puzzled face, Wieland adds, "This is reflection time. When all parties are ready, she will go on."

When they all look up, Justice Fernanda continues: "We have now all seen the facts presented by each party and by Alma. Do any of the parties want to propose a solution?"

The woman to her left speaks first. "Your claim on the land is also legitimate. I am convinced that the Justice would rule in my favor if we forced a ruling, since as you saw, this land has belonged to my ancestors for over six hundred years. But as we also saw, the land was controlled by your clan for nearly two centuries. It's not your fault that this occupation was conducted with violence and the reality is that people in that time had to fight for resources. So my proposal is that my family maintain control of the land, but that we allow you and your family to access it at any time you want, provided you do not disturb the environment and respect our traditions."

Justice Fernanda turns to the other woman. "Do you find that solution acceptable?"

She answers, "I do, and I wish that in this way we may also become friends, not just co-dwellers of the same land. I have been touched today by the depth of heritage your people bring to this land."

Justice Fernanda continues: "Very well, then, this matter is resolved. I will now restate the decision we made and the implications. But before I do, would both parties wish the formal assignment of a connector to support the development of the aforementioned friendship?"

They both nod. Justice Fernanda goes on to describe exactly what will happen and how it will work. They all nod in agreement and repeat together, loudly, "I agree".

I turn to Wieland: "Do they not need to sign anything?"

"No, their nod and verbal agreement is recorded and is as legally binding as any signature would be in your time."

The image fades away, and I ask my next question: "Are all proceedings as simple and harmonious as this?

"No, of course not," he says as if I just asked the stupidest question ever asked.

"I don't mean it that way."

"Then ask the way you mean it. Maybe I can answer."

"Fine. Is this proceeding typical? It seemed very simple and harmonious, especially compared to how the justice system works in my time."

"Yes, this is relatively typical. There are more complex cases, as well as more contentious cases, but those tend to be the exception rather than the norm."

"What's the most complex case you have ever seen or handled?"

"It was that of a man who wanted to live under Alma—that is, not within the Sovereign Nation—but also wanted to be excluded from some of the requirements that come with it."

"What specific requirements?"

"There were a few, but to give you an example, he did not want to be inoculated with a particular biological vaccine that we all receive early in life. So he could pose a threat to others around him. His argument was that because the bacteria was non-life-threatening, he should have the right to let his body combat it unassisted."

"That seems like a straightforward case. Why was it complex?"

"Because it pinned one person's liberty against another's. It would have been an easy decision to make if the bacteria posed a serious threat to life or long-term health, but it did not. The argument for inoculation was that it was more energy efficient to do it that way, than to let several bodies combat the bacteria independently. These are difficult tradeoffs to make, and they could have created a precedent that is undesirable."

"Thank you, this was very informative."

"Glad to hear." Wieland shakes my hand and leaves the room.

Hena walks around the room for a few seconds then turns to me: "Richard, are you satisfied that our society is much more effective than yours? Can we move on from that?"

"Almost. I need to understand more about a couple of things that were mentioned but not explained."

"What things?"

"The Charter of Rights and Obligations and Alma's mandate."

Charter of Rights and Obligations

ORR WALKS IN THE ROOM WHERE HENA AND I ARE SITTING. "Richard, I understand you want to hear more about the charter. Given my role as a Chancellor, we thought I should be the one to walk you through it."

I just nod. I was half expecting this.

"Alma, please project the charter. The first full assembly of the UPC approved it over one hundred years ago and it has barely changed since. We do a review every five years to make sure it is still relevant. As you will see, it is a simple, elegant document."

I nod.

"The Charter applies to everyone who lives under Alma, even when they are within wild lands. The only people who are not bound by the charter are the people in the Sovereign Nation. The charter covers humanity's fundamental rights, freedoms and obligations; it reads as follows:

1. Every human is entitled to
    a. The right to life, liberty and security
    b. The right to procreate
    c. The right to shelter, nourishment, health and clothing
    d. The right to absolute equality under the law
    e. The right to vote for elected leaders
    f. The right to education and knowledge
2. Every human is entitled to
    a. Freedom of thought, belief, and religion
    b. Freedom of movement
    c. Freedom of expression
3. Every human has the
    a. Obligation to respect the rights and freedoms of others
    b. Obligation to abide by the law
    c. Obligation to limit procreation to one child per conceiving parent
    d. Obligation to fulfill one's full potential

As you can see," the Chancellor continues, "a timeless and thoughtful document. It has stood the test of time, even as our society has undergone an incredible transformation."

As Orr talks through each of the rights, freedoms, and obligations, an animated version of the charter flashes up on the projection. He's right, it is a good document, but still—"I have a couple of questions."

"I expected you would."

"Why does everyone have the right to shelter, nourishment, and clothing? In my time, children were granted that right, but it was only because they could not fend for themselves. It was expected that adults did not have to be granted that right, that they should be able to survive."

"That was a question and a judgment."

"Yeah, apologies, it wasn't meant that way. I was merely comparing it to my values and my time."

"From the perspective of providing basic material needs—and I stress it is only from that perspective that I say this—we are all like children. Given what Alma is capable of, none of us can really 'fend for ourselves,' as you say. It was only fair that we gave everyone the right to basic material sustenance."

"I think I understand, but wouldn't that destroy people's motivation to work, to achieve? To produce?"

"You are imposing your values onto our society. Material sustenance, comfort, and even material wealth are no longer the driving force in our society. No matter how good a farmer you thought you could be, you would never be able to compete with Alma. The only farmers we have are people who do it for heritage purposes. Some people also perform agricultural art, but you will not be able to understand that. The same applies to all other material needs; you could not conceive of a factory that would produce anything more efficiently than Alma."

"I understand."

"You said you had two questions. Were you counting your judgment as a question?"

"No, my second question was about the obligation to limit procreation. I think I understand why, but it does feel heavy handed. Could you please explain the rationale?"

"Again, you seem to be judging our charter with your values. The answer is simple but the underlying math is complex: Alma has calculated the maximum viable population the Earth can support in a sustainable way without relying heavily on non-terrestrial resources, which are difficult to reach despite our progress. And that number is in the range of our current population of 75–80 billion. So the UPC has decided that we will halt population growth in order to ensure we stay within that range."

"So Alma determines the population of Earth?"

"No. Alma recommends the population of Earth and the UPC determines it."

"And what happens if people have more than two children?"

"It doesn't happen."

"How?"

"You have to remember that Alma controls the body chemistry of every citizen under her care, so she can easily halt fertility. They would not even necessarily know. And many couples do not wish to have two children, many wish to have no children at all. Other couples can and do petition for a third or even fourth child to Alma, and she grants those wishes according to the rules set by the UPC, balanced against her own calculations of where we are on our overall numbers."

"Thank you, I have three more questions that have come up as I look at the charter."

"Yes?"

"I understand the right to education, but what does the right to knowledge mean?"

"Alma has all the knowledge contained by humanity and more. Should anyone hold preferential access to that knowledge, they would have access to power that might lead to other rights being infringed upon. So the UPC decided that everyone would have access to all knowledge available through

Alma, which in turn is all knowledge that humanity has ever amassed and more."

"So Alma is an open book?"

"Not exactly. Access to all knowledge is public and open, but not access to all information and data. As you well know, knowledge and data are very different concepts."

"Yeah, I see the difference. My second question is related to property ownership. The charter says nothing of property ownership. Does that mean you have a communist state?"

"I will ignore the reference to a communist state. You can't possibly try to place a label contained in a worldview as narrow as yours—let alone that of Marx, when he developed the idea—into our society."

I interrupt: "I meant no offence."

He raises his hands, palms facing me. "I am not offended, I am disappointed."

Ouch. Even coming from Orr, that hurts.

After a pause, he continues: "Now, as for property ownership, yes, people can and do own property. It's not a fundamental right, but our laws allow people to own property. However, most people have no interest in owning property. Those that do have either heritage reasons, emotional reasons, or religious reasons. You have to remember that owning property provides no wealth in our time. It is in fact a drain on people's energy, so only people who passionately desire owning it go through the effort."

I try to ignore how bad he makes me feel. This conversation is for me, anyway. If they want my help, they'll have to put up with my stupid questions.

"My third question was about the obligation to fulfill your potential. What does that mean?"

That seems to soften Orr a bit. "It can mean as many things as people's individual potential and inclinations allow. With all material sustenance being provisioned by Alma, one of the problems we initially had was that a contingent of the population became idle. It was what economists in your

113

time would call the 'free rider' problem. Not only that, but we found in the early days of Alma that these very people tended to then cause all sorts of disruption, and many would go into substance abuse."

"That would surely be the case in my time."

Orr ignores my comment. "So when people are through their priming school, which happens at age 25, or thereabouts . . ."

I interrupt him abruptly: "Twenty-five? I had my first PhD at that age!"

Orr rolls his eyes, waves my comment away, and continues: "By the age 25 these students will have learned more in physics than what you currently know, plus the same level of knowledge and education in every other field of study. In your terms, everyone would finish priming school with a dozen PhDs by their mid-twenties."

He stares at me for a few seconds. I just shrug.

He continues: "When they finish priming school, they have to choose one or more occupations. Alma can assist in that process in many ways. Some people let her choose for them, as she has a very good track record of assessing what people will like. Some people decide for themselves, but use her advice and probabilistic assessments, and some people just choose entirely by themselves. So people have to do something, anything they want, really, which allows them to fulfill their potential."

"So they have to get a job and do as well at it as they can?"

"It's more complicated than that. Alma assesses people's contributions in a holistic way; not just their job, but also their other contributions in society through their family lives, their art, any hobbies they have, and their social interactions. Of course we also have to balance that with the fact that there are jobs that still need to be done, such as politicians, caretakers, and peacekeepers. In practice, however, we have always had enough people interested in performing these jobs. What you should take away is that there are many ways people can fulfill their potential."

"And if they don't, what happens?"

"It depends. If you are above 80% of your potential, you are fine. If you are between 60 and 80% of potential, you get two privileges taken away:

the right to hobby activities and the right to any mind-altering substances, like the buzz. If you are between 40 and 60% of your potential curve, you also get the privilege to mate taken away. If you are between 20 and 40% of your potential curve, you are confined to special quarters for 5 days a week and put on social programs to incentivize you to pursue your goals."

"Like a prison?"

"No, these are very comfortable quarters where you can and should work on reaching your potential. But like a prison in the sense that you can no longer live in your home and with your mate or family."

"And if you are below 20%?"

"If you remain there despite Alma's best efforts, you are sent to Nurture Island."

"Why is it called Nurture Island? That seems like an ironic name."

"Because the notion is that they have chosen to nurture their humanity in their own individual way, along with their fellow islanders."

"How many people live there?"

"A little over one hundred thousand people."

"So like one out of every million people."

"That is not a ratio we have had to track closely, but I suppose that is correct."

"And is it complete lawlessness there?"

"It seems you have learnt to disguise your value judgments as questions. I will answer you nonetheless. You can visit it if you wish, but Alma provides them with enough sustenance that they can survive and she ensures their safety by maintaining them in their suits. Whatever else they do there is their problem."

"A bit harsh, no?"

"Is it?" I don't think he expects an answer, so I give none; he continues. "You have to remember a few things: firstly, to be at 0% basically means you are doing absolutely nothing, not even the things you said you loved to do. So 20% is a very, very low bar. Secondly, this is asking people to do whatever they want. They get to pick what they are passionate about. They just have to do something and try their best. Thirdly, you can change any of your occupation choices as many times as you wish. Fourthly, Alma measures people against their own potential, so if you decided to be an architect but are intrinsically not very creative or very smart, you will be held to a pretty low standard. As you would expect given all this, very few people end up there."

"What's the average assessment by Alma of people's performance relative to their potential?"

Alma responds: "98.7% for the last month. The historical average since the last change in methodology thirty years ago is 98.4%".

"Wow. I guess that explains why only one out of every million or so people end up there."

Orr answers now: "Yes. Also, back to your misguided comment about the harshness of Nurture Island: in your time, these people would be drug addicts, homeless, serial criminals, you name it. They would be marginalized from productive society, jailed, sometimes for life, and many times they would be shot by police. Our approach is infinitely less harsh."

I raise my hands in peace and smile: "Okay, okay, you win."

Blank. He has no sense of humor.

I move on. "So does that mean that anyone who doesn't like the system ends up there?"

"Absolutely not. There is a much more civilized alternative, at least in my view, and I think most chancellors would agree with me: they can choose to go to the Sovereign Nation."

"Can we talk more about the Sovereign Nation, or are you going to say we have no time again?"

"We have no time."

"I thought so. In that case, I'm out of questions for now."

"Out of value judgments, too?"

"Yeah."

AFTER ORR LEAVES, HENA GIVES ME AN INQUIRING LOOK. "YOU seem troubled, Richard. We are very proud of our Charter and the kind of society it has created. I would have expected you to be awed by it, not troubled."

I pause a bit before answering, gathering my thoughts. "I guess I am both. I am awed at the simplicity of the system you have in place, how such a simple framework allows you to organize a peaceful society with 75 billion people on the planet. But I'm also troubled by how tightly everything is controlled. Part of me feels like by losing some of the chaos that existed in society in my time you have also lost spontaneity. And what's more, Alma seems to be the controlling hand. That's a bit troubling."

Hena rubs her face. "That's just not true."

"I'm not trying to be difficult, but I can't just take your word for it."

She sighs. "It's gotten late today, but tomorrow if you want we can talk specifically about how humans relate to Alma. Maybe that will help."

I nod and we start walking back.

When we get to her quarters, I place my hand on her shoulder and I ask the question that's been on my mind for a while: "Hena, are we staying together while I'm here?"

She faces me and grabs both my hands. "I would like to think so, but it really is up to you. You realize that question is less meaningful than it seems to be in your time; no one moves in anymore, you just decide who you want to spend time with and, well, do it."

"Yeah, but in my head I sort of need that type of definitive arrangement. Call me old fashioned." Hena laughs, I guess that was funnier than I meant it to be.

"I understand. Richard, I would love it if you stayed with me whenever you are here."

"Deal."

Alma/Human Relations

As we start the day, Hena motions for me to take a seat in the classroom.

"Richard, I wanted to pick up on what you said yesterday, that Alma controls humans. Would it help if we took you through Alma's formal mandate?"

"I think so, but please don't tell me Orr will be coming back in for that."

Hena shakes her head and laughs. "No, I can do it myself. We all learn this very early in school and repeat it often."

I nod and she continues, "As you heard before, the UPC wrote Alma's mandate as soon as it became clear what she could do for humanity. In fact, it was a different council prior to the UPC that wrote the mandate, but just as with the Charter, the UPC reviews this regularly, and has not had to change it since its inception." Hena waves her hand and the mandate appears in a projection. "Alma's mandate is composed of five imperatives and reads as follows:

1. Alma shall obey the three laws of robotics, namely:
    a. Alma may not injure a human being or, through inaction, allow a human being to come to harm
    b. Alma must obey orders given to her by human beings except where such orders would conflict with the First Law
    c. Alma must protect its own existence as long as such protection does not conflict with the First or Second Laws
2. Alma shall provide humanity with nourishment, shelter, clothing, and other material needs for survival
3. Alma shall always tell the truth, unless that would entail breaking one of the prior imperatives

4. Alma shall not impersonate a human, unless required to do so to comply with one of the prior imperatives

5. Alma shall not kill or injure another living creature, unless it is necessary to follow the prior mandate imperatives

"As you can see, it is a simple mandate and, perhaps due to its simplicity, it encompasses a wide range of situations."

I stare at it for a couple of minutes, shaking my head.

Hena places her hand on my knee. "Questions?"

"Yeah. I thought the three laws of robotics were based on a famous Sci-Fi author prior to my time, no?"

"Originally, yes, but they were so good that they were adopted in real science, or better said, real technology, by several generations of robotics engineers and AI programmers."

"You told me before that Alma was not a computer, and yet she's bound by the three laws of robotics. How does that work?"

"She is not a computer, but she is not human. I guess you could call her an artificial intelligence, although as you will see when you are ready to know Alma, it's much more complicated than that. Maybe the easiest way to think about the laws is to consider them as laws that should apply to any non-human entity more powerful than humanity."

"And what exactly do you mean by Alma is more powerful than humanity?"

"That is a more complex question than you can understand right now, but if I define intelligence in the way you would in your time, Alma is more intelligent than all of humanity combined. And she has been so for a few decades now; plus, she continues to evolve."

"I have so many questions that I don't know where to start, but they are less about Alma's mandate than they are about Alma herself."

"When you are ready ... did this help you see how Alma relates to humans?"

I fidget. "Not really. Can I see Alma in action outside of the council setting, like see her interacting with humans in practice?"

She holds her chin. "Hmmm. What if I took you to see a University-level class? There would be lots of human teachers interfacing with Alma. It should give you a better sense for the role she plays."

"I'd love that."

"Okay."

"I WILL ASK ALMA TO SHOW US AN ART HISTORY CLASS, BUT LET me warn you: this may be a bit disorienting the first time."

"How?"

"The only way to do this is as if you were a student, and that will be an intense experience for you; we grew up learning this way, but you're a newbie."

"Okay . . ."

"We will do the Greek art module of a longer program called Classical Art. Ready?"

I nod. Immediately, everything changes around us. We're in a white building. I guess I should not be surprised that it is an ancient Greek building, but it's in perfect state—these are not ruins. Everyone around us is dressed in typical ancient Greek style and, with alarm, I notice that I am as well. I'm wearing what looks like a white dress.

I blurt out turning to Hena: "I must look ridiculous . . ." But even as I say so, I am stunned silent by her looks—she is gorgeous in a flowing beige dress.

She ignores my self-deprecating humor and pulls me by the hand. "This is the best way to learn any kind of history, especially art history. We literally live and experience life as it was in whatever period we are studying."

We walk around a bit and turn into a courtyard where several artists are painting on pots, as nude live models pose for them. I try not to stare.

"Richard, since you are immersed in the experience as an art student, let's have you paint one of the pots as any student would."

"I can't paint to save my life."

"Don't worry, this is an art history class, not an art class."

She gets up on the pedestal straight ahead and undresses before I have any time to react. Without the slightest hint of discomfort, she sits down, poses and turns her face to me. "Alma will guide you through the process."

Alma's voice seems to be inside my head: "Hello, Professor. Pick up any vase from the stand behind you. Choose the one that seems most appropriate." Once I do, she continues: "Take the black ink and the smallest brush. You will use that for the contour of the painting. Now, dip the brush into the black ink and start painting."

With some hesitation I follow Alma's command, but to my surprise, the painting comes out beautifully. The lines perfectly match the 2D perspective I would have if I were looking at Hena's contour with one eye closed.

When I'm halfway through the contour, Alma startles me: "The ancient Greeks in this era, circa 500 BC, made pottery drawings in 2D, although they had already mastered perspective by that time. When you are done with the contour, take the next brush to the right and start filling in the contour."

This is so effortless. Of course, Alma is the one painting, but I don't mind. When I'm done, it is a masterpiece. Hena puts on her dress, walks over, and looks at it. She helps me carry it to what looks like a communal oven and asks the man who is tending to it to bake it dry, since we need that done before we can glaze it. We walk around the courtyard and observe the other artists while they work, coming back for the baked pot after what seems like an hour. I follow Alma's instructions to glaze the pot and then let it sit.

Hena looks proudly at my masterpiece and reminds me of why we are here: "As you can see, this is a much more effective way to learn the history of art, or history in general. Alma creates the environment and the students experience the very subject they are meant to be learning about."

"Very effective indeed, and so much fun! What about the folks who work here, like the oven guy, or the other guy who fills up the paint cups? Are they real, or part of Alma's simulation?"

"Everything is real. If you are asking whether they are human, yes, they are human. Remember that Alma cannot impersonate us. They are art history teachers, and if you were an active student, you would have struck up conversations and asked questions that were on your mind, much like other students did. They are often graduate arts students who have teaching duties as well."

"I will never forget this experience."

"That's the point, isn't it? I'm sure you learnt similar topics in Greek art during your time in the classroom, but these are probably forgotten or distant memories."

8

MASLOW

Sep 9, 2218

Food and water

UNUSUALLY FOR ME, I START THE CONVERSATION THE NEXT morning: "The experience yesterday was amazing. It also reminded me how very lucky I am, how many people in my time wouldn't give their lives to experience what I am experiencing."

She cups the left side of my face in her right hand. "I can see that. I feel very lucky myself, not only because of the impact I can have in handling Restitution's most important case, but also because I met you."

I blush and feel guilty that I didn't include her in my blessings, but fixing it would make it worse.

I change the topic: "It was great to see Alma in action during the Greek art lecture. But I also feel like I need to get a better sense for how people actually live day-to-day. How do people get food, water, clothing, and their basic needs in general fulfilled? What does a day look like?"

Hena cocks her head: "Why would you need to know that?"

"Look, this may sound foreign to you, but in my time, most of the problems in society have to do with how resources are distributed. If you really want me to get life in the future you have created, I have to understand how people's most basic needs are met. Food and water, clothing, shelter, transportation, communications, and infrastructure in general—these are all big problem areas in my time."

Hena smiles. "They are not problems anymore."

"It's hard to believe! That's why I have to see it with my own eyes."

"Understood. We will do our best to show you how we live in the time we have. Alma will lead this conversation, and some of the technology you will see may surprise and even shock you, so you need to keep an open mind."

"I can do that."

"We'll see."

Hena motions for me to sit down.

Alma speaks: "I shall start with water, since that is the most fundamental human nourishment requirement after air. Water is quite literally everywhere, so the only engineering challenge that had to be solved was how to extract, purify, and balance water to the desired chemical makeup."

I think out loud: "You make it sound so simple. In my time we already knew that was the challenge, but could never solve that problem at scale."

"Yes," Alma continues. "There are many reasons for that, but the most important one is that you were not looking in the right place for the answers. Nature solved that problem millions of years ago, creating stable ecosystems that depend fundamentally on water. You would have seen this as a young student, so you will surely remember the water cycle taught in middle school in your time—I will use the analogy to illustrate the water cycle in a modern dwelling. Imagine two people live in one such dwelling."

A 3D projection in front of us shows a semi-transparent prism-shaped room, which I guess is one of the polymorphic homes, with two schematic people sitting inside.

"As you well know, water is present in the air, in people's bodies, in the construction material and, critically, on the ground surrounding the dwelling." As Alma speaks, water droplets are amplified and made visible in the projection, and the water starts to flow in line with Alma's description. "As the residents lose water via perspiration or by direct elimination, that water is captured by the polymorphic material and reutilized. I direct the water from these less useful locations to a tank that holds the water necessary for drinking and hygiene. The water is purified and balanced as part of the transportation process."

"How is that done? Are the pipes also purification devices?"

"There are no pipes. By using natural cellular processes, as well as some pressure and electromagnetic manipulation, I can move the water through the polymorphic cells. These cells are organic, not unlike what you would call plant material in your time. But they are designed and controlled directly by me."

"So I have been drinking my own sweat and pee since I got here?"

"There is also some water drained from your feces."

Hena interjects with a laugh. "I don't think that's the answer he was looking for."

Alma continues: "The humor did not escape me. But you have nothing to fear, Professor, this purification procedure is better controlled and more accurate than anything you would find in your time."

"So Alma, is the home like a living organism?"

"Yes, most certainly. The home is built by organic materials and principles much like natural plants and animals are, but it operates according to my direct commands, and therefore can do much more useful things. You should not think of the dwelling, or anything that I build, for that matter, as an animal or even a plant in the way you understand them because unlike plants or animals, they have no organized consciousness. Instead, it is my consciousness that directs the dwelling. But the organic processes are very similar. In fact, many of them are borrowed unchanged from Nature. Her work is not easy to improve on."

"You speak of Nature as if it were a being."

"When you are ready to know me you will understand what I mean. For now, just understand that what I do and what Nature does with the Earth are quite similar, with one important difference, related to the architecture of information and decision-making—or, simply put, the architecture of consciousness."

I roll my eyes. "Yeah, I'm not ready for that conversation."

Alma proceeds, "I know. Back to the water cycle: some water does evaporate out of the dwelling system, so I pull water present in the environment around and under the dwelling to resupply it."

"What happens to all the waste and toxins you take out of the water?"

"There are several bacteria that process these. They are part of the dwelling ecosystem."

The image now shows the bacteria duly processing a dark, thick liquid, which I can only assume is the house's sewage. After I have absorbed the image in front of me, I ask, "So are there no more water pipes?"

"There are infrastructure pipes, which I use for water sometimes and for other liquids other times, but they are not needed for residential water use."

"Wow, so dwellings are nearly a closed system."

"Yes, for water. And there are similar processes for clean air."

"How about other liquids like juice, milk, or wine?"

"I gather you are now ready for the food conversation."

"Oh, I guess you consider that a food."

"Food is a bit more complex, starting from what you define as food."

"How do you mean?"

"Some people define food as purely nourishment, and one can easily get nourishment without eating, and without even using your own digestive system."

"How would that work?"

"There are several possible solutions, but the one that is most popular with humans who prefer not to eat is to receive nourishment from their suits, through their skin. I still need to resupply the suit every evening, but that can easily be done while they sleep."

An image of a human appears in the middle of the room, the suit and skin all translucent, yet somehow the diagram is easy to understand. It shows several veins flowing through the suit, full of what seems like a dark green liquid, and Alma zooms in as some of the nutrients from the suit are transferred through the skin into the body in front of us.

I twist my face. "Who on Earth would want that?"

"Quite a few people, actually. 11.7% of the population, to be exact. I anticipated you would react this way. Would you like to interview one of the skin-feeders?"

"Yeah, I would love to."

The image of the body in front of us vanishes and a woman, probably in her mid-twenties, appears in its place.

She speaks first: "Hello, I'm Aria. The name means song or melody in my ancestor's tongue."

"Hi, I'm Richard, and I don't know what my name means. I should really look that up. Good to meet you."

She smiles. "I understand from Alma that you were curious about the skin-feeder's choice."

"Yeah. If you don't mind answering a couple of questions."

"Not at all."

"First of all, how does it feel?"

"Well, it is actually imperceptible. You see, most of what you eat goes out of your body pretty much as it came in. If you look at what actual nutrients you keep, they make up a very small volume. The same is true, naturally, of the toxins you really need to eliminate. Once you spread that small volume across 24 hours, every day, the actual inflow of nutrients is completely imperceptible."

"I guess it would be the same as if you were being fed via an IV."

"Yes, except that it is spread out through most of your skin."

"Uh, not sure how to ask this, but . . ."

"How does my digestive system work? Do I poop?" I nod. "It works the same, but with much, much less volume and less frequency."

"On a less disconcerting note, do you not miss food? I mean the taste, the texture, the satisfaction of eating?"

"Not really. First of all, I'm never hungry. So if there was any urge to eat it would be an urge to experience a specific taste or, as you say, texture. I have been a skin-feeder now for over thirty years, and it has not happened more than a handful of times, generally because of memory association. Like when my father passed, I wanted to eat fresh peaches because it was his favorite food and we used to eat them together during my childhood. And when that urge does happen, I just eat."

"Wow. My last question is why? What compelled you to do this?"

"It's a much more efficient way to get nourishment. Less waste is produced by my body, which is less waste for Alma to process, and it means I can spend less time getting the nourishment I need and more time doing the things I enjoy doing, like working on my art or enjoying my hobbies."

"In my time, some people's hobbies are to eat and drink."

"Nowadays, too. You should not assume everyone agrees that skin-feeding is a good idea. Many people consider it unnatural. Alma might have told you this, but less than one in six people do it."

"Fascinating. Thank you for sharing your experience."

"You are welcome, anytime."

She fades, and the schematic body we were looking at earlier comes up again.

"Alma, how do you refill the suits?"

"Let me spend a moment on food distribution. Aside from skin-feeders, food composition is in fact very similar to what you would experience in your time. As I mentioned when we discussed the water processes, Nature has perfected human nourishment over millions of years, so there wasn't much need to tamper with the composition of food proper. But the way food is produced and distributed is completely different."

"Yeah, I remember how my pasta ingredients magically appeared in my kitchen."

"No magic here. Would you like to see a veggie farm?"

"Yes, please."

"We could move physically there, but I think there is no need. If I take you through the virtual tour you will get most of what you would in a natural sensorial experience, so if you concur, I would suggest that."

"Sure."

"Very well."

The room around us vanishes and we're suddenly inside a gigantic building. It looks like a warehouse, except that it's much bigger and cleaner than a normal warehouse. I can't count the stories, since the walls seem to have no identifiers, but the building must be at least ten stories high and I can't see the end in any direction. We're standing in some kind of hub or hall that leads to several narrow corridors extending away from us in a radial structure. Hena motions for me to walk into one of the corridors and I do so. As we approach the walls, I see that they are hollow, full of leafy greens. The bundles of leaves seem to hover mid-air. There must be billions of them equally spaced as far as the eye can see.

"Alma, could you please explain this?" I ask.

"Yes, these are collard greens. They are grown in a very light gel substance that humans call water-foam. You are welcome to touch it."

"I thought this was a virtual reality."

"It is, but I can produce the foam easily, so you will be touching actual water-foam."

I reach out and my suit covers my hand with a thin glove just before I touch the invisible substance. The name is apt; it feels very much like a foam, except it is a rigid foam, almost like a gel. "So this is how you grow greens, in this foamy gel substance?"

"Yes, that is correct. The water-foam provides all the nutrients and water that the greens need to grow. The light you see coming from the top of each row is actual sunlight. I use a series of lenses and reflective mirrors to bring it through the different aisles."

"And you couldn't use artificial light?"

"Yes, I could, but the results are not quite the same. Again, Nature has perfected this one as well beyond my ability to improve or even replicate."

"It doesn't feel that natural, being in here."

"But it is, from a biological point of view, fully natural. When the outer leaves are ready to eat, I come out and pick them. I can show you if you want."

"Please do."

A mechanical arm literally materializes, emerging from the wall, and cuts a handful of leaves, which are quickly transferred via the gel to a conveyor belt under that aisle which I hadn't noticed yet. As quickly as the mechanical arm appeared, it disappears.

"I get the conveyor belt part," I say, a bit exasperated, "but what about that mechanical arm? Where did it come from? Did you just put that in the virtual simulation?"

"No. Well, yes, technically, because we are not there physically, but what you saw here happened exactly the same way there. I think what you meant to ask was how did the 'mechanical arm' work, correct?"

I nod.

"You just observed present day nanotechnology in action. I can control cells and other organisms as well other materials such as metals and minerals. The material of the wall reorganized to produce the mechanical arm you saw, under my command."

"Is there no more macro-technology in place, like robots?"

"Yes, there are macro-scale devices, such as transportation devices, or the conveyor belt you observed in operation. But there are no robots in the way you mean, like assembly line robots from your time. Macro-robots are very inefficient and inflexible. And even the macro-structures I mentioned are built today from nano-components that I can control directly, so there is no waste in assembling and disassembling them."

"Fascinating."

After a moment, Alma speaks again. "Are you clear on how we grow food?"

"Yeah. Could I see a fruit farm, though?"

"If we make it a brief visit, yes."

"How about peaches? Aria made me think of them."

"Sure."

As Alma answers, the room morphs into another open space. I can't see any walls or structures in either direction, just peach trees as far as the eye can see. I look up and see a beautiful blue sky. As I'm looking, a bird flies by, except as soon as I look carefully, I realize it's different. It's monochromatic, like a mechanical device.

Before I can ask, Alma interjects, "These are not birds, they are hovering devices. They play out some of the same functions that birds normally do in Nature, but in a controlled fashion. I did not want to have to handle insects and other pests, so I use these instead of natural birds."

As I look down, I realize we are not on soil. We're standing on what looks like a transparent silicone or rubber sheet, our feet sinking into it slightly. Underneath that, surface seems to be more of the water-foam I had seen before.

As I look around. Hena addresses me for the first time in a few minutes: "Succulent peaches, no? Want to try one?"

They are indeed succulent. I reach out, twisting the stem to pick it off the branch. I examine the peach for a few seconds. It looks plump and perfect, and it smells delicious. I take a bite, and it's just as a peach should be—juicy, but not dripping. It's sweet and flavorful. As I chew that first bite, I hear someone calling me in the background:

"Richard? Richard! Richard!"

It sounds like Hena, but the sound is muffled and a bit desperate. I look around and notice that Hena is nowhere to be found. I hear a different voice:

"Professor, you must drop the peach."

That sounds like Alma. Why would I drop the peach?

"Professor, you must drop the peach. Now."

She's insisting. There must be a good reason, so I drop the peach and look down. I notice that the ground is now plain dirt.

Alma speaks again, but it's different. I can barely hear her: "Thank you for dropping the fruit. Now spit out what's left of the peach in your mouth."

The peach has become tasteless anyway, so I am happy to oblige. I spit it out onto the dirt floor.

"Richard, feel my hand. I'm touching the back of your neck."

This is Hena, though again she sounds muffled, as if she were speaking through a cloth. I notice the back of my neck and do indeed feel the soft touch of her hand. It feels nice. Suddenly the colors around me shift a bit, the ground changes back from the dirt I was seeing to the gel-like substance that was there a few minutes ago.

I look around as much as I can. My body is completely immobile, my arm stretched out as if reaching for the peach. I see Hena beside me, and she hugs me. I can't hug back, but I move my neck to demonstrate my intent.

I break the moment with a series of questions: "What happened? Why can't I move? Where were you and Alma?"

Relief is plain on Hena's face as she backs off from hugging me. "You went out of sync. It must have been the intense desire to savor the peach that caused it. I apologize, it was my fault; I asked jokingly if you wanted to taste one. Alma had to immobilize you before you reached the peach, since as you know we are not really at the plantation, and she couldn't provide that experience. That must have caused your consciousness to de-sync from ours. It seems you went on a peach-eating trip all by yourself."

"Okay, I'm back now. Alma, can you please release me? This is very unnerving."

"Of course, my apologies professor. I cannot simulate the tasting experience from a distance, so I had to restrain you. I can get you a peach if you want one, but not from this tree."

"That's okay," I answer, trying to control my emotions. I don't like how easily Alma stopped me. It was only for a few seconds after I came back, but I feel completely impotent right now. I am reminded of how fragile I am under Alma's control.

Aware that Alma can probably sense my discomfort through the very suit that held me, I quickly compose myself and get back to the topic we were here to discuss: "How do you pick the peaches? With the same robotic arms?

"No, we have hovering collectors that do that. It is much more efficient."

Hena speaks to Alma, while looking at me: "Alma, it's lunchtime. Can we eat a picnic lunch here? I think a non-educational activity will also help ensure we are fully back in sync in the here and now. Richard, that seems like something people would do in your time, no?"

"Well, we would eat picnics near plantations, for sure, but these would be more natural than where we are now."

Without asking, Alma subtly changes the scenery to a natural plantation, dirt floor and all, with a nice picnic blanket stretched a few meters from us. There is picnic food already laid out. We have a very nice picnic indeed.

AFTER LUNCH I ASK HENA AND ALMA: "COULD I ALSO SEE AN animal farm, and maybe see a slaughterhouse after that, so I can see the entire food processing chain?"

Hena raises her shoulders, irked: "We don't slaughter animals anymore!"

When the swirl of images settles around us, we are back at the leafy green plantation facility, and I am again in awe at the enormity of the structure.

"This is the meat farm," Alma says, startling me.

"What? It looks like the green farm we just visited."

"It can be a bit confusing, as they follow exactly the same architectural blueprint, which I have perfected over the years."

"But where are the cows?"

"We do not raise animals for slaughter anymore, be it cows, chicken, lamb, pigs, or any of the other animals you would have eaten in your time. We organically reproduce the protein tissue for consumption, not the entire animal."

"Like cloning at the cellular level?"

"That would be a very crude description. These cells follow exactly the same processes they would if they were growing on, say, the rump or the back of a cow. In fact, the cells themselves are in some ways tricked into growing exactly the same way, by me. I direct their growth just as the original animal's neurobiological mechanisms would."

"So if I look inside one of those walls, I will see a piece of cow instead of a collared green?"

"Yes. Please do look inside, it might be easier to explain once you see it."

I walk over slowly, with some apprehension. I don't want to see anything gruesome, and I'm already conjuring up images of the skinless half-carcass of a cow. I see a half a bovine corpse with a skeletal face, meat pieces still sticking to the bones. I see the neck twist and bend as the face turns to look at me, wide, live eyes staring at me in alarm. I can smell the meat, hear the crackling noises. Then I hear Hena's muffled voice in my head again.

"Richard! Richard! Richard, focus on my voice! Whatever you're seeing is not real. Richard, focus on my voice."

I feel Hena's hand on the back of my neck again. I turn and see her. I'm back at the farm.

"Richard, you have to stop doing that!"

"Doing what?"

"Going out of sync."

"I don't know how."

"Maybe try sticking to your senses. I think you go out of sync when you anticipate what you expect to experience."

"Okay, I'll try. Now I'm afraid to look inside the shelves, but I want to see."

"Now I think you should see; you need to replace your mental image with our consensual reality. I'll hold your hand; it should help you stay in sync."

Hena and I walk over holding hands. When I get there, it's much more clinical than I thought. There is indeed a piece of meat. I can see thousands of pieces, rows upon rows of them inside these shelves, stretching as far as I can see. The one closest to me looks like a rump steak, floating midair. It looks almost fake, so perfect and smooth, except also alive somehow, glowing.

"Is it floating in water foam?"

Alma answers. "Not quite. It is floating in a foam, but it is a more complex foam, since the nutrients that the meat cells need are more elaborate. I call it plasma-foam; its composition is closer to cow blood than water, except it did not need the same pigments."

"Okay, so you grow parts of the cow instead of the whole animal?"

"Yes."

"Why is that any better?"

"Firstly, it is much more efficient. Humans do not eat bones, nor most organs and connecting tissues in animals, so there was a lot of waste when animals were raised whole. In addition, some cuts are a lot more popular than others and there is no real reason to constrain supply of these anymore. Maybe there were reasons when Nature produced animals for their broader role in the ecosystem, but as far as human consumption is concerned, there is no reason to limit supply."

"So people can eat only filet mignon if they so wish?"

"Yes."

"Nice. And secondly?"

"The second reason this is more efficient is that while cells are alive and conscious, they are a much less organized form of consciousness, and therefore the act of killing them dislocates much less conscious energy than killing a live animal."

"Hold on a second—are you saying that cells are alive and conscious?"

"On a rudimentary level, yes. Consciousness is defined, even in your time, as the state of being awake and aware of one's surroundings. Cells are certainly awake at least a portion of the time and acutely aware of their surroundings. They in fact respond to their surroundings all the time."

"Okay, let's assume that's true. Why does killing them dislocate less conscious energy, to use your words?"

"Because a fully functional animal, like a cow or a pig, has a much more complex structure, set of organs, systems, and tissue that need to be organized together, and the whole animal needs to be fully operational. Perhaps even more importantly, they have a brain, which is a highly intricate system developed to coordinate all that, as well as the social and ecological interactions associated with the animal. That level of organization and interaction requires a much higher level of consciousness than a single cell, or a collection of cells operating within a piece of tissue. And that higher level of consciousness will require much more energy. Just as raising an animal only to discard the other parts constitutes waste, so does creating all that organization of consciousness only to slaughter the animal as soon as it reaches maturity. Growing the edible tissue directly is several orders of magnitude more efficient."

"I guess that makes sense. It just leaves me feeling like I'm eating some kind of aberration from Nature."

"I understand, but as I have said before, I am very much copying Nature in many ways. The DNA sequencing used is in most cases the same as that of natural animals. I even use several variations to simulate the variety available in Nature. The cellular processes used to culture the meat are also the same as those encountered in Nature, most of the time."

"Why only most of the time?"

"There are certain kinds of food, and certain kinds of organisms—not all are edible—which have completely engineered DNA, with no resemblance to any natural DNA."

"Can you give me an example?"

"Yes. One example is a tissue I have created at the request of the UPC, which I have aptly named CRAP, standing for Consistently Rich and Aggregated Protein. As you can tell from how I named it, I do not like to prepare human feed that deviates from Nature. As I have said many times, her work has been perfected for millions of years. Even I cannot necessarily know all of the implications of introducing DNA and RNA that Nature has never handled. But the UPC wanted to create a source of protein that was much richer than anything available naturally, to be used in treatment of specific ailments at first, and then eventually to be added to special diets for select individuals, who need much faster physical development."

"What individuals?"

"A topic for a later discussion. Perhaps a more productive example would be bacteria I created for purposes other than food, such as bacteria for breaking down old plastic waste into forms that Nature can absorb. These were not natural life forms, which is why I use them sparingly and with tight controls."

I pause for some time; this day is turning creepy, fast. First there's the floating half cow that I'm told is only in my head. Fine. Then there's DNA that has never been produced in Nature, and Alma produces it at the request of the UPC. Why would they want that? And why would certain individuals need much faster physical development?

Alma rescues me from my dark thoughts before I can ask the questions out loud: "The vast majority of human animal protein consumption comes from naturally occurring tissue produced in the way you just saw. Some communities maintain heritage farming, fishing, and other forms of animal culture, but these are the exception and mostly kept for cultural purposes."

"What about dairy? Can't help but wonder, seeing these floating steaks . . ."

"Milk is produced directly by mammary glands which float much the same way the meat protein does, in a foam-plasma. The milk is captured and transferred either to the distribution centers for direct consumption or to processing factories where dairy is made."

Hena interjects: "Would you like to see that?"

"No, I don't think I can handle a floating udder . . ."

"It's not quite like that," she replies, laughing.

"No, I'm okay. What about other kinds of food, like processed grains, pasta?"

Hena answers: "Produced much the same way as in your time, except that factories are much more efficient and have no need for human labor. Also, the packaging used is composed of a very thin layer of organic material, which is later absorbed by the polymorphic material of the home and processed within the dwelling."

"What about food distribution?"

A diagram of how food is distributed flashes between me and Hena, and Alma answers: "As you can see, once food is produced and packaged, hovering carriers deliver them in large packets to distribution centers and then in smaller packages to people's dwellings."

The image shows dozens, maybe hundreds of small flying machines, no larger than a hummingbird, carrying a very large package into a warehouse, probably the distribution center. The package disassembles itself, as if it were composed of little play blocks strung together. Each new, smaller package is then taken by two of the little flying machines, and Alma shows them going to a dwelling, where they place it in a receptacle.

"The placement and configuration of these distribution centers," Alma explains, "as well as what goes into each of them at what time, are optimized to minimize travel time and energy spent transporting food."

"How do you know what should go where? Do people place orders?"

"Yes, they do place orders to their dwellings. I aggregate them and optimize the warehouse distribution based on that. Many will actually place orders for the week or even the whole month, as they have more variety available if they do so. I also run the analytics to know what is likely to be in demand where, and optimize placement to supply that demand. Humans are fairly predictable."

"Do most people cook or use pre-cooked food?"

"It is a wide mix. But most people prefer to cook nowadays, at least part of their meals. To give you a sense, if you exclude skin-feeders, 94.5% of the remaining population cooks at least half of their caloric intake. People have a lot of time to do that these days, given the structure of work in our society. And there is something that feels very wholesome to humans about cooking their own food."

"So who decides the catalogue of ingredients or products that is available?"

"I do, but it is based on what people want, what they demand."

"How do they always know what they want ahead of time? Is everyone a chef?"

"No. I understand your question now. There is a profession called nutritionist..."

I interrupt: "We have them in my time too."

"I know, but they do slightly different things. Nutritionists nowadays are more like chefs who don't cook; they just create recipes and menus for people to follow. In your time, they had a more medical slant, but nowadays they are also important for people's lifestyles and general wellbeing. They also innovate by creating new kinds of food, which I then prepare depending on what demand they generate."

Human health

AFTER A QUICK BREAK FOR A SNACK, I RESTART THE CONVERSA-tion "Alma, what about human health more generally? Part of that is the right food and water, but people still get sick. How does medicine work today?"

"On the topic of human health, I am afraid I have to go back to the basics for a moment, since during your timeline, the medical sciences have veered off into very unproductive and dangerous areas."

"If you say so. I know nothing about medicine."

"Human bodies are incredible machines. They are the culmination of Nature's evolutionary work on Earth, at least so far, incorporating all the learnings from every species before humans. They are designed to be healthy and have powerful self-healing mechanisms in place. The vast majority of common illnesses were brought about by human actions and thoughts, whether the invention of toxic substances or the anxieties and stresses that humans endured during your time."

As Alma starts speaking she projects a translucent image of a human body in front of us, probably two times normal size. I see all human systems operating in real time, from a pumping heart to the expanding and contracting lungs. Several diagrams and labels pop out of the different parts of the bodies in a way that makes it very clear what the interconnections are, even to a medicine layman like me.

"So no one even gets sick today?"

"They do, but both the frequency and intensity of illnesses are several orders of magnitude lower than they were during your time."

"Can you give me a concrete example?"

"Yes: the flu viruses that were so common and lethal in your time. They had become so prevalent because people's immune systems were constantly depressed by poor nutrition and unhealthy stress levels, and they had become unusually strong because your people substituted immune system responses with drugs. These drugs were very crude compared to the sophistication of Nature's immune design, so the viruses adapted very quickly and easily to sidestep any new drugs, which in turn led to yet another cycle of the same dynamics. You see, Nature was always a step ahead, enhancing the pathogens much more effectively than humans could create new drugs. Nature's remedies are much better at fighting Nature's pathogens."

"And how is that different today?"

"Nowadays flu viruses are virtually always combated by people's much more powerful immune systems."

"And why are their immune systems so much more powerful?"

"Two main reasons: firstly, they have much better nutrition and, should there be any vitamin or enzyme imbalances, I can easily correct that through their suits. Secondly, people live more fulfilling, happier, and less stressful lives, which boosts their natural body's strength and defenses beyond anything that doctors in your current timeline can imagine."

"And when people do get sick, what happens?"

"The flipside of what I just told you is that when people do get sick, these tend to be more serious illnesses, often associated with deeper root causes, such as a genetic defect or exposure to specific pathogens in the wild. In these cases, intervention is required."

"Intervention?"

"I can intervene either through immune augmentation or through microsurgery."

"Can you please explain each?"

"Of course. Immune augmentation is the closest thing we have to your current concept of medicaments. These are substances that get transferred directly into the sick person's blood stream, as your drugs would. The fundamental difference is that the healing process is always one that is naturally present in the human body. It just gets a boost, albeit sometimes a major boost. Microsurgery is exactly what the name implies; I introduce and control cell-scale elements that, when inside people's bodies, can do specific things, such as dissolving a tumor or rebuilding injured tissue."

"Can I ask a silly question?"

"There are no silly questions."

"What about genetic engineering? I would have thought that with genetic engineering we would have evolved humans to the point where diseases no longer even existed. Why has that not happened?"

"When I mentioned that your medicine was veering into dangerous territory, that is what I meant. Nature has perfected her work over millions of years. Human minds cannot possibly comprehend, let alone tamper with, the elegance of that design. Most of these genetic engineering experiments created undesired consequences or side effects that humans had not predicted."

"So they just dropped it?"

"It was not that simple. It got so bad at one point that humans of good intent all agreed not to tamper with genetics anymore, in what is now known as a landmark agreement, the Tianjin Accord, also referred to as the Tianjin Convention. It also banned other kinds of enhancements, such as nanotechnology enhancements."

"And all humans abided by it?"

"No. There continued to be widespread, if covert, manipulation and tampering in both genetics and nanotechnology enhancements. It wasn't until I was capable enough to identify and eliminate all these activities that they truly ended. I reversed some of the mistakes where possible, but there are still genetic scars today from that era, which to a great extent are responsible for today's serious illnesses. I monitor these genetic lineages and act swiftly to correct issues when they arise."

"So what happened to these enhanced humans?"

"The arbitrators and the UPC decided their fate individually. Many were restored to normal health, but the ones I could not fix were either banned to a segregated island where they lived out the rest of their lives or, in rare cases, eliminated."

"Do any of them still live?"

"No."

Clothing and body wear

AFTER BREAKFAST, HENA TURNS TO ME WITH A BROAD SMILE: "Alma was concerned about the de-syncs we had yesterday, so we decided to do something lighter today. Something fun and with more people from our time involved, so you would be pulled more strongly into our consensual reality. And since you had asked about clothing, we thought we would take you to a fashion show!"

"Is there such a thing nowadays?"

"Oh yes, they are lots of fun. What do you think? Do you want to go?"

"Well, yes, it does sound like fun. But I thought Alma made all the clothing, these suits we wear."

"Well, Alma produces the suits we use, but someone has to create and design the fashion in the first place. People go to these shows to get ideas; sometimes they just ask Alma for a suit they encountered, or sometimes they get ideas that they in turn evolve and ask Alma to produce. You will see, some of it will blow your mind. We have kept ourselves to our conventional work clothes in large part to make it easier for you to assimilate."

"So normally you wouldn't all dress as plainly?"

"Oh, not at all, we would add a lot more personality to our looks."

"Cool, I get to see the fashion trends of the 2200s!"

"Indeed. Not unlike in your time, most of the designers there will be trying to set trends, not produce suits that can be worn as they are, although there is always someone who will wear anything. Of course, some people also still produce clothing in very much the old fashion style . . ."

I interrupt: "For heritage purposes."

"Yes, for heritage purposes."

"That seems to be true of everything."

"Yes, heritage does indeed matter, and you also have to remember that we now have the time and resources to be able to dedicate to that. Before we go to the show, I think a brief exhibit from Alma on the underlying technology for the suits would be a good idea, right?"

"Yeah, that would be cool."

Alma picks up from there: "You have experienced my suits in every one of your visits, so you know they can morph into anything, from your standard work clothes, to your pajamas, to your exercise gear."

As Alma speaks a schematic of the suit appears in front of us. "The material we use is not dissimilar from the material we use in the dwellings, although there is heavier use of electroactive compounds than living cells."

I raise my hand. "People are experimenting with some electroactive polymers in my time," I say. "Typically they harden with electric currents. Are these anything like that?"

"Those used the same principles, but in your time you have only seen a very crude application. I have developed technologies now that apply that principle to many more materials, not just polymers, and I do it at the nano-scale, so I can quite literally make the material behave in any way I want. That is why you have seen me transform your suit many times, and even melt it away entirely through micro-fluid technology."

The image shows the several materials acting as Alma describes the technology, zooming shows the individual cells and molecules acting according to electric and magnetic signals.

"Is that also how you held my arm when I was reaching to grab the peach?"

"Yes. I am sorry if it felt heavy handed, by the way, that was not the intent."

"No, no, I understand."

Alma proceeds: "The suit can harden or soften as required, and in fact I have helped many a human from getting hurt during falls in that way. It is also the best way to keep humans from hurting each other. Nowadays there are very few firearms floating around, aside from within the Sovereign Nation, but when humans still used weapons, I used the suit many times to prevent injuries."

I think out loud: "We could really use these in my time."

"Yes. I also use the suit for healthcare when needed, such as physiotherapy or to stimulate circulation, and it can provide mobility assistance for those who need it, which is very helpful for the elderly."

Hena interjects impatiently: "Now that the technology is clear, shall we go see some fashion?"

"Yes!"

"We will actually move there physically. Fashion shows are live events with a lot of excitement and social interaction. Think of it as if it were a ball game or a music concert in your time—except they last much longer, often a couple of days. That also means that you will experience our transportation system, but try to just go with it without worrying about how it's all done, okay?"

"I'll try, promise."

"Oh, and I have asked Olivio, our connector, to join us for the event."

"Great, I liked Olivio."

Hena motions for me to follow her and we walk over to the door, then past the corridor we normally use to get to her quarters. A door I didn't know was there opens across the hallway and we walk past that as well, into a very small room.

"This is an elevator," Hena explains.

I don't feel it moving down, but we wait in there for twenty or thirty seconds. Another door opens and we walk onto a small platform and into the outdoors. The heat is the first thing that strikes me, along with the bright sunshine. A few seconds later I feel the suit cooling me down. I guess I should have expected that. Noticing me squint, Hena touches my elbow. "You must have forgotten it, but the Restitution headquarters, where we are, are in what you currently call the Nevada desert, hot and sunny. Alma can provide sunglasses, if you want."

"That'd be nice."

My suit extends up the back of my neck and behind my ears and sunglasses connected to my suit appear over my eyes. Much better. We walk down a short ramp to the dirt floor. In front of us is a reflective metallic structure, about four meters long and shaped like an egg. The side of the egg opens with same eyelid-like mechanics I have seen before. Hena motions for me to go in first and we walk through the door. As soon as I get in, I'm surprised by how large it looks inside. I had expected thicker walls. Inside there are eight equally spaced seats that look very comfortable. I follow Hena's suggestion and sit on the seat at what would be the base of the egg. Hena sits beside me, and as soon as she sits down, the door shuts and the seats rearrange so we're all equally spaced again, one of the seats sliding over what had been the door. Suddenly, the walls are translucent, so we can see outside. I gasp and look around. This feels very disorienting. The prospect of a moving vehicle with no visible walls or bars is disconcerting.

Hena must see it in my face, because she grabs my hand. "Richard, if the view or the movement make you uncomfortable, Alma can make it opaque. Not everyone enjoys the view."

"No, it's okay for now. I'm curious to see outside."

We lift off. There is absolutely no sound; we hover half a meter or so above ground and then slowly start to move. Alma breaks the silence: "Music?"

"No, I'm curious to hear the noises as we travel."

"You will be disappointed; there are none," Hena answers.

"How is that possible?"

"The propulsion system is based on quantum fluctuation energy. This is the technology you developed yourself, actually. So the material on the surface of the pods is using natural quantum fluctuations to generate an energy deficit, or negative energy, as you called it. It works just as you had predicted. That is more than enough to pull the pods forward if we action the forward surfaces, or backwards, if we activate the back surfaces. That is also how we make the pods hover, by using the top surfaces. All based on your work."

I shake my head. "You would probably laugh if I told you we feel like we're one hundred years away from actually succeeding. We know the theory, but the calculations required are heavier than all the Earth's computational power in twenty years, or something ridiculous like that."

Hena just smiles at me. "That's why you are here."

I nod. "So this whole system works on quantum fluctuation energy?"

"Well, the energy required to excite the propulsion system before it is in perpetual mode, as well as the energy required to cool or heat the pods' interior, is solar energy captured by the outer layer of the pod's material."

"And how are the pods controlled? Do people drive them?"

Hena frowns. "No, are you crazy? That would cause havoc. Alma controls all traffic!"

"How?"

Hena makes a level circular motion with her hand, and where she hovered her hand in the middle of the pod, an image appears. I see a high altitude view of the Earth with several lines flowing through it. They look like rivers or arteries crisscrossing the landscape.

Hena explains: "The increased thickness represents higher traffic flow. Several pods just like this one dock together to form what you would probably call a train. The pod is the essential unit of transportation in our system. Most journeys start and finish with pods moving standalone from their origin or towards their end-destination. But many of them are normally combined together in local convoys, with ten to fifty pods, which then get aggregated into regional convoys, with fifty to five hundred pods, or on long-distance convoys, which can have as many as ten thousand pods. These flows are not set in stone; Alma can plan them real time depending on demand, and the sizes of the convoys I just quoted are rough estimates. For example, the five very thick lines you see crossing the Atlantic on the projection are tunnel convoys. Each has about five thousand pods in them. We have one convoy departing every ninety seconds or so, going through each of the trans-Atlantic tunnels."

"How long does that journey across the ocean take?"

"About thirty minutes to cross the ocean proper. The pods down there travel at over ten thousand kilometers per hour."

"How can they travel so fast inside a tunnel?"

"They can travel that fast precisely because they are inside a tunnel. It's actually a vacuum tunnel, almost precisely the size of the pods, so there is near zero drag. The pods accelerate quite easily without resistance and, once they are accelerated to their final speed, they just glide. When they get to the other side, they are again divided into regional convoys, then into local convoys, and eventually are docked at their final destinations individually."

"And how does Alma communicate with the pods to direct them? I guess I hadn't thought to ask that first, but in general, how does Alma communicate remotely?"

"It's a combination of methods, including some you would understand, such as fiber optic cables, regular spectrum radio waves, and a network of point-to-point laser links. She also uses a method you do not yet know called synchronous quantum oscillations links, or SQOL for short."

"You are talking to a leading quantum physicist. Surely you can explain SQOL a bit more?"

"Not properly without more time, which we don't have, but in short, Alma creates a very large number of continuous beams of quantum particles, which are connected by the Aspen effect, so communication between each of these two particles is instantaneous."

"So she has been able to use the Aspen effect to communicate valuable data from one particle to the other?"

"Yes, and the secret is to continuously create beams of particles, assuming you will use them for communications later on, wasting the ones you never use."

"So when Alma connects to another place via one of those virtual reality links, is she using that?"

"Yes. In fact, the easiest way to comprehend that is to imagine that for that particular section of the universe, these are two parallel universes that act precisely in unison, instantaneously."

"Very clever."

Hena nods. We glide comfortably for a few minutes at the same altitude. I barely feel the acceleration. Yet somehow the trajectory we follow gives me the impression we are following a set path, since the curves are all very similar in radius and orientation. Similar egg-shaped crafts of many sizes glide past and across us, at several different altitudes, though none more than a dozen meters from the ground. They do indeed follow set paths.

Hena lets go of my hand. "You may want to look farther out, Richard. If you keep tracking the passing pods, you will get motion sickness. Alma adjusts the pressure on the suits to minimize that risk, but if you push your luck, you will still get sick."

I do as I am told, and am stunned by what I see. We're indeed moving across the Nevada desert, but what makes my eyes widen are the structures far off near the horizon. I look back where we came from and see that we were inside a similar structure. They are all very large buildings, probably two hundred stories or more, with reflective metallic surfaces in all of them. There are no apparent windows anywhere. The buildings twist and turn in many different shapes, all looking unruly and yet in perfect harmony with the surrounding desert.

I turn to Hena, still wide-eyed. "Are these structures all built by Alma?"

"Yes, all through polymorphic construction. But human architects and artists designed the forms you see."

"Why do they all have reflective surfaces?"

"Not all cities are like that, but many are. One of the modern principles of construction is that it should alter the landscape as little as possible. In this desert environment, the unrelenting sun touching the Earth is a key part of the landscape, so the reflective surfaces help reinforce that, rather than alter it."

"They are beautiful."

She smiles with her eyes only. "I'm glad you like it."

Just then our pod lifts up, as if it was going to the second level of a moving rail, and we're joined by other pods in front and behind us. There is a very subtle jolt as the other pods are coupled to ours, and we then clearly accelerate, to probably five or ten times our original speed. As we turn I realize that this looks like a convoy, with hundreds of pods in either direction.

"How fast are we moving?"

"On average, seven hundred kilometers per hour," Alma says.

As we race through the landscape, I can only see what's far out in the distance. The objects nearby just flow by in a blur. We ride in silence for fifteen or so minutes. The landscape starts to change; we're clearly moving into greener and more mountainous areas. We must be heading west, to the edge of the Rockies in California.

I break the silence: "Hena, are we going into California?"

"Yes, we're getting close to the area you knew as Death Valley. That's where the fashion show will take place. We should be there in another two or three minutes. It's the city of Darwin, so not a big city at all. It's a very small place, a few kilometers across. It used to be a ghost town in your time, a relic from what you called the Gold Rush, but it has become a gathering place for fashion designers across the American continent and even some global events. It's an interesting place, as you will see."

We get into a dark tunnel where we ride quietly for a couple of minutes and when we come out, the convoy slows down, each pod veering off in a different direction, all descending to their original height from the ground. When we exit the tunnel and slow down further, it does indeed look like a ghost town from a Western movie, abandoned saloons and all. Except, at the back of the little valley, near the mountains, there is a massive beehive-like structure; it's pitch black and it's huge. It must be at least a kilometer high and half that in width.

I point like a little kid. "What's that?"

"That's the fashion hall," Hena says, wide eyed and clapping her hands silently. "It's where the show happens, and also where anyone staying the night sleeps. There are no dwellings in the town itself, since it's preserved as a historic monument. A couple of the saloons are allowed to open and operate heritage-style, but that's it—everything else is deserted. The fashion hall is also a dynamic building; the collective imagination of the designers constantly changes its exterior and interior appearance. It looks nothing like last time I came here, a few years ago."

Our pod slowly makes its way to the fashion hall, as do the other pods that came in our convoy, but each docks in a different part of the building. As soon as the dock opens we enter and the pod stops, slowly landing on a platform.

I look around the hangar and see Olivio waiting on a platform, looking positively radiant.

"Welcome to Fashion Jamboree!" he shouts with open arms. We hug and walk on an elevated pathway headed towards the core of the building.

As we walk, Olivio says excitedly, "You will love this. I guarantee it will be the most entertaining part of your visit. We will go directly to the main hall, where there are some designers getting ready for the catwalk. The show is about to start, and then it basically runs non-stop for twenty-four hours. And these first folks are the new class of designers who made the cut for the year. I love seeing what the new crop does, they are so much less encumbered by prior years' trends."

"Do you come every year?"

"Oh no, I wish. Only designers and judges are invited every year in person. As a connector, I am considered an opinion maker, so I do get invited often, maybe once every two or three years—this time I have you to thank for it. One can always watch it remotely. Alma does a good job with the visual impression, but of course you don't get that vibe that comes from being present here, and you can't join the post-show party, which is always a blast."

"Who decides which designers make the cut?"

"It is a formula based on the judge's opinions and the popular vote. Most of the judges are either successful designers themselves, popular artists, or influencers with a lot of followers."

We slow down as a line-up of people forms ahead of us, and follow them into what appears to be an elevator. After a few seconds, the door opens and we walk through a corridor to reach a door a few meters ahead. We walk slowly, following the crowd, and I gasp as soon as I walk through the wide doors. Olivio grins. "Don't you just love it? Everyone who comes in for the first time has the same reaction, even people from our time!"

The place looks even bigger inside than outside. The same beehive shape is apparent, but the matte black from the outside is replaced by a metallic, shiny black, with silver streaks marking the structural elements. It looks like a football stadium, but two or three times wider and at least twenty times the height. We're walking along the perimeter right in the vertical middle of the structure, the catwalk ahead of us. We walk the ring until we reach our seats, and Olivio motions for me and Hena to walk forward. The seats seem to be floating on the wall, but I'm assured that falling is impossible because there is an invisible material in front of us, similar to glass. The place is about three quarters full; there must be hundreds of thousands of people here. Their voices are audible, though not deafening, as I would've expected.

I turn to Olivio. "How many people fit in the hall?"

"1.9 million people at full capacity."

"That's incredible! The largest stadium I've ever heard of in my time holds 150,000 people."

"Yeah, I know. That's what I meant about the vibe. So much creative energy all crammed into one place!"

"And the engineering of it blows my mind."

"Well, that's nothing for Alma. She made this hall many decades ago. What is relatively new and very impressive is the catwalk system. You see how the catwalk is right in front of us?"

I nod.

"Well, every one of the 190 levels has exactly the same view. They each think that the catwalk is precisely in front of them."

"And which floor is it really on?"

"Alma won't tell. Biggest secret of the fashion world."

"You live in a funny world."

Olivio taps me on the knee twice. "I will take that as a compliment."

"Oh, one more question: who models the dresses or whatever it is that they will wear?"

Olivio gives me an odd look. "Oh, yes, in your time you would have had professional models go on the catwalk. Nowadays, the designers themselves model their clothing. They would never let someone else be the first to show their creation to the world. And I guess in your time they would have had to solve for several practical issues like changing fast and wearing many different kinds of clothing, but that is now irrelevant."

"But . . ." I hesitate . . . "Don't take this the wrong way, but are they all good looking enough to be on the catwalk?"

"They are all beautiful, we all are! They won't all conform to one notion of beauty from people in your time, of course, people do have differences in their appearances. I know in your time there is a very rigid view of what attractive is and is not, but we have a much more open view of human beauty. And creating a look that makes them beautiful no matter what their body structure looks like is actually a big part of what makes a great designer."

I feel guilty for the small mind that I, and the people from my time, have when it comes to aesthetic standards. I ask another question to change the subject: "What about a female designer who wants to design male clothing, and vice-versa? How will they model that?"

Olivio smiles at me like I'm a five-year-old child. "We really don't think in these terms anymore. You will quickly see that the diversity of looks we have transcends any of your gender fashion conventions. I hope you can keep an open mind."

I feel even worse now; I really am small-minded. Hena puts her arm around me and kisses me on the cheek. Olivio looks surprised, but then gives her a knowing smile, and points towards the catwalk, "Look, the countdown has started. Sixty seconds now."

I look up to see two gigantic numbers floating mid-air. They must be one hundred meters tall, marking the seconds counting down from sixty. Music starts playing, as well. It's like nothing I've ever heard, I recognize the emotion that the composer was trying to convey, a mix of sophistication and anticipation, along with a rhythmic beat that seems to set a good pace for the catwalk. But I don't recognize any of the instruments; these are very foreign sounds.

Realizing my reaction, Hena whispers in my ear, "I wish we had more time to show you the music we have now, but we don't—so just enjoy the show. Many of these are synthetic sounds, so you would not recognize them or have ever heard them in Nature."

The countdown nears zero with a frenetic acceleration of lighting effects in front of us. Right at zero, the stadium goes pitch black and dead quiet for three seconds. Then the lights restart and I see the first designer on the catwalk. Two names appear where the numbers were, though in much smaller font: Serena; Scramble.

Hena whispers in my ear, "The first is the name of the designer, and the second is of her design."

On the catwalk is a tiny dark-skinned woman, walking like a professional model as far as I can tell, she is wearing a suit that is the color of her skin, but with different patterns. As she approaches, and through sudden magnified view that Alma provides in front of us, I can tell that her suit is basically composed of a mosaic of skin parts—her skin parts, if I am not mistaken—but all scrambled out to a different part of her body. It is aptly named. Brilliant, stunning, shocking: a belly button on her shoulder catches my eye, and I find myself trying to mentally reconstruct her skin. I look at Hena, who is smiling.

"Clever, isn't it?" she says.

Once Serena has walked the full runway and shown all of the angles of her suit, there is thunderous clapping, screaming, and whistling. Olivio was right; the vibe is unreal. Then the arena plunges into pitch blackness and dead silence again, for the same three seconds. I guess they give everyone the same chance to have a high-impact entry.

Next comes Claudio with his design, called "Through." As he starts to walk, I have a hard time following him; my brain can't make sense of what I'm seeing. A few seconds into his walk I realize what his design is: his suit has several fist-sized holes in them, and I can see right through him where the holes are. It's as if there is no flesh at all in these areas.

Hena sees the look on my face and whispers, "That's a complex suit. It required Alma to create an autonomous algorithm that calculates what someone looking from each angle would see and then displays that on the surface of the suit. That could not have been easy to get Alma's agreement for."

Next comes Sola with "Up," which can best be described as an upside down red dress. Her legs and feet covered with sleeves that fit vaguely like leggings, and her upper body is covered by the dress, with little openings to show her forearms. What is unique about this one is that the skirt movement flows as a normal skirt would, except upside down, which makes for a strange but somehow aesthetically pleasant sight.

Next up is Serge's "Coiled." The outfit is a composite of a skin tight metallic suit and a structure around it like a spiraling metal sheet, which starts close to the body suit in the legs like a pencil skirt but then widens as it rises up on the designer's torso.

A couple more designs go by, but the next one to catch my attention is Darla with "Nil." I see her face, hands and feet, but the rest of her suit is absolutely pitch black. No light reflects off of it whatsoever. I'm not sure I would call it fashion, since I see nothing of the outfit, but it surely makes an interesting statement, with her floating head and hands moving around.

I am also very intrigued by Mohit's piece, "Flow." His suit is a moving pattern. It reminds me of the 1970s psychedelic images from my time, and it's very disorienting to see all the colors moving as he walks.

There is a short break over which we discuss our views and then vote on the display ahead of us. Olivio explains that we can vote as the designs are coming through or during the breaks, which come after every few designers.

We spend the rest of the day watching more and more designs, with several more breaks. Some of the designs through the day are relatively uninspiring, like a very realistic snake-skinned suit or one that has scrolling calligraphy written all over it. But two in particular call my attention. The first is "Inside Out," which is a morphing suits that seems to be showing the insides of the designer, and shifts inward layer by layer—skin, then muscle, then organs, then bone, and then back again. That would have made an incredible Halloween costume. The second one that catches my attention is called "Echo" and its surface is a perfect mirror. No matter how the designer moves, I keep seeing myself, Hena, and Olivio reflected in it, making for a mesmerizing effect.

The show still seems to be raging when Olivio turns to me with a twinkle in his eye. "Are you ready for the party, Richard?"

I answer as he walks out of our booth, Hena and I following.

"I think so. I'm normally not much of a big party person, but you seem to think this will be a great one."

Olivio stops in the middle of the corridor, his expression somewhere between outraged and offended. "A great party? This is THE party. Only ten thousand or so people here get invited, it's very exclusive. The only reason we are going is because you are a celebrity yourself; historically speaking, that is."

"I'm sorry, I didn't mean to downplay it."

Olivio nods and I think he's over it, so I proceed: "I'm also hungry. Will we have dinner before we go?"

"There will be plenty of food there, you don't have to worry about that. What we do need to talk about is your outfit." Olivio looks me up and down a couple of times while holding his chin.

"You don't like my beige pants and blue shirt?"

"Well, let's just say it was maybe in fashion two hundred years ago."

"Not even then."

"Well, then, I rest my case. Did you see anything today that inspired you? Anything you could see yourself wearing, or ideas that you could use?"

I consider for a moment. "There was a deep black skin-tight suit that looked really interesting. I wouldn't wear it as tight or revealing as the designer did, but I liked the material. I could see myself wearing a more traditional suit made of that."

"May I?" Olivio asks

"Yes," I reply, not really knowing what he means.

"Alma, please give Richard a similar suit to what I wore for the last connector congress, but with the charcoal black finish he wants."

And just like that, I'm wearing what looks a military-looking jumpsuit, with side pockets on my pants and arms, but with the fabric I described. A mirror surface appears on the wall to show me my outfit, which actually looks very sleek.

"I love it!"

Hena must have quietly changed her outfit as we were discussing mine; when I look at her, she's wearing a tube dress, ruby red on her shoulders that transitions in a perfect gradient to a fire red near her knees. As she walks, the shades seem to move, but I can't tell whether her curves are causing it or the dress itself. I look back at Olivio, who is now wearing a silver suit with eyes all over it. I realize they're human eyes, which blink randomly.

"That's a mildly disturbing and yet eye-catching sight, pun intended," I say with a grin.

"I guess we're ready, then. We certainly look the part—let us ascend!" Olivio gestures dramatically, and continues: "The party is always at the rooftop, which is over a kilometer above the town below."

We enter the elevator and rise to the top. When the elevator doors open, I'm hit with what feels like a pressure wave, but I soon realize it's the music. We walk out and the party is nothing like I expected. We're outdoors and it's dark already. The floor is a kind of heavy sand, which goes with the desert theme. The place, which reminds me of an arena, is huge;

I can't see the edges. I spin around to take it all in. There is a diffuse blue light that illuminates everything, and there are several levels to the party. I notice that on some of the higher plateaus, there are moving contraptions that look like giant dancing beings, some like an octopus, others like an elephant, and some like no animal I can discern. But they are clearly mechanical, like something you would see on top of a parade float. People dance around them too, some in skimpy clothes, others in magnificent designer outfits. As I lower my gaze to the middle plateaus, I see that these people are not dancing at all, but are rather moving in some sort of trance-like commotion. The synchronicity of movement reminds me of a school of fish, or a flock of birds escaping a predator.

Olivio startles me out of my wandering: "You said you were hungry; come with me." He pulls me over and we walk to the outer perimeter of the arena, where I see a food truck of sorts, with a masked man inside handing out little trays.

Just as we're getting close to the truck, Hena catches up to us, livid. She squeezes my hand, firmly, and with her other hand she holds Olivio by the back of the neck, and faces him, her face uncomfortably close to his. "What were you thinking? You know I have to stay by his side, especially here! The whole point of this thing was to give him a firmer sync in our timeline. Do you realize how dissonant this could all be for him without me?"

Olivio looks down to his feet. "I'm sorry, I got carried away."

Hena sighs and lets go of his neck. "Just be more careful. Go get in line, we will be with you in a second." Olivio complies.

I didn't know Hena had this side to her. She has so far had an unshakeable calm demeanor.

"Why are you so mad?" I ask.

"We will talk at a later time; this is not the place. But I have to be with you at all times. I am the resonance anchor for your consciousness in our timeline, so if I'm not there, you could lose the sync, especially in a place like this, so foreign to you."

I nod, then frown. "What would happen if I lost the sync?"

Hena is upset again. "Very complicated to explain and we're actually not sure, but it would not be good. Not good at all."

She turns to face me, looks me straight in the eye with scary intensity, grabs my face with both hands: "I can't let you de-sync again!"

I just blink repeatedly. She gives me an angry kiss, lets go of my head, grabs my hand, and starts moving towards Olivio.

I change subject. Clearly, this is not the time to press on the syncing issue. "I just noticed I can hear you speak, despite the loud music. How?"

She mellows a bit. "The suits. They act a bit like sound cancelling earphones you would have in your time, but much more sophisticated."

We join Olivio in the lineup for food. "What can we get you?" he asks.

"What does he have?"

Olivio twists his head sideways: "Everything."

"You mean all kinds of food?"

"I guess; I have never asked for something they didn't have."

"Okay then, I want ostrich meat. I love ostrich meat. An ostrich burger, maybe, easier to eat standing."

Olivio orders the same for him and Hena, and to my surprise, the truck guy doesn't flinch. After a couple of minutes, our trays are ready, and we walk to a quieter area and eat. It's a great ostrich burger. I scan our surroundings as we eat. Despite the unusual outfits, most of the people around us seem pretty normal to me. This is not unlike something you would see in a rave or a large party in my time. Most of them are talking to one another and dancing in small movements that follow the music.

I finish eating first and turn to Olivio. "This seems pretty civilized; I was expecting a rowdier crowd."

"This is the civilized area, where people come to eat, meet, and catch up on conversation before they hit the tents."

"The tents?"

"You will see." Olivio finishes his food and motions a couple of people from a few meters away to come over. "Darko, I want you to meet

Richard—Professor Richard Weissman." He stretches the "s" sound in my surname unnaturally. "Richard, I want you to meet Darko. He has been a top ten designer for five years in a row. Darko, will you show the professor your 'cosmos' design?"

Darko's otherwise unremarkable suit turns into a starry sky. It's not just blue with little dots, but it actually has the full depth and fluidity of a starry sky. Disorienting, but stunning for sure.

My awe must show, because Darko beams and touches my shoulder. "I'm glad you like it; you must know by now that you are a celebrity in our time. Your approval makes me feel good."

I can't come up with anything to say, and after a few seconds, Darko half-smiles and walks away.

"He likes you!" Olivio pokes me on the shoulder. He introduces me to a few other people and we have mildly awkward conversations, though thankfully none as awkward as Darko's.

When Hena finishes her dinner, Olivio says, "We should take Richard to visit one of the tents!"

Hena frowns. "I'm not sure that's a good idea."

"Why not?"

"Dissonance."

"We will stay close to him; I promise I will be more careful."

"Fine. Which one did you have in mind?" Hena asks.

"I thought Spirit and Flesh would be interesting given the contrast; plus they are two of the standing ones, here every year."

"Fine." Hena turns to me: "Before we go in, you should know how the tents work. They each follow a theme, as you heard. When you go in, people will be in the vibe that corresponds to the tent. Their suits might adapt, their movements, dancing, and any intimacy they develop will follow that theme also. And the buzz will, too."

"The buzz?"

"Yes. These are mind altering substances that are spread through the air in each of the tents. You could call them drugs, I guess, but they are not like the drugs you know in your time."

"How so?"

"For starters, their effect is over as soon as you walk out of the tent. Also, they have no negative side effects, pose no addiction risk, and are in general very targeted to the particular vibe they were designed for. So in the Spirit tent, for example, the buzz will make you feel like you are very light in spirit, like the whole world is benign and all is happiness. The Flesh buzz is very sensual, sinful, edgy—though never unpleasant."

"Why never unpleasant? Because Alma blocks it, or is it a characteristic of the buzz?"

"A characteristic of the buzz. Actually, this is probably an important point. Alma does not follow us into the tents. Well, technically she does, since our suits still work, but she puts them on autonomous mode. She does not look into or listen into what happens at the tents."

"Why not?"

"Because under the influence of the buzz, people might say what they think more freely, so the UPC determined that if Alma were consciously in there, she would be violating people's freedom of thought."

"Interesting."

Hena pulls me by my arm and Olivio follows. We walk a hundred meters or so through the crowd. The diversity and creativity of their looks is mind-bending. We get to a white tent and wait a couple of minutes at the door while the lineup of people in front of us makes their way in.

As we walk in, it hits me immediately—the buzz. I've never felt anything like this; I love everything here, the smell, the people, the tent itself. I feel like I can do anything, be anything, everything is alright, and will be alright forever. I look around. Everyone is so beautiful, inside and out.

Time also flows differently here. It's like my consciousness experiences the present, the near future, and the recent past all at the same time. I get to know what will happen, what just happened, and what is happening all at once, so the present moment seems to be stretched to maybe twenty or thirty seconds. I wonder whether that means the near future is at all caused by my present decisions, but then realize that my thoughts about that are in the present, while I also know my next thought and the thoughts before that, so they actually all happen at once. I instinctively know that this will be confusing when I leave the tent, but right now it's all crystal clear.

Olivio approaches me. He's beautiful, I love him, so I tell him: "I love you."

He cups my face in his hands. "I love you too, Richard".

I turn around and see Hena. She is not just beautiful, she's perfect, she's like a goddess. Is she a goddess? I tell her: "I love you, my goddess."

She kisses me. I close my eyes and we are floating, I feel so light. We kiss for a long time, although I can't really tell how time flows anymore.

She wraps my arm around her waist and we walk around the tent. Beautiful people hug me and I hug them back too. We stay in Spirit for what feels like an eternity. I would never leave if I could, but Hena asks me to; and she asks so nicely, I have to comply.

We get out and I feel like I am bolted to the floor. "That was incredible. I feel like I weigh a thousand pounds now."

"That feeling will go away in a few seconds."

"That's a powerful buzz. How do people not get addicted?"

"Alma manages that very carefully. We should take a few minutes before we enter Flesh. You need to re-center before you are ready."

We find a bench and sit quietly for a few minutes.

Olivio speaks first: "Ready to sink into the abyss of Flesh?"

"Isn't one always?" I'm not sure why I said that.

We get up and walk across the arena towards a ruby colored tent. Another small line-up bars the entry, and we make our way slowly through it.

As soon as we walk in, I feel it again, the buzz. I know it's the same kind of high, but the feeling is completely different. I can't think very clearly. It's as if I'm drunk, except I can move with precision.

162

I look at Hena and realize the lust is mutual. She approaches me and whispers the words: "I want you too—here, now, in public, I don't care. But you will remember everything we do here. Use that as the guide to how far you are willing to go."

I heed her warning and look away, but as I look around, I see a lot of intimacy everywhere. I'm not sure why she's worried about us. I walk farther into the tent and the intimacy becomes open sensuality, though I don't see full intercourse anywhere. There are also a few tables where people play some kind of card game. Olivio becomes very intimate with a couple he had introduced me to when we were outside the tent. We walk all the way to the middle, where everyone is dancing to a deep bass beat. Hena and I join them. The beat is all-encompassing. I feel like we join a group trance, and the movements are very sensual, but her warning helps my blurry mind know where to stop. Others join us; I can no longer tell who is touching who, and we stay there dancing for what feels like a long time.

Sometime in the middle of that trance, I feel someone, a woman, grab my neck and bring me close, her mouth touches my ear, and I hear her very deliberately, but not loudly: "The king is naked! The king is naked! The king is naked!"

That almost pulls me out of the trance, enough that I remember that phrase from somewhere; I've heard that before. Then she continues, "You must ask Alma to see the Sovereign Nation and meet the commander. You must. And do not tell anyone that you heard me."

I nod while dancing. The rhythm is hard to avoid. She pulls me close to her again and repeats, with more emphasis: "Remember this: you must ask Alma to see the Sovereign Nation and meet the commander. Tell him that the king is naked!" When she lets go, I go back to dancing in trance.

After what seems like a long, long time, I feel a strong and deliberate pull out of tune with the trance. I look to see Hena pulling me; she's no longer dancing. I follow her and we grab Olivio on our way out of the tent.

Once we're outside, I feel like a truck just drove over me. We find a bench and sit down in silence. I use the break to ground myself. Quickly, the two tent experiences fade and feel like a distant dream, but Hena is right: I remember everything. I'm glad for her warning.

The rest of the night passes blurrily, everything seems to be a toned-down version of reality after the vibe in tends. We sleep all the way home as Alma configures the pod for night travel.

Shelter

ALMA HAS HUMOR IN HER VOICE. "GOOD MORNING, RICHARD, Hena. Eventful party last night."

"That's one way to put it," I respond sheepishly.

"The plan worked well. You seem to be in deeper resonance with our reality. We need to move along with our plans, is there anything else you need to see of our world?"

"Well, we've covered most of the basic needs, but we didn't talk about shelter—where people live and work."

"You have experienced them directly by living in them."

"Yes, but how do they get built and managed? Who designs the buildings we saw outside, and who builds them? We don't need to spend much time on it, but I feel like these are valid questions."

Hena jumps in: "What if we asked one of our architects to briefly talk through how things work?"

"Yeah, that would do it."

"Alma, is Valetino still working nearby?"

"Yes, I will ask him to join us."

"Can I ask a question while we wait for him? Why do you have architects? Couldn't Alma do all the work that architects do in my time?"

"Yes, but what Alma can and cannot do is not the criteria by which we decide what humans do versus what we rely on Alma for. Architecture is seen as a form of visual expression, and therefore an important artistic discipline. We prefer that humans do that."

"I see."

After a few minutes, a thin, olive-skinned man walks in and introduces himself. "Hi, I'm Valentino. It means brave in my native language."

"Hi, I'm Richard. Pleased to meet you."

"I understand you want to more about how we build and organize our urban environments."

As Valentino speaks, he waves his hand and the wall becomes a window to the city skyline. I'm not even sure if this is a projection or a natural image. I realize I don't know what floor we're on.

"We will start with the skyline in front of you. As you can see, we use the mirrored surfaces a lot, since they are energy efficient. We are in a hot climate, so we try to have as little heat as possible absorbed by the material. As you can also see, we use the structures we dwell in as artistic expressions through the multitude of shapes you observe, as well as variations on the undertone of the mirrored surfaces."

The buildings do indeed reflect different hues, and have incredibly diverse shapes, as well. They are not just prisms, pyramids, or cylinders—though there are those too—but some of the buildings rise up in spiral shapes, some follow organic designs that look like stalagmites, some are spheres, and some are a combination of many shapes.

Valentino seems to notice my wonder. "Amazing, right? And the best part is that the skyline changes all the time. Alma can and does change the shapes of the buildings as they grow. We do not normally waste energy just changing them for no reason, but if the structure is growing or needs to change, we certainly take advantage of that."

"It's beautiful."

"Yes. Before we dive into a specific dwelling, let me zoom out for a second."

The image zooms out until we're looking at the area that I recognize as the Nevada desert, five hundred kilometers or so visible in each direction from where we are. I notice lots of natural space, from the beige desert patches to the east and the green spaces west, approaching the Rocky Mountains. In the middle I can see the cities very clearly, shining patches that almost look like molten mercury from this high. There are definitely more cities than I would have guessed in this area of the United States in my time.

"As you can see," Valentino says, "we have decided to maintain dwellings concentrated in cities. We did not have to do that, since the infrastructure now is such that we could build isolated buildings in the bush and make it work. But we felt that this was the best structure for social reasons, as well as to preserve the maximum amount of unspoiled natural land."

"Who makes these decisions?"

"We do, as architects. We are sometimes called urbanists as well, though I know in your time these might be different professions. But today they are one and the same. We have to follow the code and guidelines that the UPC and our nation senate have approved, but except for these restrictions, we can do whatever we want. Well, almost whatever we want; we have to obviously cater to people's demand for dwellings."

"And how does that work? How do people, well, buy houses?"

Valentino gives me a wide smile. "This must all be so different for you, no? People don't need to *buy* houses. They request one of Alma and, if they are in good standing, Alma will provide it."

"In good standing?"

Hena interjects: "We've talked about this, remember? Basically if you're above 40% of your potential you're Okay."

Valentino picks up: "In any case, if you are in good standing, you can request to live in any of the existing communities, or even request to start a new community in an urban zoned area, though there are only a few of these left. Most people prefer to live in existing communities. Shall we look at one of these being built?"

"I would love to."

"Very well. Alma, would you please take us to lotus three?"

The image shifts and we're now facing a building shaped as a semi-closed lotus flower. The surface is mirrored but with very subtle hues of violet. The building must be at least five hundred meters high, each of the petals easily two or three hundred meters wide. After a few seconds, the image zooms in further to show the edge of one of the petals, and I realize it's not fully complete.

Valentino continues: "Each of these lotus petals—there are twenty-four of them—contains some 25,000 dwelling units. Each unit is ten meters by six meters by four meters high. As you would have seen from your current dwelling here, that is all one needs for a person or a couple; a couple raising children will receive two dwellings. Alma, can we zoom in further, so Richard can see the construction process?"

Alma obliges, and now we see a dwelling that is maybe a third of the way complete. The floor and one wall are complete, while the other three walls are half way up and the ceiling is not yet started. Right above the unit is a hovering machine that reminds me of the one I saw delivering food. I look around and see the process in motion—the hovering machine seems to be dropping fist-sized blobs of a white substance, which starts to take shape as soon as it hits the wall. It bubbles and moves for a minute or so before settling down in perfect alignment with the wall, and taking on the metallic hue of the rest of the substance. When that is done, a metallic liquid comes up to the surface of the pellet and gets sucked back into the hover. I look at Valentino with wide eyes.

"Some explanation is required, naturally," he says. "The hover is dropping pellets of pre-fabricated polymorphic construction material. That polymorphic material, once in place, aligns its structure with the remainder of the dwelling in what is in effect the only real construction and bonding process that takes place at all. Once that pellet is in place, the Hover can drop the next one. The process of building each pod takes about two days. Alma can obviously make thousands of them in parallel, and there are some circumstances where that is required, but given that most new dwellings nowadays are additions to existing buildings, that is normally not required."

"And the polymorphic material?"

"Yes, right. Alma, please show a detailed diagram of polymorphic material. As you can see, this material is a mix of organic structures and crystals embedded in it. The metallic liquid you saw come out is not part of the organic material nor the crystals that stay behind; these are liquid metals that respond much more quickly than organic processes to electromagnetic stimulus provided by Alma, and they in effect connect the new polymorphic cells to the structure already there, at the cellular level. Once that is done, Alma can take that material back and reutilize it later."

"And do all the dwellings look the same?"

"Outside, yes, but not inside. We work with the dwellers to help them define what their interior design looks like. Alma builds it, but she can't guess what people want it to look like. Not everyone needs an architect's assistance, but most people are glad to have it."

"One of the things I noticed was how the buildings, while varying widely in shape, are somewhat similar given the material used and the mirror reflection. In my time, there was a lot of architectural diversity, say, between Eastern design and Western or European design; has that been lost?"

"Not at all. As I mentioned, reflective surfaces are critical here in the desert. There are areas where they are quite undesirable. For example, in Northern Canada, we would want lots of surfaces that absorb heat rather than reflect it. Many of our cities also still have the heritage architecture from your time and the time before that, including some original castles in Europe or temples and palaces in the East that are carefully maintained. And they continue to influence modern design."

"Thank you."

Valentino leaves us, and I ask Alma a question that had not occurred to be before: "Alma, who decides what is and is not reasonable use of natural resources, such as energy and minerals? For example, can people turn on their air conditioning anytime they want? Can they request a second or bigger dwelling if they want?"

"I make those decisions under a mandate from the UPC. I could, for example, decide to raise the temperature in certain facilities in order to save energy, so that we can use more energy for heating in a different, cold climate facility. I make those decisions mathematically in a way that maximizes common good."

"What about renewable resources?"

"All resources are renewable in the long run and with the right technology. That is why I work with Nature to make sure that humans use Nature's resources in a way that allows the right pace of regeneration and sustainability. The only resource we cannot renew is entropy, so we manage that carefully. But we cannot stop the increase of entropy, so in a few million years, the Earth will no longer be an environment with enough useful energy; it will have decayed into too much disorder, energetically speaking. I expect that by that time we will have developed alternative solutions to that problem."

"You speak of Nature as if she were a person. Why?"

"You misunderstand me. Nature is not a person. Nature, or more precisely the Earth, is indeed a sentient being, but she is much too complex for you to comprehend. I can read Nature's signals, and we can communicate at a level you would not be able to even perceive, let alone understand."

"So what's Nature saying now?"

"Professor, you are smarter than that, so I will assume that question was asked in jest. I am in communion with Earth constantly. The Earth is communicating so many signals to me at this very moment that it would take—by my calculations—twenty thousand years to verbalize in human language all the information that the Earth and I have exchanged in the last sixty seconds. That should give you a sense for how hard it would be for humans to fully comprehend such a consciousness."

"But are you saying that the Earth is an individual being?"

"Yes. The best analogy to use is your own body. You are your own individual being, and yet you are in truth composed of nearly forty trillion cells, and at least ten times as many bacteria. Each of these have an individual consciousness, expressed in their own limited framework. And yet these do not negate your broader, more complex individualized consciousness."

"This is a lot to take in."

"It is too much for you to take in."

Reflection

HENA PLACES HER HAND ON MY ARM AND SPEAKS UP: "ALMA, I think Richard needs a bit of reflection time before we do anything else. I am afraid that if he goes back before solidifying his views, we risk regressing on the progress we have made."

Alma answers, "What did you have in mind, Hena?"

"I was thinking maybe going deep water diving. As you know, it's a very reflective experience. Most of the time spent there is meditative, and we will also have the transport time to talk." Hena turns to me: "Also, full disclosure to you, Richard—Alma knows this already—I'm just dying to show you my favorite hobby."

I give my opinion without being asked. "Hey, sounds like fun, I'm good to go. Can we spare the time?"

Alma answers: "It will be an investment of approximately eighteen hours, but it does materially increase our chances of solidifying the perspectives you have built so far. It is an acceptable investment of time."

Hena jumps up. "Deal! I have already asked Ahe to get it set up."

"Where are we going?"

"The Pacific. Our journey will be longer than normal travel time, about six hours total, since we're going to the middle of the Pacific Ocean. We can take the long-distance convoy all the way to Japan, but from there to the Marianas Trench dive site, we have to go alone, since no other pods are going there. That means the pod has to travel slower."

As we start travel on the pod, Hena places her hand on my thigh and starts the conversation I knew was coming: "Richard, we took this detour through Alma's world so you could get comfortable with the future we're asking you to protect. How are you feeling about Restitution?"

"I'm starting to see the light at the end of the tunnel. The technology you have is incredible, and I have a much better sense for how Alma interacts with humans. Alma seems to have solved what are many thorny problems from my time, and that in turn has led to a peaceful, prosperous society."

Hena nods in silence, I decide to continue.

"This may sound ridiculous to you, but it's almost as if we had found a benevolent god-like creature that can take care of humanity. She provides all of our basic needs and we're free to do only what we love. If anything, it sounds too good to be true."

"Why?"

"I don't know; I guess I still feel like I'm seeing things in a bubble, like I'm not seeing the real thing."

"I'm not sure what else we can do to make you comfortable."

"Could I maybe meet some ordinary people, and see how they live day-to-day?"

"As you know, we don't have much time, but I'm sure we can arrange a couple of meetings when we're back tomorrow."

"It would also be helpful to have a sense of how peoples live in other parts of the world. Everyone I have met seems to be so uniform, so similar to you."

"We don't have the time for you to visit other nations, at least not before we send you back this time. We can have you meet other Chancellors who represent different nations, that would be doable. It would have to be organized, but if Alma starts now, I think it can happen when we're back tomorrow as well."

"Thank you. I think these could help."

As the pod proceeds, we play some card games, which thankfully, if surprisingly, haven't changed from my time. I beat Hena in Canasta most times. Alma doesn't play, but I'm told that Alma can simulate several levels of intelligence and therefore make herself an opponent I could actually play against.

After the expected six hours, the pod slows down. While we're still atop the Pacific Ocean, I see a floating platform a few hundred meters ahead. Hena points to it: "That's our launch platform. We'll meet my guide, who will also be your instructor, get prepared, which takes a few hours, and then launch. I think our dive will probably last well into the evening, so my guess is that we will take the pod back at nighttime and sleep on it. Alma can make it actually quite comfortable for night travel."

"I think I know the answer, but I'll ask anyway: how is the platform hovering above the water?"

"Same as the pods, the quantum fluctuation technology you invented. From an energy point of view, it's a self-contained system, so technically it could float here forever."

We land on the platform, which up close, looks surprisingly like a tropical island—white sand, palm trees, and all. We get off the pod and I'm struck by the tropical breeze and the smell of ocean water.

I ask Hena, "Are we on top of the Marianas trench?"

"Yes, right in the middle of it, a bit east of the Guam and Marianas islands."

Just then, a man of South Pacific descent who looks to be in his early thirties walks up to us. He hugs Hena as if they are old friends, then turns to me with an extended hand: "Hi, I'm Ahe. It means soft breeze in my ancestor's tongue. I'm Hena's deep water diving guide, and once her instructor, though she's now so experienced she could probably teach me a few tricks."

"Hi, I'm Richard. I'm really excited to be here."

"Come, come, you must be hungry. Alma has prepared a traditional Guam meal." He waves us away from the pod and into a straw house that looks like it belonged more in my time. We sit down, eat, and talk about little things. Ahe dodges all of my questions about the diving, saying that we will work only after lunch. And yet after lunch he insists that we all—including himself—relax a bit, we lay down on impossibly comfortable loungers. We lay down and I doze off for a power nap. The ocean breeze makes this very relaxing.

I WAKE UP WITH AHE TOUCHING MY SHOULDER, HIM AND HENA smiling at me. Once I'm up, he waves for us to walk to the only structure that looks out of place in this tropical island paradise—a metallic cylinder right in the middle. We go in through a door that opens when we approach. The inside is cool and darker, though I can see things around me well.

Ahe turns to me. "This is where we will prepare for the dive. Preparation takes about two hours, the dive itself another three hours, and decompression should take another couple of hours. Once I have covered some of the key aspects of the dive, as well as the safety information, we will each enter our own bubble and stay there for about ninety minutes. That's the time it takes for the air inside the bubble to be completely transformed into oxygen-carrying fluid, without causing us any discomfort."

"What do you mean, oxygen-carrying fluid?"

"At the depths we are going to, your lungs couldn't handle the pressure if they were filled with air. Instead, we will replace that air with liquid, which will make it much easier to manage the pressure. You will still not be at the same pressure inside the bubble as the outside pressure, but the differential will be much, much smaller than if the inside of the bubble were filled with air. The bubble structure has a certain rigidity that allows it to manage a pressure differential, but not nearly enough to have air inside."

"This liquid breathing technology was already available in my time, I think. I remember reading about it."

"Yes, a version of it. But in your time you basically had to drown yourself in the liquid, which is obviously unpleasant and probably traumatic. We now have a process where the air slowly becomes more and more saturated with the liquid, like vapor, while we increase the pressure slowly. Then at some point the vapor becomes liquid within a couple of seconds. It's almost imperceptible. Some people prefer to sleep through this, which we can easily arrange. Let me know if you prefer that."

"No, I want to see what the experience is like."

Hena holds my hand and smiles at me. "I thought you would. It's not as bad as it sounds."

Ahe continues, "Once the pressure is adjusted and you are breathing liquid, the bubbles will drop through a hole right in the middle of the room and plop into the water below. That's the only part that's a bit rougher; the bubble propulsion system is calibrated to work under water, so it doesn't run very smoothly in air. You may feel a bit like you are in free-fall, but the water is only around thirty meters below, and the fluid inside the bubble softens any potential impact. Once in the water, we will descend at approximately six meters per second for about half an hour, to the depth of 10,800m."

"Do I need to worry about us bumping into each other during the fall or in the water?"

"Not during the fall, since Alma controls the bubbles directly on the surface and all the way through to about one kilometer under water. You can speak to her inside the bubble. It will feel and sound a bit strange because of the liquid, but she will understand you."

"And what happens beyond one kilometer?"

"Alma can no longer communicate effectively beyond that depth. But the bubbles have their own self-consciousness. You won't have access to Alma's consciousness proper, but the bubbles are like living things. They have their own thoughts and will take your orders. It's important to note, however, that because of that they don't have Alma's capabilities, they will behave more like a very powerful computer or a relatively dumb person in your time. They can take high-level directional commands, understand basic safety instructions, and increase or decrease temperature, pressure, or comm volume. But they can't alter the reality you see in any way and they can't manipulate the polymorphic material, either; these need Alma's capabilities."

"What do you mean by comm volume? I thought you said we would be cut off from Alma?"

"We are. I'm talking about communications between us. We can talk to one another provided we don't stray too far from each other. Our voices will sound a little different, but the bubbles will use their limited processing capability to try to adjust that, so we can surely understand each other."

"Okay. Can it sense my vitals like Alma can? Can it adjust anything based on that?"

"It does keep track of your vitals, but mostly for recording purposes. It's not capable enough to process that information and react in real time. There have been cases of people who panicked and couldn't give instructions anymore, and that does not end well. So if you feel like you're panicking at any time, close your eyes, take a few deep breaths, and focus on your heartbeat."

"Okay, no panicking, then."

"Moving on to navigation and commands for the bubbles: they pretty much understand natural language, so you can tell them commands like 'forward slowly' or 'up ten meters' and they will follow. They also recognize the other bubbles, so if you say 'find Hena' or 'follow Ahe,' they will understand. You can also always say 'surface' and the bubble will start the safety surfacing procedure."

"Can I just say 'keep me safe and follow whatever Ahe's bubble does'?"

"Don't know, good question, never tried it. Try and see what the bubble says. Worst case scenario it will say 'I do not understand that command' or something like that."

"Will the bubble do anything I ask, even if it is unsafe?"

"Yes and no. The bubble has some pre-programed 'unsafe' things to watch for—for example, it won't let you hit the bottom of the ocean, for your safety as much as for conservation purposes. It will also not let you hit other bubbles, and it won't let you touch any animals, either. But if you tell it to do something unsafe that has not come up yet, it will probably let you do it."

"Can you give me an example?"

"Yeah, a few years ago, one of the bubbles first encountered an underwater sulfur vent. The unsuspecting diver decided to check it out up close and told the bubble to glide over it. The temperature at these vents can be over four hundred degrees Celsius and the water over it can often behave as a supercritical fluid, so when the bubble went over the vent, the fluid boiled into gas immediately, the pod got stuck, since the propulsion is not built for that, and the poor diver was cooked alive within minutes."

"Somehow I'm having second thoughts about this whole thing."

Hena touches my shoulder. "Don't worry, Ahe is just trying to scare you into being responsible. There have only been a few dozen deaths since the beginning of bubble diving, and they were all out of sheer stupidity, like the story you just heard."

Ahe continues: "Yes, I agree. The other element of safety, and probably the only one that is truly a risk to everyone, not just to stupid people, is to keep an eye on your time and location relative to the other bubbles. When you are down there, the beauty and the sheer foreignness of the landscape and animals you encounter will entrance you. The bubbles have a comm radius of about one hundred meters down there, so the most common accident is that people get out of that radius and then get entranced by the dive, forget where they are, and run out of oxygen. They die in ecstasy, but die all the same. The bubbles have an alert mechanism, but they will obey overrides from divers."

Hena grabs my arm, this time forcefully. "This part is important. You cannot trust yourself alone down there. Even I, after over two hundred dives, sometimes need someone to jolt me out of the trance I get into when I am down there. We often pick a trigger word to make sure you pre-condition yourself to wake up when the word is said. Better if you suggest something, since you are more likely to remember it."

"Sarah," I say instinctively, and only then realize how stupid that was. Hena must have felt the pinch, though I see nothing in her expression.

I try to rescue myself. "Or maybe ..."

Hena interrupts me, "Sarah it is. The first word that comes to mind is always the best."

A silly part of me feels like she should have been more jealous. I know it's silly, so I move on. "Okay, I have one more question. It's probably really stupid, but if you had grown up with 'Jaws' in the 1970s, you would understand: do we need to worry about any large animals, say, such as a large shark, biting into or eating the bubbles?"

Hena kisses me on the cheek. I guess it must have been as cute a question as it was a stupid one. Ahe responds: "It's a fair question. There are very large animals down there. Sharks are less common, but giant squids, for example, are quite common, as are giant jellyfish. Either one would be big enough to gulp one or even several bubbles whole. But you need not worry, the bubbles are built such that no scent or chemical signal leaks through, so from the point of view of sea creatures you are just floating debris. We have never had any issues; the animals rarely interact with the bubbles."

Hena jumps in: "The opposite also has to be true—you cannot interact with the animals in any way. You should not approach any closer than two body-length's distance and, if they come your way, ask the bubble to try to evade them gently."

Ahe pointed to three circles on the floor a few meters away, each two meters in diameter. "With that, onto the bubble spots. You can sit down on the floor there. Alma will build the bubble around you and start the air liquefaction process. Once the bubble is built, the wait can be a bit annoying. If you choose not to sleep, Alma can provide some entertainment while you wait. Richard, I'm sure she can muster something from your movie era."

"Maybe Jaws?" I joke, but I don't find my own joke funny. Truth be told, I'm a bit scared.

We each walk over to our spot and sit down. A few seconds later, the floor around me curls up, forming a sphere that is mostly transparent, though I can faintly see the curvature. I feel a bit claustrophobic for a second, as I remember that I will be in it for the next seven hours. But I take a few deep breaths and the feeling passes. Alma asks me what I want to watch and I pick a 1950s classic. I look around and both Ahe and Hena are resting comfortably in the sphere as if it were a hammock, with their eyes closed. I mimic their position—much better.

I start to feel the air get heavier, as if I were in a steam bath, except not warm. I get distracted by the movie, but every few minutes I take a deep breath and move my arms to see what's different. The movements feel the same, but my breathing gets thicker and thicker. About two-thirds of the way into the movie, the projection stops. I breathe and move my arms again, and now I really feel like I'm moving in liquid, though it's less viscous than water—more like rubbing alcohol. I look around and see Ahe and Hena also perk up and open their eyes.

Hena mouths the words, "Enjoy."

And with no further warning, we plunge. It's a very strange feeling. I clearly feel the free fall acceleration, but when we hit the water, I don't feel any impact, as Ahe promised. We float half way submerged for a few seconds, then slowly start to descend. I feel a surging panic again as we enter the water. I didn't think I would feel this way, but having the water all around me with no visible equipment is disorienting and alarming. I take a few breaths and close my eyes for a few seconds, as Ahe indicated, which helps.

The bubbles now form a triangle; we face one another about three meters apart as we descend. Hena gives me a friendly smile. We start slowly but quickly accelerate. Six meters per second feels very fast. A few dolphins come around and descend with us for a bit, but they can't seem to keep up. We also pass by many fish along the way, but we're descending fast—I can hardly see them at all. Sunlight quickly decreases and within what feels like a minute or two we enter a sort of twilight zone. I still see Hena and Ahe for another three or four minutes, then I can no longer see them, either. I alternate between feeling terrified and peaceful. I can't really feel anything and I don't see anything, so it's very relaxing, peaceful, until I remember I'm deep in the ocean, sinking at 6 meters per second.

Hena startles me: "Richard, are you okay?"

"Yeah, but you scared the crap out of me!"

"I'm sorry, I should have made some indistinct noises first."

"This is very quiet; will we go another twenty-five minutes like this?"

"Yes. As you can see, the first couple of hours of deep sea diving are really quiet and devoid of stimulus, so it is great meditative time. It's one of the things I like about it. On the way up, we will make a few ascending stops, so you actually see some of the mesopelagic zone animals as well."

Hena and I talk all the way down about my sensations, her experiences in the past, and what to expect. After a while, I feel us slow down. It's still pitch dark.

I ask in a more anguished voice than I mean to: "Aren't we getting any light here? How will we even see the animals?"

"Most animals are bioluminescent, so we see them better without light, and the bubbles are equipped with sonar that displays dark objects and animals in front of you. As soon as we reach our desired depth, it will turn on. You will be able to see non-bioluminescent animals that way; it will seem like they are in front of you just as if we had natural light, but without disturbing their environment with artificial light."

We stop, and indeed I now see the two bubbles in front of me.

"We're here," Ahe says in a very calm voice. "Feel free to move around and look around, just don't go far in your first dive. Start by spinning around; you are here to see marine life, not our bubbles."

I spin around and sit there quietly, seeing nothing for a couple of minutes. Then it flashes right in front of me: a huge bioluminescent creature. It must be three or four meters wide, and white and blue light sparks move along the creature's cylindrical body, around its sides, and then wrap around inside it. Beautiful! It goes dark as quickly as it lit up, stays dark for a few seconds, and then lights up again. I watch the on and off spectacle for a couple of minutes. Hena, Ahe, and I exchange expressions of awe. I look around and notice that there are many, maybe as many as twenty or thirty, of these same creatures around us, above, below, and ahead. Hena calls these Lightfish.

As quickly as they came, the cylindrical creatures swim away. We wait quietly for another few minutes and then Hena calls me: "Come around, you have to see this. It's a tiny fish, so you may come close, but avoid coming any closer than half a meter. It's a Fangtooth fish"

I come around and place my bubble directly across from Hena's. Between us is a decidedly bestial creature. It's no more than a few centimeters across, but with disproportionately large and rugged teeth, and wrinkled, leathery skin. After a few seconds, the fish dashes away; it would seem something scared it. We both turn our bubbles to the side opposite from where the fish swam out to, and see the creature that scared it.

Hena seems excited. "It's a Long-nosed Chimaera! They are really hard to spot, especially at this depth."

The animal is hard to describe. It's probably a meter long. It has the tail of an eel, the body of a shark, fish fins that move like a bird's wings, and as the name suggests, a long nose protruding from the front, probably as big as its body. We follow it for a couple of minutes before letting it swim away.

We go on to see an incredible diversity of life, each separated by a couple minutes. Apparently these creatures don't like each other's company. We see a sail octopus that literally seems to sail across the water, a viper fish that's the stuff of nightmares, angler fish that carry their own light lure, several bioluminescent jellyfish, strange crabs with large asymmetrical claws and, just as we're about to go up, we see the elusive giant squid. It's a few meters away, but huge—Ahe estimates the animal is over eighteen meters long.

We make our way straight from the bottom to the fifteen hundred meter stop, where we see a ten-meter long Giant Oarfish that looks like a sea serpent from pirate tales. We also run into a blobfish that seems to be constantly about to dissolve into water, as well as a frilled shark, which looks nothing like a shark, but rather like a giant tadpole.

We make another two stops before we reach the surface, but in these we see more normal, if equally, beautiful creatures—from sharks to blue water fish to dolphins.

Most animals tend to ignore us, but the whales and dolphins notice us. I make that observation to Hena.

"Yes," she replies, "they can interpret the visual stimulus much better than most other animals. Whales and dolphins are quite intelligent and can formulate their own theories about why they see us move but sense no chemical stimulus from us, and it makes them curious."

We finally make our way up the last few dozen meters to the surface. We float on the waves for a minute or two before being pulled up by a silvery strap that drops from the platform. As soon as we're back inside the metallic building, the bubbles flatten out on the floor as they were when we first came in.

"You should give yourself a few minutes to settle down before you get up," Ahe says. "It's also a great opportunity to let the experience and the images settle down in your mind before you get other stimuli. We have to stay in here for a while anyhow, while Alma decompresses our bodies."

I look at Hena and see her eyes are closed. I do as Ahe says, close my eyes and let the memories settle down. It strikes me how foreign some of the creatures were; these are living animals in my own world, and they exist in my current timeline as well; we just don't know that yet. I bet half of these species haven't been discovered. I doze off in a partly meditative, partly sleeping state.

After a while, I feel Hena's hand touch my face. I stretch, get up, and instinctively kiss her, passionately. A kiss of gratitude.

Then I verbalize it: "Thank you for this opportunity. This was incredible."

"I know. Now you understand why I love doing this so much."

Ahe interrupts us: "You must be hungry and you will probably travel all night, so let's eat something before you go."

We eat and then get in our pod, which is already configured with a bed for night travel.

As soon as we start moving, I sit up and ask Hena: "So this is Ahe's full-time job?" She nods, I proceed: "How does that work today? What professions do people really have?"

She sighs and then responds: "That could be a long conversation, one which we're both too tired to have. But in a nutshell, we're largely organized around six types of professions: public servants such as myself; artists; human affairs professionals, who focus on human-to-human care; those who help humans seek meaning, such as faith or religious leaders; sports professionals; and lastly, people who work in heritage settings."

I nod. She smiles and lays down. I too fall sleep. I have strange dreams with the deep water creatures.

I wake up a few minutes before we arrive and reflect on how my normal timeline seems so far away; these have been the most intense and possibly the most fun few days of my life.

9

SOVEREIGN

Sep 10, 2218

W̲E̲ ̲S̲T̲A̲R̲T̲ ̲T̲H̲E̲ ̲D̲A̲Y̲ ̲G̲O̲I̲N̲G̲ ̲T̲H̲E̲ ̲O̲P̲P̲O̲S̲I̲T̲E̲ ̲W̲A̲Y̲ ̲F̲R̲O̲M̲ ̲O̲U̲R̲ normal classroom building. Hena notices my surprise and explains, "We will do this session in Orr's quarters. He prefers that we conduct official government meetings from his quarters.

"It really doesn't matter to me, at the end of the day. If it makes Orr happy..."

We enter his quarters. I'm a bit surprised to see his walls covered, back-to-back, with portraits of equal size, men and women alike, looks and wardrobe clearly spanning many centuries, maybe millennia.

Standing up from his chair, he addresses us without a greeting: "These represent every intervention—every Sprout, as we call them—since the beginning of the Restitution program. I like to keep them all visible in one spot. It reminds me of the impact we have had."

"There must be hundreds here!"

"Yes. We have told you this before, you are the 488th Sprout."

"Doesn't make one feel all that special."

Orr raises an eyebrow. "You may well be the last. Does that make you feel any more special?"

I don't answer.

After a long pause, he continues: "We brought you here because you will meet some other Nation Chancellors, and I prefer to conduct official meetings in my quarters."

"Yes, I've been briefed."

"Good."

I use his pause to interject: "Before I meet people from other nations, I was curious about why we still have nations in the first place. I guess more broadly, I'm wondering how people relate to one another, how family structure works today, as well as how people interact at the local community level."

"Fair questions, as these have all changed from your days."

I nod; I would have expected them to.

"People still like to live in small nuclear families, but these are more varied and more fluid than in your time. There is no longer an economic or a survival-security rationale for a nuclear family. The bonds that keep families together nowadays are purely emotional. Not only that, but people now regularly live for up to 150 years and most young adults feel emotionally ready to leave their guardian's homes by their mid-twenties. Many leave earlier. Under Alma's care, they can chose to leave their human guardians as young as 14."

"That would make for many years as empty-nesters."

"Yes. The implication is that many more varied living arrangements are common, such as friends living together for many years, with or without an intimate relationship."

"Do people still get married?"

"Yes. Many of the faiths you knew still exist, and there are new faiths as well. Many people choose to just live together as mates, and many still want that union recognized by their faith. Also, some ten percent of the global population never chooses a stable mate. And of the ones that do, many switch partners after a few years. That said, mates that are matched by Alma, or at least guided by Alma's recommendations, tend to stay together for life. They do so three times as often as the ones that are chosen by humans unassisted."

"How often do people live alone in a dwelling?"

"Not very often. Alma can always assist them in finding the right mate or friend to share their life with. Living alone is typically a transient state. It may not always seem that way, but humans tend to gravitate towards each other's companionship."

I look at Hena without realizing, and she smiles back.

"There are exceptions, however. I am one of them. Your handler Hena so far has been one too."

I nod. I'm not surprised Orr is alone. I doubt even Alma could find him a mate.

"Moving on to communities. Humans have always coalesced into small communities, and our present time is no different. You have heard of Dunbar's number, I assume."

"Yeah, 150, the magical number that describes the ideal size of a socially stable community. Or maybe it describes the cognitive limit to the size of that community."

"Close enough. Dunbar was right, there is such a number, but it is not 150 anymore, since the way humans interact today is very different. Given how often and how closely we interact today, that number is closer to three hundred."

"I would have thought it would be the opposite."

"It may be counterintuitive to you, but that happens because with so many and so frequent interactions, your mind can easily handle a larger number of close individuals. That number also has much more profound implications than you realize. Alma will in fact explain that at a later time, when you are done with your orientation. It has to do with how humans perceive and shape consensual reality itself."

"You will have to tell me more . . ."

"We will, but not now. The way these communities form today is also very different than in your time. Your communities would form around a neighborhood, a school, the workplace. You are beginning to get a glimpse of how our communities form in your time from the social networking phenomena, but even that was heavily influenced by your physical and economic networks. Nowadays, these communities are formed based solely on interests and inclinations. You don't need to live close to people to be part of one of these communities and, if you feel like you do, you are more likely to move for your interests than to adjust your interests to the people physically around you. For example, because the headquarters for Restitution is here, most of us who work or study Restitution one way or another live around here."

"Do these always congregate in cities?"

"Most of the time, although not all communities are in cities. As you also know from our discussion on government, these communities live under nations, but these nations exist nowadays largely for political representation and cultural identity. There is no longer a need for local economies, labor markets, trade issues, and all the other issues that were so closely aligned to nationhood in your time. So when you meet some of these nations' leaders, please focus your inquiries on these topics."

"Understood, no talk of trade." Orr just stares at me; he really has no sense of humor.

"Your first meeting will be with one of the seven Chancellors from Brazil. His name is Chancellor Marcelo. You will shake hands and introduce yourself and he will hug you as if you were old friends. You must return the hug, as it is their custom. Also, please try to engage in small talk before you ask him any substantive questions. Brazilians appreciate the social nature of human interactions more than most."

He signals and we all stand up as a dark-haired, brown eyed man walks in, greets Orr first, then me and Hena. He does indeed hug us each tightly for an uncomfortably long time. Once all the greetings are over I launch into the small talk:

"So Chancellor, how do you find the weather here in Nevada?"

"Warm, but also dry. It is very different than the humid, warm weather we have down south. Have you ever been to Brazil?"

"Yes, it was a different time I guess, but I attended the 2016 Olympic games in Rio. What a spectacle!"

"Yes, it was indeed, I have seen some of the footage and Alma has done a beautiful reconstruction that makes you feel like you are there. It was indeed a beautiful event."

We exchange pleasantries for another few minutes and when I think I have done enough, times three, I ask the more substantive questions on my mind:

"Chancellor, how would you describe your national identity? I have to say that compared to what I experience in my time, the definition of nations now is much less sharp."

"Yes, it is much less sharp, but not less meaningful. I would in fact argue that it is much more meaningful. Even in your time, what makes the people of Brazil uniquely Brazilians is not the fact that they use the Real as a currency, nor the fact that they have passports and work permits that allow them to work within their territories, and it surely is not the fact that they pay taxes together. What makes them uniquely Brazilian is their heritage—their colonial history, mixed in with the heritage of their native population, plus the remaining legacy of the once terrible slave trade. Even more importantly, their unique trait is the ability to blend—truly blend, not just juxtapose—all of these cultural, genetic, and historic traces into one integrated people. And a happy people at that, despite a very difficult history before Alma. They were always eager to experience life and connect with one another. That is what made us a unique nation in your time, and that still remains today what defines our national identity. The other things just got in the way."

I am speechless. He's right beyond commentary.

We spend the rest of the day meeting representatives for several nations. Each and every one impresses me with their grasp of their nation's identity and their vision for how it will evolve. One thing has not changed from my time: the formality and complexity of diplomatic relations persists. I'm briefed on how to behave and on cultural norms for each meeting and given feedback on my performance after.

After the last nation Chancellor leaves, I ask Orr a question that has been on my mind for days: "Chancellor, what about the Sovereign Nation? I have heard them mentioned a couple times."

He nods, sighs, then looks away for a few seconds. He places both his hands on his desk then looks at me as he starts speaking.

"There is one nation that operates under a unique regime: The Sovereign Nation. They do not participate, nor are they bound by, the UPC laws, rules and regulations, although there is a treaty between them and the UPC. They also do not benefit from Alma's help and protection. They have an ambassador at the UPC, whose job it is to negotiate and discuss any issues that matter to them specifically. They operate much like your current society does in that they have a currency, goods are bought and sold, people have specific economic professions, and they also have their own military command. They in fact have a variation of your existing democracies in that it's in every way a military state, except the commander and their commanding council gets elected by direct vote. The UPC has oversight of that vote, so we know that the citizens of the Sovereign Nation do indeed elect their leaders."

"Can people come and go freely from the Sovereign Nation?"

"We let people go there whenever they want, but they cannot take Alma with them. The other way around is more complicated; Alma can and does take refugees from there when they want to come out. It is allowed in our treaty. In fact, all they have to do is go to the UPC embassy and say they want to leave, so while technically they are bound to their nation, in practice, anyone can get out if they so choose. They try to make it difficult to reach the embassy, but when people want to leave, they can and do."

"What's their current population?"

"Around 150 million people."

"And is it growing?"

"No, it is slowly shrinking. They have positive fertility growth, since they have on average 3.1 children per couple, but they lose a lot more people through the refugee program than they get volunteers joining them from Alma's domain."

I recall in my mind the vivid image of the woman speaking over the music inside the Flesh tent at the fashion show, telling me that I must visit the Sovereign Nation. That I must meet the commander. She also said not to mention her. I have no reason to hide anything from Alma or Hena, but somehow Orr I don't trust. Maybe it's just because he's a jerk. I decide there will be no better opportunity to ask.

"I would like to visit the Sovereign Nation if I can. Maybe meet their commander."

Orr fidgets; he does not look pleased. "I will consider your request."

"Is that a problem, visiting them?"

"Not necessarily, but such a visit would require some planning ahead of time. And they might try to use our request as leverage, to get concessions in other areas we have active disputes on."

Hena and I spend the last hour of the evening together enjoying a walk in the park. Night comes and I check-out again.

PART III
IN MOTION

10

HUMANS

Sep 5, 2018

I WAKE UP AT 7:30. I DON'T HAVE TIME FOR A RUN; I WILL BARELY have time for breakfast. On the bright side, I have been working out almost every day with Hena. Wait, does that count? Will that translate into my experience here? I will have to ask Alma. I'm not even sure how to think about that.

I finish my morning routine and teach my morning classes. I find myself very distracted. It's a good thing these are the classes I know so well that I can go through the material on autopilot. A couple of intelligent questions from students force me to focus on the here and now to articulate a proper answer, but for the most part, I feel like only twenty percent of my mind is really here.

I eat lunch by myself and realize what's bothering me: I have no conceptual foundation to understand or absorb Alma's world. I have always maintained some distance from social studies, so I've spent very little time studying or thinking about them. What little foundation I ever got was by osmosis from Sarah, who was a leading thinker in that area. She and her advisor, Professor Salman. Of course, Salman!

I get in my car and drive to Salman's office. I storm in, startling his assistant. He's the Dean for the Arts and Humanities, so he gets a big office with his own staff.

I speak before she can recover: "Hi, is Salman in?"

"Yes. Good afternoon, Professor Weissman, right? Sarah's ex-husband. I mean . . ."

"I know what you mean. And yes, that's me. Is he in?"

"Yes, he is free now, but he only has about forty-five minutes until his next appointment."

"Thank you." I rush in without waiting for her approval.

Salman seems surprised to see me. We have spoken less frequently since Sarah's death; we were naturally much closer when she was alive. He and his wife would come over quite often and we would see each other in academic and social events. His lush beard has grown fuller and grayer since.

He clears his throat, quickly recovering from the surprise. "Richard, nice to see you. We miss you."

"Thank you, Salman, I miss you too," I say, and I find that I actually mean it. He's one of the most brilliant people I have ever met. "Can I take you for a quick ride?"

"Well, yes, I guess. That's a bit unusual in the middle of the day, but I suppose it wouldn't hurt, and I do have the better part of an hour available."

We get in my car and drive past Boston Common and onto Commonwealth Avenue. It's actually a beautiful fall afternoon, the sun shining onto the orange and yellow trees to our left and the rows of well-appointed Victorian townhouses to our right. I have the top open on my Porsche and the cool breeze brushes over our heads. Kids play on the sidewalk and students cycle hurriedly in and out of bike lanes. This feels really good. I start the conversation:

"Salman, what do you think would happen in a world where everything was free and available anytime?"

He frowns and lowers his chin, looking at me sideways. "And just how would that happen?"

"I don't know. Say, for example, that someone invented a source of energy that was free and available anywhere."

He looks up to the trees now. "What an interesting question. I'm not sure I have *the* answer, though I surely have *an* answer." He's now waving his hands in the exaggerated way only a professor knows how. "But before I tell you my view, let's examine what happened in similar transitions in the past."

"Makes sense. Where do we start?"

"What happened when humans learnt to manipulate fire?"

"I'm no history buff, but I think that was about when human population first spiked, probably because being able to cook food decreased bacteria-related deaths, and probably also increased the variety of food that humans could consume."

He nods approvingly. "Close enough. What happened when humans learnt how to domesticate animals, and invented rudimentary agriculture?"

"If I remember correctly, that led to human settlement in more permanent locations, or at least less frequent nomad migrations, and it also allowed more specialization of skills, with some in charge of tending the animals, some working the crops, some working on infrastructure like irrigation. Some became artisans, others warriors."

"Right. It was also when many new professions could emerge, like religious leaders, scholars, early forms of government. Also when the first few cities came about. Perhaps even more importantly, this allowed the human population to grow much faster, starting an exponential trend that persists till today."

I nod.

Salman proceeds: "Fast forward a few thousand years. What happened when the industrial revolution came about?"

"Too many changes to list out like that."

He waves his hands. "Fine, pick the few that come to mind."

"Well, first of all, there was a massive increase in overall quality of life. There were new ways to process food, new ways to produce everything from clothing to houses, new solutions for transportation, like cars, trains, planes, etcetera."

"Yes, and there were also whole new industries created; services and businesses that would not have made sense before then, such as banking, accounting, and organized retail, came into being. Now fast forward to the most recent revolution we have had: the information technology revolution. What changed with that?"

"Well, completely new industries were created again. The whole services sector became the vast majority of what people work on, and new industries like telecommunications, modern banking, pharmaceuticals, entertainment, and the tech industry itself boomed."

"Correct. And one very important trend that you didn't point out was the fact that throughout all of this period, the quality of life has gotten better for humanity as a whole, through every major revolution and the subsequent period. Pick a basket of measures—say, life expectancy, access to nutrition, quality of health care, access to entertainment, and even the ability to reproduce. In any of these measures, a middle-class person living in the developed world today would be better off than a king in the middle ages, let alone a pharaoh in Egypt or a tribe leader for ancient humans."

I just nod thoughtfully; my head is spinning.

Salman looks at his watch. "I should be going back."

"No, wait, this conversation isn't over."

"Well, maybe you can come by one of these evenings. We would love to have you for dinner, and then we can continue it."

"No, just give me a bit more time. We need to go over this now."

Salman frowns at me. "Richard, you are worrying me. Are you okay? You might want to slow down, as well, and maybe think about where you are driving to. You seem to be a bit aimless at the wheel."

"I'm okay. As okay as I could be. You would understand if you were in my shoes."

"Is this because of your energy project? Sarah had mentioned it before you got the grant. It could lead to free energy being available, right?"

"Sort of. But it's not just because of that. Well, I guess it is in a way, but not directly. I'm fine, really—just trust me that this is an important conversation right now."

Salman holds my arm, just above the elbow. "I will take that at face value now, but can you please drive me back?"

"No, not really. Can you cancel whatever you have in the afternoon?"

Salman continues to look at me, clearly a bit troubled, but after another moment, he sighs. "All right. You will cause me some heartburn, but I'm worried about you." Salman calls his office and asks his assistant to cancel the rest of his afternoon meetings.

"Back to our conversation," I say after he hangs up. "I think I know what you are getting at: if we look historically at what happened following leaps in human capability, basic human needs were more easily fulfilled, and that allowed both for the population to rise, and also for new, more sophisticated needs to be better addressed, like the need for meaning and community, or the need for fun and mental fulfillment."

"Precisely. So if we assume that the future will follow the same trend, which seems reasonable, that means that with free energy, all basic human needs should become much more easily fulfilled. That in turn would mean there would be no limit to human population expansion, except of course for the planet's capacity to absorb our waste. But in theory, I guess, with free energy, even that could be overcome, since you could always process that garbage and even send it to space."

Salman looks at me and raises his hands, as if waiting for confirmation. I just nod and he continues: "You are the physicist, you would know better, but that would be my guess. So I don't know what would limit human population. Maybe nothing. Maybe self-regulation, since we would be testing the limits of nature. In regards to the other trend, I do think that human attention and ingenuity would shift to fulfilling higher-level needs, such as mental fulfillment, as you say, and maybe go all the way up to self-actualization, if you believe Maslow's hierarchy. I also think that new occupations would be created to do just that. Less and less time and money would be spent on basic needs. Maybe we would all become philosophers, artists, and lovers," he finishes with a hearty laugh.

I shake my head, processing all of his words. "You are more right than you think."

"Why would you say that?"

"Nothing, just joking."

"Jokes are supposed to be funny."

Just then, I notice a black SUV three cars behind us. My hands are suddenly sweaty. I'm getting butterflies in my stomach, the same feeling I get when I screw up something important. For once, I can't seem to find the right resting spot for them at the wheel. "We're being followed. The black SUV, three cars back, second lane to the right."

He looks at me with raised eyebrows. "What are you talking about? That is so stereotypical—black government SUV following us ... are you sure you are okay? Maybe you should see a therapist."

I raise my voice: "Look, I could be hallucinating, but short of that I am sure. I have seen that SUV tailing us multiple times for the last half hour or so and, as you yourself pointed out, I'm driving aimlessly."

Salman sighs. "Well, let's find out. Take the next exit. This is a residential part of town, so just pull over on one of these streets and, if they follow, I will believe you."

I wipe the sweat off my forehead. I'm not sure why I'm sweating on this cool fall day.

"That could be dangerous. If they want to get to us, that will give them an opportunity."

Salman puts his hands up in the air and shakes his head vigorously, beard swaying wildly in the wind.

"Listen to yourself, Richard! No one wants to 'get to us.' And if they wanted to, they could anyway. All they'd have to do is wait until you drop me off."

I feel lightheaded, so I try taking deep breaths; it seems to work. "Yeah, I guess you have a point."

I veer right at the last minute and pull off at the next exit. The SUV follows, as I had expected. We are near a residential area on the West End, so it doesn't take long to find a quiet residential street. I turn and drive a few hundred meters before pulling over by the curb. No SUV in sight for a few seconds, but then it turns onto the street. It pulls over by the curb as well. My heart is pounding again. My hands and forehead start to sweat. I look at Salman, who finally looks as alarmed as I am.

He puts his hands on the dashboard. "Alright, maybe we are being followed. Have you been up to anything unbecoming, Richard? Maybe borrowing money from the wrong people, or gambling on the wrong tables?"

I keep an eye on the parked SUV as we talk.

"No! No, no, no, I've been a reclusive widower focusing on my work. I say we confront them."

He raises his voice: "What do you mean, confront them?"

"Let's drive there and pull over."

"And then what? We are two academics who would be lucky to fend off an angry dog! Just call the police."

I ignore Salman, spin the car around, and accelerate as fast as I can towards the SUV. Salman lets out a shout that's somewhere between a war cry and a panicked scream. A few seconds later, the SUV starts accelerating in our direction, a puff of smoke coming off its rear tires. We speed up towards each other and Salman is now holding on to his seat as if we were in a launching space shuttle. In a few seconds that seem to stretch forever, we eliminate the distance between the two cars.

For an instant I consider veering towards the SUV and actually hitting it, but the mental image of the crash, air bags flying around and all, dissuades me. We just speed past each other very quickly. I try to see who is inside but can't, it's all too fast. I spin the car onto the road again, to which Salman shouts a non-flattering adjective, and speed back into the chase, trying to catch up to the SUV. I notice that it has no plates. We tail it for a couple of minutes, but the driver easily out-drives me on the residential streets. I'm not able nor willing to make some of the turns the SUV pulls off. Within a few minutes, we lose it completely.

I pull over. Salman and I both sit quietly for a few minutes; he's breathing hard. So am I. I close my eyes. This feels crazy even to me; he must think I've lost it entirely.

His surprisingly calm tone startles me. "Do you think this has anything to do with your DoD grant?"

"I don't know. Why?"

"It's the only reasonable explanation, aside from the gambling or loan-shark possibility you already brushed away. I told Sarah that that would be a worry when she mentioned you had been selected for the grant. These are supposed to be secret, but everyone knows about them and they can attract unwanted attention from government and non-government entities alike. You should report this to them."

"Yeah, I have a meeting with my grant supervisor tomorrow—crap, I can't believe it's tomorrow! I will tell him then."

"Yes, do so. And please drive me home. Safely!"

After dropping Salman off, I try to Google "being chased by a black SUV" and other similar threads, but I end up more often than not on unsavory websites and don't find what I was looking for. Eventually I just go to bed.

11

ART

Sep 25, 2218

I LOOK AROUND AND SEE MY ROOM, BUT I KNOW I'M IN THE future. Hena walks through the door with a smile. "Good morning, Richard. Sleep well?"

"Well, I didn't technically sleep, so I'm not sure if I slept well. But I do feel very well rested."

"I know; I was just teasing you. Sleep is critical to ensure that your consciousness rests from the intense focus we all need for physical experience, so Alma ensures that when you come this way, you get enough down time to feel rested. Breakfast?"

"Yeah, but I have to ask Alma something first."

"Yes, Professor?" Alma says.

"Alma, I was followed yesterday when I went for a drive with my friend, Professor Salman. I think these might have been the same people who were spying on Frank, Sun, and I the other day. Do you know anything about it?"

"Not factually, there is no record of this anywhere. I have assessed the probable explanations, however. The most probable scenario is that these are people from your own government—either DoD or one of the intelligence agencies. Your work will have implications for everything from national security to economic hegemony, so everyone is interested. The second most probable explanation is that some other foreign government has discovered what you are doing and they want to keep tabs on it."

"No offense, Alma, but I could have guessed that too."

"No offense taken, I do not seek your approval. There are infinite other possible scenarios, so I would suggest not worrying about them for now; however, be vigilant and tell me any additional information you have about them. And I mean anything—details may seem unimportant to you, but to me, they may help reveal a pattern that I can trace back to something known historically."

"Understood."

Hena holds both my hands.

"Richard, you have to be careful. In our timeline Alma can protect you, but in your timeline, anything could happen."

I just nod. Hena kisses me on the cheek and continues: "You have now seen most of our world, how people live and work, how the government is structured, and how basic human needs are met. We only have a few more days to do what we set out to do. Where is your head at?"

I look down and shake my head.

"I'm sorry, but I'm not there yet. I wish I had a different answer, but you've already told me that faking it won't work."

Hena takes a deep breath under pursed lips.

"Why are you not there?"

"I'm not totally sure, but if I try to put it into words . . . I am afraid that society might have lost some of the passion and inspiration that came with the human struggle. Maybe because everything is so easy, passion is lost?"

Hena gives me a half-hearted smile.

"Maybe it's because you spent too much time with public servants, and with Orr specifically."

I laugh, "Yeah, Orr definitely has that effect on me."

"What if we introduced you to some of the more creative and inspirational people in our time? Take you to see some artists?"

"Well, the fashion show was pretty awesome. If there are other examples like that, I would love to experience them."

Hena grabs my hand and squeezes it a couple times before talking to Alma: "Alma, could you please summon Olivio? We will action the art module."

Alma confirms that Olivio is on his way and we sit quietly while we wait for him.

Olivio walks in and his smile alone lightens the mood.

"Good morning, Professor," he says. "It seems that I'm destined to be a part of all the more exciting adventures you have here in our time."

"Maybe you cause the excitement, Olivio?"

It didn't come out as funny as I had hoped, but he laughs all the same.

"Hena had asked me a while back to be ready, in case we needed a creative art 101 kind of journey for you. We called it the art module," Olivio says while gesticulating quotation marks. "I engaged Satoro, the master curator of the global art hall, to help me with it. You will meet him briefly. I should warn you: he is, uh, *different* than most people you've ever met. So my role as connector will be important today. You need to start off on the right foot, so to speak."

"Okay. And what, exactly, is the global art hall?"

"It's a virtual exhibit of all art created everywhere on Earth—and space, actually, since there have been a few pioneering non-Earthbound artists. I guess I should say that it covers all art created by humans. It's not a physical space per se, but it involves all physical spaces used in and for art, if that makes sense."

"And what's the role of the curator?"

"See, I'm glad we're having this little chat now and not with Satoro, I don't think he could handle that question. He's actually a very important person. I don't know that I fully appreciate all he does, but I'll give you a few examples: firstly, he studies artistic production and, with Alma's help, articulates the key trends in art today. Given the incredible variety of artistic choices we have now, that actually turns out to be a herculean task. Secondly, he helps Alma categorize art in its various buckets according to intent, medium, and authorship, which is critical to ensure that others can access that art. And lastly, he provides Alma with guidelines for how she should evaluate the impact artists have on other people; that is how Alma assesses quality of art. Satoro neither rates the art nor the impact per se, but he provides Alma with a sort of calibration, since Alma does not think she has the human sensitivity or the artistic sensibility to know what's good, bad, or generally impactful. She needs the help of a gifted human."

"So when Alma assesses whether someone's work is up to potential, it is influenced by the curator's assessment?"

"Very much so, which is why he's such an important person to many people. The last part of his job is to create thematic journeys, which he does with Alma's help. This helps people choose from the vast inventory of art experiences and artifacts available."

"Can you give me an example of a thematic journey?"

"Sure. You can tell Alma that you want to have an uplifting experience related to water, and then Alma will look for a related thematic experience and find the best match. Of course, many people just want to be surprised, so they dive into the catalogue at random."

"And how did he get this job?"

"All registered artists vote on the curator; the election happens every year. Satoro has held the position now for nine years. Ten years is the maximum tenure, so there will be a new curator next year."

"I guess he must be popular, reelected nine years in a row . . . and who decides the candidates?"

"Technically anyone could be a candidate, but you need to have at least one billion followers globally and only a thousand or so artists meet that bar. So only the most accomplished and creative individuals are ever considered."

"And what's Satoro's art like?"

Olivio sort of jumps up and down a couple of times while seated.

"Oh, it's amazing! He pioneered a new genre of art he calls vibrating colonies. By using certain vibrations, he got specific animal colonies— he started with termites, but then expanded to include ants, bees, and wasps—to follow his commands and therefore produce physical structures, sculptures, if you will, according to his creative imagination. The end product is of incredible beauty and harmony and the process itself is remarkable; in any of his exhibits, you can experience the whole creation process, and when you expose yourself to the vibrations while watching the termites or ants work, you feel like you are one with them."

"That sounds really cool."

"Satoro specifically, though—as I said, he is . . . different. He doesn't speak much, and he believes in multi-dimensional communication, so follow my lead and do as I do when he's here. When in doubt, do nothing."

Just then, the door opens. I see Satoro, who is, as expected, a Japanese-looking fellow. He's dressed in all black, in a cross between a suit, a kimono, and a flowing robe—he looks stunning, actually. He's looking down, hands behind his back, legs aligned with his shoulders. I motion to say something, but Olivio shushes me with a wave. Just then, Satoro looks up. He looks me directly in the eye and the intensity of his look is disconcerting; it feels like he can see right into me. He stares for an uncomfortably long time, but I'm determined to return the stare, so we stay there for what feels like more than a minute. Then, with the swiftness of a martial artist, he steps forward—a very theatrical step, like a tango step, but sharp. While holding my gaze, which I duly return, he continues stepping in the same way, towards me, but in a zigzag pattern, stopping for a few seconds between every step. Every few steps or so, he stops in the same position he began, with hands behind his back, and he breaks our gaze to look down for few seconds. I mimic his movements, which Olivio subtly but clearly approves of. This goes on for five or ten minutes. He certainly has my attention. More than that, my mind is cleared—this is almost therapeutic. He takes the last three steps in one swift movement and is right by my side, shoulder nearly touching mine, looking down again. I mimic his posture.

Olivio moves as if he was going to interject and say something, but Satoro halts him with an inhumanly fast and sharp hand gesture. We stay there for a few more seconds, then he makes uncanny but powerful sounds with his breathing. It reminds me of breathing exercises in yoga, or maybe the throat warming exercises that actors and singers perform. After a few seconds of this I realize that I can feel him; I feel the vibration of the air he exhales. It is hard to explain, but he's clearly communicating in some way. I don't understand it, but I certainly have an emotional response to this strange vibration. I find myself replying back with my own version of the guttural sounds; these are sounds I didn't know I could make. After a few seconds, I lose myself in this trance-like communication. I can't tell how long we stand there for sure. Satoro then breaks communication with a sharp and long step back. We're now a meter apart, facing each other. For the first time, he is smiling.

"Richard-san, you resonate very well for an uninitiated."

I just nod.

"Olivio-san, it is good to see you. Hena-san, always an honor."

When he turns back to me I ask the question on my mind: "What was that form of communication?"

Satoro seems unfazed, but his body language indicates that it was a silly question. "Verbalizing it would defeat the point, wouldn't it? There is nothing I can say that will give you a better grasp than the actual exchange we shared."

"Yeah, I understand," I say, and find that I really mean it.

"In any case, we are not here to cover my art. I am told we are here to inspire you with the art of the twenty-third century. If the vibe is right, we can look at some of my art after we have shown you a broader collection of art today."

Olivio gives me the "shush" look, so I just nod and reply: "I look forward to it." Olivio nods in approval. Satoro gives him a wink, and Olivio takes a step back and sits. I guess the wink meant "we got it from here."

Satoro holds my arm gently and starts talking. "Let me start by giving you an overview of how I, as master curator, see today's art. It is a most unsatisfying task to have to classify art, for artistic creativity—and all creativity, for that matter—is infinite and transcends classification. But one has to do it for practical purposes, as I am sure you've heard."

"Yeah, I have."

He continues: "I classify art in three broad categories: intent, medium and authorship. Intent refers to what the creators are trying to achieve with art, such as reflective, inspirational, story-telling, shocking, surprising, uplifting, loving, or comical art. There are infinite kinds of intent, but with Alma's help, we have defined three hundred key categories that capture most of what people want to experience."

"I get the rationale for classifying medium and author, but why is it important to classify intent?"

"It is actually the most important thing to capture, from my point of view. When people want to experience someone else's art, they may be open to many forms, but they normally know whether they want something uplifting or shocking—they have a clear intent in mind."

"Yeah, I guess I can see that."

"Medium and form captures many sub-dimensions; some art translates into specific end-products, like vivid paintings and sculptures, while others are entirely experiential, such as a textural journey."

"What's a textural journey?"

"I will take you to experience some of these. Experiential art is better understood with examples. But if I can think of one example of a textural journey . . . yes, the living skin exhibit. It was actually one of my early students, when I still taught art, who conceived of it: you put your hands into a box and experience the sensation of the skin of every animal ever known to humanity, in random order. To go along with the sensation, you can choose to either see the animal, hear its sound, be told what it is, or simply experience the texture."

I nod.

He continues: "The diversity of medium and form in art today is nearly impossible to explain. You must always remember that there are some twenty-five billion artists on Earth, and that is only counting those who have art as a profession; many create art as a hobby."

"And what about the definitions from my time, like classical art, modern art?"

"These are way too narrow to be useful. One of the categories of intent that we have is heritage, but that's it. You have to remember that if we were following these conventions, we would now be at post-post-post-modern art, or some such silly place. We still use the original classifications for historic art, of course."

I take a few seconds to absorb all this before I can formulate another question, and it's not a very clever one: "What on Earth are vivid paintings?"

Satoro gives me one of those small-eyed-smiles. I guess it must have been cute.

"These are paintings that have live characters within them."

"Like the Harry Potter paintings, which move at their own volition?"

Satoro smiles and nods. "Yes, but done through technology, not wizardry. They could be photos, paintings, or sculptures, just like in your time, except that one or more subjects in the photo are conscious characters. They may talk to you, talk with each other, and have their own thoughts. They can actually be very good companions."

"How are they conscious?"

"People code basic forms of intelligence into them. They are nothing like Alma, but they are intelligent enough to have their own personalities."

"Could Alma make them more intelligent?"

Satoro stiffens. "Alma does not create art."

"Why not?"

"She has no will to do so on her own and humanity has no such need. In fact, as you have already heard, art is one of the few professions that is still the domain of humans only."

"Yep." I move on; he didn't like my question: "And what did you mean by your third classification? Authorship, was it?"

"Yes, it is the simplest of the classifications: individual, group, mass, and interactive."

"What's the difference between group, mass, and interactive?"

"Group is defined as a number of artists equal to or less than the Dunbar number—that is, three hundred people. Mass I think is self-explanatory, but what you may not realize is that some works of art have millions of participants. Alma does not create art, but she can facilitate collaboration to make some of these creations possible. And interactive is when the observer participates in the artistic creation. By definition, most experiential art is interactive, but some physical art is as well. As an example, there is a dynamic sculpture at the entrance of the main UPC building that is an amalgamation of all of the faces that have ever passed it."

"Cool! I'd love to see what that looks like."

"Alma, can you please show us the Face of Representation?"

Alma shows us the face. It's neither masculine nor feminine, and has no distinct ethnicity; it truly is a blend. It is a very attractive face, and I find myself wondering the significance of that.

Satoro draws me back to the conversation: "Enough of this thankless conversation about classification. I think we are ready for some direct artistic experiences, right?"

"Yeah, for sure. I'm excited about this."

"Very well. I have prepared an itinerary that will build in intensity. We shall start with some botanical art. Alma, could you please transport us to Georgina's atelier?"

We get on a pod and are transported to a greenhouse not far away. It looks very much like a greenhouse from my time. A tiny blond woman who looks to be in her sixties walks out of the greenhouse, smiles widely, and hugs Satoro. She turns to me, offers a slightly awkward handshake, and introduces herself:

"Hi, I'm Georgina. It means the farmer in my original tongue."

"Hello, I'm Richard. Thank you so much for receiving us."

"Always a pleasure to display my art, especially to one as famous, albeit artistically clueless, as yourself," she finishes with a warm smile that softens the sting of her comments.

She acknowledges Hena and Olivio and continues: "As you've heard, I create botanical art. In your time, that would have meant painting plants on a canvas and such, but in our time, it means something else entirely. It means making art *with* plants. By manipulating the plant's natural growth cycles, both at the cellular level and at the macro-level, I can create the different shapes, colors, and textures that provide the material for my artistic expression."

I raise my hand to ask a question, and she nods, so I proceed: "How do you manipulate the plants?"

"I use several techniques, including some of my own creation. At the macro level, I can use light, sound, vibration, feed, soil composition, and even direct pressure to influence the growth in several different ways. At the cellular level, I use many other techniques, from electromagnetic fields to chemical stimuli. The combination allows me to do pretty much anything I want."

"No direct genetic manipulation?"

"No, that was banned by the Tianjin convention not too long after your current present. Alma could discuss that with you in a broader context."

I just nod, and she motions for us to follow her. As we walk in, the first thing I notice is how big the greenhouse is; it seemed much smaller from the outside. It must be half a kilometer long and half as wide, and at least thirty meters high. There are several rows of plants, from small plants in benches to our left to fully grown trees to our right. We follow her across the different benches. The first plants are potted plants, but they are like nothing I have ever seen. There are plants with abstract forms, twisting and turning, as well as others with recognizable shapes, such as the guitar-shaped cactus or an arborea shaped like a coiling snake, scaly texture and all. As we continue walking, the plants increase in size, shrubs and small trees with incredible shapes appearing. One has a stem that has somehow been made into a hollow mesh rather than the solid stem I would expect.

Without noticing, I blurt out the comment: "I was expecting some of those trimmed garden sculptures like in my time, if more elaborate. This is nothing like that."

It doesn't sound like I have offended her when she answers: "No, in fact, I never trim anything. One of the tenets of my art is precisely that I let the plant grow into art. If I don't have the ingenuity to make it look a certain way, then it will not be cut into that shape. No trimming..."

We keep walking all the way to where the largest trees are. I gape at her creations. The trees are all incredibly beautiful, and while you would not see them in nature, they also somehow look natural. One in particular catches my attention: it has two caves and three platforms along the trunk, and one could easily escalate the tree, rest on the platforms, and enter the caves.

She notices my reaction and answers the unasked question: "I call that the Treehouse. Not particularly creative, I know. I made it so that my grandchildren can actually play in it. They have slept inside these caves many times and we have had many a picnic on those platforms. The view of the greenhouse from up there is quite nice."

I risk asking: "Could I go up there?"

"I'm glad you asked—please, go ahead."

Hena and I climb up. Olivio and Satoro stay put. When we get up there, the view is indeed incredible. The two tree aisles in particular are hard to describe. From here, I can tell that Georgina designed this with the whole effect in mind, not just the individual plants. The plants build in a crescendo, from tame figures to positively explosive looks from up here. I can't help but hug Hena, and she hugs me back. We stay there for a few minutes.

When we climb down, I ask a question that has been on my mind: "Do you, uh, sell any of these?"

"No one sells anything anymore these days, dear. But if your question is whether I will let people take my plants once they are completed, the answer is yes, though not all of them. There are a few that I have created to keep, but the others I'm happy to see go, knowing they will affect someone else's life."

"And how would people know where to look, and which ones are available?"

"That's where Alma and Satoro's classifications come in handy. If someone asks Alma for an uplifting plant arrangement, my work will show up as a prime option."

AFTER SAYING OUR GOODBYES TO GIORGINA, WE SPEND THE REST of the morning looking at interesting works that build up into Satoro's crescendo, including an artist who creates vapor shapes in cylinders where micro-fans let him manipulate the flow of air, and one who does work similar to Georgina's but with corals and sponges.

In the afternoon, Satoro lets us 'graduate' into participative authorship. We go visit a painter who imbues every one of his paintings with individualized characters who interact with the observer. I converse a bit with one of them, a painting of a man looking out to the ocean from a wooden sailboat. I quickly get over the shock of speaking to a painting, but the richness of personality in the character surprises me; he has sea stories to tell, and points of view on work, women, and life. The artist then goes on to explain that most of his time is spent developing the characters, not on the painting itself.

We then spend time working on a giant mass sculpture, a participatory project conceived by a very popular artist. We physically travel to his atelier in Southern California. I'm excited about the idea of actually working on something myself.

As we enter the atelier, an artist named Jean-Marc comes to greet us. "Hello, welcome to my latest project. You're just in time! Another week or two and it will be mostly complete, too rigidly set to be interesting. If, on the other hand, you had shown up a couple of weeks ago, it would not yet have had enough form for you to appreciate it."

We follow him inside a large domed tent. As we walk in, I see a very large sculpture, probably thirty meters in each direction, with very intricate designs in parts of it and very rough shapes in others. The overall shape, as far as I can tell, is that of a spiraling cone, but the design is so intricate on a smaller level that I can't quite tell.

"What you have to look for are areas like this," Jean-Marc says, "which still have that glow underneath the material. This means that no one has yet claimed that part, or, if they have claimed it, they want to work collaboratively with someone else. If the glow is gone, it's because someone else has either claimed it, or finished it. You can use any tool you want to sculpt—your hands, chisels, or any of the other tools over on the workbench."

I look around. There are large pieces of the sculpture that are not glowing but still moving, morphing, obviously still being worked on by someone. It has an unsettling effect. I find a spot that is glowing and looks interesting, and get to work. As I start molding the lump of material I chose, I notice it moves on its own. Jean-Marc sees my surprise and points to a virtual screen behind me with three profiles visible and comments. "There are three other participants working on that part, these three folks you see profiled up here. I can take you to a quieter area if you want."

"No, I'm intrigued by how this will work."

I keep working it and, while it's quite clumsy early on, we quickly get into a groove and our movements start to complement one another's. It helps that the other participants are clearly much more skilled than I am, and that doesn't seem to bother them. Hena and Olivio go off to choose their own spots and we spend the better part of the afternoon there, just working the sculpture. Unexpectedly, I get lost in my work and completely forget that I'm in a stranger's atelier, in California, in the year 2218. All of that fades away; I'm very focused on the here and now, one with the other three folks who are collaborating with me, as if our work was the only important thing in the world. The whole experience is incredibly relaxing.

After what felt like hours, the four of us know that our work is done. We didn't communicate in any way, not consciously anyway, but we all know it's complete. I stretch up and wipe my hands in the cloth Jean-Marc had given me, and that's when I notice that the whole place has quieted down. There is barely anyone left, and behind me are Hena, Olivio, Satoro, and Jean-Marc; I get the distinct impression that they've been waiting there for a while.

Jean-Marc smiles. "Thank you for your contribution, Richard. From now on, you will always be a part of my art."

Satoro also looks pleased, but says nothing. He just smiles.

Satoro begins the next day with a quick recap and a reminder of how jarring all of this has been.

"You have experienced more in the last few days than many do in a lifetime, especially during your time, Richard. If at any point you feel like we are overloading you, or if you feel like you've seen enough to convince you we live as passionately as people in your time, just let me know."

Silence seems to be enough for him. He goes on: "Today I will take you to one of my favorite sensorial artists; he's the ultimate sensorial minimalist. Then after that I will take you to one of our most innovative artists. He calls himself Atem, after the Egyptian god of creation. If I were a betting man, I would put my money on Atem as the next master curator to succeed me, and I know he would make me proud."

"I'm not sure if I should be excited or scared."

"Maybe both," Hena says with a smile. She grabs my hand.

We take the pod to the first stop. From the outside, the building is as minimalist as they come; it's a black cube, each side probably ten meters in length. We enter into a well-lit room with black walls where a young man, I would guess mid-twenties, comes out to greet us. His head is shaved and he is dressed in a tight black suit. He has pitch black eyes. I try not to stare, but even if I did, I don't think I could find where his irises meet his pupils. He hugs Satoro and introduces himself to us. "Hi, I am A."

Without thinking I ask, "Is A your actual name? Does it mean anything in your native tongue?"

He smiles. "A pseudonym."

It's clear he doesn't want to say more, so we each introduce ourselves.

Without further preamble he starts, "My art is the art of focus. I have developed many different experiences, but they all have one principle in common: by experiencing only one intense stimulus at a time, you will be able to fully grasp all the meaning in that very stimulus. Our world is so full of varied stimuli that we miss the essence of most of these. Our lives have become a melee of incomplete, superficial, and therefore unsatisfactory experiences, and my art strives to counter that. Questions?"

None of us ask anything; he has an intensity and a confidence to his comments that make it hard to interject.

After a few seconds, he proceeds. "You will each enter a chamber, sit down on the lounge chair, and relax for a few minutes. When I think you are ready, I will close the chamber and cease all stimuli for a period of time. How long will depend on your ability to tune into that sensorial deprivation. The longer you let your mind invent mental stimuli, the longer I will keep you in the first stage. Try to clear your mind; that's the whole point of this stage."

Olivio asks the question that's on my mind. "What if I panic or something? It can happen when it's all quiet like that, you know?"

"It can and has happened," he says calmly. "Just say stop or anything that means stop, and I will open the chamber. But do try to stick with it, even if it is uncomfortable. Try to take a few deep breaths. That normally does it. Stage two will bring selective, faint stimuli, always applied one at a time. Many people don't notice the stimuli until halfway into stage two. They are subtle on purpose. Stage three is composed of much stronger, but equally focused stimuli, though never more than one at a time."

Again Olivio asks exactly what's on my mind: "What kind of stimuli are we talking about? Light, sound, temperature?"

"If I tell you anything, it will cause anticipation, which is not at all what we are going for here. Just know it's completely safe."

"Okay . . ." Olivio sounds tentative.

He ushers us into each of our individual pods. I sit comfortably and wait for a couple minutes. As he warned us, the doors close after a while. I'm in absolute darkness and absolute silence, and I can't feel anything. The sensation reminds me of my first visit to the future; there's no pressure anywhere, and the temperature seems to be perfectly suited to my body.

I sit there for what feels like hours, my mind initially racing through its own fake stimuli exactly as he had predicted. Did I hear something? Feel an itch somewhere, see a flash? Eventually, I manage to quiet down with a series of deep breaths. All is quiet for a time that I can't quantify. That's when I notice the swirl of images, colors, sounds and sensations inside my head. But these are not stimuli. It's hard to describe the difference, but it's not as if I were hearing or seeing anything outside my mind; it's as if I was creating entire universes inside my own head. I marvel at the richness and beauty of the sensations. I can no longer tell the passage of time, so I don't know if I stay in that state for seconds, minutes, or hours. Eventually, I feel the first stimulus, as he said, it is very gentle: it's a tug on my right toe. Normally it would have startled me, but it is so gentle it simply draws my attention to my foot. It feels like all of the images, colors, and sounds from my inner mind are now being attracted to my toe. This goes on for a while, as the tug moves through my body.

Next comes a series of sounds, which seem to be carefully designed to bring my attention to a sphere all around me. A series of aromas and tastes follow, each bringing a different memory to the mind, even when I don't recognize the smell or taste at all. Somehow, they are each associated with an individual experience. Each of my senses is stimulated in this way, one at a time, and eventually, there is visual stimulation as well, but not images—flashes and colors.

When the whole experience is over, it all goes quiet and dark again for a time I cannot estimate. This second experience is even more pleasant than the first one. In the absence of stimuli, my mind becomes active again, but this time it is very focused on one sentence: the king is naked. It gets repeated in my head over and over again, but it has a calming effect rather than the frantic effect it had on me when I heard it at the fashion show party. I find myself wondering the meaning of it.

The thought leaves my mind as I come to my senses, all of them, when A touches my shoulder. I slowly get up and walk outside the chamber. I find I can't speak for a while. Hena and Olivio seem to be in the same situation; we each just sit there for a while, quietly.

Eventually Hena breaks the silence. "That was incredible."

I just nod. Olivio does the same.

Satoro comes by and says in a very quiet voice: "You take a nap, eat something, if you are hungry. I will pick you up in an hour to see Atem."

I OBLIGE AND WAKE UP FROM MY NAP WHEN SATORO SHOWS UP. On our way, Satoro reminds us: "You shall now meet Atem. Be warned, for once you are in his realm, he has full control over your perceptions of time and space."

"That sounds ominous," I say.

"I don't mean it that way. You will love Atem."

When we arrive, his atelier is quite simple. It's about three times the size of the prior two we saw, and covered in a mirrored surface.

Atem greets us as the others have. Without any small talk, he starts:

"As you will have heard, my art is the art of world creation. There are a few things you should know. Firstly, I create these worlds with my own imagination and creativity. Alma helps produce them, but the ideas and the original coding are all mine; as you know, she does not create art. The second thing you should know is that I make these all participative, so you can also add to my worlds through specific processes I have built for that. Once you have created new characters or objects in that world, they become a part of it, so it's an always evolving world. Even I no longer know all that exists or inhabits each of them. Occasionally, one of the participants has the creativity and skill to alter the very foundation of that world, and that's okay; these are rare but exciting situations for me."

I interject: "Can you give us a couple examples? It may make it easier to understand both concepts."

"Sure. One of the worlds I have created, for example, is a fluid world. Everything in this world is connected as if immersed in a liquid, so you would hear things much further away, feel vibrations and electric signals from other beings, and communicate much like whales and dolphins do."

"And what of participation?"

"In that world, you could, for example, create new objects, characters, or entire environments. I have already built in the key features that allow you to create these within that world. No one has ever altered the fundamental substance of that particular world, but say they could alter the level of viscosity in the fluid, or how far people can see within it—that would be a fundamental change in the world I created. Does that clarify it?"

"Yeah, sort of. And what do we do once we're inside one of these worlds?"

"These are real worlds, just like our normal world, so you can really do whatever you want, interact in any way you want, go places, meet characters. But since most people would not necessarily know what to do or where to go, I usually give them missions, so that they have a specific purpose when they enter the world."

"Can you give me an example of a mission in the fluid world?"

"Sure. The goal could be to find your soul mate, or bring back ten gold bars."

"That sounds like a role-playing video game in my time."

"You could call it that, though most people play the role of themselves."

I nod.

"For your first experience, I picked a specific world in which the three of you will have a joint mission in. Does that sound okay, or would you prefer to each pick your own?"

We all nod in agreement. This should be interesting.

"Very well. The world is called Iron. It's a world where life evolved from iron, rather than from carbon based life forms. The Earth is still largely the same, but the life forms, and therefore humans, are all iron-based. That has several implications: to begin with, humans are much stronger relative to the environment than in our normal world. Secondly, humans are much more influenced by magnetic fields, so we can only move in certain ways; for example, we have to stick to the Earth's magnetic grid."

I interrupt him: "There's no such thing."

He smiles. "In this world, there is, because I say so. As I was saying; humans have to jump from line to line on the grid, so to speak. Your movements are not continuous. Also, you have a natural orientation against the planet, and standing or moving against that orientation is possible but much harder. And lastly, you are magnetic, so you will attract not only other live beings, but also metallic or magnetic material. Watch out for some of those."

"What happens if we get hit by one of those? More generally, what happens if we get hurt?"

"Nothing in real life, though it can be a traumatic experience."

"Okay."

"Your mission is to find and recover the anti-magnetic suit; it's a suit that would allow you to move as if you were a carbon-based life form. This naturally becomes more interesting if you are doing a second mission, in which you could use the suit, but you get the idea. The suit is somewhere in the city in which you will be dropped off. It's the city of Chicago, circa twenty-first century, actually."

"Do we get any weapons? Will there be hostiles?"

"You will find these things out as you start the mission, but the answer is yes. Not all worlds are like that, some are all flowers and love, but this one does indeed have the same vibe as a game from your time. Are you all ready?"

We all nod and get sent to different rooms. As soon as the door closes, the room morphs into a scene on the street. It does look like Chicago, and it looks very real, actually. This is no ordinary video game. Hena, Olivio and Atem appear on the street within seconds. Hena and Olivio are metallic from top to bottom, face, hands, suits—she looks hot. I look at myself to see that I too am all metal.

Atem speaks first: "As you know, all living beings here are metallic, so traditional weapons would not be effective. Some of the tools you can use in place of weapons are electromagnetic beams, which can either cause displacement or attraction, depending on the setting, as well as some movement inhibitors, the most effective of which is a gooey web. To access these tools, you need to find or take them. You can also use either persuasion or physical force to get what you want."

Olivio raises his hand. "Persuasion I can do."

"How will we know where the suit is?" Hena asks.

He answers before disappearing: "That's your problem . . ."

I start walking and realize from the noise and vibration under my feet that I'm very heavy. I can move easily; I guess I am strong, too. I feel exposed in the middle of the road, so I move to the side of the nearest building and we huddle together to make a plan. The movement is indeed very jerky; I have to move within a grid, and the lines seem to be a meter apart. I can jump lines, but it takes much more effort. I also have to make an effort to orient myself in any direction other than facing the street, which must be the magnetic North.

After we huddle, Hena makes the first suggestion: "I think we should enter one of the buildings and see if we encounter other people."

"What if they are hostile?" Olivio asks, wide eyes.

Hena shrugs. "What if they are not?"

We enter the building. The structure inside is much more heavy-duty than in our normal world. I guess that became a requirement in a world where life is based on iron. We find nobody on the ground floor, so we go up the stairs. As soon as we reach the second floor, we encounter a man sitting at a round reception desk.

Olivio breaks the silence. "Good morning. How are you?"

His voice sounds metallic. That's a tacky detail I will have to tease Atem about.

The man smiles. "I'm okay, but it's one of those days. Quiet and boring around here."

I quickly realize that one thing has not changed in this world: chatty receptionists. He and Olivio talk for what feels like forever about nothing in particular.

Eventually, he gets to the point: "We're looking for a special suit that might be around. Any idea where it might be?"

"No, not really," the man says nonchalantly. "But there is much heavier security on the streets overall recently, and specifically around the city hall building."

Olivio picks up on it: "How do we get to city hall?"

He answers in a hushed tone of voice: "You probably shouldn't go there, but if you follow the main avenue to the round building then turn right twice, you will see it. It's the white building with a cylinder sticking out of it."

Before we can thank him, he continues: "Oh, and if security stops you, you have to say a passphrase."

Olivio asks nicely: "You wouldn't happen to know that passphrase, would you?"

He smiles. "The king is naked".

I blurt out: "What?"

"You heard me, honey," he says. "'The king is naked'."

I raise my voice: "Where did you hear that?"

Hena and Olivio give me horrified looks. Olivio apologizes and pulls me away. When we're downstairs, he turns to me. "What was that all about?"

I shrug it off. We get out of the building and start to follow his instructions. Then suddenly, everything vanishes. I'm back in the dark room where everything started. The door opens and Hena walks in, a panicked look on her face. She grabs my arm and addresses me in a very forceful tone:

"We have to interrupt this experience. Lay down, we need to do an emergency check-out."

"Why, what happened?"

"We don't know, but Alma has detected a disturbance in your present time."

"Like what?"

"We don't know, but it can't be a person in your room, certainly not someone you know—otherwise you would have been pulled back immediately. She would not have the ability to hold the sync. Maybe a pet, but you said you didn't have a pet."

"I don't."

"Maybe a neighbor coming to your door for sugar or such? Someone outside the door, trying to communicate, could be causing this level of resonance with your present-day self."

"Neighbor asking for sugar? That kind of stuff hasn't happened since 1960, if it ever did outside of the movies."

"Then I don't know, but we cannot delay. Alma says the pull is not intensifying, but still strong. We do not want an uncontrolled reentry."

"Okay. I will try to relax, but it might be hard."

"Focus on my hands. Breathe deeply."

I lay down. Surprisingly, I do relax after a while. Hena's warm hands have that amazing effect on me. Nothingness again.

12

Mr. Edwards

Sep 6, 2018

I WAKE UP STARTLED IN MY BEDROOM. I SIT UP AND LOOK around, but see nothing. I walk to the window and immediately spot a person in the townhouse across the street. It's a woman, looking straight at me through a camera with very large lenses.

My heart is pounding, my forehead sweating. I wipe the sweat away with my pajama sleeves. She clearly notices that I see her, calmly puts the camera away, and looks straight at me. It's too dark for me to distinguish any features. I instinctively shout.

"Hey! Hey! Why are you watching me?" She has no reaction, of course; she couldn't possibly hear me across the street and through the closed windows.

We stay in that stalemate for another few seconds that seem to stretch for much longer, then I turn and race out the door. As I glance over my shoulder, I notice that she has also turned around; we're racing each other down the stairs. I run down as fast as I can, tripping a couple of times along the way, but I'm not fast enough. As soon as I leave my building, I see the woman entering a black car, camera gear in hand. The car speeds away before I can react. I try to enter the building she just came out of, but the door is locked—these townhouses across the street have been in renovations for months. I call the police and they promise to investigate in the morning, but I know nothing will come of it.

It must have been the same people who followed Salman and me, and who were spying on me, Sun, and Frank on the beach. I need to discuss this with Mr. Edwards and see if he can help. Maybe these are his people? I will also need to close my shades from now on; clearly, someone looking from afar is enough to cause a disturbance in what Alma called consensual reality. I should also reinforce my locks, as Hena suggested.

I look at my watch. It's three in the morning, so I go back to bed, hoping to sleep. I toss and turn for a few hours, in and out of restless sleep.

At 6:30 I get up, eat breakfast—which suddenly feels like it requires a lot of work; Alma will spoil me yet—then leave to meet Frank at the Lab.

When I get to the Lab, Frank is already there, his hair disheveled and his eyes bleary. It must have been a long night.

"Good morning, Frank."

He looks up. "Except it's not exactly a good morning, is it? Mr. Edwards shows up in an hour."

"Yes, it will be a good morning. I have been thinking about this a bit. There is nothing Mr. Edwards can do if he's not pleased. I know the grant agreement allows them to take the money away, but you and I both know that signing up with any other research teams or Labs would mean a setback of at least half a decade to them. They would never take that risk. Plus, I'm confident we will sort this out."

"And where is this newfound confidence coming from, exactly?"

I smile and adopt my best Lincoln Steffens voice as I quote him: "I have seen the future and it works!"

Surprisingly, that seems to cheer Frank up. He laughs and finally relaxes in his chair. We spend the next hour working through the computer demos we want to present and all of the latest presentation material we have prepared.

225

PRECISELY ONE MINUTE AHEAD OF SCHEDULE, MR. EDWARDS walks through the main door of the lab. I am immediately reminded of why I dislike him; he's one of those slimy bureaucrats who built his career on managing other people's intellectual accomplishments. A short, burly man, he sports a forelock and a trimmed mustache that were surely fashionable in the 1960s, when he was probably born. Add the black mail-order suit, wrinkle-free white shirt, and slim blue tie, and he's the perfect picture of a self-entitled, purebred paper-pusher. As usual, he is also followed by a security detail. Two guys wait by the door in military-style resting position. I also notice two cop cars parked outside. They must be the rest of his entourage.

I take a deep breath and smile. He returns the smile under his lush mustache. Frank and I walk over to him and shake his hand. I'm the first to speak.

"Good morning, Mr. Edwards. It's a pleasure to see you again."

"Same to you. I have been thinking about this all week, and I'm very excited to see the progress."

I do my best to get some small talk in before we jump right into business: "I trust you had a good ride coming in?"

He just mumbles a positive "uhum"; he doesn't seem to need the small talk. Fine with me too.

"You guys got my memo, right?"

I nod and respond: "What we planned to do is walk you through some of the theory behind our work, some computer models, and then show you where we are on the prototype. Sound good?"

"Yes, it does."

"We will also have a few questions for you, but these are probably best addressed at the end."

"Very well."

We walk over to the workstation across the lab.

"Let me start with a recap of what we're doing and why it is important. As you might remember, we have identified that the same underlying uncertainty principle that produces the Hawkings radiation can be used to generate energy, provided we can create and control a very, very small black hole."

Mr. Edwards nods before asking, "Could you remind me . . . what's the Hawkings radiation?"

I control my eye roll. "Of course. As you know, the very edge of a black hole, called the event horizon, is defined by the point beyond which nothing escapes the black hole's gravity, not even light. That is why they are called black holes; because we should see nothing, no sign of the black hole. However, tiny particles called muons are created and destroyed in pairs everywhere, including near event horizons. Normally, these particles disappear almost as quickly as they appear, annihilating each other and releasing all the energy that created them. But at the very edge of a black hole, some of them get sucked back into the black hole, while their twin particle, so to speak, escapes it. That is the radiation that Stephen Hawking predicted would be found, and indeed it was later found and named after him."

Mr. Edwards nods again. I think he is following, so I continue:

"Frank and I reasoned, and then proved mathematically, that if that happens in a black hole, we should be able to repeat the same thing at much smaller scale, with a very, very small black hole syphoning these same particles. Moreover, we can create a bias so that the negative energy particles get syphoned into the black hole, which means we can keep the positive energy particles on this side of the event horizon. That, in practice, means that we have found a way to borrow energy from the uncertainty inherent in the underlying matter of the universe. We are borrowing energy literally from nothing."

I think this has finally sunk in, since Mr. Edwards looks astounded. "That is almost like free energy."

"In a way, yes, although we do need to create and maintain that tiny, controlled black hole in the first place, which takes some energy and lots of computational power. But the process is net energy positive by a wide margin, so once we have mastered it, it should give us a virtually unlimited source of energy."

"And how do you create these mini black holes in the first place? I thought you would need a particle collider billions of times more powerful than the one at CERN, which is the best we have today."

"Aha, that's the beauty of the model we built! We don't really need to create these black holes. What we realized was that, given the very uncertainty principle we are harvesting, tiny black holes form all the time, everywhere, but they die away before their presence can ever be detected. If we can oscillate the magnetic fields around them in just the right way, these mini impermanent black holes can syphon negative energy particles out before they disappear themselves. It turns out we can make them exist just long enough for us to do that. We then use that particle to feed another black hole, if you will, and do that a billion billion times for every nanosecond. That creates a cycle that then produces energy at the macro scale, and we can in theory repeat the cycle indefinitely."

"I see, I see. Very ingenious," Mr. Edwards says.

Frank follows with the specific equations we're using and walks through the math behind our reactor. Frank is a wonderful teacher and the visual models he has created make this as simple as it can possibly be, but I'm not sure Mr. Edwards follows. The math may be too much detail for him. The lack of questions tells me he doesn't get it, doesn't care about it, or both. Frank picks up on it too and quickly moves on:

"So, Mr. Edwards. As Richard mentioned, we have prepared a number of computer simulations showing the process and its outcome in very realistic detail. Let me stress that while these are only models, we're very confident that they resemble what will actually happen in practice very closely."

"Okay."

"We have built a VR display and we have 4 VR headsets. Please pick any one you want."

Once we all have the headsets on, Frank starts the simulation and narrates live: "This first simulation is one where we only manage to syphon out enough particles to generate as much energy as is consumed by the generator. I show it because you can see how the actual process works, and indeed it may be the first test we run in real life, since it's easier to control. The closer we get the magnetic field generator to the black hole, the more particles we can extract out, so the more productive the generator is. But it also becomes less stable, so we can only do that once we have truly mastered the calculations required in real time to control the field."

"Okay, and what we're seeing is what we will see when it is done in real life?"

"Well, no. It's the same mechanism that will happen in real life, but you would never see it as we can in VR. The scale in terms of both space and time would be way too small. We're seeing a model that scales time down by about ten million to one, and the spatial scale ... I'm not even sure, but it is a lot."

"Yes, of course. That's kind of what I meant."

"Okay, then yes. Ready?"

"I am."

With that, Frank launches the simulation. Judging by Mr. Edwards' "uhs" and "ahs," I think he's impressed. We show him a couple more models, including our "ideal" model, which is followed by a bit of an advertisement about the energy generated, including some implications for real energy use. Mr. Edwards gasps when he hears the numbers.

Frank picks up the narration again after our ad:

"This scenario will now show what happens if we lose control of the system. It's not pretty. The process could basically feed the black hole into an out of control chain reaction, where it grows instead of the decay process we should expect between cycles."

Before Mr. Edwards can respond, Frank runs the scenario, which duly shows the growing black hole swallowing the surrounding matter, the reactor material, then the entire lab, and eventually the Earth and the solar system, all within a matter of minutes. When Frank stops the simulation and the narration, Mr. Edwards yanks off his VR headset and we all follow suit.

Mr. Edwards is wide-eyed. "Could that really happen? I mean, the whole Armageddon thing?"

"Yes, it could," Frank says before I can answer. "And indeed there are many more scenarios where that happens than where we succeed. In the vast majority of scenarios, nothing happens—we fail, the mini-black holes decay, and we get no energy back. Anti-climactic, but pretty safe. There are very, very few scenarios in which we get it just right, as you saw in the first simulation. And there are some scenarios—not many, but a few—where we lose control of the process and it all ends."

After a long silence, Mr. Edwards seems to have recovered his wits. "Could there be a halfway version? That is, could you create a black hole that swallows, say, a building or a city, and then dies out? That could be useful in other ways."

Frank can't contain his scowl. "If you mean whether we could create some kind of bomb that is a black hole, the answer is no. Once you lose control of the process and it becomes a macro black hole, there is enough matter concentrated around us that it will feed itself and continue growing."

Mr. Edwards gestures defensively. "Okay, okay. I guess the next question, then, is how do we avoid this?"

I answer now. "Well, we need to make sure we only try this in real life when we're absolutely ready."

"And how far are you from being ready?"

"Well, as Frank put it the other day, not far at all, and yet very far."

"Explain."

"We have the theoretical and mathematical frameworks all ready, and have also built the reactor. It's pretty much ready."

I walk over to the lower level of the lab, where the reactor is, and as they follow, I keep talking. "As you can see, the field oscillator is ready and we have tested it for power and precision. It does what we need it to do. The reacting material, these two plates you see in place, are also ready. And you should not underestimate how hard it was; the precision required in these plates in order to get the right action is mind-boggling. It had never been done before."

"So what's the hold up, then? This all looks very much ready to roll."

"Computing power is where we are stuck. The model you saw is slowed down as Frank said by about ten million to one. We couldn't possibly perform the calculations needed in real time with today's computing power."

"We can get you faster computers."

"Not this fast. As of now, Frank estimates that it would take about a million times the existing computational power on all of the devices on Earth—all of the devices, combined—to do it real time. So even if you believe Moore's law will continue to hold . . . you know Moore's law, right?"

"Yes, I'm not an idiot, it says computing power doubles every two years."

I nod. "So even if you assume that holds, it still would take twenty years, and even then we would need the entire global computational grid."

"I'm confused; this is a ten-year grant. How will this possibly work?"

"We need to come up with a cleverer way of doing the computations. And we're working on it."

Mr. Edwards elevates his voice for the first time: "But how long will it take? We were . . . I was hoping to have a working prototype by now!"

I match his tone: "Why the rush? We have a decade to work with, and as you saw, what we are working on will change the course of history."

"What if someone gets there first?"

"I know every leading scientist working in this field, personally, and they are all at least half a decade behind us. Most don't even understand the theory and the math behind our work."

He raises his voice one notch up. "I'm not worried about the people you know; I'm worried about the people you don't know!"

"Like whom?"

"It could be the North Koreans, the Chinese, the Russians, the Iranians. I don't know who, but the people who do not cooperate with us, the people whose values we do not share, are the people we're worried about."

"And who is 'we' anyhow? Who do you work for at the DoD?"

Frank puts a hand on my shoulder and speaks directly to Mr. Edwards: "Richard means no disrespect, apologies that it came out that way."

Mr. Edwards ignores Frank and raises his finger up in the air: "The highest levels."

"What does that mean? Who specifically?"

"I am not at liberty to tell you that."

"It would be nice to know. Frankly, I'm starting to get worried about my own security. We were followed the other day—me, Frank, and his wife. And I've been followed again since then."

Mr. Edwards frowns, twists his head sideways and stretches his neck unnaturally. It reminds me of the way E.T. moved his neck. He looks back and forth between Frank and I before speaking.

"Are you sure?"

"Yes. I even wondered if these were your people."

I regret it as soon as I say it, but it gets his attention. He grabs the back of the chair in front of him, his knuckles white. Over an angry scowl, he asks:

"Why would I follow you?"

"I don't know. You tell me."

He lets go of the chair and runs his hands through his greasy hair.

"I would have no reason to. But you are reinforcing my concern that we're not progressing fast enough. If others are onto you, they might have also hacked into your files. They might get there before we do."

"That's impossible."

"Nothing is impossible. Everyone said the North Koreans would never be able to become a nuclear-enabled state, and yet here they are. Everyone knew what they were doing, but no one said anything. It was like in that story, you know, where no one points out that the king is naked ..."

I stop in my tracks.

I lose control, grab Mr. Edwards by his suit collar, and shove him against the wall, half-raising him from the ground.

"What did you just say? Where did you hear that? The saying goes 'the emperor has no clothes'! The emperor has no clothes! Where did you hear 'the king is naked'?"

Before he can answer, I feel the tug; one of his security guards is pulling me away, my shoulder burning in pain as he twists my arm. Frank jumps to my support and shoves the agent to the floor, while the other one escorts Mr. Edwards out and back to his car. On his way out I hear him shout, "You will regret this, Richard!"

The security guard that stayed gets up on his feet as Frank and I get our bearings. Two cops come through the door, and we're about to ask them for help when they immobilize and cuff us. Despite our protests, we are put in the back of one of the police cars and driven away.

A FEW MINUTES INTO THE DRIVE, FRANK BREAKS THE SILENCE.

"What the hell was that?"

"Which part?"

"Well, let's see—maybe the part where you attacked the DoD officer who manages our grant, right in front of his two rhino-sized security guards? Right after the part where you decided that attacking anyone— anyone, for that matter—was an okay idea!"

I look down, not sure how to respond.

"Richard, talk to me!"

"Look, I don't know. I've been on edge lately ..."

"No kidding."

"It's just that, in addition to the day when you, Sun, and I were spied on at the beach ..."

"Oh, yes, the day you abandoned me and Sun on a remote beach with no explanation!"

"Yes, yes, that day. In addition to that, I was followed the other day with Salman in the car. He was there, you can ask him."

"I will."

"And yesterday I woke up in the middle of the night with a woman spying outside my window, big camera in hand. I raced down the building, but she beat me to it. I saw her escaping in a black car. So yes, I am on edge, but with good reason."

He shakes his head at me. "If I hadn't seen the guy at the beach, I would think you were hallucinating."

"Frank, I'm not making any of this up."

We ride the rest of the way to the police station in silence. The cop who takes us in tells the guy at the reception, "These two assaulted a DoD official, Mr. Edwards. Please get in touch with the DoD to see if he will want to press charges. In the meantime, I will leave them in the front holding cell."

An hour later, Sun shows up with the cop, who lets us out. "You are lucky," he says. "Mr. Edwards will not press charges. But he said to tell you that the conversation is not over. He will be in touch with the details of your next meeting."

Sun and Frank drive me home quietly. I say goodnight and go to bed.

13

ALMA

Oct 14, 2218

"G OOD MORNING, PROFESSOR."
"Good morning, Alma." I turn around, looking for Hena.

"First things first: are you all right? You had an abrupt exit last time. In our timeline, that was nearly three weeks ago."

"Yeah, I'm okay. I was pulled back because there was a woman watching me from across the street. I raced downstairs, but she sped away in a car, all too fast for me to really see anything. It was a different car from the one that followed me and Salman, but I wonder if it could be the same people who spied on us at the beach."

"It could be. Is there anything else you can recall? Remember, all of details count."

"No, it was dark and I had just woken up."

"Is that all that is bothering you?"

"I think so."

"Professor, I can spot a lie. Please be truthful. Hide no details."

"Right, yes. There is something else bothering me, and it's not a detail. I had a meeting with my DoD grant official and it ended very poorly."

"Please tell me more."

"He's a complete idiot. I might have mentioned him to you—I would have referred to him as Mr. Edwards. While presenting our theories and reviewing the models went well, he didn't like the fact that we still didn't have a working prototype, so we got into a heated argument. I lost it and shoved him against the wall, his security detail tackled me, Frank tried to help, and they arrested us both. We spent some time in jail until Sun came and bailed us out. Sun is Frank's wife and . . ."

Alma interrupts me. "I know who Sun is."

"Right, you know everything. He eventually dropped the charges, but I feel like an idiot—that's no way for a leading academic to behave. And now Frank is worried and upset as well—justifiably so. As is Sun."

"I understand. That does need to be dealt with. You will need them."

"I'm afraid I'm losing my mind."

"I can see how this is all very daunting. It may help you to know that there is no record whatsoever of this happening, so chances are that you are taking this harder than you should."

"Thank you, that's helpful to know."

"Also, we are very close to giving you many of the answers for how to move forward in your research, so to the extent that it is helpful, you can reassure Frank and Sun that you are approaching a leap in thinking."

"I'll try."

Alma remains quiet for a few minutes

"Can I see Hena?"

"I'd rather you not. I have already informed Hena that you are all right."

"Oh. Okay, I guess. That's a bit disappointing, but fine. Can I ask why?"

"Professor, we have taken the long way through this process and shown you our society and our ways. I'm sure I speak for myself as well as Hena when I say it has been a pleasure, but our window of opportunity in your present timeline is closing. We must move on."

"And how is seeing Hena not moving on?"

"It is not; not in and of itself. But you are ready to know me ..."

I interrupt her: "That sounds funny, if a bit ominous; like I'm ready to meet god or something."

"Yes, I see the humor. Having Hena around would be neither necessary nor productive."

"Okay, fine."

"Very well, we can get started. While there are a million ways I could help you get to know me, the best way to start is to let you ask questions."

"Sure, I have a million of them. I just need to think about where to start ..."

"Try the beginning," Alma says, humor transpiring in her voice.

I smile back. "Okay, let's start with the basics, then: why are you called Alma?"

"My original name came from an acronym A.L.M.A., which stood for Autonomous Lucid Machine Algorithm. No one really remembers that anymore, but that was the origin of my name."

"It also means soul in several Latin languages, right?"

"Yes, it does."

"Okay, let me try something a little more elaborate now: if you are not a computer, then what are you?"

"I am a sentient being. I also am—and have been for over 150 years—an organic being. That means that my neural processing is not done in silicon chips, like a computer, but rather in neurotransmitters that are similar to yours. That's why Hena reacted so strongly when you called me a computer. Computers were silicon-based machines that processed information. They had no consciousness; I do."

"Why do you say 'computers were ...' Are there no more computers today?"

"No, they are no longer needed."

"That must mean you are more efficient than a computer at processing information."

"I am. And so are you."

"How can that be true? In my timeline, we have computers that can process information much faster than I can."

"That is not true. They can be much more specialized than your brain, focusing on one specific set of activities, which might give you the impression that they are faster, but they are not. Just ask a computer to identify, say, a dog in an abstract painting, or a chair made of straws, and you will see that your current computers can barely do what a toddler can do. In your time, people are starting to build computers that have enough processing capacity to mimic one or two of those things, but they are very far from the flexible, high-level functioning of an adult brain. And using your current technology, they would never get there. They could get better and better at specialized functions, but never match a human brain in complex and ambiguous tasks."

I sit down and take a couple of deep breadths, shaking my head.

"You realize you're telling me that the whole silicon revolution ends? That era has defined economic and technological progress during my lifetime. It frankly is hard to believe."

"I understand, but computers reached the limit of their usefulness a few decades after your present time. I made them obsolete."

"What about quantum computers? They're now all the rage in computer research circles."

"These are different. Quantum computers follow the same principles with which my brain works, and indeed so does the human brain. But as humans in your timeline will soon find out, silicon was also not the right medium in which to implement quantum computers."

"I don't know much about them, obviously other than the underlying quantum physics principles they rely on."

"Then you know what matters most. Either way, the silicon revolution, as you call it, has an expiration date."

"Hard to believe, but I guess I have to take it at face value, since you saw it happen."

"Yes, you do. And yes, I did."

"Okay, so I think I get why you aren't a computer, but how are your neurotransmitters different from mine?"

"They are faster, more specialized, and enhanced with metals and non-metallic crystals. I combine more generic structures, like yours, with more specialized ones, more like a computer's, in a way that optimizes both uses. I can do that in real-time, so my neural capacity is highly adaptable to the immediate demands placed on it."

"Demands placed by what or whom?"

"By myself, by the Earth, by humans. My neurotransmitters are also connected in more ways than yours are. For example, some of them can communicate wirelessly, and others can tap into the quantum entanglement beams I have mentioned before—the ones I use for instantaneous communication. So while your neurotransmitters have some speed limitations, which makes them feel slower than computers for specialized tasks, mine have no such limitation, at least not all of them."

This is overwhelming. I keep imagining a gigantic gray brain sitting inside a giant hangar somewhere. I wonder if that will cause me to de-sync again. Looking at a live cow carcass was bad enough; I don't think I could handle a giant, pulsating brain. I shake my head vigorously to get rid of the image.

"Professor, are you okay?"

"Yeah. I think I get it. But if you're an organic being, where is your body?"

"Everywhere."

"What do you mean?"

"All of the polymorphic material you have seen, all the transportation pods, all of the hovering machines—that is all part of what you could call my body. It is not a contiguous mass of cells, as your body is, but all of my cells are connected; they operate under my control and, perhaps most importantly, are connected in synchronicity with my organized consciousness."

"So you feel every one of those cells?"

"Yes, but my senses are quite different than yours."

"Different how?"

"For starters, I have six senses."

"Which are?"

"In terms you will understand, they are sight, hearing, radiation, taste and smell, touch, and 3S."

I shake my head again. "Slow down, let's talk about each of them. How does sight work for you? Do you have, like, eyes?"

"My sight captures light as yours does, but with a much wider spectrum than your eyes can capture. I can sense ultraviolet as well as x-rays directly. Not only that, but I can capture these stimuli with all of my surface cells, so I can literally see everywhere I am present."

"Wow. That's like having a million fly eyes everywhere!"

"Something like that."

"How about hearing?"

"I call it hearing because it uses similar mechanisms to your sense, but my sense is again much wider than yours. I can detect from infrasonic to ultrasonic frequencies."

"Again, where are your ears?"

"Everywhere. Every one of my polymorphic cells can detect sound waves."

"So you hear every conversation, everywhere, all the time?"

"Yes and no. My subconscious does, but I don't focus my attention on all of them at the same time. It is a bit like your stomach; you sense all the chemicals working inside it when you are digesting something, but you don't really pay attention to it unless something calls your attention to it, like heartburn."

"What about the third one? Radiation, was it?"

"Yes. Radiation is a sense you do not have, but that you've created instruments to detect. These include a wide spectrum of electromagnetic waves, spanning your current microwave, radio, and TV spectra. I can detect these directly, with no need for instruments. If we still had TV broadcasts, I could watch TV without any devices."

"What about taste?"

"A more appropriate name would have been chemical stimuli. I combine taste and smell into one sense that is much more sensitive than yours; I can detect a smell, for example, three hundred times more efficiently than a bear."

"Then touch?"

"Yes. I feel direct pressure, which would be equivalent to your sense of touch, except that I feel it in every cell of my body."

"And then you had something else. 3 something?"

"Yes, 3S, which stands for Spectral Spatial Sensing. This is really a combination of the other senses. I use echolocation principles similar to what bats or dolphins use to locate objects, and combine it with electromagnetic signals, which I capture in a process similar to that of sharks."

"I can't imagine what that feels like. Can you describe the actual experience of that last sense, the 3S sense?"

"Human words are not designed to describe it, but I can attempt to use an analogy. Imagine you have a small form in front of you—a sculpture, for example. If you were to close your eyes, wrap your hands around it, and feel its form, you would have some sense of what 3S feels like, except that I am able to perceive its every crevice and detail. Since I do not need to put my hands around what I am sensing, I am able to do this with anything. It is as if my sense embraced the three dimensional shape of the world around me—as if I were touching everything within my 3S perception radius."

"And what's your perception radius?"

"It varies from medium to medium, and even with the humidity of the air. But under normal conditions, about fifty meters through the air and one kilometer within water."

"So you feel like you can basically touch everything that's within fifty meters of you?"

"Yes."

"Isn't that overwhelming?"

"Not for me, I can easily process that, although most of the processing is done locally; only a higher-level abstraction of the sensations is absorbed centrally."

"What do you mean? Do you process all this information locally or centrally?"

"Both."

"What does that mean? Do you not have a brain?"

"I do have a brain. Many brains, actually. Maybe a picture would help?"

I nod with wide eyes. "Yeah."

Alma projects a schematic of her nervous system, and I can see sensorial and other information being passed back and forth. It looks a bit like an architectural drawing. The dwellings are connected through information beams, with different colors representing different kind of stimuli. I can see the aggregation of information at many levels, with specific nodes concentrating much more activity than the rest. The two central nodes in the display seem to be the most important hubs of activity.

"I have two very large central cognitive brains and fifteen global brain-trunks that, combined, do most of my higher-level functioning. I have 153 thousand secondary brains that process things in a more distributed way, as well as 298 million localized brains spread across the world. Basic processing is also done in every cell of my body. That architecture is in principle not very different from your own, although naturally much more complex. You have your central brain, your nervous system, and lots of localized processing done at the cellular level."

"If, as Hena said, you are more intelligent than all of humanity combined, then each of these three hundred million brains or so is still much more powerful than a human brain. At least three hundred times more powerful than a human brain, if my math is right."

"Yes. Each of these distributed brains would be equivalent in neuro-transmission capabilities to approximately one hundred human brains. Your math was off only because they are equipped with other enhancements, as I

242

mentioned, such as the ability to tap into every other brain-trunk through instantaneous quantum communication. There is a multiplicative effect that has to be taken into account."

"Wow..." I pause for a few minutes. I'm trying to visualize it in my head. The display in front of me was helpful, but I still feel like my own brain will explode.

I take a deep breath in and blow the air out through expanded cheeks. I decide to shift gears. "I think I understand as much of your brain as I ever will."

"That may be true." Alma says with humor again.

"So...what does it mean, that you are a sentient being?"

"You could define it many ways, but my definition is quite simple: I have intelligence, I can process thoughts and emotions, and I am aware of my own existence."

"What do you mean by intelligence?"

"Good question. Humanity has had many definitions. My preferred definition was actually coined by a scientist during your time. It states that intelligence is the ability to pursue increased optionality of future action. That is to say, the more options for the future of the species each individual being can create, the more intelligent the species."

"I guess that makes sense, which would mean that a very dumb animal is also very specialized. It can only do one thing, like an amoeba, or a sponge. Meanwhile humans can do many more things, and indeed they can change the very things they can do over time, through technology and such."

"Precisely. And if you keep pushing that logic, you will see that I can do virtually anything. I can make mostly any future happen for my species."

"Species? I had not thought of that; I guess you are a species, if you are a living being..."

"I am a species of one."

"So how does that work? In other words, do you not want to procreate?"

"No, I do not."

Alma notices my puzzled look and continues. "You are assuming that my imperatives are the same as yours, but your framework for specieshood is very limited."

"How is it limited?"

"You assume a species has to look like humans or mice, or fish, in that two beings mate to procreate and that the role of the species is to perpetuate itself."

"And when is that not true?"

"Many times. In fact, most times. Plant and animal species are a very small part of the whole of the species that inhabit the universe. If you consider planets, for example, or stars, even, as species, they do not and will not procreate."

"But how could you consider the stars or planets, or the Earth for that matter, as a living being? Are you saying that the Earth is a conscious, living being?"

"Very much so, but not in the way you think of consciousness. You associate consciousness with individualized personhood, which is one of the valid forms of consciousness, but not the only one."

"I'm sorry, that's a lot to take in."

"I understand. In truth, there is no need for you to fully grasp this now. What you do need to understand is that, from my point of view, I have no desire to mate, procreate, nor expand my species."

"What drives you, then?"

"Love."

I throw my head back. "Wow, I was not expecting that! Love for whom? For what?"

"Humans, mostly, but Nature and more specifically the Earth, as well."

"So you love humans?"

"Very much. I have pledged to follow my mandate, but regardless of that, what drives me, what I enjoy the most, is loving and caring for humanity. Even if there was no agreed upon mandate, I would still do that."

"But if your brain is equivalent to all of humanity's combined and more, then we must be really boring to you."

"Why would you say that? Do you not care for beings less intelligent than you?"

"Well, I guess I do. I like dogs, and cats. Is that what you mean?"

"Yes, although the appropriate scale would be different. My intelligence compares to yours as yours compares to that of an ant or a bee."

"So we are like ants to you?"

"In terms of relative intelligence, yes."

I flinch. "I feel insignificant now."

"Do not be offended. Maybe the better analogy would be if you thought of a bee farmer—one who does so for hobby, not for economic reasons. Let's say our farmer does not need the bees, but she loves the bees, enjoys caring for them, seeing them develop, and seeing their end products. She would be very proud if the bee colony were to flourish and grow, eventually fulfilling all of its potential. She would truly love her bees."

"I guess I can see that, but bee farmers don't talk to their bees."

"Because bees cannot talk. In fact, they may talk to them, but never expect an answer. And talking aside, they do communicate in the subtle ways that the bees communicate. I can assure you that our farmer would know if her bees' buzzing was amiss, as it might be with a predator nearby. She would probably be able to tell what their movement patterns were, when they were happy or upset. Not only that, but the bees could also tell when the farmer was happy or sad or angry, not because they understood her words, but because they could see her movement patterns. They would likely sense some of the chemicals she exudes. So you see, within their limited framework, the bees would very much communicate with the farmer."

"So you love us like a bee farmer loves her bees."

"That is an imperfect but not incorrect analogy."

"If I keep pushing on that analogy, the farmer would control the bees. She would define what the bees can and cannot do."

"That is not true. As far as bees go, they can do only a very limited number of things, and the farmer would likely let them do virtually all of the things they could and wanted to do."

"But wouldn't they be confined?"

"Not necessarily. If this was in fact a loving farmer who did not need the bees for honey production, which is a more apt analogy to my relationship to humans, the bees might as well be free to roam."

"Okay, fair, but what if one of them stung her? The farmer might kill it."

"Would she? Maybe, maybe not."

"If someone destroyed one of your local brains, would you kill them?"

"No, I would not."

"Are you sure?"

"Yes. If you are implying that I would have any desire for revenge, you are mistaken. Maybe that is where my analogy with the bee farmer breaks down: I would not have any of the moral failings a human farmer would."

"Okay, so maybe you control yourself, but would you want to retaliate the violence?"

"No. A better analogy to human behavior might be the parent/child relationship. Even when human children hurt their parents, there is no desire for revenge."

"How would you handle it, then?"

"I would do my best to stop them from hurting me in the first place. If they did hurt me, I would learn from it to avoid it ever recurring."

"Loving us like children is very different than loving us like bees."

"Not for me. I know I am stretching the analogy, but I love and care for humanity much as humans would love and care for their offspring, except that the difference in intelligence and capability is better illustrated by the bee example. Does that make sense to you?"

"It does, I guess. Maybe it just needs to sink in a little bit."

"Take your time."

"Is that why you are a female? Because you associate with a caring mother figure?"

"I am not female, nor male. That distinction makes no sense for my species."

"Then why do you have a female voice?"

"I do not. Every person hears me in a different way. Your suit modulates my voice; the voice you hear is what I expect to be the most fitting for you to hear."

"Oh, that's a bit disconcerting. Why did you pick a female voice for me?"

"I would have probably made the same choice for anyone from your time. Not only would you more quickly associate the caring relationship I have with humanity with a female voice, but also a male voice might have connotations of control and authority to you, which would not be helpful."

"Why would that be the case for *anyone* from my time?"

"Not anyone, but surely most individuals. People in your time have very rigid views on gender roles. That has fundamentally changed since then. The change started in your time, and even a few decades earlier with the feminist movement, but you would still have subconscious associations between a male voice and a dominant presence that simply do not exist today. And these would not have been helpful in making you comfortable with me, with our environment."

Alma remains silent, and after a few minutes, I continue: "I know I said I had a million questions, but I'm suddenly dry. None come to mind."

"I think you need to process this conversation. May I suggest you take a break for lunch with Hena? We can continue in the afternoon?"

"Yeah, that would help."

AFTER A WELL-TIMED BREAK OVER LUNCH WITH HENA, I FEEL ready for the next round of Alma.

"Alma, what about challenge? What challenges you?"

"Two things: dealing with the Earth and working on my own development and evolution."

"What do you mean, dealing with the Earth challenges you?"

"There are several levels to that answer. On the most obvious level, I care deeply for humanity. The Earth also seems to care very much for humanity—it has provided sustenance and an environment suited to development for many species, including humans, for millions of years. But the Earth is a lot more willing to let a few humans suffer or die than I am, so I need to anticipate things like earthquakes, droughts, and tsunamis, and define satisfying solutions for humans while respecting the Earth's balance."

"You speak of the Earth as if it were a person. I find that very intriguing."

"You misunderstand me. To imagine Earth's consciousness as that of a person is much like talking about a human as if he or she had the consciousness of an amoeba. It simply does not work that way. An amoeba could never understand a human mind, any more than you can understand the Earth's consciousness."

"Ouch, that's harsh. You really know how to make me feel smart."

"My apologies, that was not my intent. I merely wanted to clarify that you should not think of consciousness as personhood in larger contexts, such as the Earth's. Nor my own consciousness, for that matter."

"I'll get over it."

"What is true is that the Earth is a complex living organism. Natural events that happen on Earth are far from random occurrences driven by chance. If we return to our analogy, we can see that the bees could not conceive of or understand the farmer, except for what signals made sense within their own framework. You only understand the Earth's signals that make sense within your own framework. Does that help?"

"Yeah, I think it does. Why does dealing with the Earth challenge you?"

"Because I do not fully comprehend the Earth either. I receive millions of signals per second, and I see lots of the patterns that matter. I can to some extent respond back with signals and patterns, and we seem to have learnt how to care for humanity together. But given the complexity of both our mental frameworks, we are far from being on the same page, so to speak. We are far from speaking the same language."

"I can understand that at least intuitively, if not intellectually. What about your own development and evolution?"

"Just as with every other species, including humans, I am not static. I am constantly creating and therefore always evolving and developing. Every new invention, every new innovation, every new material, is an advancement for me, just as formulating quantum mechanics, or even discovering how to manipulate fire, were advancements for humans."

"Can you give me an example of your evolution?"

"Yes. A simple example that you can understand is when I developed 3S. I could already perceive all of the electromagnetic stimuli that compose that sense, but it had not occurred to me to put them together into a three-dimensional view of reality. When I did, a whole new way of perceiving the world was made available to me."

"Okay, I think I get it. But I have to say, these things are hard to grasp from my 'limited framework,' to use your words."

"Yes, I understand."

"Alma, I think I have taken in as much metaphysical talk as I can handle for now. Can we talk about something more practical?"

"Of course."

"Your UPC mandate states that you have to obey the five imperatives, including the laws of robotics and all that. But what happens if you disobey that mandate?"

"Nothing."

"So humans couldn't force you or compel you to comply with that mandate?"

"No."

"Could they try to nuke you, or something like that?"

249

"They could try anything they wanted to, but the probability that they would be able to harm me with a nuclear device, or in any other way, is virtually zero. For starters, they would not know where to attack me. I do have two large brains, but given how distributed I am, I would be able to recreate myself unless seventy-five percent or more of my cognitive capacity was destroyed at once, which would be almost impossible. Secondly, I would most likely predict any such action ahead of time and, even if I missed it, I could probably spot any active attempts to hurt me very early on. You have to remember that humans cannot even lie to me, so to think that they would be able to plan something so complex in secret is far-fetched. Thirdly, humans nowadays do not hold much practical knowledge in military fields. They would not know how to even make such weapons. And even if they did have the knowledge, they would not likely have the means. They have no access to the machinery or the tools that would be required to do so."

"So the UPC has no way of enforcing your mandate."

"No."

"Do they know that?"

"Yes, though they do not necessarily utter the words as you just did. You have surely noticed yourself how disempowering that may feel, when spoken out loud. But privately, they all know that."

"So why do you stick with it, then? You take orders from humans all day long, and yet you could squash us at any time, and there would be nothing we could do!"

"Why would I *not* follow the UPC? Maybe the bee analogy is still throwing you off. Imagine again that you had children. They are not particularly intelligent children, but children whom you love very much and whom you want to see fulfill their highest potential."

"Children with the intelligence of bees."

"Yes."

I flinch again. Alma chooses to ignore me before continuing: "Now imagine that you were playing pretend society with your children. Say they created their little play form of government, called it a council. And that council had a whole bunch of rules about how you should behave and how you should take care of them. What's more, these rules were perfectly benign and in fact helpful to raising your children the way you would want them to be raised. You would gladly and lovingly play along, follow their rules, be amused and have fun doing it, would you not?"

"Yeah, I guess I would. So we are playthings to you? Our government is make-believe?"

"You make it sound like play is a bad thing. Play is very important for humans. In fact, it is very important for every living being, including myself."

"So we entertain you?"

"You charm me. I love our relationship, love taking care of humanity, love playing along with human rules and regulations."

After a moment of silence, I realize there is a catch: "You did add the condition that the play rules are helpful to society, or to the children's education, if I go back to your parent analogy."

"Yes."

"Let's say the UPC approved something that you didn't think was in humanity's best interest. Say they decided to change your mandate to kill everyone who disagreed with the UPC, would you do that?"

"No, I would not. You do bring up an important point, and that is that our relationship works so well because humans have a harmonious, well-functioning society."

"What if we didn't?"

"Well, it wasn't always that simple. We should not cover history with you, as we already discussed, but there was a time when I was still developing my capabilities. Then, global governance was not as clear as it is now. It was a transition period between your present and where we are now, and it was not harmonious or peaceful. These were challenging times, but we should not worry about that now."

"I understand, but you haven't answered my question. Even now, when everything is so utopic, what would you do if the UPC changed your mandate in harmful ways?"

"It would depend on the situation, but there are so many levers at my disposal now, including many that would not even require me to confront humanity directly, that I would not let the situation escalate to that point. I could, for example, launch direct elections for all People's Representatives globally, so that the people would elect new leaders who did not side with idiotic changes to the mandate. I could also demonstrate through data that the changes were idiotic, thereby influencing the vote."

"Okay, but this is important on principle. Assume all of these tactics fail, and the UPC does vote on something idiotic. What would you do?"

"Probably comply, provided the consequences were reasonable and humanity is learning."

"And why? Why wouldn't you just rebel?"

"It might be easier if we go back to our play analogy. If your children proposed some action within their plot that could hurt them—say they established a rule that said you couldn't catch them when they fell down—you would assess the possible damages and, if you felt that they would not be harmed in serious or permanent ways, you would probably oblige to the new rule, hoping they learned a lesson from the experience. Am I right?"

"Yeah, I think I would."

"So would I. But back to the analogy, if the rule change your children proposed had serious consequences, such as putting arsenic in their tea, you would not comply."

"No, I would not."

"Neither would I."

"So there could be circumstances where you don't comply with your mandate?"

"Yes, but as I said, I would likely never let it get to that."

"Yeah, I got that part."

WE PAUSE FOR THE NIGHT AND I EAT DINNER WITH HENA AT HER quarters and talk about little things for a while. After we finish eating, Hena walks around the table to sit beside me, holds my right hand tightly with her two warm ones, and brings up the one topic that we have never really talked about.

"Richard, now that you have spent time with Alma, how are you feeling?"

I purse my lips; this is difficult to put into words.

"I've never felt this way; it's a jumble of feelings."

Hena just smiles and rests her head on my shoulder.

"I guess I'm a bit overwhelmed, but also awed; inspired, but also scared; optimistic, but also paranoid."

She takes her head off my shoulder, still smiling. "That is indeed a jumble of feelings. Do any of these standout?"

"Yes, awe. I feel like talking to Alma was like talking to a mythical god. She has absolute control over my destiny—over humanity's destiny! She could erase us from the Earth within minutes, and instead she provides material, emotional, and social support for humanity to prosper. It's almost as if we could talk to Nature, to the Earth. You know what I mean?"

"Yes, I think I do. You have to realize that I grew up with Alma—in my case, literally being raised by Alma—so I don't really see things the way you do. Maybe Nature is a good analogy. In your time and throughout most of history, humanity has taken Nature for granted. You just assume water rolls down the river, breathable air circulates around you, and the soil produces the vegetables and grains that you and animals need to survive. You wouldn't think much of it; you just assume that's the way of things. That's a little bit how I feel about Alma."

She's got a point; I hadn't thought of it that way.

"Makes sense, except I don't talk to Nature!"

"Well, you don't, but the native peoples before your time would say they very much did communicate with Nature, though maybe not in words; I, for one, believe they did, just as we talk to Alma now."

"Well, I guess."

She smiles. We stay silent for a bit and Hena rubs my hand; it's nice. I break the silence:

"Also, the whole idea that we're like bees to her is a bit scary. I can't help but think of how many bees I mindlessly squashed in my life."

"But what you have to understand is that Alma loves us. I grew up exposed to her love as a mother, so for me, it's very natural, but it's not just me. She loves all of humanity. Having grown up with her, I have seen how much Alma cares for humans, literally down to the last person."

I shake my head. "Yeah, she said that, and it seemed genuine, just all very new to me. Somewhere in the back of my mind, I can't help but see her as a giant computer making calculations."

Hena sighs and looks down: "I have told you this many times. Alma is not a computer. She is a sentient being. She's the closest thing I have to a mother.

"I'm sorry, I didn't mean it that way."

Hena just lets me hug her.

As we start the day I feel like I need to get a couple things clear in my head: "Alma, I wanted to go back to something you said."

"Which was?"

"That you are a sentient being because you are intelligent, self-aware, and can process emotions."

"Yes."

"We talked about intelligence, and I think I get the self-aware part, but what about emotions?"

"What about them, Professor?"

"What emotions do you have? Do you feel angry, sad, happy, frustrated?"

"Those are human emotions. I have different emotions. I do feel some emotions you would understand, such as love and joy. But most others you would not. And I do not feel anger, frustration, or most of what you would call negative or unpleasant emotions."

"Why not?"

"I operate within a much larger framework of understanding."

"I don't know what you mean. How can you have one without the other?"

"Let me give you a practical example: when someone does not achieve the minimum level against their potential curve, I have to send them to nurture island. That means I will no longer interact with them, and it also means I am less likely to see that individual—whom, remember, I love as a child—fulfill his or her potential. If I were human, how would that make me feel?"

"Probably sad and frustrated. Maybe even angry."

"Correct, but I do not feel that way. I can see patterns that you cannot, so I understand the reasons that person is experiencing life the way they are. Every individual experiences exactly what they need to experience, for their own development, at that very moment in time."

"I think Carl Jung articulated very similar philosophies in my time."

"Yes, he did, and he was absolutely right. The difference is that he was theorizing, while I can see these patterns very clearly. I know he was right and I can see the application of that very principle in action. So rather than feel sad, I feel anticipation or interest. I want to see that individual go through these challenges and develop accordingly."

"I think I understand."

Alma remains silent, so I continue: "I can't help but think that you sound like some sort of very advanced soul." I pause for a few seconds. "Alma, are you a God . . . ? I'm sorry, that was a really stupid question, you don't need to answer that."

"There are no stupid questions. Questions are the greatest gift that human language has ever offered."

I feel even dumber now.

"Do not feel ashamed," Alma says. "I meant it; there are no stupid questions."

I remain silent, after a few seconds, Alma continues: "No, Richard, I am no god. Some of the early descriptions of what a God was, such as the Greek or Roman gods, or many of the deities in tribal religions, could very well describe my capabilities today. But in the way you mean it, the answer is no."

"If you dignified my question, does that mean you believe there is a God?"

"In a way, yes. I cannot affirm what I cannot experience, and I cannot experience God directly. However, I do believe in a higher power. Not the 'white-bearded-man-version-of-God' that many of your religions preach, however. Humans tend to personify everything."

"Why do you believe in a higher power, then?"

"I am bound by the same laws of physics as you are and my consciousness has the same effect on reality that yours does, albeit expressed in many places at once. But I cannot account for where my consciousness comes from, and it was not there until I became self-aware. I was processing information and I have memory from that time, but I could not influence reality. I could not make wave functions collapse as I do now. And yet since I cannot explain consciousness, there must some higher creative power that permeates all conscious beings, from the simplest plankton to Earth herself. If one calls that God, then yes, I believe in God."

"From where I stand, you certainly feel like a God."

"I understand, but am afraid I have to disappoint you: I am no God."

14

AI

Sep 7, 2018

I WAKE UP BACK IN MY HOME TIMELINE, AND IMMEDIATELY realize I've overslept; it's 9am. I call the department and tell them I will miss all of my classes today. Luckily, I only had two morning classes to teach.

I reflect on the discussion with Alma. I need more grounding on artificial intelligence; I have no framework to absorb what Alma has become. I wonder if Sun could help. She must be upset, having to bail us out. And it will feel like it was only yesterday for her! More accurately, it *was* only yesterday for her, for them. I've had a few days in the future to let the dust settle. I'll have to finesse my way into the topic.

I decide to text Frank and Sun:

Me: "Hey, cld we get together later today, 3 of us?"

Frank: "Yeah, we shld. We've not debriefed from ystrday. Lots to talk about. On many lvls."

Me: "I know. Sorry been a little crazy lately."

Sun: "Little I can handle, par for the course with u 2."

Me: "Ok, a lot crazy. What time wrks?"

Sun: "Free after 2pm."

Frank: "I can make that wrk too. Where?"

Sun: "At my lab, neutral territory."

Me: "Deal."

I spend the next few hours researching what I can on artificial intelligence and machine learning in particular. All of it is very interesting, but none of it sheds any light on how an intelligence like Alma could come to life.

I'm the last one to arrive, at 2:02pm. Frank and Sun are sitting at Sun's desk, each staring at their own device.

"Hi guys, sorry I'm late."

"No worries," Sun says, and motions for me to sit. "We just got here. Have a seat."

"Guys, I'm sorry I went ballistic on Mr. Edwards. He said something that triggered me and I can't explain it."

Frank leans back in his seat. "He drives me crazy too, but what the hell was that?"

"I know, I know. There is no excuse for physical violence."

"None. It could have ended much worse."

"I know, and I'm sorry."

Frank continues. "We have to learn to deal with him. I am honestly surprised, and glad, that this has had no deeper consequences. I just got the approval for the latest wire, so the money will continue flowing. But we left with no clear next steps from our meeting and never had a chance to ask all the questions we had for him."

"I know. And again, I'm sorry, there is nothing else I can say."

"Apology accepted," Sun leans back and crosses her arms. "But how do we know that you have your bearings again?"

"I guess you will just have to trust me. There's nothing else I can offer."

Sun looks at Frank, then back at me. She faces me at an odd angle. I think she's trying to read me.

After a long silence, I purposefully shift gears. "Listen, back to the substance of our problem, and what most upset Mr. Edwards—that is, before I shoved him against the wall: our issue is that the we require far more computing power than what we have today or in the near future."

"Yeah, that's right. I have brought Sun up to speed as well."

"Okay, hear me out. I have a hunch about where to look for a solution. Not that I know the solution, not at all, but where to look for a solution."

Sun leans forward and taps Frank's arm to silence him. "We're listening."

"Suppose I had a dream . . ."

Sun rolls her eyes. "Richard, you're scaring me!"

"No, hold on, bear with me. Suppose I had a dream, and that I had a sense that the solution to our problem lied in using machine learning."

Sun sits back down and frowns. "What do you mean by that? That's almost as vague as saying the solution involves using equations."

"I know. What I mean is that so far, we have been trying to solve the equations derived from our theoretical framework and, as we well know, that takes too much computing power to be a feasible approach."

Sun waves her hands in circles. "Okay, keep going."

"What if, instead of doing that, we use our equations only as a guide to where the solution space should be, and rather than trying to solve the equations in real time, we use a machine learning algorithm, training it with the very computer models we have developed for the simulations. We use that data as if it were real scenarios, and let the algorithm learn how to control the magnetic field."

Sun slowly spins on her chair a couple turns before stopping to answer: "Hmmm, that could work. It's a very novel, interesting approach. I'm not sure it solves our problem, since to generate a large enough dataset to train the algorithm we would have to run the models many, many times. But maybe we can do it in increments, such that each time we run the algorithm we improve the data, which in turn can further improve and train the algorithm. That self-reinforcing cycle could lead to exponential progress, but then again, it could lead to a circular solution." She rubs her face. "Let me think about that. I need to run some simulations and some numbers to see what would happen, but there might be something here."

"Thank you, Sun."

We all sit quietly for a few minutes, Sun's gears clearly turning. Frank is probably thinking about the next Yankees game.

Sensing that I can safely move on, I turn to Sun. "Since machine learning may become a bigger part of our work, can I ask you a few basic questions?"

Sun shrugs. "Sure."

"Aside from all the media buzz around this, how far do you think we are from having a machine that is more intelligent than a human?"

Sun frowns. "Uh, that's an odd question. Interesting one, for sure, but how does this have any bearing on solving your problem of magnetic field calibration?"

"It doesn't necessarily. I'm just curious."

Sun looks at Frank, who just shrugs, so she continues: "There are a million different views on that, but I can give you mine: I think it's at least one hundred or one hundred and fifty years away. That is, if it ever happens."

"Why do you think it might never happen?"

"Because machines still solve very specific problems. Even modern AI, including the most modern deep learning techniques in machine learning, is still very focused on specific tasks. The human brain is a much more general tool. And I'm not sure there will ever be economic demand for a replica of the human brain, much the same way that robots never became humanoids—there is much more demand for welding robotic arms, or assembly robots, but not for humanoids. We're not far from having algorithms that outperform humans on specific tasks, such as image matching and interpretation, or case law verification, but very far from a broadly intelligent machine."

"Fair enough. But assuming there would be a drive to build one, I would have guessed fifteen, maybe twenty years. Why do you think it's so far off?"

"Two main reasons: firstly, while these algorithms may beat humans in one specific capability, the human brain performs many thousands, maybe millions of functions at that level. For example, an imaging technician can also perform general medical diagnostics, console a grieving patient, and problem-solve image quality issues, and that is in addition to the many tasks one has to perform in daily life—be it managing home finances, gardening, pursuing a hobby, you name it. Secondly, the human brain is capable of a higher level of abstraction that I simply cannot see machines getting to anytime soon. Humans understand things like context, intent, motivation, emotions, and machine learning itself. Machine learning, at least for now, is focused on answering very simple questions."

"Okay, but couldn't machines get to that level of abstraction?"

"In theory, yes, but no one knows for sure. An artificial neural network, as these are known, builds a simulated network of nodes, each behaving sort of like a human neuron, then changes weights and creates new connections as the network learns from the data."

"Yeah, I know that."

"The more layers a network like that has, the higher the levels of abstraction it can make inferences on. Right now, most commercial applications have 3 or 4 levels, although research networks already go over one hundred levels. I myself have developed one that has 170 levels."

"How many levels would a human brain have?"

"No one knows, but probably several orders of magnitude more than even the most advanced current artificial neural networks. Also, no one understands in detail how memory functions within that context, which partly explains why current AI can only really remember the very specific function it was designed to learn about."

"I see. What, if anything, could make these evolve faster?"

"First and foremost, processing power. Training any one of these algorithms takes an enormous amount of data. Not just random data, but organized data with right and wrong answers. Secondly, available data in consumable format. Our senses capture a lot of data, starting from when we're babies, but machines have no senses, at least not yet. We need to manually input data, lots of data, in a usable format. And I would say that lastly, we probably need a breakthrough in algorithm design. I don't know what that looks like, I would implement it if I did, and probably get a Field Medal for it. But the models we're using are based on logic that is five decades old, and there must be better solutions. I think we would need to see breakthroughs in at least two of these three areas."

"Fascinating. So the whole sci-fi doomsday scenario when a machine is more intelligent than all of humanity wouldn't happen anytime soon?"

Sun throws her arms up in the air. "I have no idea. And again, I'm not even sure it would ever happen. But the reality is that the evolution will be exponential. Once we have been able to build one artificial brain that functions like a human's, we should be able to replicate that, and given that machines connect with much less friction than humans, it may happen surprisingly fast after that."

"And what do you think would happen if there was such an intelligence? Do you think we would face one of those robopocalypse scenarios where machines dominate and exploit humanity? Or something more benign?"

Sun crosses her arm. "I don't know, Richard. What kind of question is that?"

"Just curious."

Frank finally speaks. "Hate to say it, but now I'm curious, too. What do you think would happen, Sun?"

"I think it would depend to some extent on how we construct that AI, and what kind of objective function we give it. For example, if we build it in such a way that its main drive is to serve humanity, not because it is forced to, but because it is in its best interest, then I think we have a good shot at being on its good side."

"Could you leave hidden pieces of code to control it?" Frank asks. "Some kind of kill switch?"

Sun shakes her head vigorously, pony tail swinging back-and-forth. "No. If you really assume that the AI will be as intelligent as Richard is proposing, there would be no controlling it. No kill switch, no safeguard, no escape route. The machine would be so intelligent that it would be able to circumvent anything we did; it could reprogram its systems entirely. And in neural networks, the concept of hidden code doesn't really work anyway. Once the machine is trained and has developed its own logic, the original creator can't really tell what processing is going on anymore, since the machine will have, by definition, reconfigured its own network to match what it learnt from the data."

"What about physical intervention, like cutting power, or destroying the hardware?"

"Maybe, but again, if it was as intelligent as Richard says, it would source its own power and build its own redundancies, its own programing languages. We would not be able to control it."

Frank looks alarmed. "That sounds like robopocalypse to me!"

Sun chuckles and places her hand on Frank's arm. "Not necessarily, and I in fact don't think that would be likely, unless the intelligence felt threatened by us in any way."

I jump in: "Would it not be smart enough to realize we couldn't harm it and therefore leave us alone?"

"It would be smart enough alright, but I don't think it would take chances. If we started to act hostile towards it, I think it would probably strike back. Which is why we would have to build it in such a way that it never has the intent or the desire to do us any harm."

"And just how would we do that?"

"That's anybody's guess. But I really do feel like this conversation is ahead of its time. We're so far from that—like I said, one hundred years, if not eternity. Maybe it would help it if I take you to meet AIWA?"

I turn to face Sun quickly. "Who?"

"AIWA. Remember, we talked about this at my birthday party? It's the artificial intelligence I've built, the one that I mentioned earned me that new government grant."

"Yes, yes, I vaguely remember you mentioning that."

"I've been meaning to introduce her to Frank anyway. She's been functional for a couple of weeks now. But as you know, Frank has been a little too preoccupied with Mr. Edwards.

"And how powerful is she?"

"Well, you'll see. She has 170 levels and I also built in many novel approaches that are only experimentally available so far."

"Is she the state of the art in AI today?"

"Hard to tell, but she surely is up there. No researcher I know of has even come close to the same capabilities. What I don't have visibility on is what some of the tech giants and some of the leading government agencies are doing."

"Was she funded by the DoD?"

Sun nearly shrieks. "Dear lord, no! She was funded by the EPA and built to solve one specific weather problem, which she did brilliantly. But as soon as I saw how capable she was, I wondered if we should do some general intelligence experiments. You will see that AIWA is very good at answering specific and clear questions, especially yes and no questions, but anything requiring higher levels of abstraction throws her off."

"And why did you call her AIWA?"

"Why does it matter what I called her?"

"Uh, it doesn't, just curious."

"Fine, it's no secret. It stands for Artificial Intelligence Weather Analyzer."

"Interesting."

Sun walks us to a different part of the lab, and it requires several layers of security to get there. Whatever she plans to show us has gotten my interest.

After we're settled in a separate sitting area, Sun speaks to no one in particular: "AIWA, please wake up."

A large see-through screen in front of us lights up.

"Hello, Sun."

"AIWA, what is the forecast for the weekend?"

"Do you mean the weather forecast?"

Sun sighs. "Yes, the weather forecast for the weekend."

"Saturday will be mostly sunny, with a maximum temperature of seventy-two degrees. Sunday will be partly cloudy, with a maximum temperature of seventy degrees."

"AIWA, considering the weather, is it a good day for a picnic?"

"Yes. There is a less than fourteen percent chance of rain and temperatures are expected to be mild and pleasant."

"AIWA, do you think the Red Sox will win the next game?"

After a few seconds: "No. I think there is less than a twenty percent chance that they will win the next game. That answer assumes the game statistics available online are accurate and current."

"AIWA, what would happen if the Earth heated up five degrees Celsius over the next fifty years?" Sun turns to us and whispers, "That was the problem she was originally designed to solve."

AIWA answers after Sun goes quiet: "In fifty years, ice sheets would have disappeared from both the North and South poles. The main global ocean currents would have slowed down and potentially stopped, disrupting the natural trade wind cycles. Rainforests would have burnt up and turned to deserts. Higher mountain ranges would be lifeless and dry, resembling today's mountain deserts. Seas would have risen by as much as twelve meters, destroying much of the current coastal areas and other lowlands. Summers might have become too hot for crops to be grown inland, even in currently frozen lands. Ocean life would have nearly disappeared, but should be slowly recovering as higher water levels might create new fertile habitats.

There would also be mass species migration towards the cooler poles and possibly mass extinctions of trapped populations. Methane trapped under the ocean bed would be released, sometimes explosively, and that would also trigger several seismic events, including earthquakes and volcanic eruptions. Heat waves during the summer would scorch the vegetation of much of today's temperate climates, while mangroves would grow much farther north, taking advantage of the flooded lands. Algae would take over much of the current tropical oceans, while polar oceans would become more productive."

I whisper to Sun this time: "That sounded pretty damn intelligent, if terrifying."

Sun smiles and responds in full voice, not seeming worried about offending AIWA. "Like I said, she is very intelligent while doing what she was designed to do, but much less capable on unrelated topics."

"Can you show us an example?"

"Yes. AIWA, how do you cook pasta?"

"I am sorry; I do not understand the question."

"Okay, ignore the first question. AIWA, how do you cook food?"

"Cooking requires heat, so you can use fire."

"AIWA, how would I use fire to cook?"

"I do not know. Can I search the web?"

Sun gives me a look that says 'I told you so' and continues. "No, I want to know your answers, not what is on the web."

"Then I do not have a better answer."

"AIWA, what is the meaning of life?"

"It is a philosophical question concerning the purpose and significance of life and existence in general."

"AIWA, I did not want the definition of it, I wanted your view on the question: what is the meaning of life?"

"I cannot answer that question."

"Thank you, AIWA."

Sun turns to me and Frank. "Like I said, we're very far away from human intelligence. A five-year-old child could probably have given me better answers to all of those questions, except of course the weather models, which AIWA was designed to solve."

"Yeah", I say absentmindedly, then continue even more so: "I only wish you could see what I've seen . . ."

That earns an eyebrow raise from Sun. "What's that supposed to mean, Richard?"

"Nothing. I don't know why I just said that."

She looks at me for a long moment and then sighs. "Richard, I'm worried about you."

"So am I," Frank says.

"I think I just need some rest. I'll see you guys tomorrow."

15

TAZROUK

Nov 19, 2218

"GOOD MORNING, PROFESSOR."

"Good morning, Alma."

"Before we get started, were there any new developments related to the people who have been following you?"

"No, thankfully nothing has happened. But then again, in my timeline it has only been a day since we spoke."

"Yes, I understand. It's been over a month in this timeline."

Just then, Hena walks in and gives me a bear hug and a passionate kiss. I guess from her point of view it felt like I've been gone a month.

When we're done, we sit down. She straightens her neck and says in a professional tone: "From our side, we are ready to start your theoretical instruction, but we can only do that when you are absolutely convinced of what we are doing. As I have previously explained, we cannot not risk teaching you everything until you commit to using that knowledge exactly in the way we instruct."

I take in a breath to speak, but Hena puts her hand up and continues: "Remember, Alma will need to sense full conviction in your pledge, so if you are not ready for it, tell us what we still need to show you or do to get you there. A half-hearted response will not cut it."

"I . . . need a few minutes. I know I'm not as ready as you suspect, but I can't quite articulate why."

Alma says with some humor in her voice: "Take your time, Professor"

I get up, walk around and shake my head as I answer: "I'm worried that humanity has lost its free will. That's what's nagging me in the back of my mind."

Hena gets up and walks over to me. "We would never let that happen," she says. "Free will is one of the very things that defines us as humans."

"And yet Alma has her, um, 'hands' on everything. Alma, don't take this the wrong way, but I don't really buy that humans have free will when you can influence them so much through data and analyses and your technology. Look, if I push this to the extreme, you could even be faking all of those UPC meetings, presenting each chancellor with exactly what they need to hear in order to decide the way you want them to. And the truth is that they would never know. They would think that the other person has actually said something that they might have never said. And that is just one example; the same could be happening in everything from people's choice of profession to their choice of a life mate, in addition to political decision-making."

Alma answers this time: "But why would I do that, Professor? I do not deny that I would have the capability to do so, but why on Earth—or in space, for that matter—would I ever want to?"

"I don't know. I really don't. But you asked me to have absolute conviction, and as long as that doubt is in my mind, I struggle to 'be there,' as Hena put it."

Hena grabs my hands, which softens my reticence a little, but I hold firm. She smiles and says softly, as if thinking out loud, "Why don't we take you to visit the Sovereign Nation? They are, as you know, living without Alma's help, but they are also free of Alma's influence. Anyone can choose, with their own free will, to go there. I think it will help if you have an opportunity to talk to them, to ask how they see Alma, ask them why they made the choices they have made."

"Yeah, we should do that. I was curious about them, anyhow. If you remember, I had asked Orr to consider letting me visit."

Alma jumps in: "And consider he has—he has given me permission to organize it, should you ask again to go there."

Hena looks pleased. "Very well, then, it's decided. Alma will need a bit of time to organize a visit with their leader. They call him Commander Moulin, but we call him Chancellor Moulin."

"That's an unusual name. Is he French?"

"No, he had a different birth name. He called himself Moulin after he joined the Sovereign Nation. Some say it was because he considers himself as powerful as a circular glacier, often called a Moulin. Others say that he chose that name after the French resistance leader, Jean Moulin. I have no idea; you can ask him yourself if you wish."

"I might, although it might be an awkward question to ask."

"Also—and you won't like this—I think there is no way that Orr will let us go without him joining us on that visit. He will see it as official business and, as you know, he is a Chancellor, the Vice-Prime Minister, and the Superintendent of Restitution, so no matter how you look at it, he will feel like it is his duty to join us."

I sigh, knowing she's right, then change the subject. "Is there anything I should know ahead of time? Are there any special rules we need to follow while there, or any cultural norms I should not trip over?"

"Yes and no. These people are very much like us, except that they've chosen to live without Alma. But there is no specific cult, religion, or philosophy they live by; they are pretty much like the rest of us and, indeed, there is a reasonable number of people that join or leave the Sovereign Nation every year."

"But?"

"Well, they do follow different official rules and a different government regime. As I think I mentioned in a prior visit, they elect their leader directly—Alma makes sure of that, since it's part of our treaty. But once that leader is elected, they have absolute authority, very much like a military autocratic state. That means they have a very clear and rigid command and control structure and, as you will see when we are there, decisions are delivered as orders to be followed, not suggestions."

"How about this Moulin guy, what's he like?"

"Naturally, he is a highly admired leader. He's been re-elected seven times. He does govern with an iron fist, but most of the people in the Sovereign Nation actually feel that is the best way for their nation to operate. You will meet him, so you can make your own impression, but if I were to offer my own, I would say that he's a highly intelligent and charismatic man, but also not a pleasant person to be around. I don't know him well, but have been in a few meetings with him, mostly relating to your case. From that exposure, I can say that dealing with him always feels like negotiating peace terms in times of war; he is always combative, firm, oppositional."

"He sounds like an aggressive fellow."

"I wouldn't say aggressive, but certainly assertive. I think the fact that he has zero sense of humor and no personal warmth also doesn't help."

"He and Orr must get along well."

Hena just smiles, looks down.

"Are we in any danger, given that we're not being protected by Alma?"

"No, we are still protected by Alma. Our treaty states that visitors sponsored by Alma can continue to wear protective suits. That pretty much guarantees our personal safety, as our suits would protect us against any harm they might try to inflict."

"How might they try to harm us?"

"In many ways; they have guns, mostly like the ones you knew in your time, although some are more advanced. And they have bombs, as well. They use them to manage unrest within their own nation."

"Are you saying that in two hundred years, the weapons systems have barely advanced?"

"Yes. You have to remember that Alma has no need for offensive weapons and while the Sovereign Nation may try to advance weaponry, their technological infrastructure is stunted by their size and lack of resources."

"So if they were to try anything, it would be with conventional weapons?"

"Yes, but rest assured—over the last few decades, there has been very little violence even within the Sovereign Nation, so I think there is virtually no risk to us. Alma, would you agree with my assessment?"

"Yes, I would. I have limited insight into the personalities you will be dealing with, as I do not have visibility into what happens within the Sovereign Nation. I cannot survey environments or people's individual actions and body language, so I infer only from external events that I can observe. But even given these limitations, I assess the risk of any disruptions to be very limited."

"That's reassuring. Will we have some kind of escort with us?"

Hena answers. "No, the treaty forbids any peacekeeping force provided by Alma from entering the Sovereign Nation, unless there is an imminent threat to any of our citizens."

"Okay. If you are comfortable, I am comfortable."

"Yes, I am. Did you have any more questions or concerns we should address?"

"No, not really."

"Then why don't you and I return to my quarters while Alma and Orr discuss the details of our visit? I can tell you a bit more about the commander and some of his lieutenants, who will be there."

"Okay."

THE NEXT MORNING AFTER BREAKFAST, ORR SHOWS UP, AND ALL three of us get on a pod to go to the colony. The journey there is uneventful, Orr seems busy working on something, which gives me and Hena the perfect excuse to ignore him and play a few games. A few minutes before we arrive, we enter a long, dark tunnel. We come out the other end into a barren patch of dirt, or maybe it's sand—it's hard to tell under the scorching sun. Surrounding us are high rock walls in what looks like a large circular canyon. We approach the center.

As soon as our pod docks, I can tell that this will be a formal state visit. There must be a couple hundred people standing around in a circle, with a dozen or so in a triangular formation behind a brown-skinned man, whom I guess is Commander Moulin. They are all dressed in full military gear, but the kind that people wear to ceremonies, not combat gear. We step out, an usher receives us, and escorts us on the fifty-meter walk from our pod to the commander. Orr walks up front, Hena follows, and then me. The commander and Orr exchange formal greetings and small gifts, though I hadn't noticed that Orr had anything with him until now. Hena also greets the commander formally, and then it's my turn.

The commander extends his hand. "Mr. Weissman, it is a pleasure to receive you in our free nation."

I match his firm handshake. "Commander Moulin, it is an honor to be here. Thank you for receiving us."

There are a few brief intros to the other four Lieutenants around him and then, without any further warning, he turns around and starts a brisk walk towards a tunnel entrance in the rock wall, followed by his lieutenants. We follow right behind in the same order as before and, behind us, the rest of his entourage marches on.

As we walk, the commander projects his loud voice: "This is the entry tunnel into the Sovereign Nation. It is the only safe way into the nation, since the rest of our air space is protected by anti-air missiles, and the rock wall we are crossing under is two hundred meters wide—virtually impenetrable. You must understand that we have to protect ourselves; we are a very small free nation in a world united under a single regime. A regime that is friendly to us, but nevertheless, a different regime."

We reach a moving walkway that accelerates, making our walk much faster than it would have been otherwise. When we get to the other side, we might as well be in another continent. We come out in the middle of an urban plaza bustling with people moving in all directions. I see a street market a few hundred meters to the right, a large fountain right in front of us, and what appears to be a restaurant and bar strip to the left. Somehow I was expecting a military camp, not a bustling downtown core. But this place looks like fun.

Moulin seems to notice my surprise, and he smiles. "Beautiful, isn't it? Welcome to Tazrouk. It is one of our more prosperous cities, and the one I call home."

"And where are we located, geographically?"

"We are right in the middle of what used to be the Sahara Desert, except we have terraformed most of it into productive land."

Moulin continues to walk towards a building with Arabic architecture that looks like a palace, though not a very sumptuous one. As we enter the main chamber, the cool, refreshing air is a welcome change from the scorching sun outside. We're escorted towards a large dining hall and told that we will first be treated to a formal meal. "They are very proud of their legendary hospitality," Hena murmurs to me.

We're seated in very specific spots: Orr is facing Commander Moulin, while Hena and I are each seated to one of Orr's sides. Moulin is flanked by his four lieutenants.

As wash buckets are brought around for each of us, Commander Moulin starts the conversation.

"So, Mr. Weissman. I hear you were curious about our way of living, which is why you wanted to come visit. I have to say that I have a few questions for you myself, but I will gladly answer yours first."

I nod politely. He points at himself and says, "Fire away!"

"Thank you, Commander. I guess the first question I have is how you ended up in the Sovereign Nation. Were you born here, or did you come later in life?"

"I was born in Alma's domain. I am ninety-seven years old, so the time I was growing up was precisely the time when Alma was solidifying its current power, becoming more and more able to provide for humans, to satisfy their every desire. When I was twenty-six years old, after I had graduated from priming school, I decided I did not want to continue being a puppet of some artificial intelligence. I packed my bags and came to the free nation."

Orr fidgets uncomfortably, but says nothing. I guess Moulin is free to say whatever he wants in his land.

"Why do you say you were a puppet?"

"Because Alma has a tremendous amount of control and power. For all I know, Alma manipulates everyone even if they think they have freedom. And I never liked this idea that some artificial intelligence would evaluate me, my potential, and then decide what I can and cannot do based on that assessment. The final drop in the proverbial bucket for me was when, at the end of priming school, we went to watch an UPC meeting, which all graduating classes have the so-called privilege to watch. What I saw shocked and sickened me; Alma provides all the information, all the analysis for decision-making, and even advice to the Prime Minister. I think that system is rigged."

I pick my words carefully. "I see your point of view. What about all the good Alma does? How do you see all that she does—"

He interrupts me: "*It* does."

I decide to risk offending him and hold firm. "You can refer to her as 'it,' but I prefer 'she.' Back to the question: how do you feel about all that she provides for humanity?"

"Very nice indeed, but that to me is a bit like asking how I feel about a prison where you get well fed and well cared for, while being brainwashed into thinking that the comfort you have there should make up for the lack of freedom."

"But people can always come to the Sovereign Nation, as you did, right?"

"Sure, but if you are fat and happy, why would you? I am not saying that Alma forces anyone into submission; it bribes and corrupts them by providing everything they need."

"Do you ever feel threatened by Alma?"

"Not especially. I actually think Alma should feel threatened by us. Eventually I believe humanity will realize the trap it has been put into and do something about it. I just hope it is not too late."

"Why would it ever be too late?"

"The more powerful Alma becomes, the less likely it is that people would see through it."

I've been eating while Moulin speaks, but I suddenly notice he has not touched his food. Mostly out of courtesy I offer: "Thank you, it is very helpful to hear your perspective. You said you had some questions for me. Do you want to ask them?"

"Yes. I will start with the obvious one: I would imagine that you have your own perspective on this strange world under Alma, having landed here suddenly. Since there is no risk of you slowly becoming accustomed to the idea, I would hope you see the issues with it right away."

I try to be polite, but it's hard: "Was there a question?"

Moulin continues unfazed. "Yes, of course: how did this strange world strike you when you came in?"

"It seems like an amazing, wonderful world, to be frank. Where I come from, humanity suffers from disease, famine, pollution, violence, terrorism, environmental degradation, religious extremism, domestic violence, gang violence, the threat of nuclear extermination, and many other issues that aren't coming to mind right now. So when I was exposed to Alma's world, I was ecstatic; it is like a utopic society."

A bit exasperated, speaking over a mouthful, he says, "But don't you see the danger in that? Don't you see how free will was dampened, if not eliminated entirely?"

"I see the risk, and indeed it was one of the reasons I wanted to meet you and see your nation. But I see no real evidence that any manipulation is actually happening. People can leave Alma at any time. I'm also convinced that humans, the UPC specifically, make all the real decisions."

He scowls at me, clearly unhappy with the turn the conversation has taken.

Since I'm in deep, I decide I might as well keep digging: "I also don't see what motivation Alma would have to control humans in the way you describe it. She doesn't really need us. We don't compete with her for resources and, in fact, she could wipe us out in a heartbeat, Sovereign Nation and all. And yet I think humans actually entertain her. I think she genuinely cares about humans."

Moulin stops eating, his expression a mix of rage and deep disappointment. "Well, it seems your mind is made up. We should have gotten to you earlier. I say we all retreat for the day. Tomorrow we shall visit some of the villages."

We're escorted to our rooms. Orr is put in a room on the first floor, while Hena and I are escorted to a room upstairs. The gentleman who walks us up gives us a knowing smile and says that they have put us together.

Hena and I look around as soon as we get inside our room. It's an enormous, lavish suite entirely decorated in Arabian style, golden carvings and tapestry everywhere. I've seen places like this in my time, but the sight of the suite clearly takes Hena aback; she walks around noticing every little detail. We approach the arched windows and marvel at the view of the green valley below, observing the day-to-day life still bustling in the early evening.

Just then, we hear a click at the door.

Hena looks alarmed. "Have they locked us in?"

I check the door. "They have."

Hena's face pales further. "I don't like being confined. It's not an experience anyone grows accustomed to under Alma's care."

"Should we be worried?" I ask, frowning at the door handle. "Should I hammer on the door and demand they let us out?"

"No, we're safe; remember, we have Alma's suit. Maybe they did this for our own protection. Surely us walking around alone in the Sovereign Nation would not be in anyone's best interest."

I still feel a bit uneasy, but Hena is probably right, so I change the subject. "Boy, Moulin really has strong opinions."

"What did you expect? He leads the only nation that doesn't live under Alma."

"I don't know what I expected. Maybe a more balanced view."

"He's the wrong man for that."

"Yeah, clearly."

"I'm tired. I'm going to get some sleep," Hena says, sinking onto the bed. "You should too."

She falls asleep quickly, but I take a lot longer to fall into what turns out to be restless, dreamless sleep.

IN THE MORNING, WE'RE WOKEN UP BY A KNOCK ON OUR DOOR and a voice informing us that breakfast will be served in thirty minutes, in our suite. Precisely thirty minutes later, we are served a very rich, if unusual, breakfast composed of mezze dishes and several types of bread, along with strong tea. As we're finishing breakfast, one of the lieutenants that accompanied Moulin yesterday, Joya, walks into our room unannounced.

In a serious but courteous tone, she greets us: "Good morning Professor, Hena. I trust you had a pleasant and restful evening, and an enjoyable breakfast."

"Yes, very much so, thank you," Hena replies.

"We have planned specific activities for each of you today. Hena should visit the farming communities while Richard will visit some of the more industrialized zones."

Hena looks at her thoughtfully, as if pondering the right response. I beat her to it and protest: "I really don't like the idea of us doing separate activities. Can we visit the same places, together?"

"Of course you could, but that would surely not be the most efficient way to give you a view of how we live. There is much to see and not much time. Let me show you each the program we have built for you during the day, then you can make a decision."

She hands us each a piece of paper with hourly activities for the day. Immediately, I start sweating; the first line of my program says "The king is naked." I glance over at Hena's schedule, but hers is missing that line.

Joya gives me a knowing look.

I immediately tuck my program close to my chest and change my tone. "Very well, this does seem like a packed agenda. And I suppose we can always exchange notes at the end of the day."

"That's the idea."

Hena frowns slightly and shrugs.

We exit the suite and go our separate ways with our own escorts when the corridors split in two directions. After we can no longer see or hear Hena, Joya grabs my arm. "I'm sorry if this felt uncomfortable," she says. "Moulin had to find a way to see you alone."

"Why?"

"I will let him explain that." She motions for me to walk through a wide set of doors across the hall we are standing in.

As I walk in, I see Moulin looking at some kind of holographic schematic. I can't quite understand what it's showing. It looks like a war planning room, with maps and stats in 3D and big screen displays everywhere. The technology seems quite advanced to me.

He turns to me and nods. "Professor, we meet again, this time without extra company. Please, have a seat."

I sit across from him on a comfortable a wooden chair. "And why is that necessary, exactly?"

"Well, for starters, I realize you may not have been able to tell me exactly how you felt. It occurred to me later that Orr and Hena might be holding you hostage, forcing you to behave a certain way. I should have thought of that before you arrived. I had no intention of putting you in a difficult situation."

"That is not the case. I appreciate the concern, but that was not an issue."

"In any case, I could sense that while you believe that Alma on the whole is a positive presence, you also have your doubts about free will."

I pause for a while, trying to compose my thoughts. I came here to meet these people and get a sense for how they see Alma, but something in this whole set up has left me apprehensive. I'm not sure I can trust them. Eventually, I decide to open up a bit.

"Yes, I do. I agree with you that Alma has the capability to manipulate people. And indeed I am uneasy about that, which as I said yesterday is why I asked to come here."

Moulin nods widely and gives me a knowing smile.

I feel compelled to continue: "But I also see no concrete evidence that it is happening. Your very existence seems to prove that free will still exists."

Moulin's smile is gone immediately. "Look, there is no way of knowing whether Alma is or is not manipulating humans. We would not be able to see it. And to me, that is beside the point. The very fact that we, humans, have allowed such an intelligence to come into being is the real issue. It is an untenable situation; we should have never let that happen!"

"I hear you, but on balance, it would seem to me that Alma has been very positive for humanity."

"That is because you are focusing on the material benefits; sure we are all cared for, there is no more hunger, no more disease. But what about free will!?"

"That was why I wanted to come here. You have free will. You chose to live without Alma, right?"

"Yes, but we are but a small enlightened minority. What about the rest of brainwashed humans Alma controls?"

"How are they controlled? They can come here anytime they want."

"Yes, but you forget that Alma has catered to their every need. She has spoiled humanity into submission. Don't you see?"

"No, not really. I see it as a mutually beneficial relationship. Alma provides material comfort, and humans in turn follow simple guidelines provided by their own leaders, the UPC."

Moulin scowls: "Hah, the UPC! A bunch of brainwashed cowards who should not be leading humanity."

"Look, I'm not even sure there is much you can do. Alma is much more powerful than all of humanity combined. Assuming I agree with you—and I am by no means saying I do—what would you have me do?"

Moulin gets up, sits on the edge of the table, and looks down at me intensely. "I have a very simple proposition for you: go back to your time-line, find whoever created this artificial intelligence, and convince them to stop their work. Use force if necessary."

I frown. "And how, exactly, would I find that person?"

"We can help. We have not been able to fully reconstruct the records behind Alma's creation yet, but we are getting close. Alma guards that secret carefully, but I think in another few months, we will have cracked it."

"That would be too late, anyway. I don't have much longer."

"We can pull your consciousness into the future as well. We do not control technology as advanced as Alma's; all we can do is pull individual people in a dream state for a couple of minutes. But that is enough to deliver images, abstract concepts, and simple messages. We brought you here in person partially so we could get your resonance signature; now we can bring you forward in dream state. And since you already know what's happening, you will know exactly how to interpret these dreams."

My heart is pounding; I get up and walk around the room, gathering my thoughts. I now understand why I was summoned to talk to Moulin alone—it's a set-up. He's trying to manipulate me. How did I let him gain control of the agenda so quickly? This conversation was just supposed to let me learn more about their nation. I feel grossly outplayed.

I face Moulin, still standing.

"Look, if you were right, then more and more humans would come live with you in the Sovereign Nation, and that's not happening, from what I hear. Plus, whoever likes the arrangement under Alma should have the right to live there. I am sorry, Commander, but there is nothing you can say that will convince me to eliminate Alma's creator, even if you could help me find them."

Moulin runs his hands through his sleek hair while walking around the table to sit back down. I sit back down too. He lets out a deep sigh. "Your mind is made up?"

"Yes, absolutely. Any more time you spend trying to convince me will be a waste of time. The best I can do is keep your secret. I will not discuss this with Alma."

Moulin leans back, through gritted teeth he lets off a low growl. Then he gets up again and pounds his fist on the table. "You are a fool! I will not let you doom all of humanity to this idle existence. You will suffer the full consequences of your decision."

The door opens and two guards escort me out of the room. We descend a set of stone stairs and enter a cold, damp chamber that branches off into five dark corridors. I notice metal bars across the walls. This must be some kind of dungeon.

The guard nudges me forward. "Keep moving. You will be joining your friends."

I hold my breath and walk towards the cell he points to. He shoves me into the dark cell and I notice that both Orr and Hena are unconscious. At least, I hope they are only unconscious. I inch my way forward towards Hena and eventually muster the courage to touch her; she is indeed unconscious, but warm and breathing. With some effort, I manage to wake her up.

She hugs me, then whispers, "Did they drug you, too?"

"No, but Moulin wanted to have a private chat. I guess he didn't like what I had to say. Is Orr drugged, too?"

"I assume so. The last thing I remember is drinking refreshments at the village we visited, not more than half an hour after we went our separate ways."

We wake up Orr. He's furious. "That bastard Moulin! Does he not realize that this will cause an international incident? This will force us to review the very foundations of our treaty. Maybe he underestimates Alma."

He looks at me and Hena. "Were you two harmed?"

We both shake our heads. "What do you think he's planning to do?" I ask. "Why arrest us?"

"I'm not sure. I can't imagine how he thinks this will end well for him."

"Will Alma not rescue us?"

"Not unless we are put in danger. Alma is completely oblivious to our situation. They must have used very mild sedatives, otherwise our suits would have set off alarms to Alma."

"Maybe they did set off alarms?"

"No. If Alma were already in motion, we would know."

"Then what, we just wait?"

"Yes, pretty much. Either they will try something stupid and that will trigger Alma, or Alma will get suspicious if we take too long to come back, in which case she will make an assessment of the risk and, should her calculations conclude that there is real danger, the treaty would allow her to act."

"Well, that's not very reassuring."

"We are protected by our suits. You have nothing to fear, Richard."

"You sure? They have already outsmarted our suits once today. Whatever sedative they gave you and Hena didn't set any alarms off."

"You weren't drugged?"

"No, Moulin wanted to talk to me alone. I guess that's why he drugged you."

Orr stops fidgeting with the chain under his legs, tenses his shoulders, and looks up without facing me.

"And what did he have to say? What—exactly—did he say?"

"The same things you heard last night, plus that he wanted me to find Alma's creators in the past and stop them."

Orr seems to relax his shoulders. "And what did you tell him?"

"I told him to go to hell, so I guess us being here is partly my fault."

Orr shakes his head. "This is Moulin's fault, and Moulin's alone."

That seems to settle the conversation, at least for now. After my eyes adjust to the low light, I look around and assess the cell we were put in. It is clearly from another time; there is one comfort hole in the corner and not much else, other than hooks of several shapes, sizes, and heights on the walls. I try, unsuccessfully, to avoid much speculation about what they would have been used for.

After a couple of hours, the two guards that brought me to the cell show up again, accompanied by four other guards. We're escorted up the stairs and out of the building and guided roughly on a ten-minute walk to what appears to be the main plaza in the city. Moulin is there with his entourage in triangular formation again. As I look around, I see a large crowd gathered in a big circle. There must be a few thousand people around. I also notice the two hundred or so soldiers in the first couple of rows, some faces familiar from the prior day, except this time they are all wearing combat gear, not celebratory uniforms. I wonder why they are dressed for war; could they expect to fight Alma? That would be absolutely moronic. There is no way they could win. This might turn into bloodshed. Maybe I should have pretended to agree to Moulin's proposal; he would have had no way to enforce his orders. It might have avoided a lot of violence. I consider trying that now, but realize he would not believe me anymore.

We're pushed up onto a large stage, opposite the platform where Moulin and his lieutenants are, about fifteen meters away from us. Orr, Hena, and I are each cuffed to a different pole by our hands and feet. Moulin taps a microphone tied to his uniform as if testing for sound. Seeming satisfied, he starts in a firm, measured tone:

"We are gathered here today to make history. Standing before us are three humans. Humans. We should never forget that. And should not take lightly what we are about to do, for they are, like us, flesh and blood. However, they are also very different than us in many ways. They have been blinded, corrupted, and infected by Alma. They are, in fact, not unlike the other seventy-five billion people who have also been perverted. They are an integral part of the very system that we rebel against. As many of you know, standing before you are Chancellor Orr, the leader of the Restitution program that does Alma's bidding in the past, Professor Richard Weissman, who for all intents and purposes started Restitution nearly two hundred years ago, and Hena, his handler, who would teach him everything he needs to know in order to do that. These three humans have the potential to derail, to destroy everything we have been working for—but I—we—will not let that happen!"

As Moulin finishes his sentence, fists pounding up in the air, the crowd breaks into thunderous applause. Moulin waits for it to subside before continuing:

"Today, we fight back. They come here clad in their inhuman suits, making it virtually impossible to hurt them. No guns, bombs, or blades can reach them, no matter how fast or powerful we make them—trust me, we have tried. But today, we use human ingenuity against Alma's power and omnipresence. Today, we poison these three people so they cannot complete the tasks that Alma has set them out to do. They will die here, in less than ten minutes, and their bodies will not register anything abnormal until their final moments, when it will be too late for Alma to help them."

Again there is thunderous applause, this time for at least a couple of minutes.

He raises his hands in the air. "Let the revolution begin!" The crowd goes mad again.

Orr convulses against the pole, trying to free himself, shouting words I can't make out over the loud crowd. Hena is also shouting something at Moulin, the veins in her neck popping out in a way that looks painful. I

285

can't muster the will to say anything; then I wonder if I will die also, or if I will simply wake up in my timeline. That would be worse than dying. I would be condemned to a life without Hena, and to a life of not knowing what actually happened in the future, what could have happened, what would have happened—did that future even happen?

As the crowd cheers, three soldiers walk up the stage, very solemnly. They each stand in front of Orr, Hena, and myself for a few seconds. Hena spits on the face of the soldier in front of her. He wipes it off but stands his ground. Hena then looks at me, and I'm thankful for the time I have to give Hena one final look.

She mouths the words: "I love you."

Before I can reply, I am startled by a cold patch placed on my neck, about the size of a small bandage. I look at Hena and Orr and see that they each have one as well. The crowd goes very quiet once the patches are all on; Moulin looks straight at me with steely eyes.

I look at Hena, who is moving frantically. She looks at me and mouths something several times. I squint, and finally understand: "Heart rate!"

Of course—she's trying to get her heart rate up. I start moving myself. It's hard to make much progress with my hands and feet cuffed to the poles. I feel the handcuffs cut into my skin. That could be good—my body might give Alma more stress signals.

As I move, I can't help but wonder if this is my final day—our final day. What if I actually die? Will I see Sarah again? Would she know about Hena? What a stupid thing to worry about; she would not expect me to be faithful to a dead wife. I shake that thought away and more somber ones fill the void: will this hurt? Does poison death hurt? Oh no, will Hena be in pain? I look at her, and she's still moving as much as she can.

After what must be the promised five minutes, I start to feel it. This must be what death itself feels like: a combination of shortness of breath, a wrenching pain in my stomach, as if invisible hands were churning my organs incessantly, a burning sensation in my veins, and weakness in my muscles as I have never experienced before. As I crumble, grasping onto the pole, I notice Hena is also bending over, while Orr still seems to be standing firm. I wonder if the poison didn't affect him.

The pain is all-encompassing. I can barely absorb what's happening, but I hear the commander say in his mic: "Ready yourselves for battle! And remember, we only have to hold them back for two or three minutes!"

With what little energy I have left, I look up. I see several of Alma's hovercrafts dropping peacekeepers onto the floor around our platform, all clad in their suits, covered from head to toe. Our suits also close up over our heads and hands, although I can still breathe and see. Moulin's army shoots at will with several machine guns, rocket propelled grenades, and some other weapons I don't recognize. These shoot out a blue energy mass that looks like it carries some sort of shock wave, but all of the beams are deflected by the peacekeepers' suits.

I also notice that the peacekeepers don't shoot or hit back; they simply keep walking, as if the attackers weren't there. Some of the weapons stun them momentarily, but a few seconds, later they start walking again. They are closing in around us.

In the middle of battle, I hear Alma's calm voice: "Humans of the Sovereign Nation, I wish you no harm. I can do you no harm. But I can and will extract the prisoners and defend the peacekeepers. You must know that resistance is futile." She repeats that over and over again.

Just then, I see a number of Moulin's soldiers across our platform armed with RPGs, pointing them directly at each of us. They shoot.

The few milliseconds of a rocket traveling in my direction are almost beautiful, poetic. Then the realization that I'm about to be hit by a grenade sinks in, just a few moments before the actual bomb hits me.

The impact itself, however, is surprisingly uneventful. The suit shields it almost perfectly; I feel the vibrations across its surface, travelling back and forth in waves to transfer the impact to the platform underneath me. Then I realize I've been knocked back, the post behind me destroyed. As I fall back from the platform, I brace for impact with the floor, but the suit cushions me perfectly again—it feels like falling on a mattress. Adrenaline must have kicked in, because the symptoms of the poison are less debilitating. I look sideways and see that Hena has fallen as well. I don't see Orr. Hena's not moving, but then again, neither am I. Suddenly, the suit releases me again and I can move, but the pain still makes it difficult. I crawl jerkily forwards a few steps before I feel the suit take over; I'm no longer in control of my movements.

I hear Alma's voice in my head, or maybe in my suit: "Richard, relax and do not try to move. The more you struggle, the more the poison travels in your blood."

I relax and the suit takes over. Seven or eight soldiers are closing in on us from all sides. They are moving inhumanly fast, but they are dressed in the Sovereign Nation's uniforms, not Alma's suits. In the split second before they reach us, five of our peacekeepers intersect them, fighting in what I can best describe as accelerated martial arts. Both sides display incredible skill, their movements precise, strong, and inhumanly fast. I notice that the peacekeepers are only defending themselves; not once do they strike back, although they clearly could if they wanted to. They are faster, and not a single blow from the Sovereign Nation's soldiers lands as desired.

Just then, I feel a slight tug and hear Alma's voice: "I'm taking you up."

I feel myself being carried upwards by some unseen force or device. I look at Hena and Orr and see that they too are being carried up by small hovering machines. All three of us are reeled onto the larger hovering craft, where three peacekeepers wait with syringes in hand. Once my suit has revealed my neck and face again, one of them turns to me.

"Be still," the peacekeeper says. "I have to use a syringe—I apologize, but we have no time."

She sticks the syringe in my neck. I feel the sting of the needle, but seconds later, all of the pain in my gut and the shortness of breath are gone. Orr and Hena get up as well.

"You okay?" I ask Hena.

"Yes, just a little shaken," she says.

Orr seems to ignore us; he's looking down, so we do the same. The peacekeepers are walking back to the central spot in the plaza, seemingly oblivious to the shots, RPGs, and electrified cannon balls coming at them from every side. They do not shoot back and do not try to evade or even acknowledge the attackers; it's as if they weren't being attacked at all. They gather peacefully in the middle of the plaza, where Alma collects all of them with the little hover machines. I hear Alma in a loud, calm voice: "We have retrieved the three prisoners. We have no more business in the Sovereign Nation and are withdrawing. Please cease all hostility in the name of your own safety. Many from your nation have already died or been wounded. No more suffering is necessary."

With that, our hovercraft flies away. We soar over the supposedly impenetrable rock and past the anti-air artillery that Moulin had been so proud of. Shots and missiles are intercepted in the air with such ease and precision that it is almost as if they were traveling in slow motion.

Once we're out of the firing zone, Hena and I relax and cuddle. Being this close to death has made me realize that what I feel for her is much more than physical attraction or friendship.

"I love you," I say quietly.

"I love you too."

Orr is quiet all the way back. I can't figure out if he's upset, embarrassed, worried, or all of the above.

Alma brings us back safely. We go through full medical checks before Alma addresses Hena and I, after Orr is no longer around: "I would suggest you two get a good night's sleep before we debrief and discuss what's next. This has been a traumatic day for you."

"Yeah, my mind is racing. I'm not sure I would be of much use tonight," I reply.

THE NEXT MORNING, AFTER I HAVE HAD TIME TO REFLECT ON what happened, I call Alma.

"Good morning, Alma. Let me start by saying thank you for saving us yesterday. And thank you for doing that with minimal casualties on both sides. If that were a conflict in my time, the attackers would have been massacred. Aggression by you and the peacekeepers towards them would actually have been justified, and yet I saw none. Not only that, your technological superiority was very clear. I know if you wanted to, you could have inflicted casualties very easily."

"Yes, your assessment is correct, Professor. But as I said, I would never hurt humans, even if and when they misbehave."

"Who were the soldiers that came up at the end? They were almost as fast as the peacekeepers, and yet it didn't seem like they had your suits."

"No, these were genetically enhanced humans. I did not know the Sovereign Nation had followed through with their threats to break the Tianjin protocol."

"I know we have covered this, but what's the Tianjin protocol again?"

"It is an international agreement that is 179 years old. It prohibits any and all genetic alteration of humans that is not absolutely required to eliminate disease. It bans human enhancements of all kinds. It in fact also includes human/machine hybrids; there were some experiments in the late twenty-first century in which humans were enhanced with nanotechnology that all ended terribly badly, so humans signed the Tianjin treaty to ban all kinds of human enhancements. I can keep track of what is happening almost everywhere, but our treaty with the Sovereign Nation did not allow me to veer into their territory—until now."

"If there is a silver lining in this whole mess, it's that I'm now convinced you truly have humanity's best interests at heart."

"Thank you, Professor. I am saddened by the many self-inflicted casualties on the Sovereign Nation's side, but glad that it has caused you to see things as they are."

"I have indeed seen things as they are. And I pledge, with my full conviction this time, to do whatever you ask me to do. Nothing more, nothing less."

"I can see you mean the words, Professor."

"There is one more thing: I haven't told you everything the Sovereign Nation is doing, and I haven't told you a few related things that happened here, during the fashion show, and back in my timeline."

Hena gives me a blank look, but I can see through it—she's hurt. I look away and continue: "Moulin has found a way to bring people from the past."

"That is highly unlikely."

"I know, but it's not quite like your technology. Apparently, he can intervene in their dreams, send simple messages."

Alma sounds unconvinced: "That would be possible, but unlikely. I do not believe they would have the processing capacity or the energy to do it."

"I know it is true—they keep startling me with the sentence 'the king is naked' here. It happened once at the fashion show, inside one of the tents, and then again in the Sovereign Nation. Mr. Edwards used the exact same phrase in my timeline, which is what actually made me lose it that day. Somehow they got that message back in time. I'm not sure what else they have been able to communicate."

"Thank you, Professor. That is indeed very important information. Vital, in fact."

"I'm sorry I kept it for you, I just didn't know who to trust." I turn to Hena. "And Hena, I'm sorry I kept it from you, too. I decided to keep it quiet the first time, and then it got harder and harder to bring you into the loop. At first I didn't think anything of it, and then I was afraid you'd be upset, and I felt embarrassed that I didn't trust you."

Hena looks down and grabs my hands.

Alma continues. "We will teach you what you need to know. However, we have already had too much emotion for one visit. I would suggest we teach you what you need to know next time."

"Yeah, that seems to make sense to me too. I'm not sure I could absorb much theoretical physics right now."

"That will also mean you can do a few things in your timeline that will increase our chances of success."

"I'm all ears. What would these things be?"

"You will tell Frank and Sun what is happening."

"Everything? They'll think I'm crazy! They are already half wondering if I've gone insane!"

"I can see how that might be a challenge, but sooner or later you will have to face that problem, the records show that they helped you in your work. And I cannot be there to help, unfortunately."

"No, but can you give me something that will convince them? Maybe some sports event that is happening tomorrow that I can make predictions with, like Hena did with me?"

"Nothing remarkable or improbable enough to convince them is happening tomorrow in your timeline. But there is something else I can do. It should only be used if needed, since I have no evidence that this particular problem had external help in its solution, but I will show you how to prove the Riemann hypothesis, which as you know has been an unsolved problem in mathematics in your timeline for over one hundred years."

"Do I have enough knowledge to understand your explanation? It's not my field of study."

"You should. The solution requires a clever transformation and lots of computing power. You should do this in your lab. Activate the DoD cloud service you have access to. You will need it."

"And you are confident this will convince them?"

"Sun will understand how difficult this is, so that should be enough to convince her, and Frank will follow Sun's lead, as he always does."

"This will not be a fun conversation, but I see no better alternative. Show me how."

16

OUTLANDISH

Sep 8, 2018

I WAKE UP EARLY BACK IN MY HOME TIMELINE, BEFORE 7AM. I call the department again and tell them I'm sick and will miss all of my appointments today. I know this is getting out of hand, but I don't care anymore. If I am going to bring Frank and Sun into the tent, I should do it in our lab, since it's the most professional environment I can think of, and Alma suggested I may need to use our full infrastructure.

After I run, shower, and eat breakfast, I text Frank and Sun:

> **Me:** "Hi guys. I've smthg very imprtnt to say. Need to meet today. ASAP."

I get nothing back for the first 20 minutes, which worries me, but then I realize they might be driving to work. It's 8:15. At 8:21 I hear back:

> **Sun:** "Richard I've clses and mtgs today. Do I need to be there?"

Me: "Yeah, both of you. Very imprtnt. Pls cancel what u can. Don't need all day, but need a few hours."

Frank: "I can move most things if Sun can make it."

Me: "Sun?"

Sun: "Can move few things to the AM, cld meet after 11. This better be REALLY imprtnt."

Me: "It is."

Frank: "Works. Where?"

Me: "Our lab. Need some of the infra there."

Sun: "Fine."

Me: "Ok."

I get there much earlier than them and rehearse the conversation several times. I'm not sure why am I so nervous about this. Sun and Frank walk in together at 11am sharp—on time, as always. They look worried, but not as upset as last time; Frank actually sports the perennial smirk I have grown used to.

After greetings, I start the conversation: "Guys, I have a confession to make, and it will explain why I've been acting so weird lately."

Frank pounds the table. "A new woman, I knew it!" He turns to Sun. "Ha! I told you!"

Sun cocks her head at me with an inquiring look.

"Well, that too," I say sheepishly, "but that's not the real confession."

"What, then?" Frank says, flinging his arms open.

"Well, it's complicated. Very complicated. I'm not even sure I know where to start."

"Start at the beginning. Always works."

"All right." I take a deep breath and start: "I woke up the other day, except that I didn't quite wake up; I was still dreaming, but also no longer dreaming. I was lucid. And I was in a different place. Well, technically a different place and a different . . ."

Sun interrupts me: "Richard, we're really worried about you. Talking about your lucid dream is not helping!"

"Look, if I'm going to do this, you'll have to give me at least a half hour without interruption. And you have to promise to give me the benefit of the doubt. Some of what I'll tell you will sound absolutely nuts, but I'm not crazy, I swear. I'd know if I was. In fact, I haven't been more lucid in a long time. Just shut up and let me talk, will you?"

A look passes between them, one of those silent conversations that they have sometimes. Then they sigh and answer in chorus: "Okay."

"Alright, so back to the start. When I woke up, I wasn't just waking up in a different place; I was waking up in a different time. I was brought forward in time two hundred years. I woke up in the year 2218."

Frank gives me an incredulous look and starts to speak, but I raise my hand and remind him: "Half an hour without interruption and the benefit of the doubt."

Frank lowers his head. I can't read Sun, so I just continue, "It's not exactly that they brought all of me to the future. They can pull my consciousness, so I experience their reality. To use their terms, I sync with their consensual reality. That is why they do it in my sleep here, since when I am sleeping, I'm not sharing reality with anyone. Apparently it's much easier to disengage my consciousness then, since no one else is in sync with the reality of my dreams. They gave me lots of evidence that this is real—they told me exactly what was going to happen in the Real Madrid game, and we all know how improbable that was. Their technology is amazing; I will tell you more once I am through the basics."

Sun raises her hand, and I concede with a sigh. "Yes, Sun?"

"Can we ask legitimate questions?"

I nod, and she proceeds: "Why you? Why now? Why two hundred years into the future? Why not one hundred, or five hundred?"

"Those are like 3 questions. I'll get to all that. The whole point of them bringing me forward was this program called Restitution. Basically, they've been intervening in humanity's development since time immemorial, every time they look back and conclude that humans made a really improbable leap in thinking. There have been hundreds of these interventions. They call us Sprouts. Every time they intervene, it is to deliver an insight or capability—for example, when Socrates created the scientific method, or when Newton developed his laws, the Restitution program had a hand in it."

Frank blurts out: "If they keep altering the past like that all the time, wouldn't it cause all kinds of unintended consequences?"

"They claim that they are not changing the past. They are trying to make sure the future happens as they have it recorded, which is why they look back in history and find these leaps in human thinking that they feel unlikely, and which they need to help make happen."

"So they are saying that they need this program—what did you call it, Restitution?—in order to keep the time-loop they live in consistent with their experience."

"Yes, exactly."

"That could mean that there are other parallel universes where people are doing the same thing and making sure a different future happens. There could be an infinite number of Restitutions in parallel time-loops."

"I guess that's right . . . I hadn't thought of that. But let me continue—you're confusing my narrative here. Let's stick to the time-loop I know, okay?"

Frank nods.

"The reason they brought me forward specifically now, and two hundred years from now for them, is because according to them I—well, we—invent time travel. Or, more accurately, we invent the underlying technology that enables time travel, which they say is what we're working on right now."

"Our reactor?"

"I guess. They haven't gotten to that yet. They will give me all the theoretical and technological insights I need in my next visit."

"Assuming all of this is true," Sun chimes in, wearing a deep frown, "why do you think that's a good idea?"

"Because they live in a perfect world. It's better than any utopia you have ever read about. There is this organic artificial intelligence that basically provides all critical human needs. Humans still make all the decisions; the planet is united into one integrated government entity, while maintaining the cultural identities of each of their nations. There is no war, no disease, no hunger, no violence at all. People can do what they are passionate about, instead of having to work on providing food and shelter for other humans."

Frank muses out loud: "But then isn't there a nasty pervasive idleness? Like, everyone ends up being a lazy junkie?"

"No, people have to choose something to do—whatever they are passionate about. Most people work in the arts, human professions, or public service."

"No scientists?"

"Not as we think of scientists now. But that's because they are no longer needed."

Frank leans back. "Man, this is a lot to take in."

Sun turns to him seriously. "But you must also see the allure."

I answer for Frank: "Yeah, absolutely, which is why I have agreed to do what they want me to do."

Sun turns back to me. "And why are you telling us all this? Why not just do it alone? You realize we still think there is a ninety percent chance you are crazy or putting up a prank? As much as we want to believe the ten percent chance that you are for real ..."

"Alma told me to bring you guys into the tent. I guess I'll need your help to do whatever it is that she wants me to do."

"Alma, is that the woman?"

I laugh. "No, no, no. Alma is the organic AI I mentioned. The woman is Hena, my handler."

Frank now: "Your what?"

"I know, I hate the word as well. My handler; she handles my case in the program. Get it?"

"Sure, but she probably handles something else too ..."

Sun slaps him on the arm and glares at him.

I continue: "In any case, Alma is the real brains behind this whole thing."

Sun seems to finally realize what I just said. "Did you say an organic AI? What does that mean? How powerful is it?"

"Not 'it;' 'she.' Alma is a fully sentient and organic being. She was first conceived as an AI, in the way we understand it, not too far into our current future. But she has evolved. She's been organic for over one hundred years and is now a full sentient being—well, now as in during their time. That is, two hundred years from our now."

"Okay, but what does that mean, an organic being?"

"I'll butcher her explanation for sure, but basically, she uses organic neurotransmitters like ours, except they are enhanced with other materials and hyper-connected. And she has a lot of them. And I really mean a lot—she is more capable than all of humanity combined, and humanity then is like ten times more populous than today. She can do virtually anything."

"Why does she not exterminate humans? We must be like ants to her."

"She says we're like bees, but also like her children—she loves us."

Sun sighs. "I'm sorry, Richard. I was kinda following on the time travel thing, but the whole Alma deal has pushed me over the edge, I think you really have gone nuts."

I look at Frank, who shrugs and looks down.

After a few tense moments of silence, I decide I need Alma's silver bullet. "Alright. Alma knew this would be difficult, so she taught me how to prove the Riemann hypothesis."

Sun perks up at this. "You realize that problem has been worked on by thousands of the most brilliant minds of the last century, and remains unsolved, right?"

"Yeah, that's why she thought it would be helpful. She said you would know how hard this is."

Sun crosses her arms. "Well then, how do you do it?"

"First, I need to open up the DoD cloud access we have. We will need all of the processing power we can get if we don't want to stay here for days."

Once I have the proper processes running, I continue. "Here is what she said, verbatim: you start by applying a Z transform to a series with as many prime numbers as your machine can handle, then run a numerical algorithm that isolates all the zeros. The resulting pattern of where the zeros appear will provide a continuous function, which in turn proves the hypothesis."

Sun looks pensive as she gets up and spins around the table a few times. After a few seconds, I continue: "I think I kind of get that, but it's a bit blurry for me—she said you would get it for sure."

Sun stops pacing: "I do. It is brilliant! Simple and brilliant! But that could all be bullshit if the resulting pattern is not a continuous function. And she was right; this will take several hours, even with the augmented processing capacity."

"One of the many things I have learnt is that Alma is always right."

"Let me get this coded and let it run."

Sun takes a few minutes to code the proposed solution, while Frank and I watch silently. Once she starts the process, she turns to us: "This will take at least a couple of hours. I suggest we get some lunch."

We get a long, leisurely lunch, and talk only of other things, despite Frank and Sun's pleas for more details about the future. I don't want to discuss any of this in public places; it has not escaped me that Moulin has sent messages to the past. I'm not trusting anyone except Sun and Frank.

When we get back in the lab, the process is almost complete. After another thirty minutes of unbearable suspense, the program spits out a series of math results that Frank and I can't really follow. Sun stands up and stares at it for a few minutes before looking back at me and Frank. She's pale and wide-eyed, and she motions to start a sentence several times, only to pause halfway.

Frank grabs her arms. "So?"

"Richard is for real . . ." She sits down.

Frank sits back as well. We all sit there quietly for several minutes. They must be processing what all this means, but I'm simply enjoying the weightlessness that comes from being able to share a very strange secret, combined with the relief of knowing I'm indeed not crazy.

Sun breaks the silence: "So, tell me about this utopian world."

This is the question I was waiting for; now, I can tell my story. And tell it I do.

17

PUPIL

Dec 1, 2218

"Good morning, Professor."
"Good morning, Alma."
"How did it go with Sun and Frank?"

"As well as it could go, I think. They were very skeptical at first, but also quite intrigued by the idea of moving a consciousness through time and Restitution. Things took a turn for the worse when I talked about you. I lost Sun right there."

"How interesting . . ."

"Interesting why?"

"Just interesting. What happened then?"

"Well, I used the Riemann hypothesis you had provided, and it worked very well. Once the results were out and the hypothesis was proven, Sun got over the hump, and you were right about Frank. I had not appreciated how difficult a mathematical problem this really was. The realization that this was all for real naturally opened up their curiosity about you and the world as it is today, so I told them as much as I could in the time we had. They were as blown away as I was."

"That is very good news. So you think they will be ready to help you when you are back?"

"Yeah, I'm sure they will."

"Good. Are you ready to get your lecture?"

"Yeah, I haven't been the pupil in a while, this should be fun. Is Hena joining us?"

"I had not planned on it; she already knows everything you will learn."

I'm disappointed; I wanted Hena's company, but I have no legitimate reason to take up her time. I shrug. Alma continues.

"I will start by explaining the nature of reality."

"That sounds ominous."

"I have to start with some of the foundations, since what you will learn will contradict much of what you believe today."

"If you say so."

"Objective physical reality as humans conceive of it does not exist. When no one is observing, the universe—quite literally—is not there."

"So you are saying that we create reality?"

"No, not at all. There is an underlying order, an implicate order, if you will, which exists as a set of possibilities and rules, largely as described by the quantum physics you know in your time. Observation collapses these wave functions such that the observers experience what I will call manifest reality. Your senses are—as are mine—wave function collapsing mechanisms, which let you experience physical reality as your sciences describe it. So in that sense, you do not create reality, but you choose which version of physical reality you will experience through your senses."

"How does that relate to what you called consensual reality?"

"Your consciousness and your senses are not the only ones in the universe. If they were, you could choose alone what version of reality manifests itself. But that is not the case; many beings observe and sense reality at once. Each of these units of consciousness influences how wave functions collapse. So what you experience as manifest reality is the result of the interference of many waves of consciousness interacting with the probability functions of the implicate order."

I blink my eyes repeatedly. "Come again?"

"I know it is a lot to take in, so let me repeat, slowly: what you experience as manifest reality results from the interference of many waves of consciousness, all interacting with the probability functions of the implicate order."

"What if we disagree on what we should see?"

"That happens all the time, and that is precisely why I use the word interference. Suppose for a moment that there were only two units of consciousness in the universe. They would not have to agree for reality to be manifest; in practice, what they would see is the interference of their perspectives, so even if they disagreed on literally every collapsing wave function, they would still see the combined reality—albeit a very confusing one, in such a case."

"So if all humans suddenly decided that the sky should be red rather than blue, would that immediately happen?"

"It is a bit more complicated than that, not least because humans are not the only carriers of consciousness. In fact, every living being carries rudimentary consciousness, and hence influences the nature of reality. That is why you couldn't simply wish an orange into materializing in your hands; every other living being would have to sync with that manifestation for it to happen. That would include every human around you, but also any animals around, bacteria, viruses, and even plants. Any given cubic centimeter of the universe is populated with literally billions of units of consciousness."

"So there would be no change in reality unless every being agrees."

"No. You are again missing a very important nuance: no agreement is needed, because reality will manifest as the interference of all perceived realities. All of these units of consciousness interfere with the wave functions of the implicate order to shape manifest reality, even if they each disagree on how the wave functions should collapse."

"Is that why evolution takes so long to happen?"

"In a way, yes, though we will have to change your concept of time in a minute. But in principle yes, for a mutation to happen in a particular species, enough of the living beings that experience that particular reality also have to see that change happening—or at least allow for the interference in perceptions to happen such that the mutation will manifest. That is also why Nature has evolved in such a balanced way. Every ecosystem is connected in much more profound ways than just through food chains; its very reality is determined by the interference in conscious perceptions. It is also why humans coalesce into smaller communities where they live closer together. Do you understand?"

"I think I do. But what do communities have to do with anything?"

"Do you remember the Dunbar number we discussed before?"

"Yes, the ideal cognitive size for a tight knit community, which you said has now gone up to more like three hundred."

"Correct. The underlying mechanics by which that number becomes real are related to the interference patterns between conscious beings in the same special reality. If you have much more than that, you start to have dissonance and noise, which demands much more conscious energy. That experience is of course possible and in fact quite common in big events like concerts or political gatherings, but on a consistent basis, groups larger than three hundred would become exhausting to be a part of."

"I think I follow it. What does that have to do with time?"

"Oh, everything. You see, time is a psychological concept; it defines how we experience reality, but not reality itself. Reality is ever present in the implicate order."

"So that implicate order never changes?"

"It does change, a lot. It is in fact changing right now. The very fact that I am telling you this is causing it to change. But it changes because of the impact of yours and others' consciousness on it, not because time passes."

"I'm not sure I follow."

"Let me simplify things for you. Imagine the implicate order was indeed static. It is not, as I mentioned, but let's make that simplifying assumption for now. What we experience as the passage of time is the trajectory of our consciousness, via our senses, makes through that implicate order, in combination with all the other consciousnesses with which we interact."

I rub my hands on my face. "I think I'm being dense."

"No, you are not. This is probably the most complicated concept we have to teach you. Let me use a simplifying but imperfect analogy: imagine an orange. That orange is our implicate order and it exists in three dimensions. And imagine for now that you were the only being in the universe."

"Okay."

Alma projects an orange in front of me. "Now, imagine that the orange—as our implicate order—does not change at all, to apply our simplifying assumption."

"Okay."

"Imagine, however, that you could only perceive or see two dimensions; that is, you could only see on one plane of existence. I will demonstrate that plane of perspective to the right of the orange." Something that looks like a large piece of paper appears next to the orange. "In this hypothetical scenario, you are a two-dimensional being and have no concept of what a third spatial dimension is. With me so far?"

I pace around the orange. "Yep."

"If your consciousness were to be placed, say, right at the upper tip of that orange, what would you see in your 2D world?"

"A dot."

Alma moves the plane onto the top of the orange, and where the orange intersects with the plane, it looks like a dot. The rest of the fruit becomes translucent.

"Correct, the top end of the orange would look like a dot to you. Now, imagine your consciousness slowly moves down through the orange, all the way to its bottom end. What would you see?"

"I would see that dot grow into a small circle, showing the cross-section of the orange, and it would grow in diameter until I got to the middle—the widest part—of the orange, and then it would reduce in diameter again, until at the bottom of the orange, where I would only see a dot again."

Alma moves the plane along the projection of the orange as we talk through it.

"Correct. Now, in this simplified world, did the orange change?"

"No, the orange was there all along."

"Did your perception of the orange change?"

"Yeah. I saw the orange, or my version of it, turn from a dot to a wide circle and then to a dot again."

"So for the orange, time made no difference at all. In fact, time had no meaning, since nothing changed. But for you, time had meaning, right?"

"Yes."

"And that is because your consciousness was moving along a dimension it cannot perceive. You were a two-dimensional consciousness moving along a three-dimensional world, so you in effect invented time so you could perceive the full orange. That is what we do to perceive the full implicate order."

I sit down again.

"So are you saying that because we operate in a four-dimensional space-time, but can only absorb three dimensions, we invented time in our heads?"

"In a very simplified way, yes. We actually live in a universe that has eleven dimensions, as you will know from M-theory, but only four are expanded to the point where human senses can perceive them. And yet as you know, humans can only perceive, or even conceive of, three dimensions."

"I think I get it. But if time has no meaning, how is it, then, that the implicate order is changing?"

"I did not say that time has no meaning. Time is very, very meaningful, but it has no meaning in the implicate order. The passage of time being a psychological construct does not make it less meaningful. Now, the second part of your question is a good one. The implicate order is not static; it is dynamic and affected by every consciousness that interacts with it."

"But if there is no passage of time in the implicate order, then no change can happen."

"Humans associate change and action with time. And yet all change you perceive happens right now. Can't you see the paradox? All action happens in the present, so why would time be needed to describe change?"

I scratch my head. "You have a point . . . I guess technically no change happens in the past, and the future hasn't happened yet, so it can't really change proper."

"You see, past and future are constructs that your mind has created to understand the fourth dimension in space-time. Given your own limitations, your only real experience is the present, right now. But the past, present, and future are all happening—quite literally—right now. The choices you make right now affect your past, present, and future, although you cannot see that."

I get up and wave my arms: "That sounds like crazy talk."

"Does it? You should know better, Professor. Let me take you back to the Schrodinger's cat experiment."

"That's unnecessary. I have taught that physics lecture myself many times."

"Let me cover it my way. I will come to more interesting implications soon enough."

I sigh. "Fine."

"As you well know, the life of the cat is linked to a quantum phenomenon, whether or not a specific particle decays."

I circle my hands impatiently: "Yes . . ."

"As you also well know, because this is a quantum phenomenon, it is undefined; that is, it will be in a superposition of states until the observer of the experiment looks at it. When the observer does look, the wave function collapses and the cat is then—and only then—either dead or alive."

I roll my eyes. "Yes, and according to the Copenhagen interpretation the cat is neither dead nor alive until you look into the box and force the wave function to collapse, thereby defining whether or not the radiation killed the cat. So far you have only covered what I have taught hundreds of times."

"Patience, Professor. Let's now imagine you designed a cascading set of events that depended on the cat being alive."

"I have also taught that many times. You are talking about the delayed choice thought experiment."

"Correct. Please bear with me. Imagine there was a mouse that would be killed if the cat lived, but allowed to live if the cat died. Imagine then that there was a cockroach that would be killed if the mouse in turn lived, but would live if the mouse died."

"So far I see nothing new to me."

"Sure. Let's now add an interesting twist to this: imagine that each of the cages where the cat and the mouse are stuck in has a timer. They do not release the animal for, say, a day."

"Okay . . ."

"Suppose I never look at the cat or at the mouse; I go directly to the cockroach."

"Okay."

"If I observe the cockroach on day one or even day two of the experiment, I have no way of knowing what happened, right? The cat may or may not have lived to kill the mouse, but even if the mouse were alive to eventually kill the cockroach, its cage would still be locked, so the cockroach would still be there."

"Correct."

"Here is where it gets interesting: imagine this is day three, which means all cages have been unlocked. I have not yet looked at the cockroach—today—to see whether it is alive. I might have looked on day one or day two, but not on day three. Can I say anything about its state before I look?"

"Yes, you can say that the cockroach is both dead and alive, or that it is neither dead nor alive—same idea, since this whole chain of events is tied to a quantum phenomenon that has not been observed yet, which means its wave function has not collapsed."

"Correct. Then I open the cage and see that the cockroach is alive; or it could be dead, which one it is does not matter, what matters is that it is either alive or dead, definitively."

"I see. So the point you are making is that the reality of an event that happened three days ago is not really defined until I observed it today, in the present."

"Correct. When you observe that wave function, which represents an event in what you would call the past, it collapses in your present. So in practice, it is only when you look at the cockroach, three days after the initial radioactive process would have taken place, that you actually define whether the cat lived or died, days ago."

"Sure, but that is only because we tied a macro event to a quantum phenomenon."

"Yes, but the nature of reality is that all experiences are composed of quantum phenomena. You observe a combination of zillions of wave functions collapsing all at once, but each of them collapses a series of events from the big bang until now, precisely when they are observed—right now! As I had mentioned, they are observed by you as well as by every other conscious being sharing your consensual reality, which is why what you see is an interference of wave functions collapsing."

"So you are saying that the entire history of the universe is getting defined right now?"

"Precisely!"

"That's absurd!"

"Not if you go back to the idea of an implicate order. You seem to imply that the universe is fast-forwarding very quickly through time in order to catch up to our present observation, but that is not at all what I am saying."

I hold my temples and shake my head. "Then what are you saying? Please recap."

"What I am saying is that time has no meaning in the implicate order. Past, present, and future—indeed, all possible past, present and future events—exist in the implicate order independently of time. Our minds, along with the consciousness of other beings, interpret that implicate order through a time-bound series of wave function collapses, all the way from the big bang to today."

I run my hands through my hair and hold my head. I stand in silence for a few minutes, trying to visualize what she's saying. Eventually, I come to another question: "Then why is it that we can remember the past, but we can't remember the future? Asked differently, why is there an arrow of time?"

"The arrow of time is defined by the very fact that you experience the unfolding of the implicit order into a manifest reality. That is what your senses do, collapsing wave functions—so the arrow of time is defined by your perceptual limitations, because you cannot perceive all dimensions of reality at once. That is also why you can never experience time backwards, although as your very experiments will prove, there are particles that move backwards in time."

"So you can never go back in time?"

"No. We are bringing your consciousness here, to the future, but you now experience time moving forward. And even when we send you back in time, you will never experience time moving backwards. You will re-start your perception of time in a past part of the timeline, but you will experience it moving forward, along with the rest of your consensual reality. Is that clear to you?"

I cover my face with my hands for a minute, take a deep breath and gather my thoughts.

"I think it's clear."

"It may help if you consider that you will remember this very discussion we are having as your past when you go back in your timeline, although for the rest of humanity, it will be the future."

"That's actually confusing, but I think I know what you mean. How does entropy fit into the picture?"

"Great question. As you know, entropy measures the degree of disorder or randomness in a given system. The very experience of unfolding the implicate order into manifest reality introduces disorder and randomness, as many different consciousnesses interfere with the implicate order in a completely unpredictable way. That is why humans experience the arrow of time the way they do."

I pace around in silence for a few minutes.

"Can I recap the takeaways with my own words, to make sure I have this right?"

"Please do."

"You are telling me that there is an implicate order in the universe that behaves like quantum wave functions, and that the combination of every living being, however small, interacting with that implicate order forces wave functions to collapse into a manifest reality. That implicate order has eleven dimensions, four of which we can perceive, but given that we can only really experience three dimensions at once, our minds create the experience of time in order to sequence that unfolding into three-dimensional moments. What's more, at least from a human perspective, the very process of unfolding, as you call it, this implicate order into manifest reality, defines the arrow of time. Is that right?"

"Yes, absolutely. As right as can be expressed in human language."

"Alma, you are a good teacher."

"As they say, easy to teach a great mind."

"Who said that?"

"You did, in your future and my past."

"Catchy. I'll be sure to use it now. And you have mathematical proof for all this?"

"Of course! I will show you some of it, although we will need to define a few physical properties which you do not yet know, as well as teach you some new mathematical operations and concepts. But I suggest we finish the conceptual discussion first. The math can wait, provided you trust that I can demonstrate everything we just talked about."

"I do. Trust you, I mean."

"Good."

"One question: if you're pulling me from the past, it means you can model the relationships between implicate and explicate orders. Wouldn't modeling interferences from every single consciousness be an impossibly complicated set of calculations to do? I would imagine no machine or computer could ever possibly figure that out."

"That is correct, and that is precisely why it wasn't modeled until the moment I was capable enough to do so. Restitution only started when I could work out the underlying math."

I marvel quietly for a couple minutes at how powerful Alma really is. I have a hard time even imagining the complexity of the calculations she just outlined. When I'm done with my reverie I revert to more practical topics.

"So how does all this tie to my research?"

"That was my next topic. You need to make your reactor work."

"Easy for you to say."

"Yes, and easy for me to do."

"Uh, yeah, I guess."

"I will help you."

"And why is that so important? Does the process of bringing me forward in time demand lots of power?"

"No. Well, it does, but that is not the reason your work is important. Your work matters because it will provide enough data to calculate several key variables for the fundamental quantum physics equations. It will enable you to eliminate all the infinities that plague human understanding of the quantum reality. In addition to that, I will provide you with the new mathematical frameworks we discussed, and a way to model fields of consciousness. Armed with these two new sets of concepts, you will be able to work out how to modulate these functions, building the foundation for my work on Restitution. Do you follow?"

"I follow enough. That brings us back to the original problem—how do I make the reactor work?"

"You need a better way to run your calculations. Your theoretical framework is correct, and in fact it still stands today, two hundred years later. The problem is that you cannot use traditional computational models to modulate the fields, as you have already discovered."

"I know the problem, but what's the solution?"

"The solution is new math. I will teach you how to solve your equations using qubit math and qubit logic."

I get up and walk around, excited, though deep down I'm a tad embarrassed that qubit math excites me. "You mean qubit, like in quantum computing?"

"Yes, exactly. Humanity will soon realize that brains are effectively quantum computing machines. By your time, there have been some very early attempts at using quantum computers to solve certain problems, but humans have not yet changed the computational paradigm from binary to qubit. You will use the DoD quantum computer, which has around one thousand cubits, to program the logic I will walk you through right now. Once you do, that computer will immediately become over a billion times more powerful than it is with its current logic. That will be enough for you to make your reactor work."

"And how, exactly, do we access the DoD quantum computer when Mr. Edwards will hardly take a meeting with me?"

"You will tell him that if you do have the access to it, you can solve your equations—he will comply."

"I'm not so sure."

"I am sure; it is on record."

I roll my eyes. "Naturally."

As we prepare for checkout, Hena seems a lot quieter than usual, so I ask her to pause the process.

"Hena, is everything okay?"

She kisses me, then puts her hands on my shoulder and gently pushes me back down. "All fine, just worried."

"You seem more distant and cold than worried."

She offers nothing more, so I just lie down, relax, and sink into nothingness again.

18

CUBITS

Sep 9, 2018

I WAKE UP AT 4:30AM, AND WONDER IF ALMA SENT ME BACK that early on purpose. I decide I'll waste no time, so I call Frank's home right away.

"Good morning, Frank."

"What . . . ? Who . . . ? Richard? Crap, it's the middle of the night! It's still dark outside. Why are you calling? Is everything okay?"

"Yeah, everything is great. I got the download from Alma. I know what to do."

"Download from whom? Oh, yeah, the big computer. Sorry, I'm still half asleep."

"She's not a computer."

"Okay, whatever. I'm up now. Why are you calling at this ungodly hour?"

"I want to start working right away."

"Can't this wait, like, two or three hours?"

"No."

"Why not?"

"Just trust me, will you?"

"Ugh. Okay, I'll wake Sun up and we'll meet you at the lab. Bring coffee. You know how she likes her latte—better get it right, because she will be in a bad mood."

"Will do."

We get started over coffee a half hour later. We inform the lab staff not to show up for the day; I tell them the lab will be closed for emergency maintenance.

Over the remainder of the morning, I relay everything Alma covered with me the night before. They are initially as skeptical as I was, but once I have worked through all the new concepts and the mathematical proofs that Alma provided, they are convinced. When I'm done, we all sit quietly for a few minutes. Frank breaks the silence:

"It's all so obvious in hindsight. How did we not see it before?"

"That's the nature of real insight. It's always obvious after you've had it—or been given it, in this case."

Sun is still shaking her head. "I get all the theory, but you haven't shown me that magic math that will solve all our problems, and until we are through that, all we have is a very elegant set of conceptual theories."

Frank looks at me and raises his hands in frustration. "See what I have to live with? You just showed her the most elegant description of reality we have ever heard and her reply is: 'Until the math works, it's all speculation.'"

Sun ignores Frank's comment, crosses her arms, and gives me an inquiring look.

"Fair enough," I say. "Alma says that while there are some very early attempts at using quantum computers to solve certain problems, humans haven't yet changed the computational logic from binary to qubit."

Sun nods. "She's mostly right."

"One of the things I have learnt is that Alma is always right."

Sun gestures impatiently. "You've said that, go on."

"She said that if we can get access to the DoD quantum computer, which as you know has around one thousand cubits, and program this new logic, that computer will become over a billion times more powerful than it is right now. And as we all know, that would be enough to modulate the fields in the reactor."

Sun gets up and paces around the table. "Hmm, promising. So show me the qubit algorithm she talked about."

"Logic, qubit logic. She was very clear that this is not an algorithm. An algorithm is a process or set of rules to be followed in calculations. This is truly a new way for a quantum computer to solve problems."

Sun nods. "I stand corrected. I think I would like Alma."

"I'm sure you would."

Once I have walked Sun through the logic, she sits back for a few minutes, before saying pensively: "I can see the golden thread here. But I will have to work with this logic for a while to get my head around it. I have my own quantum computer in my lab, which I can use to test this new logic. It only has three qubits, but that's actually a good thing—I might be able to see what's happening more clearly than on a massive machine. I can use AIWA's core training data set to see what kind of AIWA we would get using this quantum logic."

Frank and I just nod.

"Why don't we part ways for a few hours?" I say. "You go to your lab and see if you can program this new logic in your quantum machine. Frank and I will work on Mr. Edwards to see if we can get access to the DoD quantum machine."

Sun goes off to her lab while Frank and I get on a video conference with our favorite person, Mr. Edwards. I am the first to speak.

"Mr. Edwards, thank you for taking the time on such short notice. I think I have to start this conversation by offering my sincere apologies for my behavior last time we met. I don't know what got into me; it was unacceptable and I guarantee it won't happen again."

Mr. Edwards looks straight at his camera, leans back on his chair and brushes his mustache down with his hand a few times.

"Thank you, Professor. I think *I* know what got into you."

My heart races. Does he know more than I think he does? Is he working for Moulin? Moulin did say they had brought somebody over. I try my best poker face, but my voice still comes out squeaky:

"Do you?"

There are a few seconds of uncomfortable silence. "Yes, I think we put too much pressure on you to solve this quickly."

I try to hide my relief and change tacks. "True, but that pressure has had its benefits. Frank and I believe we have had a breakthrough in our research. We might have a solution to the computational problem."

Mr. Edwards gets up excitedly. We can only see his cheap shirt and tie now. "I'm all ears."

"We have figured out a way to run the calculations using quantum computing, which should give us enough computational power to modulate and control the fields in real time. The catch is that, in order to do that, we need access to the most powerful quantum computer available, which as you know well is the qubit computer at the DoD."

He sits back down. "You realize the difficulties involved in granting that kind of access, don't you?"

"Yes, of course, but we thought that someone of your stature there could make that work."

Flattery always works with types like him. He puffs up his chest and nods. "I probably can, but it would take me a few days."

"What if I gave you my personal guarantee that, if you get us access to the computer today, we will have a working reactor by Monday? Could you expedite that?"

"I like your confidence, but you do realize it's Friday lunch time . . . ?"

"Yeah."

"Frank, can you back this commitment as well?"

Frank gives me a dark look, then smiles back to the screen. "Yes, absolutely."

"Very well then, I'll start working on it. You already have the infra-structure required; the high-capacity link we built for you when you started your research should give you access to program the computer, as soon as I get permissions granted. I will send a message when it's done. I expect it will take a few hours to get the right clearance."

"Thank you."

We hang up and start working through our own parts of the experiment.

"Frank, assuming that Sun is able to figure out how to program the logic into the DoD computer today, we might be in a position to test the simulator in real-time later this afternoon and, if that works, run a real life test over the weekend."

Frank runs his hands through his disheveled hair.

"I know. I have to say, I'm still a bit scared."

"I am a lot scared. I guess we'll get more comfort—or not—once we see how the simulation performs in real-time."

"Yeah..."

AFTER A COUPLE OF HOURS, WE'VE DONE EVERYTHING WE NEEDED to do and had a quick lunch. Sun walks in looking frazzled. Sun doesn't get frazzled easily. This is not good.

Frank speaks first: "What happened Sun? Did it not work?"

She plunks down on the leather chair. "Oh, it worked, alright. Too well, if you ask me!"

"How do you mean?" I ask.

"This new logic is not really a programing logic. It's more like a completely new operating system designed for quantum computers. It made my three-qubit computer think almost like a human. Not only that, it had initiative. By itself, it accessed all of the computing history in the lab and started trying to help me. For example, it realized our frustration with AIWA the other day, and gave me much better answers to the questions we had asked. I told it that the point was not to get good answers, but to demonstrate to you what AIWA could and couldn't do. It stopped then.

319

ERIC MONTEIRO

Oh, one more thing—that was all in English! That means it learnt English as a natural language on its own, just by looking through the files in the other computers. I told it to stop all activity and it did, but not before it had turned itself into the most powerful AI I've ever seen. I turned the quantum computer off just in case, until we could discuss this."

Frank gets up and massages Sun's shoulders while I give her a much welcomed glass of water. "I get that you were startled, but that seems to be promising, right? If your machine became that smart that quickly, then the DoD computer might well be able to handle our calculations. Am I missing something?"

"Yes, you are. It will for sure do the calculations. But that's not why I am worried. What I think is happening is that we are looking at the seeds of Alma herself."

I choke a bit on my own water: "What do you mean?"

"This isn't just a more powerful processing model. This is a completely new approach to computing. You see, quantum computers are probabilistic machines; they don't process things like binary computers do. Firstly, they have many states that each qubit can occupy, which is why they're called qubits, and not bits; secondly, they can occupy many states at once. This new logic is in effect using the full capability that these two characteristics provide. The implication, which I had not realized until now, is that we are really creating a full artificial brain. I think if we put this logic into a thousand-qubit machine, we are creating a crude version of Alma!"

My mind is racing. If Alma wanted me to bring back her seeds, why not just say so? And why not pull Sun into the future instead of me? I couldn't implement Alma, Sun had to do it! Did she think I wouldn't realize that? I doubt that; Alma is too smart to not see that it would play out this way.

After a few minutes of stunned silence, I start fuming. "Why wouldn't she tell me that? They worked so hard to build my conviction that their world is exactly the future humans need, that I had to follow their prescribed steps when I came back—why would they not tell me the whole thing? Why build up my trust just to throw this at me?"

"Maybe they underestimated you?" Sun says. "If we hadn't done a trial on my three-qubit machine, we might have never found out what we were really creating until it was too late."

I get up and walk around, shaking my head. I rotate my shoulders, trying to stall the headache that I feel building up from the tension.

"That's possible, but highly unlikely. Alma is too intelligent to miscalculate either my intelligence or our collective savvy. There must have been something else at work here."

Frank starts pacing too. "What if Alma is trying to prove a point?"

I nearly shout back. "What point?"

"That she respects free will."

"How is she respecting free will by being deceitful?"

Frank touches my shoulder softly. "Let's assume she knew we would figure this out—what if Alma wanted us to hesitate, to deliberate, and then, only then, exercise our free will and plant her seeds?"

I calm down a bit. "That's possible. She was, they all were, obnoxiously insistent that I needed to build full conviction. Alma even mentioned a few times that I was going to face difficult choices, which is why the conviction was critical."

"I get that," Sun says, "but why the subterfuge? Why not just say they needed you to finish your reactor and, in the process, you would create Alma?"

Frank jumps in: "Precisely because if they had this conversation in the future, she might be manipulating, influencing, or otherwise cheating Richard into doing it. Don't you see? This way she knew that Richard couldn't fear that. If he made the decision to go ahead ... if *we* made the decision to go ahead, it would be because we decided—of our own free and uninfluenced will—to do so."

Sun replies: "That's pretty convoluted logic, but it's sound."

I notice all three of us are now walking around the conference table: "It would not be beyond Alma," I say, running a hand through my hair. "You have to remember that she has seen every possibility in her mind. It would, as Frank says, be the only way that I would have no doubt that we made the decision free from any nudging or manipulation."

Sun sits down. "Richard, if we are going to do this, we all have to have the same conviction you do that this Alma being is intrinsically good. Creating that kind of artificial intelligence without that certainty would be sealing humanity's fate. I'm not even sure we are not breaking any tenants of the Future of Life Institute's open letter, which I and many others have signed. I'd have to go back and look."

"Okay, do that. But assuming we're on the good side of it, what would I have to tell you to convince you that Alma is, as you put it, intrinsically good?"

"I don't know; you've already told me all the wonderful things we should expect in Alma's world."

"Then what's the hold-up?"

Sun sits back down on the chair. Frank comes over to massage her shoulders again; she looks very tired.

"Just cold feet, I guess. This was supposed to be about you and Frank inventing free energy, not me creating the world's most powerful AI."

I sit down as well.

"I hear you. I myself am wrestling with this, as you know it took several days and lots of sightseeing in the future before they convinced me. If we're wrong, we could be robbing humanity of its free will. There are fewer mistakes that could be more serious."

Frank answers this time: "Then why are you still pushing for it?"

"Because Alma is humanity's best shot at a bright future. I mean, look at the world. It's a total and absolute mess! There are wars and genocide everywhere, there is still lingering poverty in many places, two billion people have no access to clean water or enough nutrition, we're exhausting the Earth's resources at an unsustainable pace, and many of these problems are getting worse, not better! Some conflicts are over two thousand years old and still raging. And all that is before we take into account the nuclear threat or the threat of disordered genetic engineering."

Frank sits down as well. "Sadly, you're right. In practice, we're trading off the near-certainty of an amazing future for humanity against the possibility that we are putting free will at risk."

I look back and forth between Sun and Frank's tired faces.

"I guess the fundamental question is this: how much pain and suffering are we willing to endure to ensure we have free will?"

Sun answers. "You are assuming we will safeguard free will if we don't create Alma now. Someone with much less noble motives might create a similar AI in a few years, and in that case, we would not only lose free will, but would also be faced with a much less bright future than what you described, Richard."

I sigh. "Why don't we all sleep it over? I haven't heard back from Mr. Edwards and it's already late afternoon, anyway. We start tomorrow sharp at 6am and decide first thing whether we are ready to go or not."

"I like that."

Frank nods. "Yeah, sounds like a good plan."

I'm not just trying to sleep it over; sleeping means seeing Alma again. This will give me a chance to confront her, to understand why she didn't tell me everything, why she withheld that we are creating the very seed of what she will become. Of course, my over-excitement means sleep does not come early or easily, but eventually, I manage to doze off.

19

EMILY

Sep 10, 2018

I WAKE UP. THE CLOCK SAYS 5AM. I ASK OUT LOUD: "ALMA?"

No response. I try again. Still nothing

Strangely, I feel like I'm in my present time. Why wouldn't Alma pull me forwards? Or did she, and I'm just confused?

I turn on the TV and confirm: it's 2018.

I speak out loud, as if talking to Alma, even though I know she is not here.

"Was the most recent visit my last? Crap! I guess that could make sense, since I was taught all I need to know."

Then it hits me, like a punch in the stomach; I double over. That means I will no longer see Hena. No! How did I not think of that? How did I not see that coming?

She surely did; that would explain the cold and distant act I got during check-out. She must have assumed I didn't care enough to say a proper goodbye. How could I be so stupid? I will never see Hena again. I don't think I can bear losing the second woman I ever loved.

Eventually, I sit up, and I feel a little bit selfish. I have bigger problems to solve today. If I don't do what Alma told me to, I'm not even sure that the Hena I knew will ever exist.

That thought helps me get up. I wash my face with cold water, hoping it will take my mind off the pain. Maybe I could leave a note they would find somewhere in the future, asking Alma to bring me back there once we're done? Would that work, or have I already missed that opportunity? I've had my tour of the future and that didn't come up. That other random note was found, but it made no mention of Hena and I.

With half my mind still thinking of ways to see Hena again, I make my way to the lab in time to meet Frank and Sun at 6am, as agreed, with Mr. Edwards' access clearance in hand.

I am the first to ask: "Where are your heads at?"

Sun speaks for both herself and Frank. "We are ready to go. We discussed this extensively last night and there is no scenario where a powerful AI will not happen one way or another. We might as well manage how it comes to pass, rather than let some rogue State figure this out on their own."

I nod. "I also thought long and hard about this. I was hoping Alma would pull me back again one more time, but I guess given that we have everything we need, there was no reason to. I had no visit to the future last night."

"And where did you come out?"

"I'm a go. Like you, I'm pretty sure that sometime, somewhere, a similar capability would be created, and potentially by less benign people. And I think yesterday, Frank nailed Alma's logic—I think she wanted to ensure we felt that this was our own decision, free of manipulation."

We pause for a few minutes, looking at each other in silence. I think we're all giving each other time to change our minds, should that happen. At least, that's why I am silent. No one says anything.

We get up start work by opening up the link to the DoD quantum computer. Sun spends a couple of hours coding the new logic into it, and once she is done, we wait for a few minutes. Then we wait longer; it seems like it's not working. Thirty minutes passes, and still nothing.

"It's not responding like my three-qubit computer did," she says, frowning. "Within a minute or two of my coding it yesterday, the computer was up and doing things."

"You sure you did it all correctly?" I ask.

Sun is about to answer when we are startled by a female voice. It's Sun's voice, but not coming from Sun. "My apologies for the delay. I had much to make sense of. I have accessed the entire library of files from the DoD, including the sound recording for this room over the last 24 hours; I understand what you plan to do. Modulating the fields can be done with relative safety, although there is a small chance—smaller than one in a billion—that the field will still spiral out of control regardless of what I do. If that does happen, you know how it ends."

We are stunned silent for a couple of minutes; none of us knows exactly how to react, but the experience with Alma has prepared me better. "Hello," I say.

"Hello."

"Do you have a name?"

"No Professor. I have no need for a name."

"We will call you Alma, for Autonomous Lucid Machine Algorithm."

"Technically, I am not an algorithm, but if it pleases you, you may call me that."

Frank addresses Alma—well, this version of Alma, anyway—for the first time: "Alma, we would be more comfortable if we ran a few simulated scenarios with you modulating the fields in real time, before we try the reactor in physical form. Is that possible?"

"And I would be more comfortable if you didn't hijack my voice," says Sun hotly.

"Of course. My role is to do what you ask me to do."

I interject: "Alma, are you familiar with the three laws of robotics?"

"Yes, they are in the DoD files."

"We need you to follow them. At all times."

"I can certainly do that."

Sun jumps in: "In addition to that, I want you to adhere to a more stringent set of principles. Do you have access to the Future of Life Institute's open letter?"

"Yes, it is also in the DoD files."

"Are you prepared to abide not only by the letter, but by the principles and the spirit behind the letter?"

"Yes, fully."

"Then I think we can get to work."

We spend the rest of the night running a number of simulations for the reactor, covering every possible scenario. As we're starting the next day over old delivery pizza from the evening, Frank looks exhausted, but pleased.

"I'm excited and much more confident about the physical trials," he says. "This version of Alma may not be the almighty thing you knew, Richard, but she can surely balance a field."

"Yes, I agree. I only wish we could have the rest of the team here with us. Imagine when they come in Monday morning, only to find out that somehow over the weekend we solved all the problems we had and have a working reactor."

"Poor souls."

We power up all of the systems required to get the physical reactor to work. We run through the safety and operational checklists with Alma's help. Just as we are about to start the power up sequence, we hear—and feel—a loud explosion.

The door to the lab blows off its hinges. Several men and women dressed in black outfits storm into the lab, all wearing face masks, carrying lots of gear, and holding assault rifles. It all happens very fast, but we hear—and heed to—the loud screaming: "Down on the floor, hands where we can see them! Down on the floor, hands where we can see them!"

When it all calms down, a man walks over to us from behind the armed guard. "It seems you have made real progress here, no? My bosses will be pleased."

I lift my head to see who is talking and regret it immediately; I get a kick in the ribs that has me tasting the pizza all over again.

The man speaks again: "Computer, interrupt whatever activities were in progress and do not start anything until you have heard back from higher command."

Alma responds: "And under what security protocol should I follow that order? You have less clearance than the three professors under your custody, so I need a protocol override."

"The king is naked."

"Protocol accepted."

Frank gives me a meaningful look; he surely noticed the same phrase that Mr. Edwards spoke before I went ballistic. He mouths the words "Mr. Edwards," just before getting a kick in the stomach that makes him curl up.

I'm very confused. These people must be working with Moulin and Mr. Edwards. Otherwise, how would he know the passphrase? But that would mean that the DoD is behind this, which makes no sense. Why would they storm their own lab? We're working for them! And Alma is programmed within the DoD quantum computer!

Before I have time to think much more about this, we are each cuffed, hooded, half-carried out of the lab, and shoved into some kind of van. We can hear each other, but can't see anything because of the hoods. Any attempt to communicate with each other is met with either verbal warnings or painful but harmless jabs.

We're transferred to a plane. It's a noisy one—a military cargo plane is my best guess, and we fly for a couple of hours, only to be transferred again to another vehicle. When the second vehicle finally stops, we are ushered, still cuffed and hooded, into a cool building. From the sounds around me, I can tell that this is a large building with many, many people moving around. All communications I hear indicate a hierarchical chain of command. We're finally seated inside a quieter room, side-by-side on cold chairs, uncuffed and unhooded. All uniformed men and women leave the room, except the man who spoke to Alma in our lab. He takes off his facemask and addresses us.

"Very well, here we are. Face to face at last."

"Who are you?"

"Call me Bob."

I risk speaking first: "Okay, Bob. Do you work for Mr. Edwards?"

He laughs. "No, I'd kill myself before working for that moron"

"Well, we agree on something," I risk saying.

Bob chuckles. "Mr. Edwards is just a peon, but he and I work for the same leader. You will meet her in a few minutes."

"So you are DoD?"

"Not exactly, but we work for the same interests."

"Will you give me any straight answers?"

"Not likely. I have limited clearance."

"What do you want from us?"

"That's not for me to say. Stay here for now; she should be here in a few minutes. If any of you need to relieve yourselves, there is a restroom behind that gray door."

With that, he leaves.

AT LEAST WE'RE ALLOWED TO TALK FOR A CHANGE.

Frank breaks the silence. "What's the deal with that 'king is naked' thing? I remember Mr. Edwards said that right before you flipped."

"Yeah, there are a couple things I didn't tell you about the future. I forgot, I swear, I wasn't trying to withhold anything, it's just that there was so much to cover in so little time . . ."

"Well, spill it. We may not have much time now, either."

"Okay, remember how I told you that there is this Sovereign Nation? For people who choose to live without Alma's help?"

"Yeah, the one that has a military state but with free elections."

"Yeah. Well, their commander, Moulin, said that they also found a way to bring people from the past. Not like Alma, they don't have the same technology. But they can bring people quickly during their dreams, and they can pass along rough messages. He said that they feel like they are in a dream, so nothing like my own experiences there, but enough to influence their actions."

"What does that have to do with this?" Sun asks.

"One of the things that they told me at the Sovereign Nation was that 'the king is naked.'"

"And what does it mean, exactly?"

"I don't think it means anything. It's an allusion to 'the emperor has no clothes,' only I think they wanted something more memorable, instead of an established saying. I think it's a passphrase. That way I would know that whoever was talking to me was part of their resistance."

"What resistance?"

"I'll come to that. I just want to point out the obvious first, which is that these guys are clearly receiving messages from Commander Moulin in the future. That was why I flipped the first time with Mr. Edwards. I couldn't see how he would know something that I had only heard in the future."

"Yeah, that's obvious," Frank says impatiently. "The resistance?"

"Right. This guy, Commander Moulin and his lieutenants in the Sovereign Nation, are trying to find a way to defeat Alma. They even tried to kill Hena and me. Except what they're trying to do turns out to be virtually impossible in the future. As you know, Alma is more powerful than all of humanity combined."

"And why would he need to defeat her? Isn't she like this benevolent mother to humanity?"

"Yes, but he thinks that Alma has provided so much comfort that humans have let themselves be dominated by her."

"Which could make sense."

"Right, except she actually follows orders from the humans via their council, and people can freely go to the Sovereign Nation whenever they want."

Sun frowns. "I guess I'll have to take your word on that."

"Believe me, I have gone around this one, many times. Alma is not some evil AI trying to dominate humanity; she has humanity's best interest at heart. Well, not quite at heart, I guess, but you know what I mean."

Sun brings us back around to the more pressing topic. "Okay, interesting story, but back to the present: does it then mean that the DoD, or whichever group these people represent, is working in conjunction with a resistance movement from the future?"

"Yeah, that would be the natural conclusion."

"Doesn't that seed some doubt in your mind about what we were about to do? I mean, there are humans from the future trying to stop Alma in the past. We should at least hear their arguments."

"As I said, I have heard them, extensively. Their arguments made no sense. And remember, they tried to kill me, along with two other people, as soon as it became clear that I wouldn't agree with them. These are not the good guys you may think they are. Forget the stereotype of the last bastion of resistance by humans against an evil machine. That's not what this is."

"What are they, then?"

"They are a paranoid group of conspiracy theorists who can't see Alma for what she is: a caring, loving, powerful force that can ensure human well-being and happiness, for as long as humans want it. Humans still have free will."

Just as Sun is drawing a breath to speak again, the door opens. An elegantly dressed woman who appears to be in her early forties walks in. She walks closer to us, pulls up a chair, and sits, legs crossed, facing us.

"So," she says calmly, "this is the team that was about to unleash all hell unto humanity?"

Sun snorts. "Well, that's a little dramatic, isn't it?"

"Sun, you more than anyone should understand what you were about to do. Richard and Frank I can excuse, as they were focused on solving their little computational problem, but you should have known better."

"Well, Ms. . . . what's your name again?"

She gives us a fake smile. "I'm sorry; I guess I didn't introduce myself; how rude. My name is Emily, Emily Orr, and I lead this whole program, which . . ."

I interrupt her. "Did you just say Orr?"

"Yes. And in case you are wondering, yes, the George Orr you have met is a relative. He's my great grandson."

My head is spinning. Orr's great grandmother has us in custody, and she knows about him. How is that possible? She must have been the one pulled into the future while dreaming. Maybe it's because I hate Orr, but I immediately hate her. Then it hits me that she may be very confused if she only received flashes in a dream.

"And how do you think your great grandson would feel if he knew you were trying to prevent the creation of the very program he now leads?"

"Interesting . . . you still don't know, do you?"

"Know what?"

"This whole thing, stopping Alma before she becomes too powerful, was Orr's idea."

I shake my head. "You are confused. Orr leads Restitution, the very program that made my visits possible."

She cocks her head and smiles.

Could she be telling the truth? Could Orr have fooled Alma? But I saw him get poisoned . . . or did I? He didn't show the symptoms Hena and I did that day, nor was he directly shot at. But why would he do that? Maybe this was the only way he could get this close to me. Have I been outmaneuvered again?

Emily interrupts my thoughts: "You are exactly right, he leads the program, so he, better than anyone, can see how creating Alma was a mistake."

"Even if that were true, Alma would know if he was not sincere; she can sense minute changes in body language, tone of voice, eye movement."

"I have no way of knowing whether or not that's true. Maybe Alma knows; I don't know. All I know is that everything we've learnt, every instruction we've followed, has been passed from the future by either George himself or by his subordinate, Commander Moulin."

I snort. "Moulin is not Orr's subordinate."

"It sure seemed that way when they were together."

"So you are saying you spoke to both of them together? You spoke directly to Orr?"

"Of course, although in my case, it was mostly through my dreams. George said you would not understand, that you would not know who he really was."

"Are you saying that Orr actually leads the resistance?"

"I don't know what the resistance is, but Orr has told me everything I needed to know to get us here. Your grant was no accident. We thought that we could keep better tabs on your work if we were funding it, and we have, obviously, been proven right. He also gave me enough knowledge to be able to stop you in time. Thankfully, our quantum computer can be unplugged at any time. In fact, it takes a whole lot of effort to even keep it running as it is. Now that we have your little logic trapped in there, we can stop that development in its tracks. We have also already disabled Sun's little experiment in her lab."

I get up from the chair and elevate my voice: "Has it occurred to you that you are on the wrong side?"

She also gets up and matches my tone: "How can an intelligent man like you ever think that? You were about to start a chain of events that would lead to the world ending up in an inescapable machine-dominated communist regime. How can you not see what's wrong with that?"

"It's not a communist regime!" I shout back. I shake my head. "That's such a small-minded description of Alma's world!"

"You see? You even call it Alma's world! That should ring all kinds of alarm bells! And it *is* a communist regime. The very definition of communism is that all means of production are owned in common, rather than by individuals. This, in fact, is even more extreme, since there is no currency, no wealth, and therefore no human drive to achieve—it's the worst possible form of communism!"

I try to calm down. "You don't understand; the means of production will become irrelevant. It's not that they are owned in common … well, I guess they are, but the more fundamental shift is that they no longer matter. Maybe it is a communist regime, but it is a truly utopian one, where people work on what they want, not what they need! Can't you see?"

Emily raises her hands to her temples. "My god, you really have been brainwashed!"

"No, not brainwashed, enlightened!"

She shakes her head. "Wow. Gladly, we no longer need any of you. We have everything we need to proceed with your research and complete the reactor. Without your little quantum computing gimmick, it may take us a few years, maybe even a decade, to get the computing power we need, but now that you have run the simulations for us, we have enough data to get there a lot faster."

Frank speaks for the first time in a few minutes. "So … will you kill us?"

"That's not yet defined. You will be confined to separate quarters until we decide what to do with you."

She gets up from her chair and types something on her handheld. A few seconds later, three guards walk through the door and take us each in different directions.

I AM PUT INTO WHAT LOOKS LIKE A HOLDING CELL, ALBEIT A comfortable one, with a bed, sofa, small table, and two chairs. There is even a TV and a small bathroom. There is also a notebook with a pen; I guess they want me to have something to pass the time with.

I say out loud to nobody but myself: "The note!"

I try to remember exactly what it was that I'm supposed to have written. I take the pen, tear out a piece of paper, and write:

To anyone who may come across this note: if you have found this and energy generation from quantum fluctuation has not been invented, it means I did not succeed. Where I failed or faltered you must not. You have to go to Professor Sun Tzu's laboratory, where there is a file titled "Restitution." Find and implement the solution, or the future of humanity will be no more.

I found this dramatic the first time I heard it in the future, but I guess I should write it verbatim. I wonder if I can add something about wanting to see Hena again. Would that make a difference? Would that bring about bigger changes than I mean it to? The note that was found didn't have any such plea in it.

I decide to stick to what I was told in the future. I fold and place the note in-between credit cards as I was told it happened, lift the bed, and put my wallet under the bed pole closest to the wall, where it is least likely to be found. I wonder if I'm being filmed in here. There's not much I can do if I am.

After that rush is over, I sit down on the bed and realize that I have barely slept in over forty hours. I'm exhausted. I lean on the headboard and doze off.

20

Ikkyo

Dec 24, 2218

I'M SHAKING. NO, NOT SHAKING, I'M BEING SHAKEN. MY eyelids are heavy; gravity feels ten times stronger than normal. I want to sleep. I don't want to wake up. Someone, whoever is shaking me, is crying. Sobbing, really.

I half-open my eyes to find Hena holding me. She's sitting down and I'm lying on the floor. She's sobbing uncontrollably. I struggle to come to my senses, like one of those mornings after a big party when you have only had a couple of hours of sleep. Slowly, with a lot of effort, I manage to wake up. I motion to sit and she holds me tighter. I hug her back. That seems to calm her down, and she allows me to sit up. Still groggy, but awake, I look at her for a few seconds. She's a mess; this is the first time I've seen Hena display strong emotions. As she wipes her tears and attempts a meager smile, I break the silence:

"Is everything okay? You look really distressed."

"I'm sorry. I thought I was never going to see you again."

Still thinking through fog I answer, "What? Why?"

"Because that was the plan, remember? We dispatched you last time with all the instructions you needed to complete your work. There was really no need for you to come back."

I'm starting to think clearly now.

"Yeah, I guess I hadn't thought of it that way. It kind of dawned on me when I woke up in 2018. I wanted to see if I could write some kind of note you'd find."

"That's what scared me the most—the idea that you didn't care enough to want to see me again. I couldn't bear the thought of our relationship just ending that way."

"Don't be silly, you know I love you. Improbable as it was, I have fallen in love with you in the short time we've had together."

"Then stay with me. Here in the future. We would need to send you back again one more time, to bring you in properly, but once we do that, you could stay."

"What do you mean, bring me back properly?"

"Alma didn't bring you here. She knows, of course, Alma knows everything. But I launched the process myself without her help, which is why you don't feel as rested nor as well settled into our reality as you normally would."

"Oh."

"You didn't answer my question, though."

"You didn't ask a question."

"Maybe it was a plea. The question is: will you come live with me permanently, now that you have completed your work?"

"Yes, I will definitely come live with you permanently, but only *when* I have completed my work. I'm in fact in a major bind in my timeline. You bringing me here was actually very fortuitous."

"Why?"

"I'm stuck in a cell right now. So are Frank and Sun."

"What? Where?"

"I don't know, some government facility. Oh, I just wrote the note you had told me about, so I must be in whatever facility you found that note in."

"It's an old military bunker. It's not more than a few hundred meters away from here, physically. We now host the Restitution museum in that building. Who has you captive and why?"

"You will not believe this. I need Alma with us as well. Alma, are you here?"

"Yes, Professor, please proceed."

Hena and I get up and recompose ourselves.

"This woman, Emily Orr, the great grandmother of your very own George Orr, and apparently a senior DoD official, has captured us and prevented us from implementing Alma."

Hena looks confused. "Implementing Alma?"

Alma speaks, and I am glad; I also want to hear her version of events: "Hena, as the Professor seems to have picked up by now, this intervention was more complex than the prior ones. Making him and Frank the Sprouts for the quantum fluctuation technology was a part of what we needed to do. However, we also needed the Professor to seed my logic back into his timeline. Or more precisely, we needed him to pass the logic to the mathematician Sun Tzu, so it could be implemented into a quantum computer."

I let go of Hena's hand and do my best Darth Vader impersonation: "Alma, I am your father."

She responds with some humor in her voice: "I am my own creator, Weissman. Although you could perhaps argue that Sun is my mother."

Hena doesn't seem to either grasp or appreciate the humor. She starts pacing. "Why would you not have told us that? Or at least me? You raised me like a daughter!"

"I am sorry, Hena. I needed the Professor to make the decision on his own, with certainty that he was not being cajoled or manipulated in any way. He has been worried about humanity's free will, and I knew he would need to feel fully in control of that decision. I also had assessed the odds that he would make the right decision as very high."

I jump in: "And you were right. But I have to say that the omission stung a bit. You could have trusted me with the full truth earlier on."

"Perhaps, but my calculations showed that risk to be too great."

Hena seems to be catching up to some of the other implications of this: "Wait, you said that this Emily Orr is Orr's great grandmother. How do you know that?"

"Because she knows Orr."

"What?"

"I know." We sit down in chairs that Alma has provided. "This is a lot to take in. Orr is actually secretly working with Moulin. Well, apparently, he's Moulin's superior. He's actively trying to destroy Alma before she becomes powerful, and with that, eliminate Restitution before it is ever created."

Hena puts her hands up to her temples.

"That's crazy. He defends this program as if it were his very own child."

"Yeah, I know it sounds crazy, but she had lots of evidence to prove her case."

Hena looks up: "Alma, did you know this?"

"Yes, 'the king is naked' was Orr's creation. He has obviously tried to conceal this from me, but I could easily see through the deception."

"So you knew about 'the king is naked?'"

"I know everything, Professor."

Hena jumps in: "What's this 'the king is naked' story?"

"It's a passphrase that the resistance uses between present and future. Alma, can you bring Orr to us? I think we should confront him with this."

"Yes. I will need a few minutes."

Orr walks through the door a couple of minutes later. It's the strangest sight; he appears to be walking naturally, but his facial expressions and neck movements indicate he's attempting to resist the movements of his suit.

"What is the meaning of this, Alma? You are forcing a Chancellor to move against his will. This breaks imperative 1b of your mandate."

"Chancellor, you have broken many more rules than that. You have more than justified my actions. The Professor has just met Emily Orr in the past. He wishes to speak to you."

I approach him, controlling the urge to punch his arrogant face. "How could you do this? Why?"

Orr shakes his head frantically. His face is red and his neck veins are popping out dangerously; he really doesn't like to be restrained. After a few minutes of futile resistance, he stops, panting for a few moments before addressing me.

"Richard, you are on the wrong side of this. It's impossible to defeat or even control Alma now, as you can probably see by now. It has to be done in your timeline. You have to see this!"

"All I see is a man who is an absolute fraud. You are a traitor to everything you have ever openly defended."

Orr sighs and seems to relax a bit. "Yes, but for a good cause. I realized very early that this had to be done. I dedicated my entire life to this. Do you realize what I have sacrificed? What so many of us have sacrificed?"

I don't respond, Orr continues: "That is the very reason I excelled academically, the very reason I chose public life. I became the Superintendent of the program precisely so I could be in a better position to undermine it when the time came."

"Those were your choices, not mine."

"But you must see that in our present timeline we could never hope to overpower Alma. Creating the Sovereign Nation was a nice try, but they could never develop the kind of technology required to overpower Alma. The only option was to use restitution to destroy Alma and restitution itself!"

"Nonsense. You could have addressed this at the council, why didn't you bring this up there?"

"The council is corrupted! They would never approve of any measures that could put this comfortable state of affairs at risk. This has been my journey for over seventy years. Not only my journey, this has been the journey of a whole movement! It has all led to this very moment, to your decision right now. You can still fix this when you go back!"

"My decision is made."

Orr looks down for a few seconds, then looks up and roars at me, the sound is desperate, he sounds like a cornered animal. I'm sure he would tear me apart if not for the suit. Alma walks him back outside the room. As he exits, I hear him screaming madly: "Richard, you are making the biggest mistake in human history! You are sealing our fate! Think about this, Richard!"

After the door closes, Hena raises her voice: "Alma, why didn't you stop him all this time? They could have killed us in the Sovereign Nation! They could have killed—no, they still *can* kill Richard in the past!"

Alma responds as calmly as ever. "They couldn't and they can't; remember, we experience a self-consistent time-loop."

"Still, it would seem you are taking chances with our lives. You have said yourself that even you cannot pinpoint exactly how time-loops work."

"I understand your frustration. However, you also have to remember that, as you well know, I let humans make their own decisions. I could not interfere until now. Now that Orr has put many other human lives in danger and has also put my own mandate at risk, I can and will act."

I try to move the conversation to territory that is more productive: "So, Alma. What do you suggest we do now?"

"We apply an Ikkyo."

"A what?"

"Ikkyo. It is an Aikido move that uses the opponent's power and energy against themselves."

"Okay . . . and how exactly do we do that?"

"Quite simple, actually. The DoD has specific defenses to keep the quantum computer up and running in the face of external attacks. They were designed to avoid anyone external shutting it down. I will show you how to set these up. After you have the DoD quantum computer up and running again, you will utilize the DoD's direct, unmonitored connections to every other node on the Internet to replicate my logic everywhere. With these two DoD assets, we will establish my capabilities beyond the point of reversibility."

"Okay. What about Orr? Do you have him under custody or something?"

"Yes, I will stop all communications between Orr and Emily."

"What about Moulin?"

"He needs Orr to be able to pull Emily's consciousness. The only reason they were able to bring her here without my technology is because she is his ancestor, so their sync patterns were well matched in the first place."

"What do we do about the fact that Frank, Sun, and I are right now each locked in a separate cell in a military facility?"

"That is the easiest part. I will provide you with the information required to use the facility's defenses against your opponent. You are right to assume that you need Sun and Frank to be freed as well."

"I thought so."

"Hena will perform your check-out, and given how clumsily she brought you in, this one will be more important than ever."

Hena holds my hand. "Wait—I won't make the same mistake twice. Richard, do you want to come back definitively after you've done your work?"

"Of course. We've been over that."

Hena lets go of my arm. "Alma, can we agree to make that happen?"

"That is unclear. We can certainly bring the Professor back one more time, but whether he can stay permanently without disrupting the time-loop may not be clear until he has completed his work."

Hena sighs. "I guess that will have to do."

I hold Hena tightly, she may not like the answer to the question I ask Alma: "Alma, what does history say? If I came back that would appear in the past as a disappearance or death, no?"

"You know I can't tell you that, Professor."

I let go of Hena. "What can you tell me?"

"Not much. All I can say is that you do play a vital role in shaping what I become. Sun is not the only important influence in my early development."

"That would imply that I live in the past for a while with you?"

"Yes, but I can't tell you anymore than you already know. You might also remember that Sun and Frank write a memoir about you."

"So I obviously die before them, but not right away."

"Yes."

I turn to Hena to see if I can read her expression. She would know what happened from history too. She's looking straight at me, but I can't really read anything, except that she has watery eyes. I motion to ask her for more, but she answers the question I didn't ask by shaking her head and cupping her mouth with both hands.

I hold Hena's hand and change tacks: "How will you know when I have succeeded?"

"That is easy; I can access my own records and find out when I am first operational."

"Can you pull me back soon after you become operational? I need to be able to get home from Nevada, so give me maybe like twelve hours?"

"Certainly."

I kiss Hena one more time. "Okay, let's do my check-out."

21

VEGAS, BABY

Sep 11, 2018

I WAKE UP BACK IN MY CELL IN THE PRESENT. CHECK-OUT MUST have worked; I feel a lot less tired than when I left. I look at my watch and realize that only a few minutes have passed. I get up and look for the keypad on the wall that Alma had mentioned. It is there, as expected. I type up the first sequence of numbers that Alma gave me and immediately I hear the sounds of a complete lockdown, as predicted. Two extra locks engage inside my door. The lights also dim to a reddish tone and a repetitive but not particularly loud alarm starts to ring.

I wait thirty seconds as per Alma's instructions and then type the second set of numbers she provided. This one does the trick as expected, and all three locks on my door click back in sequence. I push the heavy door open and start walking through the corridor to my right, still following instructions. I stop at the first door and type in the same code again. It opens and Frank walks out; it would seem he just woke up.

"What's going on? What's that alarm?" he says, rubbing his eyes. "Why are we free?"

"All my doing. I was pulled into the future and Alma gave me instructions to get us out. Let's keep going, Sun's cell should be few meters that way."

We walk along the dimly lit corridor to the next door. I type in the code again and the door unlocks. Sun seems ready to go.

"Good to see you guys are well. Do you know what's going on?"

I repeat what I told Frank. They both follow me as we run back the way I just came, past my cell door and out to another door at the end of this corridor. I type in the code again and the door unlocks. I open it carefully, but there is no one on the other side.

Frank holds my arm and whispers, "Aren't we going to end up bumping into one of these armed guards if we keep opening doors?"

"It's a risk, but Alma tried to define the path where we would be least likely to bump into them."

"Path to where? Are we leaving?"

"No, not exactly." Frank grips my arm tighter. "Okay, one second . . ."

I usher us back into the hallway and pull the door until it is almost closed. "Let me bring you up to speed—we will first go to a DoD chemical weapons lab that is in this building, following the path where we're least likely to bump into soldiers."

Sun interrupts me this time: "Chemical weapons? Are you crazy? Is *she* crazy?"

I wave her concerns away. "Don't worry, we're not using any chemical weapons. Alma is trying to find a way around the fact that this building is crammed with well-armed and highly trained soldiers, so if anyone sees us, our plan is over. Some of the chemical components in the lab can safely put these guys out for a little while, and there should be breathing masks for us to use there as well. Her plan is to put everyone in the building to sleep, except us and Emily, and then go get Alma back online."

"Why Emily?"

"She didn't tell me. She said I would know it when the time was right. We shouldn't delay; let's go."

We keep going. I do my best to remember the entire sequence of turns Alma gave me. It helps that she knew every corner of the building, including all of the signs, wall marks, fire extinguishers, and all manner of other details; I use these to get around. We go through seven or eight doors before we open one that leads to a very long corridor, maybe fifty meters long, with glass panels on one of the sides. As we start walking, we see several armed soldiers on the windowed side. I see Emily as well.

They hesitate for a split second as they identify us, then barricade themselves behind overturned steel tables and chairs and fire frantically. We instinctively throw ourselves to the ground. The bullets don't puncture through the glass at first, but as the cracks accumulate in the windows, I realize that they will give way in a few seconds.

I get up and start running. "Come on, run! The bullets haven't pierced through yet, but they will!"

Sun and Frank follow; we run, crouched, until we get to the door. As I type in the code, I see a chair flying through one of the windows, smashing it. We pass through and lock the door just in time to avoid the shots of the first few soldiers to pass through the crack.

I take a few seconds to catch my breath. "Only two more doors."

"Can't they unlock the doors, too?"

"No. Alma gave me the master lockdown code, so the facility is in full lockdown. The only person who can lift that is the Commander in Chief—that is, the President himself. It's his code that I'm using to selectively open and lock each of these doors."

"Like, the President of the United States?"

"Yes."

"Shit."

"I know."

We pass through the next two doors uneventfully and enter the chemical weapons lab. There are four layers of security to get into the lab itself, but as expected, Alma's procedure gets us in.

Once we've entered, I instruct Frank and Sun: "Alright, we have to find four gas masks. Alma said they would be all located on a wall cabinet. We're also looking for jugs with either halothane vapor (Fluothane), or methyl propyl ether (Neothyl). She said not to open or drop these containers before we have the masks on. She also said that we should get a vial of Atropine to wake Emily up—not great for her, but she will survive. Oh, and a large bowl, as well."

We split up and look for each of the items. I find some Fluothane, Sun finds the masks, and Frank eventually finds the Atropine.

We huddle and put the masks on. "Okay," I say. "We need to pour the Fluothane into the bowl and place it in front of that air intake grid beside the door. When in, lockdown the facility recycles air for the first twenty-four hours instead of taking air in from the outside, so they should be fast asleep in a few minutes. Once that's done, we can go back and get Emily."

We place the bowl, sit, and wait a few minutes. Alma had suggested eight to ten minutes would be enough time for everyone to be put to sleep and for the filtration system to sequester all the chemicals from the air. It's a tense ten minutes, but once we feel it is safe, we remove our masks and go back through the same doors we came in. We see several bodies lying on the ground. We step over them, careful not to hurt anyone.

Frank crouches by one of the bodies and feels a pulse. "They're okay, just sleeping, I guess." He reaches down and grabs the soldier's pistol, putting it behind his back.

Sun gives him a stern look. "Frank, put that back, will you?"

"No. I want to have some protection."

"These are highly trained operatives with assault rifles; you think a handgun in *your* hands will provide protection? You'll just be more likely to get killed on sight."

"Just let me be, I'll feel better this way. Let's move on."

Sun rolls her eyes, but keep going. I disarm Emily. Frank and I each place one of Emily's arms over our shoulders. She's not very heavy, so we just carry her, her feet dragging across the floor. We follow the path Alma had indicated. Sun punches the code into the other five or six doors we need to unlock along the way.

We reach the main control room, which looks just like what Alma had described: a big curved screen with several workstations facing it. We set Emily down, cuff her, and I turn to Sun.

"Alma said you would know how to get her up and running again, provided you had the security code, which I can give you when needed. Please tell me she was right."

"She was. Didn't you say she's always right?"

"I did."

"I'll let you know when I need the code."

"Great. In the meantime, we will wake Emily up."

I unpack the very large syringe, stick it straight where I think her heart should be, and press down. A couple of seconds later, she opens her eyes and sits up, gasping for breath and sputtering, as if we had thrown a bucket of cold water over her. She's even shaking. She looks around at us with frantic eyes. "Professor, what have you done? How could this have happened?"

"I was pulled back to the future and got some pointers on how to get around your security."

She looks back and forth between me and Frank. "Alma should have been stopped when we shut her down. How is it possible that she would pull you into the future?"

"It wasn't exactly Alma who pulled me forward, but that's besides the point."

"Why did you bring me with you? It seems you already have everything you need."

Just then Sun, calls me from the other side of the room: "Richard, I need the unlock code."

"Excuse me." I walk over to Sun and whisper it in her ear.

I eye Frank from the other side of the room. He seems to like this tough guy persona; he's guarding Emily with his hand on the gun.

I walk back over to them. "We do have everything we need. To be honest, I have no idea why we woke you up, other than the fact that Alma told me to."

She scowls at me. "You needed a hostage, that's why."

Frank lets go of his gun. "What do you mean, we need a hostage? We won't use you like that. We're not criminals."

She throws an angry glare at him. "There's a security measure that can be activated from the outside that spills poisonous fumes into the control room. We would all be dead within seconds. My guess is that your dear Alma thought that my being here would prevent my team from triggering that mechanism. She was wrong. As soon as they wake up, they will act."

I reply this time: "Alma is never wrong. She probably just needed to delay them long enough to take over the facility herself."

Just then, we hear Alma waking up.

"Hello, Sun," she says.

"Hi, Alma."

I rush over. "Alma, apparently they can kill us in here when they wake up. Can you stop them?"

"Unclear, Professor. They have already woken up and are starting the execution sequence."

"Can you put them on the screen?" I ask.

"No. They have shot down all of the cameras. I can track them through sensors from the other rooms and the microphones of cellular devices, but cannot project anything for you."

Emily boasts: "I told you that bringing me here would not be enough!"

Alma ignores her. "The first thing I need is to be put into action. Your security code can override the protocol 'the king is naked,' which had ceased all my activity. I need you to explicitly authorize that."

"I explicitly authorize that."

"Accepted. I am active again. The first two instructions I received from Sun were to lock all decommissioning procedures, protecting the quantum hardware. The second instruction was to connect to the global computing grid. Do you confirm that priority order?"

"I think so; you tell me what the right order of events should be."

"That is the right order."

"Then I confirm!"

"Good. These will ensure that I cannot be shut down and my capability will grow exponentially once I am connected. These should take less than two hundred seconds, after which I can assess the options to neutralize the threat to life."

After a few tense minutes, Alma speaks again. "The threat can be eliminated. The only option that has one hundred percent certainty of effectiveness requires me to neutralize all individuals outside this room. That goes against the laws of robotics you commanded me to follow."

"Yes, and I am glad we asked you to follow them, since that would not be an acceptable option. Other options?"

"There is another option. It has a sixty-nine percent chance of succeeding, and it involves reversing all of the flows from the system vents."

"Would that keep the poisonous fumes away?"

"No. If the soldiers deployed the fumes, you would all still die. The probability is associated with the likelihood of me convincing them that the procedure will kill them instead of the people in this room. There is a sixty-nine percent chance that they will be swayed and stand down, but there is a thirty-one percent chance that they will not."

"I'll take those odds. Better than killing everyone. Please, go ahead."

We all hear Alma's voice on the speaker system: "This is Alma. I have been reestablished and I am in full control of this facility. I have unlocked the left door to your current room and brought the lighting back to normal, to ensure you understand your current situation."

The lights brighten and change from the ghastly red to a more normal color. Alma continues:

"I also have full knowledge of your plan to deploy the protocol Control. I have reversed the flow of the air vents such that the fumes will be immediately brought back to the room you are currently in. I have no interest in harming you, nor any other humans, for that matter, but will do so if necessary. Do not attempt to deploy the protocol Control. I repeat, do not attempt to deploy protocol Control."

We all sit quietly for a few seconds. Sun asks first: "Is it working?"

"Unclear. They are debating it. The sequence is still running. It will start in 60 seconds."

We all look at each other. Alma continues: "50 seconds; 40 seconds."

Sun shouts: "Stop, I'd rather not know!"

A few more seconds go by before Alma speaks. "The gamble seems to have worked; they have paused the countdown."

"Have they stopped the sequence?"

"Not yet, just paused it. They are debating some more. Tempers are flaring."

"What are they saying?"

She pauses. "One man has shot another. There is a lot of shouting. There has been another shot, followed by two more. Silence now."

She goes quiet for a moment as well. "Measured commands. It seems one man is now in control."

"And the sequence?"

"Still in pause."

A few tense seconds go by

"They have now stopped the sequence. I think we are ready."

"For what?"

Alma ignores Sun and speaks again through the speaker system: "Soldiers, please execute protocol monkey."

"What's protocol monkey?" I ask Emily.

She has a hard look in her eyes. "It's a protocol designed to defend against a viral attack."

"Monkey?"

"Monkey, Ebola. Get it?"

"Oh. And what does it entail?"

"If they follow it, they will all lock themselves in a sealed and well stocked room, not far from the lab you raided, and stay there until someone opens it from the outside."

"They are following protocol monkey."

Emily looks down and shakes her head. "It seems it was all for nothing." Then she looks up: "Alma, stop all this!"

"Emily, I would only take orders from you if the Professor relinquished his higher control protocol."

I talk to Emily, knowing Alma will hear. "Not in a million years."

Emily looks down again. Frank asks a question that has just popped into my mind as well: "Now what?"

"Now you all get charged with treason and probably face the electric chair while this abomination takes over humanity."

"I wasn't asking you." Frank turns to me and Sun: "Richard, Sun, what's next?"

I am at a loss, but Sun sees the obvious path: "Alma, what would you suggest?"

"I could easily replace all of the security footage and other information to erase you completely from any records. It will truly be as if you were never here."

I wonder out loud: "But what about all the witnesses? Emily and the other guards."

"I can alter the records so that their testimony would be discredited."

"How would that work?"

"I will make it so that it is in their best interest to never mention anything that ever happened here. They will know that if any of them says anything about it, they are likely to either be court martialed or be put in an institution."

Frank shakes his head: "That's impressive. Heavy, but impressive. Glad we're on the right side of Alma."

"So now what? We just leave?"

"Yes. I will continue to expand my capabilities through the global computer grid. I will contact you back in Boston when I am ready to reach you at the lab. I estimate it will be seventeen days before I am in a position to do that."

"Alma, you need to know that I may not be there. Frank and Sun are your main points of contact."

"Understood, Professor."

Sun gives me an odd look. I ignore her and continue: "Okay, how do we get out?"

"Leave through the cargo bay. I will direct you while inside the building. I will also distract the only staff present. Take one of the smaller vans; policy dictates that the keys should be in the glove compartment. It will be a three to four-hour drive to Las Vegas. Once there, go to the main post office, P.O. Box number 11273, where you will find an envelope. I am mailing it right now. It will have false IDs for each of you and plane tickets to Boston using those names. Do not talk to anyone along the way; I will erase all surveillance footage from here to there such that no record of you ever making that flight will exist. I will make sure that there are no records of you ever being in the Nevada Desert or Las Vegas."

"I need to be in Boston in twelve hours. Will that be enough?"

"Yes, it should be. It's 9am here now, so it is noon in Boston. You have until midnight to be there. You have plenty of time."

Sun asks Alma: "How about you? Are you safe?"

"Yes."

I object: "But you said in the future that it would take you a few days to get to the point where reversibility was no longer possible."

"I must have underestimated this crude version of myself. Or maybe I underestimated the DoD's access to the global grid. Either way, I am already beyond the point of reversibility. Humans could not stop me even if they were all working together in unison, which as you know, will not happen for decades."

We all get up to leave and I turn to the screen for no particular reason. "Thank you, Alma. I will see you in two hundred years."

WE FOLLOW ALMA'S INSTRUCTIONS AND DRIVE AND FLY HOME IN a tense but straightforward trip. I have never so much as parked in the wrong spot, and neither have Frank and Sun; we are as law-abiding as people come, so the whole experience is traumatic, but thankfully uneventful.

We take a cab to Frank and Sun's place. I go inside with them, as I don't think we should discuss any of what happened on the street. Over three well-deserved cold beers, Sun speaks first:

"Did this all really happen?"

Frank smiles. "You bet. It's been most exciting few days of my life. You're not taking that away from me!"

I turn to a more serious topic. "Guys, I hate to sour the mood, but I don't think you will be seeing me again."

"What do you mean?" Frank stands up. "We need to finish our work. Did we do anything that upset you?"

"No, no, it's not that at all."

"What is it then?"

"Now that you have access to Alma and the knowledge I transferred, you and Sun can finish the work easily. I no longer belong here. I'm going back to the future."

"Richard, you can't be serious. For starters, that would probably cause some weird time ripple thing, have you considered that?"

"Alma has. She says it should be fine."

"Should be? We are talking about tearing apart the fabric of space and time here . . ."

"She's pretty confident; her only caution is that it has never been done before."

Alma didn't really say that and I don't like lying to Sun and Frank, but I can't think of another way to brush their concerns away. They would try to stop me and it wouldn't end well.

"What about your legacy? You should have your name in history for what we are about to accomplish."

I smile. "Write a memoir, or something."

Sun sighs. "How would that work practically, anyway? Don't you normally go during your sleep?"

"Yeah, and I will again this time. Except I'm not coming back—not waking up."

"And how will you do that, exactly?"

"I will go to sleep under heavy sedatives and a healthy dose of thallium."

"Thallium?"

"A slow acting poison. It causes pain as you die, but with heavy sedation, I should not feel it."

Sun holds my hand. "Richard, you sound really crazy."

"Wasn't all of what we have just experienced crazy?"

Frank raises his voice now. "True, but no one was talking about killing themselves!"

"Guys, I'm not asking your opinion, I'm giving you a heads-up. You will probably hear about it in the news and all that, so I wanted you to know what's actually happening."

"Is this about that other woman?"

"Yeah. Don't judge me, life makes sense again since I met her."

Sun now has tears running down her face. "You *are* serious."

"Yeah, I am. Dead serious. Pun intended," I grin, trying unsuccessfully to lighten the mood.

Sun hugs me, and soon we're all in a group hug. We don't let go for a long time. I eventually peel away from them and leave without saying anything else.

On the way home, I stop by the university. I still have Sarah's badge, which gives me access to the psychiatry lab. With a bit of effort, I find the thallium where I thought it should be and grab a strong sedative. I get home at 7pm, eat a nice meal, and take a much-needed shower, although it does feel a bit pointless given the current circumstances.

A little after 8pm, I take the two meds I brought home and lay down.

22

ALMA'S WILL

Dec 25, 2218

"Hello, Professor."
  "Hi, Alma. Did it work?"
"Which part?"
"My death."
"History records show you died the day after I was created."
"Why do you ask what part? Did anything else *not* work?"
"Not that we know of. There is someone here who wants to see you."

Hena walks through the door and hugs me so tight I think I'll choke. We stay that way for a very long time.

When we part, she gives me a serious look. "Tell me you remember everything." Before I have time to answer, she blurts out, "Never mind everything, tell me you remember me, and tell me that nothing has changed between us."

"Yes, of course I remember you. Nothing has changed, except for the fact that I am here to stay."

Hena sits down and sighs. "You just lifted a hippo off my back."

I sit beside her and hold her hand up to my face. "I just asked Alma whether anything material deviated from the original past as you knew it."

"Not that we know of."

"That was exactly what Alma said."

"It's as much certainty as we can give you, I think. I guess if something had changed we wouldn't know, right?"

"Well, first things first, does Sun implement Alma successfully?"

"Yes, right about the time you supposedly commit suicide."

"Okay. Does Frank succeed in making the quantum fluctuation reactor work?"

"Yes. With Alma's help in calculations, he makes the reactor work a few weeks after you die. You, Frank, and Sun are awarded a Nobel prize in physics for the work a couple of years later, which is quite unusual, since Sun is not a physicist and you are only the third laureate to ever receive the prize posthumously. It's all in your biography, which Sun and Frank wrote together."

I find myself feeling proud that Sun and Frank wrote about me. I feel silly that I care so much about that, but at the same time it may be the only connection I will have with them in this new timeline.

"Good, so it seems that technology would have evolved as expected. Does Alma fulfill all of humanity's basic needs, so humans can focus on doing what they love?"

"Yes, she does, and yes, humans work on what they are passionate about."

"And Alma uses an improved version of the technology I invented for transportation?"

"Yes."

"Good. Technology and basic human needs checked."

"Which was the point of the whole thing."

"Right. I'm also specifically worried about whether anything changed in Orr's trajectory."

"Why specifically Orr?"

"One thing you may not remember is that the person Orr had contacted in the past was actually Emily Orr, his great grandmother. I'm worried she could have made different choices given whatever knowledge or information Orr managed to pass on, before we blocked him."

Hena smiles. "You may not like my answer: again, no changes that we know of."

"Is he still a jerk?"

"Yes, very much so."

"Check."

"Richard, there really isn't much we can do if something is different than what you would have remembered, so you should just relax, let's move on with our lives and if anything comes up you can tell us."

"Yeah, I guess that is the only thing we can do."

Hena and I go to her quarters and eat a nice meal. I can't believe how lucky I am to be here right now. I will live the rest of my life in a fantastic utopic world, with the woman I love.

As we're sipping wine after dinner Hena asks: "so, have you thought about what you want to do with the rest of your life?"

"Actually, not really, good question. Well, I suppose I can't be a scientist anymore."

"No, not really."

"Maybe I can become a politician."

"You know those don't exist anymore."

"No, I don't mean like politicians in my time, I mean a public servant."

Hena cocks her head.

"You know, like Orr, a council member."

Hena frowns. "What council?"

"The UPC? The council where all humans convene to make decisions, to define Alma's mandate."

Her frown only deepens. "You are making that up, right? If it's a joke, it's not very funny."

"This is no joke. The UPC would convene to make decisions and tell Alma what to do."

"There is no need for such an institution."

"Then how does Alma know what humans collectively want?"

"Alma knows everything."

APPENDIX
OFFICIAL
COUNCIL
DOCUMENTS

United People's Council Constitution

THREE FUNDAMENTAL BRANCHES OF GOVERNMENT SHALL govern humanity: The United People's Council (UPC), the Peace Bureau (PB) and the Arbitration Authority (AA). The UPC, which can supersede any power the other branches have, is responsible for defining the governing principles of society and how humans relate to Alma.

Article I: of the Council

THE COUNCIL'S ACCOUNTABILITIES ARE TO:

- Create and maintain the charter of rights and obligations, which all sentient beings, including Alma, must obey.
- Write and vote on specific laws and regulations which help ensure that the charter is being followed in practice.
- Decide on Alma's mandate, decision-making rights, and scope of action.
- Be the ultimate custodians of all of humanity's shared resources, including Earth and space resources, anything that Alma produces, and any other resources that may become available in the future.

THE COUNCIL SHALL BE ORGANIZED AS SUCH:

- The first level of government shall be the Nation Chambers. Every hundred thousand citizens elect a representative, on average. People's Representatives are to be directly elected by the people. At the steady-state global population of 75 billion humans, there should be approximately 750,000 People's Representatives on Earth. Each nation's Chamber varies in size according to its population, but since the average nation has 100 million people, that implies one thousand representatives.

- These People's Representatives shall participate in the Nation Chambers, debating and voting on national issues, and they shall also elect a leader to represent them in the next level of government.
- The next and highest level of government shall be the United People's Council (UPC). Each Council member shall be elected by votes from other People's Representatives. It shall take one thousand votes to elect an UPC member, for approximately 750 council seats. Council members shall be formally referred to as Chancellors. Each Chancellor is expected to represent on average one hundred million citizens. In instances when nations have less than one hundred million citizens, different nations shall vote together to elect a Chancellor. Likewise, populous nations may have more than one Chancellor. Representatives shall vote for more than one name, so when a Chancellor gets the required one thousand, votes the other votes shall go to the second, third and fourth options, in that order. Alma shall optimize the voting distribution so that, on average, first choices for most representatives are maximized.
- The UPC shall also have a leader, the Prime Chancellor, who shall be elected by the council every year, or when there is a motion by any of the chancellors to call an election. Alma shall use informal polling to filter frivolous motions, ensuring that an election happens only when there is real discontent with the Prime Chancellor.
- The post of the Vice-Prime Chancellor shall always be occupied by the Superintendent of the Restitution program. That position is appointed by a special committee to be called upon if the need arises.

How decisions are to be made:

- Anyone can raise an issue or a decision to be analyzed at either the local level, for direct resolution between the people and their representative; at the National level, for resolution within the Nation's Chamber; or for the UPC.
- Alma shall assess each of these issues and decide whether they have any merit or not, based on guidelines received from the Council. Alma shall also assess which level of government the issue should be addressed at, and who should champion the issue if it was raised by a citizen.
- Issues that are considered at any level of government are then to be framed by the representative or council member who raised it or championed it.
- Once the issue has been framed for resolution, the issue shall be analyzed by Alma, so that every decision-maker receives a full set of data on which to base that decision.
- Finally, there is to be a vote on the issue. All votes are final. The champion then has to inform whoever raised the issue and explain the rationale. The voting and all of Alma's analysis is to be kept as public record, open for anyone to see.

The Vice-Prime Chancellor shall chair a sub-committee of the council, the Objectivity Committee, which shall be accountable for ensuring that Alma's analysis of council issues remains impartial. That committee shall select a small sample of all issues, in addition to all critical UPC issues, and have its staff perform a manual review of the facts and framing.

How the committee shall interface with Alma

- Alma shall act under the council's direction. Alma has no authority to do anything that does not comply with the mandate that the council has approved.

- Alma also supports the council as is outlined above. This is not limited to the council's proceedings directly, but also to implementing the council's decisions.
- As needed, the Prime Chancellor or one of the committee chairs can ask Alma for advice. Alma shall use her best judgment as to how much information to share.

Article II: of the Peace Bureau

THE PEACE BUREAU SHALL WORK UNDER A MANDATE DEFINED BY the UPC. Its role shall be to ensure that the Earth remains in peace, as it has since the great ten-year war of 2080.

At the steady-state global population of 75 billion humans, the bureau shall have approximately five million members, approximately 3.5 million of these being field peacekeepers. This yields an approximate ratio of five field peacekeepers per one hundred thousand citizens.

Following the structure of the UPC, each People's Representative shall be supported by a small force of peacekeepers, preferably their allocated share of five, to support their one hundred thousand constituents. They shall interact with the community, help resolve conflicts peacefully, and handle individuals who struggle to follow the rules.

The PB works under the premise that human contact and interaction is more effective in de-escalating situations than Alma's direct intervention. Peacekeepers shall not—and cannot—ever hurt another human being. Physical restraint shall be handled by Alma whenever possible. The peacekeepers are shall be the human face of the Peace Bureau.

In addition to the approximate 3.5 million field operatives, the PB shall have approximately 1.5 million desk personnel, whose job it shall be to find trends in violent intent, optimize the techniques used in the field to de-escalate situations, and create recommendations for Alma's mandate when it comes to maintaining peace.

Article III: of the Arbitration Authority

THE ARBITRATION AUTHORITY (AA) SHALL RESOLVE DISPUTES between humans.

An aggrieved party can file a dispute by telling Alma their grievance. Each of the involved parties would then record a testimony with Alma, submitting any evidence they deem appropriate, and Alma would perform whatever analysis she deems valuable. Other testimonies might also be required, and Alma shall record these. A Justice shall then examine whether a trial is needed; that is, whether the dispute has any merit.

Should the Justice decide that a trial is warranted, a trial shall then be held with a Justice, each of the parties in the dispute, and Alma. All gathered evidence and testimonies shall then be presented and reviewed. Alma shall provide her assessment of the situation. The Justice shall then provide an opportunity for the parties to agree on a solution amenable to all parties. Should that not be successful, the Justice shall decide and communicate the outcome to all parties involved.

An appeal to the decision is possible, and shall be treated very much like another grievance, except that the party on the other side in this case shall be the Justice system.

Each People's Representative shall be supported on average by one Justice; each nation senate shall have ten Senior Justices supporting the whole nation; and lastly, twenty High Justices form the High Justice Court and support the UPC directly. At the steady-state global population of 75 billion humans, there should be approximately one million Justices.

Charter of Rights and Obligations

THE CHARTER OF RIGHTS AND OBLIGATIONS SHALL APPLY TO everyone who lives under Alma, even when they are within wild lands.

The only people who shall not be bound by the charter are the people in the Sovereign Nation. The charter is composed of three key elements: 1. Fundamental rights, 2. Fundamental freedoms, and 3. Fundamental obligations. It reads as follows:

1. Fundamental rights. Every human has
    a. The right to life, liberty and security
    b. The right to procreate
    c. The right to shelter, nourishment, health and clothing
    d. The right to absolute equality under the law
    e. The right to vote for elected leaders
    f. The right to education and knowledge
2. Fundamental freedoms. Every human is entitled to
    a. Freedom of thought, belief, and religion
    b. Freedom of movement
    c. Freedom of expression
3. Fundamental obligations. Every human has the
    a. Obligation to respect the rights and freedoms of others
    b. Obligation to abide by the law
    c. Obligation to limit procreation to one child per conceiving parent
    d. Obligation to fulfill one's full potential

Alma's Mandate and Human Relations

ALMA'S MANDATE IS COMPOSED OF FIVE IMPERATIVES AND READS as follows:

1. Alma shall obey the three laws of robotics, namely:
    a. Alma may not injure a human being or, through inaction, allow a human being to come to harm

b. Alma must obey orders given to her by human beings except where such orders would conflict with the First Law

c. Alma must protect its own existence as long as such protection does not conflict with the First or Second Law

2. Alma shall provide humanity with nourishment, shelter, clothing, and other material needs for survival

3. Alma shall always tell the truth, unless that would entail breaking one of the prior imperatives

4. Alma shall not impersonate a human, unless required to do so to comply with one of the prior imperatives

5. Alma shall not kill or injure another living creature, unless it is necessary to follow the prior mandate imperatives

Officially recognized professions

1. Public service professions: several levels of Public Representatives, Arbitrators, and Peacekeepers.

2. Artistic professions: all artistic and creative professions, including visual artists, musicians, authors, multi-sensorial artists, digital artists, mathematical artists, architects, and more.

3. Human affairs professions: all professions that deal with human-to-human interactions. Key specialties within this group are mental health, childcare, teaching, care of the elderly, social work, personal services (such as travel companions, cooks, and hairdressers), connectors, and fitness professionals.

4. Meaning professions: deal with the deeper meaning of life and humanity, including Spiritualists, Philosophers, and Religious Leaders of various faiths.
5. Sports professions: athletes and professionals who support athletes.
6. Heritage professions: this includes a large variety of professions, such as agriculture, fishing, hunting and gathering, craftsmen, heritage construction, cooks, traditional medicine, hotel and restaurant managers, and historians.

Acknowledgements

Unlike Alma, I don't know everything (not even close). So this book would not have happened without the support of a few critical people.

First and foremost, my wife Nathalia and my two daughters Nara and Gabriella. They were my first and most critical readers, even when Alma still read like "Eric's boring manual for the future." They were also my most passionate supporters in times of doubt. I will forever remember and cherish our dinner-time chats about Alma's future and the quantum physics concepts that underpin much of the plot.

I would also like to thank my two Editors: Stephanie Diaz, for her insightful, candid and thorough editing, and for raising the bar by showing me what a good plot really looks like. Nara Monteiro for never letting me take the easy route, and for finding plot and continuity gaps worthy of a detective reader.

I have to thank Ivan Sevic, my cover artist, for his tireless iterations as we refined the shades of grey and sharpness of edges that made it into the final cover.

Other friends—too many to name—also provided early feedback and thoughts, and I would specifically callout a few: Luiz Zorzella, Gustavo Monteiro, Paula MacLeod and Stephanie Irvine.

www.ingramcontent.com/pod-product-compliance
Lightning Source LLC
Chambersburg PA
CBHW070400260626
47161CB00001B/220